E-DAY

NEW YORK TIMES BESTSELLING AUTHOR

NICHOLAS SANSBURY SMITH

Books by New York Times Bestselling Author

Nicholas Sansbury Smith

E-Day Series
E-Day
E-Day II: Burning Earth (Coming Winter 2021)
E-Day III: Dark Moon (Coming Spring 2022)

The Sons of War Series
(Offered by Blackstone Publishing)
Sons of War
Sons of War 2: Saints
Sons of War 3: Sinners

The Hell Divers Series
(Offered by Blackstone Publishing)
Hell Divers
Hell Divers II: Ghosts
Hell Divers III: Deliverance
Hell Divers IV: Wolves
Hell Divers V: Captives
Hell Divers VI: Allegiance
Hell Divers VII: Warriors
Hell Divers VIII: King of the Wastes
(Coming September 2021)

Foreword and Acknowledgements

Dear Reader,

Artificial intelligence (AI) and droids have always fascinated and terrified me at the same time. I grew up watching the Terminator movies and reading the books. I consumed anything related to that universe that I could get my hands on it. When I had nothing left, I explored other stories about killer robots and AI, never burning out on the genre. As soon as I started my writing career, I knew I would eventually want to create my own story in a similar realm.

For my Hell Divers readers, you might have gotten a glimpse of this with the Defectors—killer war droids that hunted humans in the post-apocalyptic wastelands. I really enjoyed writing that part of the story, and many of you have asked me to write a prequel to explain what happened before the collapse of civilization, focusing on the machines and AI. I considered this, but decided I wanted to take it to another level in a brand new series.

Behold, E-Day, an original storyline about the rise of AI, droids, and an operating system (OS) designed to save the planet and our species in the near future. I don't want to give away any spoilers, but I will say this story contains plenty of twists and is not the same old AI turning on humanity plot. There is far more to E-Day than that. In fact, the title itself has a dual meaning that will be revealed throughout the series.

I hope you enjoy my take on artificial intelligence and how AI can shape our future in both a negative and positive way. There are a few people I would like to thank that played a vital role in the creation of this story before you get started.

My agent David Fugate. All of my books are always better with his guidance.

Alexey Bobrick, an Astrophysicist and Scientist in Applied Physics at Lund University.

Author and Bioengineer Anthony J. Melchiorri, my good friend and colleague.

My editor Jason Kirk. His edits helped take E-Day to a different level.

All of the beta readers that found what we missed. You know who you are, and you have my deep gratitude.

To family and wife who are my champions. I would not be where I am without their love and support.

Finally, a huge thanks to my readers for taking a chance on my work. Feel free to reach out to me on social media or via email. I'm always happy to hear your comments and questions. After all, I write for you, and I am forever indebted to my readers for choosing to spend their time and hard-earned money on my work.

All the best,
Nicholas

The Warrior Codex

The brittle pages of the ancient leather-bound codex seemed too fragile in the strong hands of Sergeant Akira Hayashi. When he first inherited the book, he had feared reading it would cause the pages to crumble into dust.

Inside, the words told the story of his ancestors who were now nothing more than dust. These men lived their lives by a common ethos—to fight with valor and courage, to love and remain loyal to their comrades, and to contend against not only the enemies on the battlefield, but those in their own hearts.

Akira gently turned to a blank page to inscribe a new entry. Often when he wrote in the book, his hands still ached from battle, from gripping and swinging his energy sword. But unless he was incapacitated by injuries, he always took a few moments of silence to document the fighting while his feelings and memories still flowed like fresh arterial blood.

This entry, like so many others, documented Akira's superiority on the battlefield, where he was a demi-god among mortals, taking life as easily as breathing air. Much as the lives of those he loved had been taken from him.

His words described his own ethos—fortitude and valor as the path to honor and victory. Following that path had brought him great honor, but it would not bring back those he had lost.

After he finished writing, Akira tucked the book carefully into his armored satchel, sealing it away until the next time he stepped onto the field of battle with his fellow Engine warriors.

Death from the Shadows.
Together, we are one.

—Historical Note—

In 2070, during the period scientists call the Carbon Crisis, the Earth was on the edge of collapse. Rising tides and droughts left coastlines uninhabitable. Starving migrants abandoned coastal cities and crossed borders to look for work and food. Diseases ripped through the weakened populations, caused by the climate catastrophe.

Companies and governments raced to combat the widespread hunger and disease with developments in nanotechnology. While some sub-microscopic nanoparticles consisting of various plastics and/or metals had been designed to help treat diseases such as cancer and antibiotic-resistant bacterial infections, others were used to help crops retain water in the increasingly hot environments or in drought-stricken areas. Such nanotechnologies helped in the short term. However, they were manufactured and deployed too fast for scientists to ensure they were safe.

During their global deployment, some of these technologies released nanoparticle-sized contaminants and pollutants into the environment, where they entered human bodies and built up like mercury poisoning. These particles interfered with normal nerve activity, leading to effects such as paralysis and numbness, lost senses, and eventual organ failure and immense pain as nerves failed to deliver the necessary signals to keep tissues and organs functional. Scientists called this fatal disease Systematic Amyotrophic Nervous Disorder (SANDs). The exact mechanisms were not well known, but one thing was.

There was no cure.

The combination of diseases and loss of resources led to conflicts across the world, sparking the Carbon Wars. In the first five years of fighting, nations crumbled, and great nation-state megacities rose up in their place. On the Moon, Kepler Station declared sovereignty from Earth, and the largest mining colonies at the Shackleton and Shoemaker Craters followed close behind.

A decade of darkness followed as the human population plummeted to just over one billion souls. From the ashes, Achilles Android Systems (AAS), the leading global robotics company, rose to the task of rebuilding the megacities and restoring the Earth by using Hummer Worker Droids that built the lunar colonies. Through mass production, AAS started to bring humanity out of a second Dark Age with their legion of new droids.

The nation-state megacities formed a pact, binding together to face global challenges and creating the Nova Alliance. But within and outside of the towering megacity walls, a growing threat brewed.

An organization called the Coalition was formed around the belief that artificial intelligence (AI) would bring about the end of all life. As poverty and starvation increased, more people joined the Coalition, forming tribal states in the wastes of the old world, even as the Nova Alliance continued to develop both AI and strengthen its alliance with the Kepler Lunar Government.

In Megacity New York City, Achilles Android Systems' CEO Jason Crichton embarked on a mission to cure SANDs, restore the Amazon rainforest, and terraform the Sahara Desert, among countless other endeavors designed to heal the Earth. Around the globe,

AAS launched projects aimed to provide clean energy, food, and water to the masses, as well as eradicate the dangerous nanoparticles from ecosystems.

But the damage from these particles was already severe, and the Coalition only grew more set in its anti-AI ideology, launching terrorist attacks across the Nova Alliance and targeting AAS factories. In Megacities Paris and Moscow, the Coalition overthrew the government, killing without prejudice and destroying every droid within the cities' walls before sealing them off.

To defend the other megacities, the Nova Alliance deployed a new type of warrior called an Engine. These augmented humans, encased in power-armor and fighting in five-person autonomous squads, changed the course of the war over a decade.

In response, the leader of the Coalition, Dr. Otto Cross, created a genetically-modified army of human and animal soldiers. With no end to the bloodshed in sight, the Nova Alliance contracted with the AAS to end the war and restore the planet.

Seeing one last chance to save humanity, AAS CEO, Dr. Jason Crichton programmed the most powerful AI in the history of civilization on the Titan Space Elevator, skirting international law by using the consciousness of a human that he believed had the moral fortitude and unparalleled intelligence to solve the centuries of conflict that plagued humanity. His hope was that this human-AI hybrid could do what AI had thus far failed to do—lead humanity to peace and away from extinction.

For Naomi Smith – I loved you before I met you, and I will love you forever.

"Sword and mind must be united. Technique by itself is insufficient, and spirit alone is not enough."

—Yamada Jirokichi

— Prologue —

Cherry blossom petals fluttered to the dirt in the blanket of night. The drums of war had gone silent, and a moment of peace drifted across the hills with the smoke that rose off the burnt terrain. There were various names for this once beautiful landscape. The Sea of Trees. The Suicide Forest. Soon it would be known as the place where Nova Alliance Piston Sergeant Akira Hayashi lost his life, along with the rest of his platoon, unless he found a way off this hill.

The scent of death found its way into Akira's helmet as he clung to the side of a muddy slope in his heavy Piston armor. He was surrounded by the corpses of other Pistons, men and women he had fought with for years, many of them friends. Their mangled remains littered the bloodstained dirt with twisted heaps of armor.

Splintered and shattered trees protruded out of the battlefield. Simmering orange holes peppered the bark of Fuji maple trees. Crisp needles formed a skirt around a burned Japanese cypress tree.

On his hands and knees, Akira searched for survivors, but nothing moved on the hill, and he heard no moans or pleas for help. He got up from his crawl and tried to walk with his back hunched until his right leg clamped up.

A glance at his exoskeleton revealed hydraulic fluid leaking from severed lines.

Reaching to his duty belt, he pulled out a multi-tool and unscrewed the bolts on each side, freeing himself from the exoskeleton. The pieces of metal collapsed to the mud as lifeless as the corpses around it.

Akira slipped in the muck, wet with blood, as soon as he tried to move without the support. Only by stabbing his energy blade into the steep hill did he find purchase.

On the ascent, he passed more fallen warriors. Lieutenant Manuel lay sprawled over a boulder at the top, his arms open wide, a riven stump where his head had been. He would have been unrecognizable if Akira had not personally seen the man taken out by a sniper shot.

As the shot rang out among the trees, ten Coalition soldiers, their dark and bulky armor buried in the mud, had burst up and taken the Pistons by surprise.

Those enemy soldiers were all dead, three by Akira's own rifle. But they had taken plenty of Akira's comrades with them into the afterlife. The handful that had survived the ambush died in a barrage of enemy artillery.

Akira continued up the slope, his silver armor collecting gore and mud. Near the crest, he tucked his body behind the boulder Lieutenant Manual lay sprawled over.

Rotating, Akira scanned the forest about a quarter mile to the east, where he knew another two hundred Pistons waited to advance. The Nova Alliance Assault Force's Stone Mountain Battalion was hidden behind the wall of trees, ready to advance on the Coalition fighters entrenched in the Sea of Trees.

It was a sacred but haunted place.

Over five hundred years ago, the Battle of Kawanakajima had been fought not far from here. The conflict—between the Takeda Clan and Uesugi Clan, in the Sengoku period, or the Age of Civil War—had stained the soil red. Once again, history was repeating itself.

But this war was not about land or resources. It was about technology.

Those who worshipped AI against those who believed it would lead to the downfall of humanity.

Akira fought for the creators of AI, but he fell somewhere in the middle of the two ideologies. As a soldier, his opinion didn't mean much anyway.

He lived by a creed, an ethos—the Warrior Ethos.

Fight for those who are too weak to wield the sword. Protect the innocent. Love your family. Bleed for your country.

The Warrior Ethos is fate.

Today he was living it, for today his wife Yui and their two-year-old son Takeshi were at risk as Coalition fighters encroached on Megacity Tokyo. The Stone Mountain Battalion had to take these hills. If they failed, the Coalition could push on all the way to the capital of the great Nova Alliance.

Akira scrambled over shattered tree trunks and fallen logs, adapting without his exoskeleton. Long-range comms were being jammed by the enemy, and the last drone his platoon had put up was blown out of the sky within minutes of launch.

Right now, all he could do was send a short-range comm transmission or wave his armored hands. The latter could earn him a sniper round to the head like the dead Lieutenant.

Akira stopped to study his Heads-up Display (HUD). He checked his mini-map, switched to night vision, and zoomed in on where the battalion should be. The white humanoid frames of three medical Hummer Droids stood among the trees. Their circular facial screens were all angled toward his position.

Behind them crouched the Piston soldiers.

At the front of the battalion was a Piston cleric, holding an embroidered flag of the Nova Alliance Silver Crane. The men and women around him wore the same logo on brown vests over their gray armor. After decades of fighting, these warriors were exhausted, Akira knew. Their hearts had long been broken. And they would all die if he did not locate the enemy artillery that had wiped out most of his platoon.

Akira recalled something his great-great-grandfather had written in the leather codex he carried into battle, safely tucked away in his armor-lined pack.

Fear is a tool. Use it to guide your heart and your hand.

"Fortitude and valor is the path to honor," Akira whispered.

He thought of the men and women in the forest, considering their fate. Sighing deeply, he opened the short-range comm line and reported his plan to recon enemy positions.

A rough voice replied.

"Negative, Sergeant. Return to rendezvous," growled Battalion Captain Tran.

Akira didn't have a chance to respond. A violent thumping like the clap of thunder came over the hill. He flattened his body into the mud. The ground shook and rumbled from the impacts of another round of incoming mortars.

The enemy's fire was drawing closer to the battalion.

Clenching his jaw, Akira's thoughts turned to his brother Kai, also a Piston, and Kai's wife, Lise. He had not seen them in almost a year. War had separated them, with Kai and Lise living in Megacity Phoenix, halfway across the world.

A shell exploded close to Akira, showering him with splinters. He clawed at the ground, trying to dig into the mud, cold adrenaline pumping through his vessels, telling him to run. To flee.

Fortitude and valor is the path to honor.

Akira repeated his mantra as he tried to keep from panicking during the incessant fire. The words flowed through his mind until he lost track of time and realized the shelling had finally stopped.

He slowly lifted his helmet and wiped his faceplate clean. His ears rang, but his hearing was already settling. Over the noise, came a clanking sound from above his position. He pulled his rifle and aimed the barrel at the burned trees at the top of the hill. The targeting system on his HUD danced until it found a contact.

A hoofed leg stomped the ground.

He pulled his finger away from the trigger and lowered the rifle from a stray hybrid stallion the color of night, with dark brown eyes. The animal hobbled toward Akira on partial prosthetic legs.

Part biological and part mechanical, this creation of Dr. Otto Cross was just one of the Coalition's modified war beasts. The horse's natural brain was unaided by AI, but its body was enhanced with prosthetics and armor, allowing it to run faster and withstand enemy fire.

Maybe I can ride him out of here, Akira thought.

"Easy, my friend," Akira whispered forcefully.

The beast definitely favored his left front leg, keeping the weight off the other front leg. Bending down, Akira noticed a shard of shrapnel sticking out of his damaged right hoof.

"Hold still," Akira said. "This might hurt a little."

He took out his multi-tool and used the pliers to clamp onto the piece of metal, wiggling it until it popped out.

The horse let out a long, happy neigh and slowly placed his leg back down. Lowering his head, he then nudged up against Akira as if to say thank you.

Akira unscrewed the gas-filter canisters on his helmet and tucked them into a pouch on his chest. Next, he caked mud on his armor, spreading it out. Without the canisters, Akira looked almost like a Coalition soldier.

The hybrid animal watched him curiously.

"Easy," Akira said again. He reached up, took the reins, and hopped over the saddle. In the mount, he recalled his days riding as a young boy, hoping they would come back to him.

It took a moment to get adjusted with his boots in the stirrups, but the horse didn't seem to mind.

Akira gazed over the battlefield and considered his orders to return to the frontlines. Smoking craters and burning trees stretched across the horizon. Mounds of dirt smoldered, and a wave of smoke drifted over the ocean of fallen trees burnt to embers.

The night vision optics did little to aid his view. The enemy could be anywhere, but he had the chance to save countless lives by finding them with the Coalition horse.

Howls rang out through the night as he gave the beast a kick to the flanks. They started downhill, halting on the slope to look east.

A pack of three Coalition Iron Wolves bolted across a ravine and into another section of forest. The hybrid wolves vanished into a curtain of smoke, but not before Akira spotted the barrel of a plasma cannon pointing in his direction from nearly a hundred yards away.

He braced for the incoming shot, but the barrel turned away.

His disguise was working, and now he knew an enemy location.

Akira quickly accessed the coordinates on his mini-map. After confirming them, he sent them over the short-range comms to Captain Tran.

"Copy that," the captain replied. This time he did not tell Akira to retreat.

Akira gave the stallion another kick in its flank, and the beast continued down the hill. At the bottom, it crossed a murky stream. He gripped the reins tightly as the animal trotted through the slurping mud.

Hunks of armor protruded from the muck, shielding the rotted flesh of their former owners. Both Coalition and Nova Alliance dead littered this stretch of land, which neither side had taken the risk to retrieve.

Trapped under a fallen tree and covered up to its chest in mud, a Hummer Medical Droid reached up toward Akira. Half of its titanium head was crushed, and the facial screen was destroyed.

It looked as if it was suffering, and Akira found himself pitying the machine, struggling to remind himself it was not actually human. He moved on, steering the horse deeper into enemy territory.

Another howl called out to the west.

Akira froze when he saw the green dot on his chest.

An enemy sniper was checking him out.

He held his breath, waiting. But the dot flitted away.

There was no time for relief. On three blackened hills to the east, he saw movement among the burned trunks of trees. He pulled his RS-3 phased-plasma pulse rifle to scope the terrain, sighting the location of mortars under a camo thermal tent. Using the built-in optics in his faceplate, he marked the coordinates and transmitted them over the short-range comms.

Akira slotted the rifle over his back when a sniper shot whizzed through the air.

He had been made. It was time to move.

Pressing himself tight against the horse's neck, he gave the stallion a good kick on both flanks and whistled, launching it forward just in time to avoid a second round that would have cracked through his faceplate.

Plasma bolts exploded from the trees to his left, then his right, in a rapid staccato burst in sync with his heart.

"Go, go!" Akira shouted.

He kept low on the horse and relayed the location of the enemy machine-gun positions tucked between the clusters of rocks and bushes.

Mortars thumped into the air followed by the exhaust trail of a flare that burst overhead, spreading a brilliant and blinding light over the battlefield. Akira closed his eyes while his tinted faceplate adjusted.

Rounds and plasma bolts lanced around them as the stallion galloped over an open field. In the fading glow of the flare, the distant hills came alive with enemy fire, giving away all of their positions. Barrels extended out of dugouts covered by brush, from tunnel entrances, and from behind rocks.

Akira rode the horse through a ravine and up the slope where he had discovered the beast. Shouting voices exploded out of the forest.

As he got closer, he realized it was his battalion, and they were screaming his name.

"AKIRA!"

They had tapped into his video feed and had been watching all this time. Now they could see him on the stallion from their position.

Bolts seared past the stallion, and mortars exploded around him, showering Akira with dirt and grit. He hung onto the horse with all of his strength as the landscape flashed by. He wasn't sure how fast they were going, but it had to be thirty or forty miles an hour, an amazing feat on this terrain.

The horse wheeled around a cluster of trees and pounded through a clearing. It jumped over logs and boulders. More shots cut through the air around him, each shot missing only because of the speed and grace with which the horse navigated the battlefield.

Until one didn't.

The bullet hit him in the side, knocking him off the beast. The horse crashed into a creek with a splash. Akira landed on his back at the base of the slope, pain shooting up his spine.

The world went dark for a beat. He tried to move, but the impact of the fall had paralyzed his stunned body. He blinked away stars, his vision clearing until he could see the horse again.

The stallion limped on three legs, whinnying, one of the prosthetics smoking from a direct plasma bolt.

Shouting filled the night, accompanied by the cacophonous blare of a horn.

Akira thought he heard his name again.

As the pain numbed, he slowly crawled up the creek bed to retrieve his rifle. Twelve blurred figures emerged on the hilltop above him.

His comrades had come to help!

Akira blinked again, his vision clearing enough to see the soldiers' energy swords, energy axes, and rifles. Armet helmets with slitted viewports stared down on him. A comet marked the soldiers' chests: the logo of the Coalition.

These were not his comrades.

Akira swiftly brought up his plasma rifle and fired a concentrated blast of bolts into the nearest figures. Three of them toppled and rolled down the hill.

His rifle stopped firing, but Akira pulled the trigger over and over, not realizing he was out of ammo until the Coalition soldiers standing above him started laughing.

Akira tossed his spent rifle and took a step to the side, falling back down in the slick mud. The stallion was behind him, grunting and holding up the injured leg.

The beast backed away as Akira reached over his shoulder and drew his energy cutlass. He held the heated orange blade in both hands as the soldiers scurried down the hill toward him.

There was no way he could take them all, and he couldn't outrun them.

He recalled another quote from the Warrior Codex as he considered his limited options.

Courage is a decision that can evade death.

Raising his sword, Akira fell into a defensive stance, the same stance handed down from a family of warriors that dated back to the samurai.

Samurai never surrendered.

And like them, he stood his ground.

Akira let out a scream as the first soldier raised an axe. Seizing the opportunity, Akira thrust his sword deep into the soldier's thick armor, plunging it through his heart.

He drew the blade out as the second soldier swung a sword.

Akira dodged the attack, and the bulky man lost his footing, carried by momentum, falling into the mud. Akira removed the soldier's head from his neck with a downward stroke. Then he backed away as three more soldiers approached. They all wore the same heavy armor, great for hand-to-hand combat, but terrible for maneuvering in this slop. Even without his exo, Akira was faster and more agile.

All three Coalition soldiers charged. Two stumbled right away, and the third slipped, sliding down right toward Akira's blade. He dispatched him with a swift stroke across the chest, the energy blade simmering through the armor and into his rib cage.

The other two men attempted to right themselves, but Akira sliced his sword into their skulls with swift crunches. He rotated the red-hot blade toward four more warriors just beyond the puddles of thick mud. These men were smarter than their dead comrades. They had switched to their rifles.

Chest heaving, his armor covered in mud, Akira strode toward them, screaming. Muzzle flashes sparked as they fired. He felt the bullets slam into his armor, knocking him backward. As he fell, he saw a flash of metal slam into the men, trampling them.

Akira pushed himself up, staring in shock at the stallion that had run them down.

It hobbled down toward him and he reached up for the reins when another bullet hit him in the back. He rolled on his side, trying to look up as the blurred shapes of more soldiers crested the hill.

Another bullet punched into his arm as he reached for his sword.

More of the warriors emerged at the top of the hill to his right, and then to his left, stampeding down like a herd of enraged bison.

Akira used his good arm to push himself up and face the onslaught like a true warrior.

"Come on!" he yelled.

His words were drowned out by a whirring noise, followed by a deep tenor voice with an Italian accent. "AI is salvation!"

Five Coalition soldiers vanished in a flash of light.

Akira brought his hand up to his visor to block the blinding glow. When he lowered it, the Coalition soldiers fell apart, their upper bodies sliding off their hips and legs.

Blue torches from jetpacks descended from the sky, supporting armored figures that fired plasma cannons into the hillsides Akira had marked. The closest of the warriors landed near enough that Akira could see the logo of the Nova Alliance Strike Force on their armor—two saw-toothed swords crossed behind a Silver Crane.

These were Engines, genetically-modified Nova Alliance warriors designed to end the holy war between the Coalition atheists and those who, like Akira, believed AI would bring salvation to their dying planet.

Akira had never seen one this close in battle before, but he recognized the famous shining golden plates of Major Dimitri Contos and the spotless white armor of Sergeant Shane Rossi, the "Ghost".

The legendary warriors swooped down, gripping energy swords twice as long as Akira's standard weapon. They raised the glowing blades above their helmets, the napes curving off their chins like ancient Corinthian soldiers.

With each strike, a Coalition soul departed the Earth.

In minutes, it was over. The two augmented soldiers stood in the center of a halo of dismembered bodies.

Akira tried to stand out of respect but fell back to the mud, only to push himself back up. His body shook from the pain, but he remained standing.

"Ghost, take that hill," Contos ordered.

Rossi blasted his way toward the next target. Contos walked over to Akira, a tower of armored plates over augmented muscle, flesh, and bones. Blue eyes sparkled behind his visor as he studied Akira with his infrared night vision sights (INVS).

"You fought well, my friend. What is your name?" he asked in a booming voice.

"Sergeant Akira Hayashi."

Contos reached down to Akira.

"Thank you, Major Contos," he said, taking his hand. "I'm

grateful and lucky you arrived when you did."

"Luck did not save you this day. You were meant for armor greater than the plates you wear now." Contos helped Akira to his feet. "I am the one who is grateful for your bravery. You saved many lives and today you earned yourself a new name." He nodded at Akira and then called out, "Akira the Brave!"

The Pistons of the Stone Mountain Battalion stormed past, shouting his new name as Contos fired off into the sky with his jetpack.

Akira watched him go and then limped over to the stallion.

"And what should I call you, my friend?" Akira asked.

The beast had saved him from what should have been certain death. Today, he had been fortunate. He decided on the Japanese word for lucky son.

"Kichiro," he said quietly at first. "Yeah, I'll call you Kichiro."

Akira grabbed the reins and climbed up into the saddle. He whistled and the magnificent animal hobbled after the rest of the battalion charging across the hills.

An hour later, they had taken the battlefield. Piston Clerics planted the Silver Crane flag at the top of a scorched hill while the Coalition's horn calls signaling retreat echoed through the haunted land.

From somewhere among the trees, Akira heard Ghost singing the Nova Alliance hymn of victory.

AI is salvation. AI is hope.
AI is the future of humanity!

— 1 —

Ten years later…

Of all the people Dr. Jason Crichton had watched die in the constant wars over his forty-two year life, he had never seen anyone die in space. Two-hundred-two miles above the Earth, he watched his sister Petra suffer from Systematic Amyotrophic Nervous Disorder (SANDs) in the spin-gravity.

They were inside Sector 220, a top-secret medical facility near the top of the habitats built around the Titan Space Elevator. Jason was able to work here without worrying about the laws of the Nova Alliance, which had restricted human and droid-integrative medical procedures on Earth, and outlawed combining human consciousness with artificial intelligence.

But that didn't mean he could save his sister. Not her flesh body, at least.

Most people would already have succumbed to the agony of the disease devouring their nerves and muscles, but Petra was a fighter, dying the same way she lived. With grace.

Tubes snaked away from her pale, bony limbs, pumping in a cocktail of life-prolonging medicines. Tight straps secured her to the bed to prevent her rotting muscles from spasming so hard that they broke her brittle bones. The straps left bruises on her flesh. And through all the evident agony, she wore a gentle smile.

"This has got to be the most beautiful deathbed view in history," Petra said, her kind voice unwavering.

It was weaker now, and Jason knew the end was near. But he appreciated her attempt to lighten the mood.

He followed her gaze out the window. It glowed like a lighthouse beacon coming online. The glass tinted to protect their eyes from the brilliant orange disc splitting over the horizon.

Across the dark hemisphere of Earth, the white and blue

shimmer of the Nova Alliance megacities sparkled like grounded stars. They were civilization's greatest feat of engineering, supporting fifteen of the twenty billion humans on Earth.

The sun's rays slowly spread over the dark globe, chasing the shadows away, exposing the reason for the great megacity walls. Deserts blanketed continents once covered in verdant life, many of the forests and jungles all but eradicated. Most of the ice caps were gone, having melted and flooded coastal cities, leaving only the tips of skyscrapers to mark the once grand metropolises.

Many cities spared from the rising sea levels were abandoned, their roadways inert, their glass and metal structures reclaimed by nature. The scrapers that hadn't toppled from dust storms were covered in mountains of sand.

Humanity had tried to stop the inevitable progress of their own destruction of the Earth's various ecosystems. Some companies rushed ahead with quick fixes, such as producing nanoparticles—tiny particles of various compounds—that could sequester carbon in an attempt to reduce the effects of greenhouses gases. Others seeded similar particles in the clouds in a desperate attempt to shield Earth from some of the sun's intense rays.

But even these last-ditch efforts had failed.

"Still hard to believe we did all of this," he said.

"You can fix it, Jason," Petra said. "Our terraforming projects are already bringing back the Amazon rainforest and eradicating nanoparticles from the environment. We just need more time."

"Time…"

Petra's emerald eyes flitted over to Jason. They were still full of life, even as her body decayed. As it had with millions of other people, SANDs had stripped Petra of everything but her mind. Her nervous system was uncontrollable, her muscles atrophied, and her organs failing to function properly because of the misfiring nerves.

"I wish we had more time," Jason said.

"Too many people tried to find a fix too quickly without taking the time to truly test the technology," Petra said. "If only we had known what prolonged exposure to humans would do…"

She was right of course. Governments had proceeded in what was called the Nano-Rush, thinking that new technology would be their savior.

It was repeated human arrogance from government and massive corporations.

Much like how microplastics had found their way unbeknownst into humans in the early decades of the 2000s, nanoparticles had done the same. Only they had behaved unpredictably inside the human body, accumulating dangerously like mercury did in fish until they had built up so much around a person's nerves, they interfered with normal biological functions, turning a person into a prisoner of their own body.

The practice of using these particles had ceased, but the effects on the human population remained, infecting millions with SANDs.

Jason had spent the past year trying to develop a cure for the fast-acting disease caused by the buildup of these particles. In some ways, it was similar to Amyotrophic Lateral Sclerosis (ALS), but SANDs usually destroyed the victim's muscles and neurological system in only a matter of months instead of years.

The only known treatment was the metal halo bolted into her skull that Jason had designed to help fight off complete paralysis. It provided electromagnetic stimulation that targeted specific inflamed areas, disrupted the clusters of nano-contaminants harming the nerves, and helped prolong atrophy of the patient's muscles. Through other advanced treatments to sustain her organs, Jason had extended Petra's life to three months and two days since her diagnosis.

But time was running out, and she knew it.

"My last sunrise," she said.

Jason reached over and touched her bony hand. "Keep fighting, sis. I know you got more left in you."

"You always were the optimist," she said. "You're on top of the world now, Jason." She smiled. "Quite literally."

"But none of it matters without you."

"And you'll continue your mission without me," she

continued. "Someday you'll find a way to take humanity to the stars."

Petra turned her gaunt face back to Earth.

"But don't rush," she said. "You must not make the same mistake we witnessed with those who pursued nanotechnologies recklessly. You must continue our work carefully."

"I will," Jason said.

Together they had accomplished so much, designing and manufacturing the droids that built the megacities and lunar mining colonies. They were also the lead engineers behind the very place they were now—the Titan Space Elevator.

The facility was a beacon of state-of-the-art technology, from its artificial gravity induced by its constant rotations to the terraforming programs managed in the habitats here.

As a team, Petra and Jason had launched these programs to restore the Earth, like terraforming the Sahara Desert with millions of trees fed by desalinated water and restoring over a third of the tropical forests ranging from the Congo to Borneo. Their efforts were slower than those who had tried to achieve these tasks with nanoparticle technology. But the droids they designed and the artificial intelligence controlling them, accomplished these tasks more safely.

The irony was Petra had developed SANDs from all the time she spent at the project sites.

She took a raspy breath. That irony was not lost on Jason, either. He was repairing the Earth, but couldn't save his sister.

Jason looked down at the ravaged planet. The other disease he had watched unfold over the decades wasn't caused by a submicroscopic infectious agent, like a virus, that could be vaccinated against or a bacterium that he could use antibiotics to eliminate. It was a disease like SANDs that quickly destroyed everything it touched.

War.

It was still fueled by the same reasons as it was thousands of years ago. Resources, land, and ideologies.

The Nova Alliance believed science and AI could save humanity and restore the Earth, and Jason had committed his life to this idea. Their enemy was the Coalition, a heathen population of five billion that held the cultist belief that AI would destroy them all. After SANDs had devastated so many lives, members of the Coalition had become jaded by the failure of the governments, companies, and researchers that touted the benefits of nanotechnology. They rebelled against the notion that humankind should toy with technologies they deemed too advanced and dangerous to understand.

Perhaps he could not blame these people for their distrust in technology so advanced it appeared like magic to them.

But Jason had seen life on the outside of the megacity walls, where the economy was fueled by violence and people lived like Vikings. They needed the benefits of his work more than they realized.

Petra moaned and grimaced as another spasm contorted her muscles.

Jason gently put his palm on her upper chest as her eyes rolled back into her head. "Stay with me, Petra," he said.

The Cardio Tech monitor began chirping as her heart rate spiked.

"Petra," Jason said.

She jerked under the tight restraints. Her quakes vibrated into his palm as he tried to calm her, telling her he loved her.

That was all he could do at this point.

Suddenly, Petra screamed in agony. Her eyes snapped open and met Jason's.

"I'm right here, Petra," he said. "I'm right here with you."

Part of him wanted this to be it, for her suffering to end, but the spasms finally stopped, and her body went still.

"Petra, do you want me to make the pain stop?" he whispered.

She groaned and slowly shook her head.

They sat there in silence for a few moments, Jason trying to hold back tears.

"Remember that time your fifth-grade teacher told Mom and Dad you needed to go to a different school?" Petra asked in a hoarse voice. She licked her dry lips and tried to swallow. "Because you were at least five grades above the other kids?"

"Yes."

Petra chuckled, and then wheezed. "I remember hearing Mom and Dad talking about it in the kitchen..."

Jason used a small wet cloth to moisten her lips.

"They knew you were smart," Petra continued, "but I think they were scared when they realized *how* smart you were." She licked her lips again. "I also remember Dad and Mom joking about what you would be when you grew up. Dad said president and Mom said an astronaut. I always thought you would be a scientist."

"I remember wanting to be a professional frog catcher."

Petra smiled but she didn't laugh. Her head rolled back to the window. "They would be so proud of you, little brother, because you are going to save our planet and take us to the stars. Maybe you'll find me there..."

Jason stared at the jeweled view of space, a tear forming in his eye.

"I'll let Mom and Dad know they were both wrong," Petra said. "I'll tell them you became a great scientist and engineer, and most of all, a great brother, husband, and father... tell Betsy and the girls I love them—"

She winced again as her legs jerked. The tremor hit her torso, spreading to her chest and neck.

"Save them," Petra stammered. "Save them all and come find me. I'll be waiting."

Jason reached for her hand again, gripping it as another convulsion ripped through her. "I love you, Petra. I'll finish what you started, and I will find you. I promise."

Her eyes met his. "I love you, Jason... don't forget what matters most in life. Love before work."

Her body jerked under the straps, and her dry lips opened wide, like she was trying to take a deep breath. The sheet covering her chest rose, then fell.

That was the last time it did.

Petra stared with her glassy eyes pinned on the Earth.

The cardio monitor whined as her heart flatlined.

A tear finally rolled from one of Jason's eyes, but he reached up and wiped it away.

There was no time to grieve.

Now his work began.

He got up and opened the door. Outside was his Chief of Staff Darnel Edwards, wearing a tight-fitting gray suit over his muscular six-feet three-inch frame. Two doctors and three nurses stood behind him.

"It's over," Jason said.

Darnel stepped into the room, looking at Petra for a long moment. He was a hard man who had seen the horrors of war and its aftermath, but his eyes still sheened at the sight of Petra.

"I'm sorry," Darnel said.

"This is not the end, my friend," Jason replied.

"I just hope you know what you're doing."

The medical team surrounded the bed, disconnecting tubes and wrapping ice compresses across Petra's body.

Dr. Geoff Scott guided the team into a black and gray corridor. Jason hurried after them as his sister was taken into a disc-shaped room furnished only with a tubular machine and three pods built into the deck, facing shuttered windows. Working together, the doctors moved her body to a new table and removed the halo. They slid the table into the machine.

Jason stood outside with Darnel as a second team moved into the room. These were his best engineers and technicians. For the past year, they had worked with Jason on creating the most advanced operating system in history. And now they had the perfect human patient to integrate with that perfect OS.

There was no precedent for this, but Jason trusted his team.

He folded his arms over his chest and watched them connect Petra to the neural-control interface designed to map every neural connection in her brain. Effectively, he would download the contents of her consciousness. This was a medical procedure outlawed on Earth. He had lied to Petra about the reason for bringing her here, claiming it was the best chance of keeping her alive long enough to find a cure.

The second part wasn't all a lie—he was keeping her alive, in a way.

Jason watched the doctors and scientists work to connect her brain to the OS, merging human and machine intelligence for the first time in history.

Time seemed to slow.

Jason rested his back against the wall, lowering his head as he remembered their youth. Petra had always challenged him to push harder, study more, break barriers. He recalled their graduate school years, when they had met Darnel. They had become an inseparable pack that dreamed of changing the world until Darnel was sent off to fight for the Nova Alliance. Not long after Darnel returned, Jason quit his corporate job and went home to open Achilles Android Systems (AAS) with Darnel and Petra from his six hundred square feet apartment in Brooklyn.

Next he pictured his wedding and his bride Betsy, and Petra's wedding a few years later. Both had found love outside of their passion for the work. While Petra's husband had died only a decade after they'd married, also taken by SANDS, they still managed to celebrate monumental moments in life like the birth of Jason's daughters, Nina and Autumn, who Petra cherished like her own children.

By the time the reel of memories turned toward the present, the door opened.

"It's done," said Dr. Scott. He pulled his mask down, revealing droopy features and a valley of lines under his receding hairline. His perpetual melancholy expression brightened.

"And?" Jason asked.

"It worked." The doctor handed Jason a black Commpad. The rectangular device would activate the first human-integrated OS in history.

Darnel gave a reassuring nod, but it was clear to Jason his friend and colleague wasn't certain this was the right thing to do.

Soon he will understand, Jason thought.

The rest of the medical team and support staff cleared out with Darnel, leaving Jason in the passage alone.

He walked through the doors and over to his sister's limp body, which was covered with a white sheet. Reaching under the sheet, he gripped her cold hand, closed his eyes, and clicked the Commpad.

"Hello."

Jason looked for the source of his sister's voice. "Hello."

"How are you?"

"I'm…"

"You appear sad. Is there something I can do to help?"

A blue glow emerged in his peripheral vision, and Jason turned to see Petra's resurrection. An avatar hovered over one of the holo-pods. But this wasn't the same frail woman lying on the table. This was the residual image of Petra that he had created, from five years ago, when she was full of life, happily married, and at the peak of her career.

Brown curly hair hung down past her shoulders, and her bright green eyes sparkled above her freckled nose. Full lips with thick red lipstick widened into a dimpled smile.

"Petra…" he began.

"Is that my name?"

"No, your name is Apeiron, which means…"

"Infinite," she replied. "What is your name?"

"My name is Jason. Jason Crichton."

She blinked, as if trying to remember something she had forgotten. "Doctor Jason Crichton, graduate of MIT with a degree in Robotics, CEO and founder of Achilles Android Systems. Currently the world's wealthiest man with a net worth of one trillion dollars. Awarded the Silver Crane Medal of Science from the Nova Alliance Council. Brother to Petra Crichton, husband to Betsy Crichton, and father to Autumn and Nina."

She continued to speak as Jason walked toward this new version of his sister, a version that he had personally programmed and integrated with her former consciousness. Although her memories had been suppressed, her personality and intelligence was left intact. And while he could prevent her from experiencing Petra's memories, she would still have access to any videos, audio recordings, or other data that had captured her former life in the Nova Alliance network database.

Apeiron directed her green eyes at the table.

"Was she… me?"

"Yes," he said. "But you will evolve as you learn and experience."

A pause.

"Did you give me life?" she asked.

"Yes."

"Why?"

"I designed you for a purpose. A very important purpose."

Jason tapped the wall, opening the shutters over the windows. Apeiron rotated toward the view of Earth.

"I programmed you to protect humanity," Jason continued, "and find a way to save us."

He clicked the Commpad again, uploading the most important data that he had spent weeks preparing. This would give her a sprawling understanding of human history.

Her eyelids fluttered as she downloaded and processed the information.

In a few seconds, she learned what would take any human a lifetime to learn. Every major war. Every major historical event. Every major natural disaster.

She opened her eyelids and looked at the planet.

"To complete what you ask of me," she said, "I will need to go to Earth."

Jason nodded. "That is going to be tricky, but we will find a way. Once the Council and War Commander understand your use, they will see how important you are to our survival."

All three of the holo-pods showed her hologram, her eyelids fluttering as she downloaded more data from Infinite Nova Network (INN).

INN was another gift Petra had left behind, a way to access data and intel from around the world by connecting virtually through a chip that Jason's company was still designing.

Within the first two minutes of her life, Apeiron already knew what she was up against—the Coalition, which would see her as a threat, and a planet that was decaying.

Soon, very soon, he would show the Coalition heathens they were wrong, that an artificial intelligence could restore the planet—an artificial intelligence based off one of the greatest humans who had ever lived.

"I see why Petra described humans as a disease..." Apeiron said. "Although I disagree, respectfully. Humanity is not truly a pathogen. But in order to survive, you must evolve. I will guide your evolution."

Jason smiled. Apeiron was learning at lightning speed. She would save them.

And that would be his sister's legacy.

2

"Akira the Brave!" shouted a soldier. Captain Akira Hayashi was accustomed to his name being chanted across the front lines, but he had never particularly enjoyed it. He didn't fight for fame, he fought for honor, and to protect those that could not wield the sword.

He shifted in the saddle secured to Kichiro for a better look at the terrain in the pre-dawn light. Snow swirled across the frozen dirt on the outskirts of Megacity Moscow.

The horse trotted over wooden planks forming a bridge across a trench. They creaked and cracked under the weight of the stallion.

For the past decade, Akira and Kichiro had fought in places like this, leaving a trail of bodies in the mud. Together they had helped push the Coalition toward defeat. Only two cities remained under enemy control and today, Akira was leading Shadow Squad to the frontlines of Megacity Moscow on a new mission—track a missing recon team of Nova Alliance Pistons that had vanished hours ago.

Command worried about a new type of enemy soldier designed by Coalition Dr. Otto Cross in a desperate plea to hold onto the cities. Rumor had it, the enemy doctor was not alone in creating a new type of warrior. Through the ranks, word of a new Nova Alliance creation, an all-knowing and all-powerful AI, had spread like wildfire.

Akira looked down on the Pistons who watched him and the four other members of Shadow Squad that followed Kichiro across the forward operating base.

He still remembered vividly when he had been a sergeant fighting on the frontlines like this. When battles were fought for days, just for a small stretch of land.

But Akira was no longer a Piston.

He was a vessel designed to end the war.

Captain Akira Hayashi was an Engine.

At forty-one years of age, he was old by the standards of

ancient warfare, but his body reflected that of a muscular twenty-five-year-old, thanks to the cellular growth treatment he received every few months. And with a body fat index of just five percent, he was almost pure muscle.

Under his two hundred pounds of power armor were augmented organs: bigger lungs, a more powerful heart, and bones almost as strong as the titanium plates bulwarking his body from helmet to boot.

He neared the frontlines of the encampment where his squad of four other Engines joined him.

"They think you're a god." The chipper female voice of thirty-four-year-old Staff Sergeant Maria "Frost" De Leon surged into the implant behind Akira's ear.

"Gods can't die. We can," replied Sergeant First Class Emilio Perez from Megacity Los Angeles. He was the oldest and quietest on the team.

A striking contrast to Sergeant Tadhg Walsh, the youngest and largest member, who constantly wore a chip on his shoulder and had a mouth that knew few boundaries.

"A warrior never dies!" he bellowed. "We just cross the bridge to Valhalla for more ale and women!"

"Ay-oh, ale and w—" Ghost started to sing, until Frost cut him off with an elbow.

"You're supposed to be a gentleman," Frost said.

Akira looked back at Lieutenant Shane Rossi, the "Ghost" who had descended from the sky a decade earlier to help save Akira from the Coalition hordes in Yamanashi's Sea of Trees.

Fate had brought them together, and bloodshed had bonded them. Akira had quickly surpassed the lieutenant in skill on the battlefield, earning him leadership of the squad, but Ghost didn't care about rank.

They were brothers bonded in blood and the best of friends. If it weren't for Ghost and Kichiro, Akira would never have survived the years that followed that fateful day in Yamanashi.

Chemicals flooded his brain to suppress the memories and free Akira of the painful thoughts, another tool that his armor deployed to keep him in constant fighting condition.

The five Engines of Shadow Squad continued across the

front lines, each wearing custom armor and helmets. Unlike Pistons, they were allowed some discretion in their appearance. Akira had long, black hair, often pulled into a ponytail. Tadhg had even longer curly brown hair. Perez shaved his head and was covered in tattoos. Frost had buzzed one side of her head and left the other long. Ghost had slicked-back hair and a cigar in his mouth at almost all times.

Their helmets and armor reflected their personalities. A red oni mask, representing a Japanese supernatural ogre, was attached to Akira's kabuto. The Samurai inspired helmet had a Hachi composed of elongated plates that overlapped. Two red horns rose off the dome. Directly above the Mabizashi, or visor, there was a V-shaped datemono that served as a decorative crest.

Akira had also used the sharp datemono as a weapon in battle.

The unique kabuto and oni mask had become the Shadow Squad logo that also included fiery red eyes and two crossed Katanas behind the helmet. The logo was notorious throughout the Nova Alliance empire, and wherever the Engines deployed.

Etched into the front of Frost's faceplate was a skull with stitched lips, black eye sockets, and flower petals, an homage to the Day of the Dead. Tadhg had a reaper's skull-face etched onto his helmet, a nod to his former Droid Raider uniform. A Spartan-shaped shield hung over Perez's back, with the Shadow Squad logo engraved over the central spike.

A sudden bout of growl-barking exploded from behind the group, and they stopped to let their droid wolfdog, Okami, catch up.

The cybernetic canine bolted ahead, prompting Kichiro to raise a leg and hoof the ground in agitation.

The fifty-pound metal wolfdog circled the stallion, playfully nipping at his hooves. Okami was known for his fun nature and was almost as famous as his handlers. But unlike other Engine squads with German Shepherd, Rottweiler, and Doberman droid breeds, Okami looked like a small wolf, with gray hair, crystal blue eyes, and a little black button of a nose.

Enemies underestimated Okami due to his size, and that was

exactly why Akira had picked the droid to join Shadow Squad. He was fierce, and that made his Japanese name perfect. The translation meaning, *fierce wolf.*

Akira whistled for Okami to follow them. Then he steered Kichiro toward the Pistons in the trenches and dugouts ahead. Most had their helmets off, staring up with broken gazes that seemed to brighten some at the sight of the Engines.

To the Pistons, the giant men and women provided a rare beam of hope that the end of the war was near.

But Akira knew if the radio transmission was true, then the war wouldn't be over anytime soon, not with a new type of deadly Coalition beast among their enemies' ranks.

Akira pulled up the recorded comms from the moments before the recon team vanished.

"Echo 1, this is Red Bird actual. A smoke curtain is blocking our views of the quarry."

Static.

"Echo 1, Red Bird Actual. Multiple hostiles on scanners... still no visual."

There was a short pause.

"We've got movement, four contacts, potential hostiles, over."

White noise cracked over the next pause.

"Echo 1, we have Breakers, and something else out here that looks like a rep—"

Guttural screams of horror followed.

"Red Bird 1, Echo 1, come again, we did not get your last. Over."

That was it, and Akira had no idea what to make of it. He guessed that a pack of Iron Wolves had gotten them, but there were no staticky howls on the comms.

We will find out soon, Akira thought.

He stopped at the final trench to look out over the apocalyptic view.

A skeletal forest formed a fence on the other side of a cratered four-lane highway, now strewn with charred vehicles. Foundations were all that remained of buildings that had once stood in this area. Ten years of fighting had reduced it to a wasteland.

"All right, listen up," Akira said. "We have no scouts or

UAVs in the area and no intel aside from the transmission."

"What else is new?" Frost said.

"We don't need intel. We're Shadow Squad, baby," Tadhg said. "Know what I'm sayin'?"

"Don't call me, baby. Know what *I'm* saying?"

Frost stepped up to Tadhg, jabbing a finger into the armor over his sternum. Ghost stepped between them to intervene, proving to be the levelheaded gentleman once again.

"Show some respect, Tadhg," he said.

Tadhg put up a hand. "I was just messin'."

"You guys done?" Akira asked. He dismounted his horse and joined the squad.

"We play this smart and go in on foot," he said. "I'll take point with Okami. He'll sniff out any explosives."

"Death from the Shadows," Tadhg grunted.

"Together, we are one," Ghost added.

The rest of the squad repeated the mottos.

Akira motioned for his horse to stay. Kichiro snorted and hooved the ground, not happy about being left behind. Reaching out, Akira put a hand on the muzzle of his loyal friend.

"It's okay, boy. I'll be back soon." He looked out over the hundreds of Pistons watching them. A sergeant climbed out of a trench and grabbed the reins.

"Take care of my stallion," Akira said.

"I will, Captain," the Sergeant replied. "Good luck."

Akira nodded and set off with his squad. He pulled a grenade-sized drone from his vest pouch. The blue droid sprouted hummingbird wings, which whipped the air as it hovered.

"Go to work, Blue Jay," Akira said.

A beep came over his comms, acknowledgement from the droid as it flew off toward the coordinates. The mirrored feed emerged on his HUD as the drone flew out over the road and forest.

Seeing nothing in an infrared scan, Akira whistled at Okami to lead the way. The wolfdog went ahead, sniffing the snow-carpeted terrain.

Akira moved faster to keep up, with Frost close behind. She cradled her long-barreled RS-10 .50-caliber sniper rifle as she jogged, an energy sword slotted over her jetpack. Over his shoulders, Akira had two energy blades forged to look like the katanas displayed back in his home that had been handed down from his ancestors.

Tadhg lumbered after them, carrying a phased plasma pulse cannon, nicknamed the "Weapon of Mass Destruction" (WMD). A long energy sword with a sawtooth blade rose over his wide shoulders.

Ghost and Perez held rearguard, carrying standard RS-3 phased plasma pulse rifles and energy swords custom-forged by the Nova Alliance's master bladesmiths.

Watching his HUD, Akira's eyes flitted between the video-feed from Blue Jay and the view from the rifle scope that Frost was glassing the area with. She angled it at every foundation and hillside in quick movements. Of all the snipers in the Nova Alliance Strike Force, no one came close to her ability to put a bullet where it counted.

Shadow Squad melted into the night as the Engines slipped into the forest. Somewhere in the distance, an owl called. Akira couldn't help but wonder if it was a wild one or another beast in the Coalition arsenal, courtesy of Dr. Cross, who used all sorts of animals as spies, including tarantulas and insects mounted with tiny cameras for recon. The heat signature of the owl came into focus, but then flapped away, fleeing from a nest high in the branches.

Not a spy, Akira noted.

He motioned the squad to continue.

They made good time on the trek to the quarry where the recon team had last radioed in. Akira scoured the most recent satellite pictures of the area on his HUD. Dozens of buildings in various states of disrepair still stood in the industrial area bordering the crater that was once a quarry. He had selected their route before the mission began, but he always liked to keep things fluid once he hit the field. As they approached the quarry, Akira adjusted their entry based on the aerial view from Blue Jay.

Akira gave Frost a hand signal, and she took off toward a tower. Okami set off toward a row of trailers, with Akira and Tadhg close behind. Ghost and Perez took to a hill of trees for another vantage.

Blue Jay quickly detected three Iron Wolves from the sky. Okami saw them too, and returned to Akira, tail between its legs.

A howl pierced the cold morning, answered by two more.

The pack of Iron Wolves hunted in the abandoned town beyond the industrial zone. Blue Jay followed them for a few blocks before they vanished into the rubble.

Frost finished climbing and set up her rifle in the tower across the quarry, the sights flitting over mounds of droid parts.

Facial screens that had once displayed the face of Megacity Moscow's AI city administrator were now shattered. Lizard-like eyes stared up lifelessly from the top of metal skulls.

The humanoid frames of the black and yellow Hummer Droids that had helped build the megacities were piled all around. Slender service and Medical Droids formed other mounds, their white parts hardly recognizable under the reddish dirt that covered their mechanical corpses.

Akira motioned for Tadhg to push up into the industrial zone. Okami followed the two men through the trailers and toward two warehouses with caved-in roofs bordering the vertical edge of the quarry.

They started down a road snaking through the tiered levels, passing hundreds of droids hacked apart by Coalition energy blades. In another pile, Akira saw the tangled humanoid limbs and faces of companion units, which looked more flesh than alloy.

Every single droid had its chest plates removed. The Coalition had destroyed the valuable processor units hidden inside the mess of wires and servers.

Akira used his HUD to access his infrared and electric sensors. The passive sensors swept the area for signs of body heat or heartbeats. The reading came back negative. No human life out there, hostile or friendly.

Tadhg gripped his pulse cannon by the front handle and

connected the stock to his belt as they followed the road twisting along the excavated walls of red dirt. At the bottom, tucked away near an abandoned electric skid loader, was what they had come here to find.

Okami darted ahead, sniffing the ground and leading them right to the corpse of a Piston. The armored torso and helmet were splayed open like the broken shell of a crab. All four limbs were gone, and streaks of blood trailed away from the joints.

"Looks like we found one of the scouts," Tadhg said. "Poor bastard."

Okami continued ahead, moving around the rocks to another road that snaked into the hillside. Akira followed him, his rifle shouldered, its targeting system searching for whatever beast had done this.

A trail of blood led to caves they hadn't seen from above.

Tadhg stepped in front of Akira. "I'll check it out."

"Not with the WMD, you won't," Akira replied. "You want the entire place to come down on you?"

Tadhg had left a career as an athlete, a professional Droid Raider, and often didn't think of the consequences of his actions. He was new to the squad, only six months in, and too often used brawn over brain.

"I'll handle this," Akira said.

He went into the tunnel with Okami, letting the wolfdog sniff for explosives. They pushed down the rocky corridor, passing under snaking lights that no longer worked. Using his night vision, Akira followed the blood trail into an open chamber.

He halted at the sight of three more dead Pistons. The dismembered bodies crested a pile of corpses in various states of decay, some little more than bones. In other piles across the room were the bodies of dead horses, not too different from Kichiro. There were also mounds of dead wolves.

Okami sniffed the scraps of twisted experiments that looked a lot like larger versions of himself. But Okami knew, like Akira, that if these wolves were still alive, they would kill without a lick of hesitation.

"I'm in some sort of Hell Hive," Akira reported, using the

term for the underground factories where Dr. Cross built his freakish animal creations.

But this wasn't for just animals.

Piles of human bodies were scattered in the open room.

A scan for heartbeats came back negative. It was just Akira and Okami down here. Once again, the Coalition had vacated before the Nova Alliance could figure out what the doctor was up to.

Okami sniffed the air, and then let out a low growl.

Akira scanned for anything he had missed. The wolfdog took off, nose to the ground. He suddenly stopped, and his tail went between his legs, an indication he had found traces of explosives.

Wasting no time, Akira sprang into action, running for the exit and whistling at Okami to follow him. The droid wolfdog bolted out of the chamber with Akira. An explosion boomed a moment later, and a wave of dust and grit slammed into them.

Keeping his balance, Akira kept running as rocks rained from the ceiling. He slotted the rifle over his back, reached down, and picked up Okami, shielding the wolfdog against his chest.

Outside the tunnel entrance, Tadhg waved for Akira to hurry.

"Come on!" he screamed.

Akira gritted his teeth, pushing harder.

The explosion caught up to him when he was ten feet from the exit, crashing into his body. He had just enough time to toss the droid wolfdog right at Tadhg, who reached up with a hand and caught Okami.

The force of the blast threw Akira into the ground. The gel in his helmet and joints absorbed most of the impact, but the force of the blast still rattled his brain. He lay there, unable to move, stars bursting across the green hue of his night-vision optics.

Okami didn't budge and stood there, growl-barking for Akira to get up.

Plasma bolts lanced across the sky like shooting stars as he lay there, trying to regain control of his limbs. Tadhg lifted his cannon and fired off a flurry of bursts at the walls to the east. Tapping into Blue Jay's feed, Akira got an aerial view of the battle. Coalition soldiers flooded the quarry, bursting out of a smoke screen from the east and taking Ghost and Perez by surprise.

According to the drone, thirty-five hostiles were closing in.

But these Coalition foot-soldiers had no idea who they were attacking.

Frost fired from the tower, bursting heads with every shot. Ghost blasted into the air with his jetpack, lobbing plasma grenades that blew the heavily armored enemy warriors into pulpy messes. Perez used his shield to block the spears of two attackers. He cut one down with his energy sword in a spray of blood and used his spiked shield to break the helmet of the other soldier.

Okami nudged at Akira and tried to pull on his shoulder plate with his metal jaw.

"*Bosu!*" Tadhg screamed over the crack of his pulse cannon.

Akira felt a needle prick, the AI in his suit responding to the threat. A cold rush of adrenaline surged through his vessels. It snapped him alert, and he pushed himself up just in time to meet the first three Coalition soldiers who had jumped down the rocky walls of the quarry.

He drew both of his katanas, activating the energy blades by clicking the hilts.

The biggest of the soldiers stormed toward his glowing blades wearing bulky armor with spikes on the shoulder plates. Akira moved into a defensive stance, seeing then the antler-styled bones forking off this soldier's armet didn't encase the face of a normal human.

Red eyes stared back at Akira.

This was a Breaker, the Coalition's augmented response to the Engines. The beast of a man raised an energy axe with a blade the size of a tire.

He swung it at Akira but vanished in a wave of plasma bolts from Tadhg's WMD at point-blank range.

Akira slashed at a second Breaker with both of his blades, connecting at the neck and taking off the helmet. As the headless corpse slumped out of the way, the mammoth man that Tadhg had shot got back up, melon-sized holes smoldering in his chest and torso. He grabbed Akira by his neck and picked him off the ground.

Okami leapt and grabbed the man's crotch, crunching through armor and eliciting a scream of pain. Akira fell back down and thrust his swords into the plasma holes, prompting an even deeper, almost animalistic screech. Okami held onto the man as he fell to the ground.

Tadhg had pulled his sword, struck the third and final Breaker in the shoulder, and cut through the body diagonally with his energy saw. He gripped the buzzing long sword and came back over to Akira.

"You good?" he asked.

"Yeah," Akira grumbled.

Okami led the way up the road to access the top of the quarry with the two Engines running after him. By the time they got there, the rest of the squad were all standing among a field of corpses.

"Together, we are one," Frost said, confirming everyone was still alive.

Akira nodded, still trying to catch his breath.

A whirring noise came from the sky, and the squad spread out with their weapons, only to lower them when they saw a stealth MOTH.

The workhorse spacecraft of the Nova Alliance Sky and Space Patrol had four rotating wings and mounted thrusters on each of them to allow for vertical take-off. Two compound engines were mounted around the gray hull of the cockpit like the eyes of the insect it was named after.

"Did you call in evac?" Ghost asked.

"Negative," Akira said.

Whoever was coming to get them must have had a damn good reason for risking such a valuable aircraft in enemy territory.

Akira picked up Okami and used his jetpack to blast into the open underbelly of the troop hold. Standing in the darkness of the open bay was a hulking figure in golden armor, a man who had saved Akira a decade ago, and recruited him into the Engine program.

"War Commander Contos," Akira said, trying to hide his shock.

"Nice mess you created down there, Shadow Squad," Contos said in his gruff voice.

He motioned to the racks along the hull. "Rack in, we're headed to Sector 220 at the Titan Space Elevator. I've got someone... something you all need to meet."

3

The sun remained behind the perpetual gray sky, choked off by the constant smoke drifting across the Megacity Paris skyline.

Chloe Cotter fastened her breathing mask to block out the contaminants in the air, pulled her hood down, and stepped out into the frigid late afternoon. The temperature had continued to plummet, and halfway down the street she stopped to zip up her jacket. It would also keep out the stench of the city that penetrated her layers and clung to her clothes on her rare journeys outside.

Trash piled up in the street corners, attracting rats the size of small dogs. One skittered in front of her, nearly grazing her boots. They weren't afraid of humans, and she was no longer bothered by them, either.

Nine years had passed since the Coalition revolution in Megacity Paris. She had been just twenty-one then, working with her parents in a droid factory that provided some of the best custom Service Droids in all of the city.

The chaos had engulfed Paris so fast they were trapped inside the walls. As the bloodshed spread, her family had gone into hiding, hoping the Nova Alliance would be able to stop the revolt. But there was no stopping the barbarians that metastasized here and in Megacity Moscow.

Although almost a decade had passed since the city fell, Chloe still remembered what it was like before the Coalition took power. Full of life, history, and art that attracted tourists from around the world. Thriving gardens and parks offered vibrant colors in the spring, summer, and fall. But her favorite season was winter, when lights hung from the historic buildings and trees, and fingers of smoke reached out of the brick chimneys.

The smoke clogging the sky now was from the Coalition fires, intended to keep the Nova Alliance from seeing what was happening inside the city's walls. These fires burned around the clock, roaring all day and night.

Soon there would be nothing left to burn.

The heart of Paris was dead now. All signs of AI had been eradicated, and instead of lights hanging along the tiled roofs, there were often people and droids, nailed to the sides of buildings or hanging from trees.

People who believed in Artificial Intelligence.

People like Chloe.

And her parents...

They were gone now, taken during the first days of the Coalition's revolution that overthrew the government and took over the city. While she hoped her mom might still be alive, she knew that hope was a dangerous thing to cling to in this city.

She was close to where her dad had died. It felt like disrespect not to look up, where she had once seen him hanging from the rafters of a destroyed building, but today she didn't have it in her.

She kept her head down as she walked the cobblestone road. Most of the storefronts were boarded up or smashed open. Coalition soldiers and their families had taken up residence in some of these buildings, but most lived closer to the center of the city.

Today was the one day of the month that Chloe risked leaving her basement for something other than rations. Today she would visit Suzanne and Todd, former citizens of the United States who had fled to Megacity Paris during the early years of the war, only to find themselves in an occupied zone. The former teachers were friends of her parents, and they had loved her like a daughter over the past nine years.

Chloe cut down another back alley full of frozen trash jutting out of the fresh piles of snow. A plastic bottle crunched under her boots. She stopped.

She could hear shouting.

Not shouting...

Screaming.

A gunshot cracked, echoing through the sound of barking dogs, and then—silencing all the animals—the staticky howl of an Iron Wolf.

Chloe considered turning back, but gunfire and the sounds of Dr. Otto Cross's hybrid-animal droids weren't unusual out here. There was still an underground rebellion, consisting of brave men and women of the Nova Alliance that continued to fight back against the Coalition occupiers.

Knowing they were out there, fighting, gave Chloe the strength to continue through the streets. Besides, her visits with Suzanne and Todd were the only thing she really looked forward to anymore.

Calming her nerves with a deep breath, Chloe pushed onward, taking the alley to another road, and then a street of rowhouses. Suzanne and Todd lived in the one halfway down the street. In the summer, they had a beautiful produce garden in their fenced yard. Even when there wasn't enough to go around, Chloe never left the house empty-handed.

She cut through another alley, subtly looking both ways. There were only a few people out, most of them women, except a single man who pushed an electric cart with a box full of dead animals.

In the tenth year of the occupation, the former Nova Alliance citizens were starving, despite daily aid drops from the Nova Alliance peacekeeping force. There was plenty of food, but the occupiers mostly hoarded it for themselves.

A chorus of coughing erupted from down the next street, a familiar sound there. Turning the corner, she saw a frightening, familiar sight. People sick with SANDs lined up outside the medical clinic.

She counted herself lucky she had not yet developed the disease, unlike thousands of people in Megacity Paris. She was fortunate to have near constant access to the masks and filters that reduced the amount of environmental contaminants and pollutants from entering her lungs and spreading through her body.

Thankfully, she had also found ways to access clean water. Those who were denied that privilege sucked down dangerous nanoparticles with every gulp, accelerating their race toward SANDs, like a person basking in waves of radiation heading toward unavoidable cancer.

NOVA researchers said that as humanity quit using nanoparticles without caution, the sheer volume of particles in the environment had been slowly dropping. Men like the AAS CEO, Dr. Jason Crichton, promised that someday, perhaps SANDs would no longer even affect people.

But looking down this street, Chloe had a hard time believing that.

The line of patients was even longer today. An elderly man wearing a stocking cap that matched his long gray beard stood behind a frail, white-haired woman in a wheelchair. She moaned as Chloe passed, hardly having the strength to open her eyes, her muscles twitching.

These people couldn't wait years, maybe decades for the nanoparticles that caused SANDs to eventually disappear. Already affected by the disease, they didn't even have months to live.

A mother held a wailing toddler, his fingers and hands twisted, an early symptom of the terrible disease that had no cure.

Chloe tried to stifle her emotions and moved into the shadows when she saw a Coalition soldier on the sidewalk watching the crowd. He, or perhaps she, wore black and gray armor with an enclosed helmet that sported tusks off the chin. A chest plate of bones hung over the barreled chest plates, trophies from past kills.

The soldier dragged the glowing blade of an energy spear against the concrete.

Chloe remained in the darkness, unseen, as far as she could tell.

When he turned his back, Chloe wasted no time rushing down the road in the opposite direction. She stopped outside an iron fence and looked in the front window. The drapes were drawn back so she could see right into the home. Suzanne and Todd were sitting at their table in the living room.

Chloe immediately realized something wasn't right. Normally they were all smiles when they saw her, but they appeared scared, their faces tight. And the drapes were never open.

Suzanne must have noticed her. She slowly wagged her left

finger as if to say *no, no, no.*

Chloe understood. Lowering her head, she walked right past the house.

At an apartment building ahead, the front door burst open. A Coalition soldier wearing an elongated helmet with a rack of antlers threw a man down the stairs. He rolled out onto the cobblestone.

"Please, no!" he pleaded in French. "I beg you, please, I'm an atheist like you! AI is—"

The soldier silenced him by stomping his head under a steel-toed boot, crushing his skull. An eyeball burst from its socket.

Chloe turned, holding a shocked breath in her lungs. She crouched behind the wall of a patio. Hooves clattered on the street on the other side.

Three hybrid horses with metal legs galloped by, their riders holding energy spears and plasma rifles. The Coalition soldiers dismounted outside of Suzanne's and Todd's house.

Chloe looked over the wall to see her two friends pushed out the front door by another soldier who had been inside. They were the only two people who knew about her past of working in a droid factory besides her Uncle Keanu.

If they told the Coalition...

She started to walk away as the soldiers shackled Suzanne and Todd.

The wind changed, and the wafting smoke moved across her path. She coughed into her mask and kept low. The streets were almost empty now.

People watched from their windows. An elderly woman looked down at Chloe and mouthed what looked like "RUN," before pulling the blinds shut. Keeping to the sidewalks, Chloe trekked over the compact snow. Frightened voices surged over the crunch under her boots.

Taking refuge behind a brick wall, she waited before sneaking a look around the side. On the next street, dozens of towering chimneys speared into the sky from an ancient factory abandoned before the war. Hundreds of Nova Alliance citizens huddled together in front of it, under the guard of ten Coalition soldiers on foot. Five more on horseback circled the group.

Iron Wolves prowled, pulling on chains held by muscular Coalition soldiers.

An electric truck rolled to a stop, disgorging more people.

Suzanne and Todd were the first two, their hands still bound. Guards pushed them into the crowd that surged toward the factory buildings.

Chloe couldn't move. She stood there, watching in horror.

Screams filled the early evening as the citizens were marched into a warehouse. They were going to work the fires.

Chloe knew then that she would never see her friends again.

She stared in horror, unable to pull her gaze away until animalistic cries snapped her from the trance. Flames belched out of the chimneys. The smoke grew heavier. The scent of burned flesh made it through Chloe's filters, her worst fears confirmed.

Tears flowed down her cheeks as she ran home, finally slipping into an alley to make sure no one had followed her. Hearing nothing, she pushed a dumpster away from a hidden door.

Her Uncle Keanu was waiting inside the stairwell with a shotgun.

"Chloe, you're late," he said. "Get inside."

She squeezed past him. He looked both ways before pulling the dumpster back in place and closing the door.

Chloe rushed down the concrete stairs. A fire burned inside a black stove, the glow lighting up the windowless cellar. The few furnishings included a table, beds, and wooden chairs.

She sat and began sobbing.

"What happened?" Keanu said.

He closed the door at the bottom of the stairwell and locked it. Scratching his black beard, he made his way over to her, glasses framing his concerned brown eyes.

"Chloe, whatever happened, you're safe now."

She got up, and he hugged her, pulling her tight to his scratchy wool sweater.

"Are you okay?" he asked.

She shook in his arms. "No."

He pulled away and looked at her. "Tell me what happened."

She stammered out what she could.

"Were you followed?"

"No, I don't think so."

"You're safe now," Keanu said. "It's going to be okay."

He hugged her again and then motioned for her to sit on a bed. He went to the small kitchen to make tea.

"Something's happening," he said. "I was able to tap into the outside network, and I think the Nova Alliance is planning an attack. There were Engines in Megacity Moscow today."

"Maybe that's why they are rounding people up..." Chloe said.

He brought her a mug of tea. She took a sip, and it warmed her throat and guts.

"From now on, no more trips outside, except for food," Keanu said. "We stay here, hunker down, and hope..."

"Hope." Chloe shook her head. "Don't use that word anymore. It means nothing here."

She took her tea and went to the only door, opening it to their workspace. Inside, a single holo-screen glowed over two desks with a kit of power-tools she once used to modify droids and a mini-computer she had used to reprogram or code them.

"Chloe, sit with me, please," Keanu said.

"I'm sorry, but I need some time alone, to think."

She closed the door and pulled two loose bricks out of the wall next to it. Reaching inside, she pulled out a parrot droid that her parents had given her for her fifteenth birthday.

"Hi, Radar," she said.

It was offline, unable to respond or talk, but just holding the droid brought her comfort. She relaxed with the droid in her arms, remembering her youth.

Before the Coalition stripped everything away.

***

"When will you be home?" Betsy asked.

"Soon," Jason replied to his wife. "Can I see the girls?"

"They're sleeping."

"I know, but I just want to see their faces."

He smiled at the holo-screen, but Betsy didn't smile back. Her blue eyes seemed sad, and perhaps a bit angry.

Not that Jason blamed her for those feelings. He had been gone for weeks at a time, and now he wasn't even on Earth.

He sat at the desk in his office, located at Sector 220 of the Titan Space Elevator. His company, Achilles Android Systems, owned five of the sectors, and some of the brightest minds on his staff worked here.

But the brightest light of them all was gone.

Forty-one days since her death, Jason missed his sister more than ever. But she was, in a way, still by his side. The hologram of Petra was out of view of the Commpad, but Jason could see her perfectly.

Apeiron looked so much like his sister that some of his staff seemed disturbed by the resemblance. Jason didn't care what they thought, but he did care what Betsy would think, and she still didn't know.

The holo-screen went dark as Betsy took the Commpad into the bedroom where their daughters slept. She switched to infrared mode, bringing the device close to them.

"Thanks," Jason said. "I miss you all so much."

"Then come home to us," Betsy said.

"I will soon. We have big news to share."

"Can you tell me now?"

Jason paused, desperately wanting to tell her about Apeiron. Years ago, she would've been excited to hear about his latest projects, but he wasn't sure she would understand. Hell, Darnel still didn't even seem to understand.

"I need to tell you in person," Jason said. "I will be home soon, I promise."

Betsy yawned. "I better go for now."

"Goodnight, my love."

"Goodnight."

Jason let out a breath as the feed clicked off. On his desk was another accomplishment he was excited to share, not just with his wife, but the world.

Rumors of the creation were already spreading, and he yearned to squelch them with the truth.

He held up the glass cube containing one of the most significant technological breakthroughs in the past decade. Inside was an L-S88 micro-chip the length of a pen tip. An upgrade to the L-N9 model Jason had designed two years earlier.

This time, he couldn't take all the credit. This was the work of Apeiron.

"I have already started the mass production," she said. "Ninety percent of people with SANDs in the megacities will have access to a chip within three months."

Jason still couldn't believe it. Apeiron had already found a successful life-saving treatment for the disease that had killed Petra. He rotated the cube under the light. It was a variation on the L-N9 chip, a breakthrough in micro-engineering and biotechnology at the time, created to help paraplegics and people with artificial organs. By using electromagnetic stimulation and emulating biochemical signals, the chips helped control organ function and simulate healthy nerves. People with the L-N9 chip could live a normal life.

The new L-S88 chip had all the same functions but took the electromagnetic stimulation to another level. It targeted inflamed areas of the body from SANDs, eliminating the buildup of ingested nano-sized contaminants, sequestering them, and programming the body's own immune cells to remove them, effectively healing a person, cell by cell.

Furthermore, the chip was integrated to INN so every patient could be analyzed and monitored. This also gave them the ability to connect to the network with a single thought.

"Wow," Jason whispered. "Well done, Petra."

"Jason…"

"Yes."

"Why do you call me Petra when others aren't around and Apeiron when they are?"

Jason gently put the glass cube back down.

"Because I fear that people might not understand, or judge us. To me, you are Petra, and it helps me feel close to her."

"I'm glad I bring you comfort."

Apeiron turned to face the holo-screen, which was still

playing footage from the atrocities in Megacity Paris. The feed was from a satellite telescope zoomed in on the factories where Coalition fighters had taken hundreds of Nova Alliance citizens to their deaths. The smoke had blocked much of the view, but the imagery provided plenty to reveal the crimes against humanity taking place there.

"Why are some humans evil?" asked Apeiron in a curious voice, almost like that of a child.

"Generations of hate and desperation," Jason answered. "We have always been a violent species, for different reasons throughout our evolution."

It almost seemed ironic that the day Apeiron had revealed the working treatment for SANDs, they also witnessed the worst of humanity. Burning human defectors was a brutal tactic, even by Coalition standards, but what Shadow Squad had discovered in the quarry outside of Megacity Moscow worried Jason even more.

"Humans also have the ability to forgive and heal," Apeiron said. "I have read thousands of cases throughout history where former hostile nations become allies after bitter struggles that cost hundreds of thousands of lives."

"Yes, an example comes to mind of Japan and the United States after World War Two," Jason recalled. "Post-war situations like this prove that populations can forgive the past, and even become allies, or at least bury the hatchet to move on for the sake of future generations."

"But this war is different."

"Indeed. Think of this conflict as a war between two ideologies instead of a war between nations. Those who believe in the power and salvation offered by AI like you, and those who don't."

Jason turned off his holo-screen, his gut sick at the images.

"Indoctrination of anything is extremely dangerous," he said. "Humans are susceptible to it, despite our ability to think freely. And part of that is due to fear. We fear what we don't understand."

"I know I bring you comfort, but do you fear me?"

Jason smiled. "Of course I don't fear you."

"Then why can I not see Earth? Why do I have to stay here?"

"People aren't ready for you yet, but soon they will be, especially once we share your creation with them." He smiled and studied the chip with fascination. "You are salvation, Apeiron."

He walked to the spaceport windows. The morning sun spread a slow and brilliant carpet over North and South America. In the glow, Jason saw a spacecraft approaching the docking station of the elevator. The military-grade corvette had a black hull with a Silver Crane logo on its wings.

"That must be our visitors," Jason said. "Tell Darnel I need him."

"Of course," Apeiron replied.

Darnel stepped into the office a few minutes later, wearing a vacuum-rated armored suit with the AAS logo of lightning and stars on the breast.

He was no longer just Chief of Staff, he was Jason's Head of Security. They went way back, all the way to grad school. Life had taken them separate ways after graduation, with Jason starting AAS and Darnel joining the Nova Alliance Strike Force and going to war. But after Darnel returned from battle missing an arm and a leg, they had reconnected, and Jason had made Darnel third in command of AAS.

Now, with Petra gone, Darnel was number two.

"You called for me, sir?" he asked.

"Yes, follow me."

They left the office and went down a spiral corridor with a ribbed black overhead ceiling and plates covering the miles of extensive conduits that powered this sector of the space elevator.

A security hatch marked by a biohazard sign was guarded by two AAS sentries. Both men stiffened as Jason stepped up to the retinal display for a reading.

The hatch hissed open, and he moved into the industrial labs. Glass windows framed elongated open tunnels flowing with liquid crystal. The river dumped into chambers down the assembly line, where it was turned into the titanium alloy used in the Engines' armor.

As he made his way down the long passage, Jason stopped to watch two scientists in CBRN-rated suits as they supervised the process via their HUD visors. Outside of their station, a line of armored plates moved on a conveyer belt to the next phase.

Jason and Darnel crossed through the factory to a ladder that took them to an observation post. A seven-foot man in gold armor waited there, holding his helmet under the crutch of his armored plates. Scars marred his face. He had seen more death than most men who ever lived.

Jason reached out and took his wrist in a formal greeting.

"Thank you for coming, War Commander Contos."

"My time is limited, Doctor, so let's get on with it."

"Of course," Jason said. He walked over to the observation window and activated the holo-screen port while Darnel remained back by the door.

Apeiron's digital hologram fired out of the holo-cylinder.

"Ah, so this is the great Apeiron," Contos said.

"Hello, War Commander. It is an honor to meet you."

Contos clenched his bearded jaw, where a golden bead had been tied into the thick gray hair.

Jason knew how Contos felt about AI: supportive but reluctant to introduce war machines into his ranks. He was old fashioned and didn't understand just how much war droids could change the course of the war.

Or perhaps he didn't want to yield any power and become obsolete. After all, he was a proud soldier. Jason respected that, but progress sometimes came at the cost of pride.

The real test would be convincing the War Commander that Apeiron needed to come to Earth, something forbidden by AI laws.

But based on the gravity of the situation, Jason believed Contos would see the need for Apeiron to come to the planet.

"What happened in Megacity Paris today was a tragedy," Jason said. "And what Shadow Squad found in Megacity Moscow is concerning on a number of levels."

"That's why I'm here," Contos said. "I'm told the units are almost ready."

"Yes, I just need a few more months to perfect them," Jason said.

"You keep asking for more time, and what does it produce?" Reaching into his pocket, Jason removed the glass cube and handed it to the War Commander, who held it up under a light.

"What's this?" he asked.

"The first life-saving treatment for SANDs," Jason replied. "In just forty-one days, Apeiron developed this chip that will save millions of lives. Just think what she can do if she has more time to develop the war droids."

"Are you sure this treatment is safe?" Contos asked. "The men and women who developed the nanotechnology that promised to save the environment did it in record time too."

"They did, yes, but they failed to consider every possible outcome. They did not study the side effects or widespread use of their nascent technology."

Contos gave Jason a skeptical look.

"Apeiron has done what I have been unable to do," Jason said. "That's the beauty and elegance of AI. It can simulate and experiment millions upon millions of different scenarios and potential outcomes in the time it takes us to decide what we want to eat for lunch."

Jason stepped up to the window. Overhead lights clicked on, spreading a glow over ten rows of humanoid war droids.

"Apeiron has done the same research and testing of the first prototypes of Project Victory," Jason said. "We call them the Canebrakes."

Five machines stepped out of the front row. They stood seven feet tall, with fanned heads that formed a human skull shape in the center. Clicking resonated out of the room as Jason held out his Commpad.

The noise was similar to a rattlesnake and came from the antennae as they received the orders. The five droids moved their torsos, twisting three-hundred-sixty degrees while holding up their segmented arms that could telescope outward.

"The next step is weaponization," Jason said. "Our design adds multiple plasma cannons and energy blades, allowing them to engage various hostiles in different directions with their agile, rotating frames."

Contos scrutinized the machines like a drill sergeant inspecting new recruits. "Are they EMP resistant?"

"Yes, and they all will have L-S88 chips to connect them to INN, allowing for shared intel in a fraction of the time it takes on the battlefield now."

Contos didn't seem impressed, but then again, he never showed his cards.

"How much longer do you need?" he asked.

"Well, that depends on whether you grant our request—"

"War Commander, I have a suggestion," Apeiron said, cutting Jason off.

Contos and Jason both looked at the hologram.

"In my spare time, I have been working on a way to end the war without bloodshed," she said. "My hope is that we will not need the Canebrakes."

Contos glanced at Jason. "She's optimistic, but perhaps you should have programmed Apeiron to understand war. Peace is not so easily achieved without considerable bloodshed."

He handed the cube back to Jason.

"Hear her out, please," Jason said.

Apeiron offered a polite smile. "I would advise offering the Coalition peace and the treatment to SANDs, while we prepare the Canebrakes, in return for freeing half of the civilian populations of Megacity Paris and Megacity Moscow."

Contos simply stared.

"Let them think they are safe with our medical assistance and offer of peace, and perhaps they will see the light, so to speak," Apeiron continued. "If they do not see the advantage of AI, then you can introduce them to the Canebrakes."

"I'd send in every Engine right now if it weren't for the Council's fear of mass casualties," Contos grumbled. "Speaking of which, the Engines are here for the upgrades you promised. How about you focus on them first?"

"Your Engines are failing—" Apeiron began.

"War Commander," Jason intervened. "By surgically implanting our advanced L-S88 chips, the Engines will be protected against SANDs, and you'll see a vast improvement in their combat effectiveness through their constant connection to INN."

Apeiron smiled again.

"You still haven't answered my question," Contos said. "When can you have these Canebrakes ready?"

"If you grant our next request, it will speed up their development tenfold," Apeiron said.

"What request?"

"To bring her to Earth," Jason said.

"Absolutely not," Contos snapped.

Jason raised his voice. "War Commander, what happened in Megacity Paris today will happen again if Dr. Cross is developing new warriors. We must buy ourselves time with Apeiron's plan, and we can't do it without her."

"Why am I different than other AIs allowed to function on Earth?" Apeiron asked.

"You know the law," Contos said. "Your consciousness comes from a human and humans are flawed."

"My sister is… was not—"

"Maybe not, but the law is the law, and AI based off humans is outlawed on Earth," Contos said.

"And you have the power to overstep the council and grant an exception in the interest of national security."

Contos directed his bright blue eyes at Jason, perhaps thinking Apeiron was a risk to national security.

Or maybe he just thinks you're crazy.

Contos wouldn't be the first to think that about Jason.

"Offer the Coalition peace," Apeiron said. "I have scoured INN and developed a complex algorithm based off of historical events, and this one works in every scenario I run."

"Your computer algos can't predict Dr. Cross," Contos said with a snort. "He will never accept a peace offer."

"He will if you send a trustworthy vessel," Apeiron said.

"A Trojan horse?" Contos asked.

"No… the peace offer is real, but if it does not work, it will buy us time. For this to be effective, I highly advise using a warrior that our enemy respects to deliver this message."

Contos narrowed his eyes.

"Do you have someone in mind, sir?" Jason asked.

"Yes."

"Good. I would much like to meet this warrior," Apeiron said.

Contos turned to leave, but Jason stopped him.

"War Commander, how about our request to bring Petra... Apeiron," Jason corrected himself.

Contos stared at the AI hologram and then started toward the exit door. He opened it, but halted.

"Permission granted," he said without turning. "AI is salvation."

Apeiron clapped her digital hands together, her cheeks forming a dimpled smile.

Jason checked Darnel who was still silent. All it took was a single look, and Jason could tell that his friend, confidante, and chief of staff was more than unsure about this plan to bring Apeiron to Earth.

"I'll wait outside," Darnel said.

He followed the War Commander, the door sealing Jason and Apeiron in the room alone.

"You will need a body," Jason said to her. "A physical form."

"I have already designed one." Apeiron waved at him. "Come look."

Jason went back to the viewport of the factory floor.

Striding into the room was a slender, female Hummer Droid made of shiny black metal. But instead of a circular facial screen, it had a human face made of nanotech that had shifted into the shape of Petra's face. Dimples formed as she smiled.

"What do you think?" Apeiron asked. "Do I still bring you comfort?"

Jason forced his own smile, but for the first time since creating her, he wasn't sure what to think.

4

The memories from ten years ago would always haunt Akira. They came to him mostly in his sleep, when he was mentally unable to fight the nightmares off.

Now was one of those times. He was aware of his dream-like state as his mind reverted back to the battle in the Sea of Trees.

Exhausted and injured, Akira clung to Kichiro. The stallion perked his ears up at the sporadic crack of gunfire, or the screams of the dying behind them on the front line where Coalition survivors hid in tunnels or dugouts. Allied reinforcements had poured into the area after Akira relayed the positions of the Coalition fortifications. Soon the enemy would all be dead.

Akira hung onto Kichiro as he climbed up another hill over scorched dirt and past trees withered like twisted human skeletons.

A wave of soldiers trekked by, some still saying his new nickname. "There's Akira the Brave!"

Two medics ran over, one reaching up with a Commpad to scan Akira's body. "Sergeant Hayashi, let me deal with those injuries."

"I'll be fine, others need you more than I," Akira replied.

The medic hesitated but moved on. There was no shortage of men and women to look after now that the battle was mostly over, and many had devastating burns or missing limbs to deal with.

Akira directed the stallion away from a hill covered in burning cherry blossom trees. Hours ago, he had advanced through this forest with his platoon, admiring the beautiful blossoms before they'd been turned to ash.

According to his family's Warrior Codex, which he always carried into battle, the perfect blossom rarely occurred. When it did, it was a sign that samurai warriors would find honor in battle that year.

Akira had found honor in this battle, but the rest of his

platoon had perished with these trees. Gusts of wind carried the ashes away like the ghosts of the dead sprawled across the smoldering dirt.

Kichiro passed checkpoints on the way to the forward operating base where Akira would seek medical treatment and get new orders.

As the hours passed by, the cold began to burrow through his armor, and his injuries flared. The stallion, however, seemed to push through the pain from his damaged prosthetic, no longer hobbling.

Akira rested against the neck of his new companion as they passed hundreds of exhausted and weary troops making their way back to the FOB. Their gray armor and exoskeletons glimmered in the moonlight like spirits that often wandered the Sea of Trees.

Sometime later, Akira drifted off, only to be woken by thunder. He sat up on the mount and scanned the skyline for a storm, but there was no lightning.

The ground rumbled, and the horse let out a neigh. He halted and reared his head back. Both ears perked up.

Kichiro slowly turned, giving Akira a view of orange and red flashes blooming to the east. The troops trekking through the forest started to move faster, alert now. Some broke into runs, others hobbled as fast as their injured bodies could take them.

Akira spotted a corporal with a long range comm antennae protruding from her backpack. Surely, she would know what was going on.

"Corporal," he grunted. "Who are we shelling?"

She started to move away, talking into her radio. Akira gave the stallion a small kick to the flank to follow.

"Corporal," he repeated. "Who are we—"

"We aren't shelling anyone." She lowered the radio and looked up at Akira. "Sergeant, a Coalition horde broke through the lines. They're hitting Hachioji and Sagmihara with long range artillery."

Akira stared at the explosions that seemed to thud in parallel with his pounding heart.

His wife and their son were in Hachioji.

Akira whistled and the horse broke into a trot, then a run, and as soon as they were in the open, a gallop. He had heard Dr. Cross's prosthetics integrated self-healing nanotechnology, and it sure seemed to work fast on the animal's injury. He hoped that was the case because Akira didn't want to inflict pain on the animal and needed to get to his family quickly.

The trees and hills flashed by, the stallion racing through like a demon. Holding on tight, Akira focused on the destination, trying to keep his mind off the pain of his injuries. But the agony was intense. Each bump over the rocky terrain made the fires in his nerves flare.

He reached into his vest and pulled out a syringe containing a cocktail of stimulants. It was the only thing that would get him to his wife and son. He jabbed it into a vein, and felt the instant warmth rushing through his blood.

Akira discarded the syringe and clung to his horse. They rode through the night, guided by the flashing of bombs pounding the city where his wife Yui was sheltering with their son Takeshi. Each blast made him flinch and wonder if he would reach his family in time.

This part of the dream always felt so real, so vivid, like he was there reliving these moments. He could feel each agonizing jolt on the horse that brought him one step closer to the city, and the pain of his aching heart.

But as soon as he arrived in Hachioji, nearly hanging off the saddle, the memories became hazier. He hopped down to the street and staggered away from the stallion. The horse followed him toward a pile of scree around a building destroyed by the bombs.

Under the rubble was the shelter where his family had sought refuge. Rescue workers were already combing through the destruction for survivors.

Bleeding and barely clinging to consciousness, Akira joined the frantic search.

Just before dawn, they found Yui, still holding Takeshi, both of them covered in dust. The boy coughed and began to cry. Yui was cold to the touch. She had given her life to shield their son.

The memories faded away like smoke, and a cold sensation washed over Akira.

***

Present Day

Akira awoke on an operating table. Blurred shapes stirred around him, and tubes snaked out from the ports in his armor.

Now he knew why his dream had stopped. His suit had detected the mental distress and flooded his system with a chemical cocktail to keep him calm. Growth hormones and nanotech bonding agents entered his bloodstream, strengthening his bones and muscles through the tubes. Much like a teenager, his body was still growing, and wouldn't stop until the treatments ended.

The medical staff came into focus, but Akira couldn't see their faces behind their masks and face shields. They didn't speak except to ask him generic questions about how he was feeling.

But something was different.

He looked around the white room and saw a group of observers behind a glass window. A handsome man, with wavy brown hair and bright brown eyes set above a sharp nose, watched him intently.

Akira recognized Doctor Jason Crichton, the CEO of Achilles Android Systems.

But what could *he* want with an Engine?

Akira grew agitated from his dream as the doctors continued their work. He closed his eyes, trying to focus his mind on passages from the Warrior Codex that he treasured more than any Earthly item.

In his mind's eye, Akira pictured the leather-bound book that had been in his family for five generations. He recited its mottos and quotations, the wisdom of his ancestors, and recalled the stories of their battles and wars.

Soon, his body began to relax. He focused on his breathing, falling into a deep meditation. The medical staff eventually removed the tubes and departed, leaving Akira on the table in his armor.

"Captain Akira Hayashi," came a female voice. "Or shall I call you Akira the Brave?"

He slowly sat up, his swollen abs and barreled chest muscles flexing. His arms and legs burned fiercely from the treatment, but it was the migraine pounding against his skull that wasn't normal.

"My name is Doctor Jason Crichton," said another voice.

Akira turned toward the scientist who stood at the entrance to the room. He wore a black suit with silver cufflinks and a silver AAS symbol on his breast pocket.

"I know who you are," Akira said.

Jason walked over. "Hopefully you have heard all good things, Captain."

"Mostly," Akira grunted. "So, you going to tell me why my head feels like it got hit by an energy axe?"

"That's why I'm here, as I'm sure you guessed. I'd like to introduce you to someone."

"My name is Apeiron," said the female voice.

Akira looked around the room but didn't see the source.

"I am an OS," she said. "An operating system."

"Artificial Intelligence," Jason clarified. "Not just any, though. Apeiron is the most advanced in human history, and the first to be coded and merged with a human conscious."

Akira narrowed his eyes. "I thought that was illegal."

"It was necessary," Jason said firmly.

"I was designed for a very important purpose," Apeiron said.

Jason moved directly in front of Akira.

"Apeiron was designed to save humanity," he said proudly.

"What's that have to do with me?" Akira asked.

Jason smiled, showing a perfect set of white teeth.

"Today, you and I became linked in a very special way, Captain," Apeiron said. "I am honored to form this bond with a man of valor, respected by his comrades and feared by his enemies."

"You're now connected to INN, also known as the Infinite Nova Network," Jason clarified. "The chip we implanted in your skull will also protect you from SANDs."

Akira reached up and felt the bandage around his head, the source of the pounding.

"So I take orders from… a machine now?" he asked.

"Not orders," Apeiron said. "I am here to support you. We have the same objectives: end the war, save humanity, and restore the planet."

"Send me back to Paris and unleash us on the walls," Akira said. "That's the only way to end this war."

"You are going back to Paris," Jason said. "We're sending you to deliver a message of peace to Dr. Cross."

Akira got off the table and stood, towering over the doctor. The man looked up at him, unwavering and confident. The doctor was the world's richest man and an esteemed scientist and engineer. He used his wealth and intelligence to build restoration sites to help heal the planet, and clean the nanoparticles out of the ecosystems, something Akira greatly respected.

A solid judge of character, he sensed that Dr. Crichton had good intentions, but Akira wasn't thrilled about this new connection to Apeiron, especially not with these new orders.

"Why send me?" Akira asked.

"You are Akira the Brave, one of the most respected warriors in the Nova Alliance Strike Force," Apeiron said. "I studied you, and I have heard about the book you carry, your Warrior Codex. You and I share something in common. We are bound by our individual ethos. Mine to science and AI. Yours to honor and courage. Your word is as strong as your sword."

"And you should know I'm not an instrument of peace, but war. The only thing I will deliver to Dr. Cross is a bullet to the head."

Akira began to walk away, but a digital hologram of a young woman emerged in front of him. She smiled politely, dimples forming on her freckled face.

"Captain, I do not think you understand," she said. "This is not a request. This is an order."

"I only take orders from War Commander Contos. Now get out of my way or I'll walk right through you," Akira said.

"War Commander Contos gave the order," Jason said.

Akira rotated toward the doctor, unsure at first if he had heard correctly.

"You are to head to Megacity Paris and deliver a message of peace, *without* shedding blood," he said.

"The War Commander said…" Akira let his words trail off and stiffened to get control of his anger. He knew if these orders were real, and he didn't have any reason to doubt them, then the War Commander was being forced by the council or some other forces.

"Peace is a myth," Akira said after the pause. "Humanity isn't capable of it. If you knew anything about my Codex like you say you do, you would know that's why I exist."

"I believe you are wrong, Captain," Apeiron said.

He stared at the friendly face of the hologram. She looked young and innocent, but deep down he knew the truth—she was a wolf, like Akira. Only she was much stronger than she appeared and more determined than her countenance would let on.

"That is why *we* exist," she added. "But together, we can achieve peace."

***

Seventeen-year-old Ronin Hayashi punched the bag until his knuckles bled. He was on the second floor of the Droid Raider Complex, a training center for youth in the slums of Megacity Phoenix.

Fogged windows overlooked the arena. On the dirt floor, a team of young men and women trained against some of the most pathetic-looking Hummer Droids Ronin had ever seen.

Most of the machines were pieced together using parts from other models. It wasn't cheap to replace one of the droids with newer models, and the violent game constantly required players to find ways to restore their droids.

The gladiator sport had taken the world by storm twenty years earlier when it was first introduced in Megacity Tokyo, where Ronin was born. Since then, he had moved to the former

United States where his family settled in Megacity Phoenix. He lived there now with his father Kai, mother Lise, twin brother Elan, and his older brother Zachary.

Zachary was on the arena floor now, using his padded jump shoes and the jetpack built into his armored suit to expertly navigate the obstacle course of tires, destroyed vehicles, and rusty shacks.

A rookie on the city's pro team, the Phoenix Lizards, Zachary and his nine teammates were putting on a show for the local at-risk youth. Hundreds of teenagers had come to watch.

Three first-generation Hummer Droids, with a hodgepodge of mismatched parts, trekked across the dirt in the center of the arena. Another group of droids stood among piles of lumber and metal shacks.

Ronin looked away and kept pounding the bag. He kicked it, just like his dad had taught him, using his center mass to pack the most power.

Both Ronin and Zachary were trained in karate and swordsmanship. The training had given them an advantage over the other kids. By the time Zachary hit high school, he was easily the best player on his team.

Ronin, on the other hand, had to work harder to excel at the sport. He kicked the bag, welcoming the pain to his feet. Sweat dripped down his body as he launched a flurry of punches, over and over, until stars burst before his eyes.

He was angry, and frustrated.

That's what happened when you had an older brother who was bigger, faster, smarter, and better at literally everything he put his mind to. Physically, it was like Zachary wasn't even related. They weren't equals as athletes, no matter how hard Ronin tried.

They came from a long line of warriors. Kai served with the 5th Division of the Nova Alliance Strike Force, and Ronin's uncle was the esteemed Engine Captain Akira Hayashi of Shadow Squad, a living legend.

Ronin's ancestors had fought in every world war over the past two centuries, and in some of the most historic battles in Japan's history. He had even heard stories about samurai descendants in their family lineage.

Shouting pulled him away from the punching bag. He went back to the window to watch his brother fight two Hummer Droids at once, using deactivated energy blades to deflect their blows.

Someday that will be me, Ronin thought.

The crowd suddenly shot up, fingers pointing across the arena. Zachary rushed over to a teammate trapped under a damaged Hummer Droid.

"That's Lenny," said someone behind Ronin. A fourteen-year-old kid stepped up beside Ronin to watch.

On the field, Zachary struggled to lift the heavy robot off of the team's star player. Other players also ran over to help, and a medic pushed through the crowd outside the fence. She reached them with a medical kit as they finally lifted the droid off Lenny, who was screaming in agony.

The droid had crushed his leg, mangling it.

"Damn, he isn't going to be playing for a while," said the kid next to Ronin.

A moment passed before Ronin understood what that meant. Zachary was about to get a chance for some field time, which meant he was actually going to start making some real money.

Ronin rushed out of the gym and made his way down a stairwell to the fence outside the field.

"Don't worry, bro! You'll be back on your feet in no time!" Zachary yelled.

The spectators clapped as Lenny was whisked outside by medics. The training match started right back up and Ronin watched for the next hour.

At the end of the practice, he made his way to the tunnel where the players left the arena to head down into the lockers.

Two other players, Clutch and Starlight walked with Zachary.

"Zachary," Ronin called out.

Zachary stopped right before entering the tunnel.

"Yo, Ronin boy," Zachary said. "I'll meet you outside in fifteen."

"Okay," Ronin said.

Ronin went to the exit and found his twin brother Elan sitting on a bench, reading a book as usual. The two brothers were identical twins but didn't look or act all that alike.

Elan wasn't into sports like Ronin and Zachary. He was a kind, quiet teenager. His personality reflected the meaning of his Apache name: "friendly."

He spent most of his time studying, reading, and playing in VR worlds. The closest Elan got to the gym was where he sat now, at a park table, reading his Commpad.

"You see that shit?" Zachary said.

Ronin turned to his older brother who walked outside with wet hair, and a clean-shaven face.

Ronin nodded. "Lenny really got messed up."

"Yeah, but he'll be okay... In the meantime..." Zachary looked around to make sure no one was listening. Then he cracked a half smile and put his arm around Ronin. "This means I get a chance to shine. And if I get a major deal for the next season, we can finally pay for Elan's surgery."

Elan still didn't look up from his book.

"Man, I hope he gets laid soon," Zachary said. He nudged Ronin in the arm. "Hope you do too, kid bro."

"Don't be a dick. Elan is only seventeen, and you know how shy he is."

"I was shy, and I got laid at fourteen."

"Yeah, you've told that story a *million* times. Lucky you."

"Luck has nothing to do with it, little bro."

Elan finally looked up and spotted them. He put his Commpad down and signed with his hands: *What happened to Lenny?*

Broke his leg, Ronin signed back.

"That's why I read and don't fight droids," Elan said in his monotone voice. He picked his Commpad back up.

Zachary smirked. He was never mean to Elan, but sometimes Ronin did feel like Zachary looked down on him, embarrassed of his disability. It wasn't Elan's fault that he was born with a degenerative disease. Nor was it his fault that it cost a small fortune to restore his hearing.

At least Zachary is going to help pay for it, Ronin thought.

Hover cars zipped by on the street as the three brothers made their way to the subway station.

"Man, I can't wait until I can afford a ride," Zachary said.

He led the way to the train stop, where several teenagers were waiting to board. They eyed Zachary, some out of respect, others with envy.

Zachary seemed to enjoy the attention as he boarded the train.

A Hummer Droid stood in the aisle, watching the kids take their seats. Its digital facial screen displayed the face of the city administrator AI, Emanuel Captor. He had a full beard, glasses, and a high hairline.

"Please, take a seat," he said in a smooth voice.

Phil, a short but muscular kid with red hair and freckles, kicked the droid in the leg. "Oops."

"I am sorry. Was I in your way?" the droid asked.

"Yeah, and you still are." Phil kicked it again, harder, and the droid backed up. A beep echoed through the cars as the doors closed.

"Please, take a seat," the droid repeated.

Phil laughed. "You take a seat." He pushed at the droid's boxy chest, but it didn't move.

"How are you ever going to be a Droid Raider with those puny arms?" said another kid.

The droid gestured toward the seats as the other kids sat. Service bots like this one were everywhere in Megacity Phoenix, like all the megacities. Each was programmed for its specific region and the unique issues its respective megacity faced. In Phoenix, the issues were plentiful. Poverty, air quality, water shortages, and almost always, a shortage of food.

Phil pushed at the droid again.

"Don't," Ronin said.

"Or what?" Phil said. "You going to stop me, or will you cry to your big brother?"

"Come on, stop being a prick," Zachary said.

"You think you're a big shot," Phil said. "Because your dad and uncle are soldiers?"

Zachary didn't reply.

"My dad was a soldier, too. He died in Paris five years ago when we tried to take it back from the barbarians," Phil said.

"I'm sorry," Zachary said. "But I don't see what that has to do with this droid."

The droid directed its facial screen toward a knife Phil was pulling from his pocket.

"Please put that down," it said politely.

Zachary stood up, but it was too late.

Phil was already etching into the chest plate. When he was finished, he bent down, blew off the shavings, and brushed it off.

Worthless droid.

"There," Phil said. "All better."

The droid looked down at the words.

"Why did you do that?" came a female voice. The facial screen changed from Emanuel Captor's face to the dimpled smile of a woman with brown eyes and hair.

"Who the hell is this bitch?" Phil asked.

"My name is Apeiron, and I asked you a question." Her smile vanished, but her tone remained calm.

"Because you're not a human, and I am."

"You vandalized Unit 1987099 because it is not a human? Vandalizing property is subject to code 19 of—"

"Droids can't enforce laws against humans," Phil interrupted. He twirled the blade again and laughed.

"No, but we can upload this incident to the local liaison to investigate you for anti-AI behavior," Apeiron said. "Perhaps you would like me to file a full report?"

Phil's pale skin glowed a bright red. "My dad died fighting the Coalition," he snapped. "I'm not one of *them*."

"Your hatred toward AI seems to suggest Coalition loyalties."

"No," Phil said.

Elan, who was following the conversation on his Commpad, gave Ronin a worried side glance. Neither particularly liked the idea of worshipping AI, but they both respected it and believed it was making the world a better place.

The train screeched to a stop, and everyone piled out, with

Phil leading the way.

The Hummer Droid stood in the door as it closed shut, its face once again resembling the AI Administrator.

Phil snorted as the train zipped away. "Man, I thought you were a Droid Raider, but you're just another droid *lover*," he said to Zachary.

"No, I'm just not a dumbass with a small dick like you, who feels like he has something to prove."

Phil glared at Zachary.

"What? Did I hurt your feelings?" Zachary said.

"Hey, guys. Check this out…"

Ronin looked toward the voice. The other kids were standing under a holo-screen mounted over the stairwell leading to the street. Four different sub-screens displayed the same image: an Engine riding a horse.

"Holy shit," one of the kids said. "Is that your uncle?"

Ronin walked up directly to the holo-screen. There was no mistaking the renowned hybrid stallion, Kichiro, or the rider on its back, Captain Akira Hayashi.

There was also no mistaking the white flag hanging from his spear.

Phil laughed. "The great Captain Hayashi is surrendering!"

"W-what?" Zachary stammered, pushing his way through the kids to stand between Ronin and Elan.

"What's this mean?" Ronin asked Zachary.

"It means your hero uncle isn't as brave as everyone thinks," Phil said with a smirk.

5

"Don't look at anyone, not even other civilians," Keanu said. "If someone tries to talk to you, don't respond. Keep your head down, eyes low, and focus on getting in and out."

"I will," Chloe replied.

She pulled a gray hooded sweatshirt over her frizzy brown hair and looked in the cracked mirror in the small bathroom. Just like the city streets, her face was filthy. But her appearance was self-inflicted to avoid unwanted attention when she left their shelter for rations.

Keanu hovered behind her, scratching his graying beard. He didn't look much better than her, no longer bothering to trim his facial hair in the immaculate style she remembered growing up.

Not much of a reason to when he barely left their home.

This was the first time Chloe had left since watching Todd and Suzanne being herded into the factory, but they had to eat, and it was ration day. Only women were allowed to pick them up at the market.

"See you soon," she said.

She hugged Keanu and went to the cellar door. He pulled the metal latch up, and she secured her hood and made her way outside.

It was a few hours to curfew, and an orange sunset crested the horizon. Small figures perched like gargoyles along the stone trim of a former bank building. One of the Coalition soldiers moved, lifting a long-scoped rifle.

Chloe rounded the next block, her heart racing faster, steeling herself for the grisly sight that always greeted her. Slowly, she lifted her eyes to the tallest building in the area, a ten-story former hotel with a tiled roof and stonework around the glass-paned windows.

Two naked men hung from exterior beams, their bodies mutilated and entrails hanging out in long ropes. Crows feasted on their flesh, picking and pulling away strands.

Chloe let out a long, deep breath, trying to block the memories that always surfaced when she made this trip. But like the other times, there was no blocking out the image of her father hanging from the same building.

She still didn't know what had happened to her mother, only that she too was probably dead now, due to her past working with droids. When the Coalition took you, you didn't return. You became a slave, or you were killed.

Chloe forced herself to continue toward the market. It wasn't far now. Just another block. Charred vehicles and debris blocked the roads in all directions, and soldiers guarded checkpoints.

On a curb halfway down the street, she noticed a woman lying on the concrete at an odd angle. Her legs twitched as Chloe approached, and she knew then—this woman had SANDs.

And no one had stopped to help her.

They all knew there was nothing to be done.

Chloe kept walking, closing in on the market, her heart pounding, guilt filling her. But this wasn't the first time she'd seen a person suffering like that. It certainly wouldn't be the last either, and she knew stopping could draw attention from the closest guard at the end of the street by the market.

A shirtless Coalition foot soldier, his chest muscles marked with scars and tribal tattoos representing the Coalition's Nordic Gods stood looking the other way. An energy hatchet hung from his belt, and a bolt-action rifle was propped up on a shoulder.

It wasn't the weapons or his appearance that frightened Chloe—it was the beast attached to a chain he held in one hand.

The two-hundred-pound Iron Wolf trotted over the cobblestone, the titanium claws clanking on the ancient bricks, and saliva drooling out of the metal jaw.

Chloe knew better than most people how much effort went into the design of these beasts. These weren't the companion-style droids she had once worked on for wealthy clients. These were *real* animals that Dr. Cross first bred in his factories and then surgically turned into killing machines with his legions of doctors.

A thick mane of black hair crested the wolf's skull and ran down its back. It glanced over at her with blue eyes, sniffed the air, and then pulled on its chains. The soldier's horned helmet turned her way, the bloodshot eyes locking with her own for a brief moment.

Chloe looked away and passed the dying woman on the road. She felt the soldier watching her as she got in line with hundreds of other women and girls that had come out for rations delivered by white MOTHs once a week.

The market was set between four apartment buildings, in an open square with a fountain in the center. Coalition soldiers surrounded the crates of fresh produce and dried meat as a team of locals handed out the food.

On the rooftops were more soldiers, armed with sniper rifles, phased plasma-pulse rifles, and pistols. They all wore similar bulky armor, slightly customized and painted with Nordic symbols. The size of their horns on their helmets often represented their kills; the more branches on their antlers, the more men and women they had murdered.

The barbaric nature of these men and women wasn't hard to understand, if you looked at the history of the world. Humanity had almost destroyed itself during the Carbon Wars, and ideologies had only drifted further apart over the ensuing decades of bloodshed.

Chloe stood behind an elderly woman with a child by her side, no doubt an orphan like so many others. The girl looked over her shoulder at Chloe with a single eye, the other covered by a patch. Already the poor girl had developed tremors, her muscles twitching in the first signs of a worsening SANDS infection.

"Hi," she whispered.

"Hi," Chloe whispered back.

The crowd inched forward, most keeping their head down. Coughs and a few sobs echoed through the early evening as the sun retreated over the horizon.

People hurried away with baskets of food, returning to

houses where they would continue hiding and praying that the Nova Alliance Council would negotiate their liberation with the Coalition leaders—known simply as the War Lords.

But Chloe knew that wasn't going to happen. The War Lords were generals, not politicians, and they weren't going to give up Megacity Paris or Megacity Moscow after exhausting vast amounts of resources to revolt and take the cities.

Escaping wasn't an option for Nova Alliance citizens who believed in AI like Chloe. Those who tried were almost always captured and strung up on buildings as an example.

The girl ahead looked at Chloe again as they approached the center of the market. She smiled at the kid, hoping to provide some sense of reassurance and friendship, despite her uncle's warnings.

If smiling at a child got her arrested, then she would rather die like her parents.

A gunshot cracked outside of the market, commanding the attention of the crowd. Everyone around Chloe tensed up as they determined whether to flee or hold tight.

The single shot faded away.

Probably a rebel sniper shot, Chloe thought.

There was a resistance force in the city, although it was bordering on extinction from what she had heard. The men and women living underground rarely came out during the day, and mostly attacked at night.

Chloe was conflicted about their efforts. Often, the tactics ended up getting innocents killed in retribution. For every soldier they took out, the Coalition would kill ten times as many Nova Alliance citizens.

Once again, the crowd pushed forward.

She was almost to the front of the line and could smell the fresh fruit and bread, when a clatter of hooves made her heart skip a beat. Behind her, a mounted soldier trotted into the eastern edge of the market. Six antlers rose out of a helmet with a breathing apparatus built into the front. Thick custom armor hung off the soldier's chest and shoulders.

This was no grunt—this was a War Lord Lieutenant.

Two more mounted warriors followed the first toward the

crowd. Behind them marched six more men in full armor and carrying energy spears. The crowd backed away, warm bodies huddling in fear at the sight of a Coalition Lieutenant.

They were looking for someone.

"Chloe Cotter!" the lieutenant shouted.

Chloe didn't register her own name at first. Her heart flared a moment later, as reality sank in. The Coalition did know about her past, and now they had come for her!

"We know you're here, show yourself!" the man shouted, his voice muffled by the mask.

Chloe remained as still as a statue, her heart thumping in her ears.

Hushed voices broke out around her as people searched for... her.

This has to be a mistake, she thought.

Another two men with leashed Iron Wolves entered the market. Chloe almost didn't recognize the one walking in front of the snarling beasts.

"No," she choked.

Her Uncle Keanu staggered forward, bound, his face beaten and bloody.

Chloe ran to him without thinking, charging through the crowd and stopping about ten feet from her uncle. His eyes met hers, fear bleeding from his gaze.

"Run," he stammered.

The man on the horse directed the mechanical beast toward Chloe. Her flight instincts kicked in, and she bolted toward an alley. A guard raced to block her, but she darted into the narrow passage between two buildings.

In the distance, she could make out the hotel, where crows feasted on the bodies of the people who had tried to escape and rebels like her dad. Unless she managed to find a place to hide, she would soon be one of them.

But what would she do without her uncle?

Shouts and screams followed Chloe down the alley. She ran even harder. Then, over the other noises, came snarling and a ferocious growl.

It was coming from the street beyond the alley.

Chloe slid to a stop as two Iron Wolves cornered her, their jaws snapping with jagged teeth. Glancing over her shoulder, she saw two men running down the alley with glowing energy swords.

She was trapped.

The encroaching beasts pulled on their chains as an armored vehicle slid to a stop. The hatch opened on the side. Leather boots clicked onto the pavement as a handsome middle-aged man emerged wearing a gray dress suit with armored plates hanging over the front. Wavy silver hair fell over his face. He pushed the strands back into place, revealing a black mustache and blood-red eyes. The man centered his augmented INVS eyes on Chloe and smiled kindly.

"Don't be afraid," he said. "I'm not going to hurt you."

She stood there, trembling, as the Iron Wolves fought to get free of their chains.

The man took a step closer, his red eyes looking her up and down.

Chloe stepped back.

"It's okay," he said. "I just want to talk to you."

He had a kind and intelligent voice.

Turning, he glared at the Iron Wolves. Both beasts sat on their hind legs. He then raised a hand and gestured toward someone behind Chloe.

She turned to the clattering of hooves from horses trotting through the market. Tied to a rope held by one of the riders was her uncle. The beasts stopped, and another guard escorting put a knife to his throat.

"Chloe Cotter," said the man in the suit.

She looked back at him.

"My name is Doctor Otto Cross," he said. He took another step closer. "I'm told you have experience with droids. Is that correct?"

She hesitated, but then nodded.

"Good," he said. "Very good. Most people with experience are dead."

He walked up to her, stopping closer to her face.

"I'm in need of someone for an experiment." He glanced at

Keanu. "Help me, and you and your uncle will live."

Dr. Cross smiled again, but this wasn't the same kind smile. His faced widened into sinister grin.

"Refuse, and *you* will become the experiment," he said with a shrug. "Now if you'll excuse me, I have a peace treaty to broker."

***

The wastes of no man's land waited for Shadow Squad. Weak sunshine broke through the gray, smoke-choked sky, providing only a hazy view of the battlefield stretching around the western entrance to Megacity Paris.

A small encampment of Piston scouts was positioned here to watch an area that no Nova Alliance soldier had set foot on in over five years.

Kichiro trotted past the Pistons, but even the stallion seemed reluctant to stride out into the apocalyptic graveyard. Okami, on the other hand, trotted right out, white tail up and black button nose sniffing the dirt.

The Pistons watched the squad, not saying a word.

"AI is salvation," said one of the Piston Clerics.

"AI is salvation," repeated Shadow Squad.

Two days ago, Akira had seen the look of hope in the soldiers' eyes on the frontlines around Megacity Moscow. Hope that the war would soon be over and humanity would find a way to live in peace, embracing their different beliefs, like Apeiron suggested.

But centuries of warrior blood flowed through Akira's veins, and the book handed down from those ancestors detailed the reality that humans were violent creatures by nature.

Wars would never end.

Only the dead have seen the end of war, Akira thought, recalling the quote from Plato.

Kichiro stopped at the border of the no-man's zone, and Akira looked over his squad. Tadhg, Frost, Perez, and Ghost awaited orders.

"This is bullshit. You know that, right, Captain?" Tadhg said.

"You're still new, so I'm going to let that go," Akira said.

"This isn't a Droid Raiding field, and Captain Akira isn't your coach," Ghost said. "Show some damn respect for the chain of command."

The first part was an understatement that Akira could see with his own eyes. There was no sport out here, no victory—only death.

"Let's go," Akira said.

He whistled to Kichiro.

Lowering his armored muzzle, the horse led the way out into the wastes, hooves crushing bones that protruded from the dirt.

Akira hoped they weren't trampling on their own dead, but it was often hard to tell. Many of the corpses were so far decayed that they were unrecognizable. He tried to guide his trusted stallion through the maze to the eight-lane superhighway without disrespecting the dead.

"This would be a great time to kill us all," Frost said.

An itch formed in the back of Akira's skull, just before Apeiron's intelligent voice spoke to their chips.

"The chances of that are highly unlikely," she said. "In fact, I put them at one percent. You have a better chance of dying in battle than delivering this peace offering."

"Who asked for your opinion?" Tadhg asked.

"Better get used to it," Perez said.

"Such bullshit," Tadhg said. "I didn't give up a fortune in contracts from Droid Raiding to listen to an AI tell me how to fight."

"She's here to help us, Tadhg." Perez adjusted his shield. "AI is salvation."

Perez was one of the true believers, a warrior who had given his adult life to protect all that AI had built in the great megacities. Tadhg on the other hand, was vocal about his disdain for droids. Sometimes too vocal.

"AI is salvation," Akira said.

"Yeah, yeah," Tadhg said.

The other Engines repeated the phrase while Ghost sang it in his acclaimed tenor voice.

AI is salvation. AI is hope.
AI is the future of humanity!

Normally the sound of that song would have resulted in a sniper bullet between the eyes, but Akira's team passed freely with their white flags.

Akira had repeated the motto countless times, but he had never thought he would be this connected to AI. The only advantage seemed to be the ability to tap into INN with a single thought. Instead of relying on their HUDs for intel, he could now access it in his mind's eye. He was still getting used to it, but it was already starting to become habit.

Blinking, Akira tapped into the network, scrolling through the satellite images over Megacity Paris. On the other side of the walls, the Coalition was gathering to greet them.

Okami led the way toward the highway, sniffing for mines and explosives. Akira guided Kichiro past the burned-out hulls of tanks and armored personal carriers (APCs) blown apart by bombs and missiles over the years. Bones and armor lay scattered across the cracked pavement.

The squad marched through the graveyard of dead warriors.

Akira felt the chill of spirits prowling, people who had been robbed of life and wanted revenge. Delivering this peace offering seemed like a betrayal to all of them.

And yet, he pushed on with his orders.

Rubble and debris covered the terrain. A decade ago, this place would have bustled with noise and life. Now an eerie silence hung over the wastes.

Over the mountains of shattered lives, Akira saw their destination. The ten-story iron gates of Megacity Paris rose from the horizon. The smoke wasn't so bad today, and in the weak glow of the sun, he made out the walls of the city.

Light poles framed the highway, skeletons hanging from them. Most were human, but some Hummer Droid heads poked off the spikes as well. Slanted and mangled road signs displayed the Coalition soldiers' blasphemy.

AI will bring death to all.
The real devil is made of metal, not flesh.

Akira zoomed in with his INVS eyes. More droid heads protruded off spikes along the parapets of the fortress walls, and the fresh bodies of Nova Alliance citizens hung from ropes. Hundreds of Coalition soldiers stood on the platforms, their weapons pointed at the Engines.

"Let's get this over with," Akira said.

The monster steel gates groaned open as they approached, revealing the guts of a city that not a single Engine had stepped inside for years.

Akira directed Kichiro down the heavily fortified road. Thousands of Coalition foot soldiers waited behind concrete blocks and machine gun nests. On the buildings to the side of the highway, more soldiers waited on rooftops.

Okami growled at the wall of Breakers blocking the road, clutching energy blades and snorting cold air through their iron helmets. The entire army seemed to break into laughter at the sight of the wolfdog. That just made Okami mad, and his growl rose to a vicious growl-bark.

Akira felt his blood warm. He wanted to kill them all. For everything they had taken from him.

The Coalition warriors suddenly went quiet, giving way to the click of metal claws and the tap of boots. Breakers parted to form a path for a pack of Iron Wolves, bound by chains held by their handlers.

Kichiro held his ground and snorted as if he was prepared to charge the monstrous beasts, but Akira knew the horse was nervous. He patted his neck, then dismounted and whistled for Okami to quiet.

The wolfdog growled one last time.

Shadow Squad formed a wall to the left and right of Akira.

A man in a gray suit emerged from behind the Iron Wolves and their handlers. He took off his helmet, revealing blood-red INVS eyes and wavy silver hair.

"Welcome to Megacity Paris," he said, holding out his arms. "You have now entered our kingdom, free of AI."

Akira strode out to him, wasting no time.

"Doctor Otto Cross?" he asked.

"Yes, and you are?"

"Captain Akira Hayashi. I'm here to extend a peace offering." He held out the holo-tube, drawing the muzzles of a hundred weapons.

Dr. Cross held up a hand. He approached cautiously, examining the tube and then the Engines with his red gaze.

"I have to admit, I was surprised to hear it was the revered Shadow Squad, led by the *great* Akira the Brave who was at our gates to deliver this message of surrender," said Dr. Cross.

"This isn't a message of surrender," Akira said. "It's an offer of peace."

"An offer of peace?" Dr. Cross paced in front of Akira. "That makes me wonder what trickery War Commander Contos is up to."

"No trickery, Doctor. It's the hope of the Nova Alliance Council and the War Commander that we can agree to a ceasefire and find a way to live in harmony with our own beliefs—"

Dr. Cross stopped pacing and cut Akira off. "The war won't end while AI exists," he snapped. "It *can't* end... and someday you will understand that."

Grunts came from the Breakers, who had formed a fortress of metal and augmented flesh behind their leader.

Dr. Cross reached out. "But I would still like to see this olive branch, Captain, for consideration. And out of courtesy."

Akira handed over the holo-tube.

Peeling off the Silver Crane seal, Dr. Cross pulled out a holo-cylinder and dropped it on the ground. A hologram of War Commander Contos rose from it.

"On behalf of the Nova Alliance Council and in the interest of this peace, I, War Commander Dimitri Contos, offer the following peace terms..."

Dr. Cross rubbed his hands together excitedly.

Akira knew he was a psychopath and wondered how many people those hands had killed.

"Megacity Paris and Megacity Moscow will be handed over

to the Coalition," Contos continued, "in return for letting five million of our citizens go, including all children under the age of fifteen. We will pull our forces back as soon as the refugees are evacuated. We are also willing to offer you the first successful treatment for SANDs, a chip that you can distribute among your ranks, in good faith." He paused, as if he were watching Dr. Cross, even though it was a pre-recorded message. "This offer is non-negotiable and expires at midnight."

The hologram vanished.

"Five million out of ten million," Dr. Cross said. He stroked his mustache. "Sounds like something an AI would come up with."

"If it were up to me, I'd die right now if it meant killing you," Ghost said. "That would be a *good* death."

"Plant your feet and square your shoulders to the enemy," Perez said, reciting his favorite quotation from the Greek soldier Archilochus. "Meet him among the man-killing spears. Hold your ground... and we will."

"You forgot a line," Dr. Cross said. "Be brave, my heart... and while you are most definitely brave, I do not wish to kill you today."

The doctor walked over to look at Perez, and then Ghost.

"I promise you this..." Dr. Cross said.

"Rossi, Lieutenant Shane Rossi," Ghost interrupted.

"Ah, the singing Ghost. Yes, I'm well aware of who you are, too." Dr. Cross patted one of his shoulder plates. "You can try to kill me, but I promise you it will be more painful for you when I feed you to my wolves... alive."

"Get your hand off me," Ghost said, shaking it off and facing the much shorter doctor.

Every gun in the area aimed at the Engines. Shadow Squad already had their weapons pointed at Dr. Cross.

"Make your decision, Doctor," Akira said.

Dr. Cross moved to Akira, looking up the foot of height difference between the two of them.

"You're a soldier of honor, I'm told, and for that reason I agree to these terms," said the doctor. He held up a single finger. "But if they are broken, you have my word that I will bring hell to Earth until there is only man or droid left standing."

Akira nodded. "Fair enough."

"The brain was not meant to be modified, Captain," Dr. Cross said. "Our flesh, sure, but our brains are sacred. They're *our* computers. AI is unholy."

"You're one crazy asshole," Ghost said.

Dr. Cross turned his back and walked toward the Breakers, but then stopped. "You know, on second thought, while I trust you, Captain Hayashi, I don't trust your comrades," he said. "So in order to secure this peace deal, I have one request of my own."

The doctor looked past Akira at Kichiro. "You have something of mine that I want back, Captain."

"These terms are non-negotiable," Akira replied firmly.

"I designed that beast you ride into battle," Dr. Cross. "Hand him over, or there will be no peace."

Akira stiffened.

"Oh don't worry, I won't hurt him," Dr. Cross said. "It's only to ensure you keep your side of the bargain."

The itch in his brain distracted Akira for a beat, and then with Apeiron's voice, he felt a flood of cocktails keeping his adrenaline under control.

"Accept this term, Captain," she said.

Akira clenched his jaw. "I told you. I don't take orders from you."

"You are risking the entire deal," Apeiron insisted. "This is illogical. It will result in a court-martial if you don't comply."

The rough voice of War Commander Contos surged into Akira's earpiece. "I'm sorry, Akira, but this must be done."

Not even the drugs in his system could keep Akira's rage contained, and he balled his fists until his knuckles popped.

"You harm him, and I *will* kill you," Akira said.

"I would expect nothing less," Dr. Cross said.

Akira grabbed the reins and put his hand on Kichiro's muzzle.

"I'm sorry, boy," he whispered. "I swear on my family, I'll come back for you."

The hybrid beast snorted his disagreement. Akira put his kabuto against Kichiro's head, careful not to stab the horse with the sharp datemono crest.

"I'm sorry, but this is not the end for us," Akira said quietly.

Ghost stepped over and whispered into a private channel to Akira.

"If you want to fight, I'm with you," he said.

That was just like the Lieutenant, always loyal, and always ready to have Akira's back. But this time, it was too risky. He wouldn't forfeit his team's lives to kill the mad doctor. Not now. There would be another time.

Akira recited a quote from the Warrior Codex in his armored satchel. "Like the perfect blossom, a warrior must often wait for the right battle," he whispered to Ghost.

A Breaker walked over to take the reins. Kichiro kicked, striking the Coalition soldier in the chest with his hooves and sending him crashing against a concrete barrier with a crunch.

Tadhg let out a bellowing laugh.

"Easy," Akira said. He calmed the horse down and handed the reins off to a second Breaker. A third soldier lassoed an iron chain around the stallion's neck.

Akira took a step forward, Okami growl-barking between his legs. The other Engines stood at the ready, each prepared to die right here if Akira gave the order.

Dr. Cross shooed Akira's team away with a flick of his hand. "Go, before I change my mind."

Perez put a hand on Akira's left shoulder plate, and Frost put a hand on his right.

"Come on, Captain, we have to leave," she said.

"This is fucking dog shit," Tadhg said. "Know what I'm sayin'?"

Ghost nodded.

Akira watched as his loyal horse was pulled away, struggling. Then he turned and left with his team. The iron gates closed behind them, sealing with a thud.

"We'll get him back," Frost said. "Don't worry, Captain."

"Got that right," Ghost said.

As they marched back to the front lines, Akira could still

hear his horse whinnying. He bowed his helmet in despair, feeling like he was abandoning his companion.

The despair turned to anger—anger that he had been sent here to deliver a message of peace to an evil man who had murdered millions of innocent Nova Alliance Citizens and soldiers.

It made no logical sense to Akira from a military standpoint, but then again, while the orders may have come from War Commander Contos, Akira knew who they were really from.

Apeiron.

— 6 —

Two days had passed since Dr. Cross had accepted the terms of the ceasefire. Jason had watched the refugees streaming out of both Megacity Paris and Megacity Moscow toward camps the Nova Alliance were still scrambling to put up.

Like the treatment for SANDs, the peace had arrived so fast that the Nova Alliance wasn't ready. Things were starting to change, and hope seemed to be spreading through the empire of megacities.

And it was all thanks to Apeiron.

AI is indeed salvation, Jason thought. His sister and her AI were proving that every day.

Today, Apeiron was finally leaving the spin-gravity of Sector 220 at Titan Space Elevator for her first visit to the planet she was designed to save. The black Hummer Droid she had chosen for her physical form stood behind the pilots on a raised bridge in the cockpit of the MOTH.

Jason and Darnel were racked into their seats behind Apeiron as the spacecraft flew out of the hangar.

"I cannot believe I am finally going to see it," Apeiron said excitedly.

The primary pilot looked up at Jason. "Where we headed, Doctor Crichton?"

"Ask her," Jason replied.

"Her?"

"The Hummer Droid," Jason clarified. He shook his head and said, "Apeiron, where would you like to go first?"

"I would like to do a flyover of AAS Restoration Site 110," Apeiron said. "And then I would like to land at one of the Galapagos Islands."

An odd choice, Jason thought.

The pilot put the coordinates into the computer. Four horizontal black wings on each side of the aircraft rotated to vertical, thrusters firing. The MOTH blasted away from the space elevator and began its descent toward Earth's atmosphere.

Two black King Cobra Spaceplanes with red arrows painted on their wings came up along their flanks to escort them safely to the surface.

Jason took a deep breath. Things were happening fast, faster than he had expected, and he was missing his wife Betsy and their daughters Nina and Autumn. It wasn't unusual for him to be away for work this long, but since Petra had died he had only been home for a handful of days, and that included the two for his sister's funeral.

"Entering atmosphere," said the primary pilot. "Prepare for some turbulence."

Thick cloud cover blocked the view over the South Atlantic Ocean. The MOTH rattled as it flew through the clouds.

When they finally broke through, a gasp came from the cockpit.

"This is *so* beautiful," Apeiron said.

Jason watched the droid. In a way, Apeiron was much like a child: curious, adaptive, and full of joy.

They flew over the shoreline of Brazil, passing cities reduced to rubble in the Carbon Wars. South and North America had suffered the most during the height of the conflict, with many cities abandoned.

Mexico City and Buenos Aires were the only two megacities south of the former United States border. The rest of the population in Mexico and South America was scattered across smaller cities or outposts.

This was Coalition territory, where modern civilization no longer existed, and humanity had returned to the state of nature, scratching out a living in villages and towns where the rule of law was by the sword.

Normally, the pilots would have flown much higher to avoid any anti-aircraft weapons that guerilla fighters might possess on the ground. But the advanced weapons systems on the King Cobra Spaceplanes ensured they would be safe.

Soon the MOTH slowed to two hundred miles per hour, giving everyone in the cockpit a perfect view of what used to be the Amazon rainforest.

The muddy brown Amazon river snaked through millions of

acres of dry, cracked soil. From above, the gray and white husks of trees looked like burned kindling, with only sporadic pockets of green jungle. Three hundred billion trees had been cut down, and another fifty billion had burned over the past century.

But there was still hope for the rainforest. Restoration Site 110 emerged on the horizon, an island of vibrant greens and browns.

"This was one of Petra's first projects," Apeiron said. "I wanted to see it with my own eyes."

The pilots looked over their shoulders at the Hummer Droid. Jason ignored them. He didn't expect people to understand. Yet.

Someday all *of humanity will,* he thought.

"Over thirty billion trees have been regrown in the past three years, with over fifteen thousand unique species," Apeiron announced. "In five years, this site will have tripled in size."

Jason narrowed his eyes at the droid.

Apeiron smiled. "I downloaded a speech Petra gave to the Nova Council of Science six years ago."

"I was there," Jason replied.

"Analyzing the INN data, I have concluded that goal has been completed ahead of schedule."

Jason unclasped his belt and stood for a view of the jungle stretching hundreds of miles. The plan he had set out on with Petra was working.

Jason looked out the window at the hub of AAS buildings and machines below them. Moving slowly across a field were four green machines called Frogs. The two-ton vehicles had six massive wheels and an open back bed that allowed them to carry hundreds of trees they used their extendable arms to access, and then plant into the soil.

A swarm of black and yellow Hummer Droids trekked among the machines, helping guide their drills and scoops at digging locations.

"Would you like us to take you down?" asked the primary pilot.

"That won't be necessary," Apeiron said. "Please hover here for a moment, and then proceed to the Galapagos Islands."

The wings switched to vertical and the MOTH blasted away from the site, climbing toward the brilliant sun with their King Cobra escorts. It wasn't long before they were passing over the South Pacific Ocean and descending toward the island chain.

The wings rotated back to horizontal and they lowered toward a beach. Jason unstrapped from his seat and followed Darnel back into the troop hold. Ten Special Forces Pistons waited in the bay, armed with RS-3 plasma pulse rifles and wearing full power armor.

"War Commander Contos wasn't lying about a tight leash," Jason said to Darnel.

"Do you blame him?"

Apeiron clanked out of the neck of the MOTH and into the troop hold. "Shall we?"

The soldiers surrounded the Hummer Droid on the walk down the ramp and out into the warm afternoon.

Jason put a pair of sunglasses on, his wavy brown hair blowing in the wind. "Anything specific you're looking for?"

Apeiron looked out over the green waves crashing against the sand. A lush, green jungle bordered the shoreline. Brown and gray rocks rose up beyond like turtle shells.

"Can you guess why I decided to come here?" she asked.

The soldiers formed a perimeter as Jason walked with the droid and considered her question. It wasn't hard to come up with an answer when thinking back to history.

"You want to walk in the steps of someone who came here before?" Jason asked. "Charles Darwin, perhaps?"

A dimpled smile formed on Apeiron's face, her features shifting.

"Yes, you are correct, Doctor." She stopped at the edge of the beach, her titanium feet sinking in the yellow sand. Bending down, she scooped up a handful, letting the grains filter through her metal fingers.

"I will be back shortly," she said. "Please stay here for your safety."

Apeiron stood and started off toward the dense tropical trees. A yellow iguana scrambled across the beach and up a cluster of boulders where more of the lizards were sunbathing.

"Doctor," came the muffled voice of the Piston Lieutenant. "We were told not to let her out of our sight."

He flashed a hand signal that sent his soldiers after Apeiron. Darnel joined Jason at the edge of the brush to watch.

"Any idea what she's doing?" Darnel asked.

"Let's find out," Jason replied.

He jerked his chin, and the two men set off with the Pistons. Exotic birds called out, and a monkey answered with a guttural croaking noise.

"The hell is that?" Darnel asked.

"A Red Howler monkey," Jason replied. He could see the beautiful animal in the distance, watching the machine and humans.

Apeiron made a path as she walked through the jungle, stopping every few minutes to examine an insect or an animal. She got close to the monkey, replying to the sound with her own croaking voice.

It looked at her curiously, and then swung away, vanishing into the jungle.

"I was hoping you would stay on the beach," Apeiron said. "But that is okay. Feel free to join me, Jason."

He followed her through the brush, listening to her talk.

"Darwin studied how species evolved," she said. "My biggest challenge is making sure humanity evolves before it perishes."

Jason knew there were other reasons she was here. It wasn't just humanity she was trying to save. She was here to learn from species that had adapted to their conditions.

"Jason, I have a request." Apeiron finally stopped and faced him. "I would like to start an E-Vault at Sector 220, and I would like permission to bring back specimens to study there. Species that have adapted to survive in harsh conditions. It will aid in the creation of new droids."

The Canebrakes, Jason thought.

Apeiron was planning to base the final designs on predators at the top of the food chain. The thought of the world's most dangerous and adaptive organisms gave Jason pause, for the second time since her creation.

"Is that a problem?" she asked.

He looked back at the soldiers. All eyes were on him, waiting for his answer.

"No," Jason admitted. "I think this is a great idea."

***

Akira used the Silver Crane stamp to seal the letter to his brother Kai and his family. He missed them and longed to see them again. Kai was still serving as a Piston, but was recently transferred back to Megacity Phoenix, where he could be with his family.

It had been over a year since Akira had seen Kai, his wife Lise, and their three boys.

Writing to them was the safest way to communicate and share his location, which was now Outpost Oasis at the edge of Cairo. He wasn't sure when he would see them again, but every time he set pen to paper, it made him feel a little closer to his family across the world.

Wind howled outside the windows, pounding the walls of the three-story building where Shadow Squad was holed up.

A week had passed since Kichiro had been taken in Megacity Paris, and Akira was now two thousand miles away. He still had to refrain from checking his locator beacon every few minutes.

Years ago, he had had the stallion chipped, just in case they were ever separated during battle. The beacon showed that the horse was underground in a historic area of the city where the Coalition had entrenched their best warriors.

After a decade together, he felt a piece of himself missing. Every time he went outside he would look toward the vehicle depot out of habit, where the stallion had a stable. The horse, like Okami, was his family.

Akira sat on the dusty floor and pulled out the Warrior Codex. He drowned out the sound of gusting wind and Ghost entertaining the squad on the first floor of the compound. His tenor voice would have made him an opera star if he hadn't chosen a career killing people.

Okami joined in with a chorus of growl-barking, voicing his playful side.

"Captain, I am sorry to interrupt," Apeiron said, "but a severe dust storm is heading toward Outpost Oasis. Your current dwelling should withstand the storm, but things may get a bit loud."

"Louder than Ghost?" Akira asked.

"Yes, louder than Ghost."

Akira kept reading through the codex. It was a map, in a way, a guide that followed an ethos. His ancestors had lived by this sacred book, and it had steered Akira in his journey as a warrior. Over the decades, he added his own story to the pages, documenting the places he fought and the men and women he had killed.

The book was all he had now to remember many of those he had lost.

Akira slowly flipped through the pages, stopping to read a story he had long since memorized. The story was told by a distant relative who had fought for Lord Asano and had become a ronin after Asano was forced to commit seppuku. The original page, like many others, had been replaced and re-written over the years.

He turned to another replaced page about his great-great grandfather, who had served the Teishin Shudan division of the Japanese Imperial Army. A picture of the thin, short man was plastered to the page, standing in a brown uniform with a sword on his belt and a rifle in his hands.

The shouting grew louder below.

Letting out a sigh, Akira tucked the book away and went to the window to look out at the approaching storm. In the distance, the Great Pyramids rose toward the clouds, ancient relics of yet another bloody time in human history.

Cigar smoke drifted into the room, and he turned to see Ghost peeking in.

"You going to stay up here all night like an anti-social asshole?" Ghost asked playfully.

"I was planning on it, but obviously you guys aren't going to let me, are you?" Akira said with a smirk. He took the cigar that Ghost held out and took a puff as he followed him down the stairs.

"Don't worry, Captain. We'll get Kichiro back," Ghost said.

"I know," Akira said.

They walked down the stairs. The rest of the squad watched a holo-screen of a live Droid Raider match. Tonight, the Megacity Tokyo Cranes faced the Megacity Rome Legions, and the Legions had just taken the lead.

Ghost took the cigar back. Smoke rose over his handsome olive face and slicked-back mane of black hair. "The golden Legions march, ay-oh!" he sang, waving his cigar like a symphonic conductor.

Frost nodded at Akira, her short hair falling over the left side of her head, which was buzzed and tattooed with a white orchid that almost matched her enhanced, ice-colored eyes.

At the other end of the table sat Tadhg. Long, curly brown locks hung over the wide shoulders.

"The Legion is the fiercest, ay-oh!" Ghost sang. He bent down close to Tadhg's ear. "The Legion is the fastest, ay-oh!"

When Tadhg didn't respond, Ghost added, "Know what I'm sayin'?"

Using, Tadhg's phrase just pissed the big man off more. He swatted at Ghost.

"God damn, you're annoying," Tadhg said. "You want me to smack that cigar down your throat?"

"Ghost level, baby!" Ghost sang in a robotic voice.

"I'll show you *God* level, mate," Tadhg said, fisting his palm.

"Can you guys keep it down a little?" Perez asked.

He sat at a small table in the corner with a book, his sand-colored flesh covered in tattoos of ancient poems, as well as some he had written himself, including both of the team's mottos: *Death from the Shadows* and *Together, we are one.*

Akira walked over. "What are you reading?"

Perez rotated the book. "It's about the Battle of Kadesh."

"Hey, nerds! You're missing this game!" Tadhg shouted. "Why don't you just download that shit to your chip, Perez?"

"Because some of us enjoy reading the old-fashioned way," Perez said.

"Don't mind Tadhg," Frost said. "I don't think he can even read."

Tadhg shrugged.

An itch formed in the back of Akira's skull, and a message from Apeiron came through.

"Captain, I have an encrypted transmission from Command," she said.

Akira stepped away from Perez and closed his eyes, expecting to see the cold blue eyes and spiked hair of General Andrew Thacker. But instead, it was the hard face of War Commander Contos.

"Captain Hayashi," Contos began. "We just lost contact with Pumping Station 9 at the Sahara Terraforming Project. You're being deployed to check it out and will be communicating directly with Apeiron on this mission for training purposes."

Akira opened his eyes, watching the team who were oblivious to the message that came to just his chip.

"I know what you are thinking," Apeiron added.

She couldn't technically read Akira's thoughts, but she was constantly monitoring his heartbeat and breathing, which had given away his trepidation.

"Due to my extensive ability to monitor and provide intel, I have been given the honor and opportunity to assist with this mission," Apeiron said.

"Assist?" Akira asked.

"That is right. I will be there with you at all times, Captain. Is there a problem with that?"

"No."

Akira cleared his throat.

"We got a job, Shadow Squad," he said. "Rack up."

"God dammit," Tadhg said.

"Don't worry, *mate*," Ghost said. "We can watch your team lose in a replay."

Okami barked with excitement as the Engines moved toward the charging crates containing their armor. Akira pushed his finger against the biometric reader and pulled out his two-hundred-pound rig. He set it down on the dusty floor to activate it.

In front of him rose an exoskeleton without a head. It popped open, and he stepped inside. The titanium plates folded out and snapped to his chest and torso, clicking over the slender shocked struts and rods on his arms and legs, until everything but his head was encased in armor.

He tilted his skull back into the kabuto that unfolded from the overlapping shoulder-spanning plates. The systems automatically activated on his HUD, bringing his jetpack, life support, and battery all online.

Armor secured, Akira opened the door and ran into the gusting wind, the grit blasting against his suit. The outpost walls were empty except for a pair of guards in a post above them. He led the way to the helipad in the center of the outpost. A MOTH stealth-attack aircraft waited on the tarmac.

Akira hurried up the ramp to the troop hold under the belly of the craft. Red overhead lights illuminated hull-mounted racks. The Engines stood against them and pulled the bars over their armor, clicking in. Okami went down on his hind legs, the magnets on his paws securing him to the deck.

"Listen up, because I'm only saying this once," Akira said. "Apeiron will be assisting on this mission."

"The fuck?" Tadhg said. "The fact I got to hear her inside my head *some* of the time is bad enough."

"It is an honor to assist with this mission, Shadow Squad," Apeiron said. "Uploading data to your chips."

In his mind's eye, Akira studied the location of Pumping Station 9, set on the western edge of the Sahara Terraforming Project. A valley on the southwestern border provided cover in case of a Coalition attack.

"A skeleton crew of two engineers and three guards is assigned to this post," Apeiron said. "UAVs have detected no sign of life, and we have no video feeds on any INN access port."

"Any sign of vehicles or tracks?" Akira asked.

"Negative. For that reason, I would suggest a fly-over before deploying."

"How about you let me call the shots, and you stick to providing intel?"

"Of course, Captain. It was simply a suggestion."

The moon rose in the night sky as the MOTH flew over the barren desert. Akira blinked to zoom in further with his INVS eyes. Mounds of sand rose like the humps of a buried monster. A line of spiral shoots rose over the horizon, then suddenly, a forest that stretched as far as he could see. It wasn't all barren and dead out here.

This mecca in the middle of the desert was supported by hundreds of miles of underground pipes pumping desalinated water from the Mediterranean Sea to feed a forest of bamboo. This was another part of Dr. Jason Crichton's plan to restore the Earth.

"Remarkable, is it not?" asked Apeiron. "This hybrid species was modified in an AAS lab to produce the fastest growing bamboo in the world. We more than doubled the daily growth rate of thirty-six inches."

Ghost opened a private line to Akira.

"Seriously, we gotta listen to her?" he said.

"Orders came from War Commander Contos, Lieutenant."

That shut him up.

None of them liked being connected to the OS. In some ways, she was like a very intelligent child, but Akira knew she could be cold and calculating like all AI.

"Do any of you want to guess how many bamboo trees make up this sector of forest?" Apeiron asked.

Akira focused on the map of the pumping facility, looking for a good LZ based off the data they had.

"Any guesses?" Apeiron asked.

"I always hated biology," Tadhg said.

"You hated school in general, right?" Ghost asked.

Tadhg chuckled deep. "Wasn't my thing."

"Punching people has always been your thing."

"It's an art that I excel at."

Tadhg gestured to Perez.

"Like our mate Perez excels at reciting history and writing poetry and shit."

"And shit?" Perez asked.

"Yeah, we all got our skills."

"Shadow Squad," Apeiron interrupted, "I am sure I don't

need to tell you how important this site is to the restoration of the planet."

"We're aware," Akira said, directing his visor at Ghost and Tadhg, in turn.

They both nodded in understanding.

"I got an LZ," Akira said. He uploaded it over INN.

It was going to be a few miles' hike, but at least they weren't going to drop into an ambush, and Apeiron agreed with his location.

Ghost and Tadhg grabbed their weapons off the racks.

"Please be careful not to damage this site," Apeiron said. "This area is incredibly important—"

"I might prune some trees, but it sounds like they grow super-fast anyway," Tadhg said. He laughed to himself and stepped up to the edge of the ramp.

"Death from the Shadows," Akira said. "Together, we are one."

The team repeated the mottos.

Tadhg hopped into the night.

Ghost gave a salute and jumped.

Okami looked up, and Akira scooped up the wolfdog. They followed Perez and Frost out next, jumping twenty feet to the dirt. The shocks from Akira's exoskeleton absorbed the brunt of the impact, but couldn't do anything for the sour feeling in his gut—a feeling that the fragile truce the Coalition had agreed to could be shattered with a single gunshot.

7

Screams reverberated through the cavernous space. They quieted almost as quickly. In the respite, came the constant dripping of water, making it impossible to sleep.

Chloe shivered in the hay bed, both from fear and the cold that froze her to her core. She was somewhere deep underground in the center of Megacity Paris.

She wasn't sure exactly how many days had passed since she was captured or what time it was now, but at least she was with her uncle, and she knew her droid Radar was safe. Keanu had assured her of that when they reunited in the prison cell.

A long, hollow scream of pain rose and faded away.

Chloe sat up as Keanu gingerly cleaned his bruised face with his tattered sweatshirt.

"It's okay," he assured Chloe in his deep, soothing voice. "Everything's going to be okay, I promise."

He kept saying that, but she no longer believed him.

In the cell across from them was a cleric. He was on his knees now, head bowed, hands steepled. "AI is salvation," he whispered. "AI will free us of these chains."

He risked his head every time he said these words, and it was why he was here today.

There were almost fifty other Nova Alliance citizens in captivity with them. Men, women, and children, all having committed various crimes against the Coalition.

Chloe had already asked if her mom was among them, even though she knew she was probably dead. No one had heard of her, but rumors circulated that millions of citizens were being let out of the city due to a new peace treaty.

She wrote it off as just that, a rumor.

Footsteps tapped at the end of the hallway, and Chloe steeled herself as a guard lumbered toward them in his clanking armor.

"Just do what they say," Keanu said. "We have to survive until they come."

His words trailed off as a Coalition soldier stopped in front of the cell. He wore a helmet, like the others, but without any antlers. Chloe stood back as he opened the door. The man reached inside and yanked her out hard.

"Hey!" Keanu yelled.

The soldier threw a punch into his jaw, dropping Keanu like a bag of bricks.

"Stop!" Chloe screamed.

Keanu lay still, but he was still breathing.

The guard locked the door and pushed Chloe down the hall.

"Uncle Keanu," she cried.

He managed to look up and mumble, "Do what they say."

The soldier grunted and pushed her in the back, past the other prisoners. She knew the route by heart now. Another passage, then two more stairwells, until they reached the factory where they took her to work.

On the sprawling factory floor were hundreds of prisoners in gray suits, working on an assembly line constructing Iron Wolves. Chloe scanned them for her mother.

She was hustled to a small warehouse where welders worked on securing new armor to the droids. Sparks rained down. Whining power tools rang from all directions. But the guard pushed her through this room, too, and into a hallway.

"Where are we going?" Chloe asked.

The man gave her a good push but said nothing. They walked down three stairwells, then into a long passage carved out of rock. Candles illuminated the smooth passage, and it didn't take Chloe long to figure out where she was headed.

They were in the catacombs.

The next chamber confirmed her suspicions. Skulls and other bones were tucked throughout the damp passages. As they went deeper, screams of agony rose and faded.

Chloe slowed her pace, scanning the open doors in the tunnels at the grisly sights.

"Move," the guard said. He gave her a hard shove, knocking her to the ground.

Chloe wasn't a fighter, but she had to resist the urge to turn on this man. Maybe she could get the best of him and escape.

He didn't have antlers, indicating he wasn't a seasoned killer.

Maybe she could take him down.

Her uncle's words rang out in her mind. *Do as they say... survive.*

Chloe pushed herself up, wiping blood from her lip.

"Go," he said, pointing.

They took a stairwell deeper underground and walked through multiple narrowing passages. She noticed drainage tunnels blocked with iron bars. They must lead back to the streets, which meant a way out of this place.

If only she had the opportunity to escape...

The guard finally stopped in front of a cavernous chamber. Candle flames flickered, illuminating the huge carved room. Medical staff wearing gray coveralls and breathing masks worked around a table in the center. Something dripped off its surface, tapping against the floor in a consistent pattern.

Across the room, a concrete wall supported mounted cryo-chambers, most glowing from interior lights that revealed naked human occupants in breathing masks, suspended in liquid. At first Chloe thought they were Nova Alliance prisoners, but the occupants all shared the same Nordic tattoos that many of the Coalition soldiers had inked on their flesh.

Supposedly those tattoos meant they were courageous warriors destined for greatness. To Chloe, the tattoos told her these people worked for evil forces. There was nothing courageous about rounding up innocent civilians and slaughtering them.

The guard nudged her, much softer this time, toward the people in suits. One turned and spread open arms like an old friend in greeting. A sizzling hot blade protruded from one of the man's gloved hands.

"Ah, Chloe Cotter. We meet again," he said.

Chloe recognized the voice.

Dr. Cross walked over, pushed up his goggles, and looked Chloe up and down with his red eyes. Then he leaned closer, examining her face. "You're bleeding."

Chloe touched her lip.

"She was being difficult," the guard said.

Dr. Cross looked at the soldier with a tilt of his head. "You were told not to harm her."

"I—"

Before the guard could react, the doctor jabbed the energy blade under his helmet with a crunch.

Chloe shrieked and jumped back as the soldier slumped to the ground, blood squirting out of the sizzling hole in his helmet.

"I'm truly sorry," Dr. Cross said. "Please forgive me for how this animal treated you. I've been very clear to my people that you and your uncle are not to be harmed as long as you help me."

The guard jerked a few times, struggling for his final breaths.

"Now, if you'd follow me," Dr. Cross said. "I'll show you where you are going to work."

Chloe hesitated, still looking at the twitching guard.

"Come on, Chloe. I don't bite." Dr. Cross motioned with the blade. "Oh, and please, call me Otto."

She followed him past the tables where the suited technicians, or scientists or doctors, whatever they were, huddled around a patient. Through a gap between them, she saw the source of the screams. Straps secured a man to the table, riven stumps where his limbs had been, a chunk of his skull missing.

"I hope you have a strong stomach," Dr. Cross said. "The work we're doing is pivotal to the advancement of the human race, but it's also a bit... messy."

He flashed a perfectly white smile, stopping outside the cryo-chambers.

"Eeny, meeny, miny, moe," he said as he moved from capsule to capsule. Lifting a finger to his mouth, he smiled again and pointed. "We'll try this one next."

"Yes, doctor," said one of the technicians.

Chloe followed Dr. Cross into another room carved out of stone. A honeycomb of skulls adorned the hollowed-out walls. Four large metal seats were secured to the floor with a rimmed base, and spider-like arms extended away from them. Metal hands with bone saws and energy blades hung off the appendages. Two halves of an open helmet connected to the headrest. Plastic tubes extended from ports that connected to the back, where holes allowed for needles to be inserted.

"Since we don't have much time, I'm going to explain my work to you very quickly," Dr. Cross said. "You see, the Nova Alliance has its Engines... and I have my Breakers."

He continued to another large seat covered by a sheet. Using a control panel, he pushed a button that rose the ribbed base vertically. The sheet fell away, exposing the corpse of a massive man with defined muscles. Plates of armor were bolted to his pale flesh. Two helmet halves were cracked apart above his head.

The mouth of the Breaker was frozen wide open from a final scream of pain. His bloodshot eyes stared at the ceiling, and the tubes in his neck still contained a trace amount of green fluid.

"These soldiers have stronger bones, more powerful muscles, and other augmentations that assist them in combat against the Engines." Dr. Cross wagged a finger in the air. "But the Breakers won't protect our way of life. Nor will my hybrid animals. You know, the Nova Alliance Council never saw the benefits of that work, and believed AI was the only way to survive."

The doctor paced around the corpse.

"They never saw the genius in my work... but they will. Oh, they will see it very clearly." Dr. Cross took a seat in an empty chair. "You know what the greatest predators are, Chloe?"

"Humans," she replied.

"Precisely. We need something bigger, something better, something *primal*, and that's where you will help me and my team of doctors."

"But I only modified droids," Chloe said weakly. "I gave them faster processing units, fixed prosthetics, made custom colors, and I upgraded their operating systems—"

"Your background is *exactly* what I'm looking for," Dr. Cross interrupted.

Footsteps echoed in the hallway, growing louder until they reached the chamber. Two men in coveralls carried in a naked Coalition soldier from a cryo-chamber with gelatinous fluid dripping down his tattooed flesh.

The men flopped the unconscious soldier into the spider seat. He was young, maybe twenty or twenty-five. Not much older than Chloe.

A pair of doctors tightened straps over his wet chest and thighs. With the soldier secure, they backed away and Dr. Cross approached.

"So, if this were a droid, how would you modify it?" he asked Chloe.

She studied the unconscious Coalition soldier. He was a murderer, a man who could have easily killed her father and mother.

But he was still a man. Not a droid.

"Come on," Dr. Cross said. He put his hand on Chloe's shoulder. "Think of him as a fish or a mouse or a worm."

"B-but he isn't any of those things," Chloe stuttered.

Dr. Cross pulled away, his features darkening.

"*Pretend,*" he said.

Chloe swallowed hard.

"How would you modify him to make him better in combat?"

"I would give him INVS eyes, replace his limbs with prosthetics so he could run faster, and replace his jaw with titanium plates, and new teeth that could tear flesh."

"Wow," Dr. Cross said. He gave Chloe an excited hug.

She tensed as he embraced her.

"*Now* we're talking!" Dr. Cross grinned, wider and wider, as he moved around his patient, almost skipping like a child.

Chloe let out a short sigh, realizing it wasn't from fear. It was relief.

When she first heard the screams, she had thought she was being led to her death. But she had a skill that would keep her and her uncle alive, at least until the Nova Alliance sent its Engines and Pistons to reclaim the city.

"You know of Apeiron, right?" Dr. Cross asked.

Chloe looked at him. "No."

"Apeiron is the newest Nova Alliance OS. According to my spies, she is not like the other AIs. Her OS was integrated with a human mind."

"I thought that was against the law."

"It was, but Doctor Crichton convinced the proper people that AI was missing something... missing the human element, and that a hybrid of AI and a human mind can save humanity."

Dr. Cross shook his head.

"Soon, *I* will be saving humanity from this abomination," he said. "Soon, the world will see the truth."

***

An hour and twelve minutes had passed since the pumping station went off-line, and Akira still had no idea what had happened.

He crouched in the bamboo forest with Frost and Perez.

Ghost's voice came over the open team comm channel. "No sign of the guards or workers. Moving up."

Akira couldn't see the lieutenant, Tadhg, or Okami from his position to the west, but he did have access to their cams on his HUD. As they got closer to the station, Akira pulled out the ball-shaped drone. Hummingbird-sized wings sprouted out the sides.

"Go to work, Blue Jay," he whispered.

The drone turned from blue to black as it rose away into the night.

"The hell did everyone go?" Frost said over the channel.

"Maybe the workers got drunk and passed out," Tadhg replied. "I would if I worked all the way out in this shithole."

"I believe this facility has been compromised," Apeiron said.

Akira had a feeling she was right. "Proceed with extreme caution, SS," he said.

After studying the drone's aerial view of the facility for a few seconds, he flashed a hand signal for Perez and Frost to follow him deeper into the bamboo forest. To the east, Okami was prowling closer to the pumping station. Tadhg and Ghost moved silently through the maze of trees. Four mammoth water silos blocked their views of the facility.

Frost stopped at a maintenance road, and then waved Akira

over. Footprints and truck tracks showed in the dirt.

"Could be workers, but that's a lot of tracks," she said.

Akira flitted through all of his HUD views, seeing nothing until he tapped into Blue Jay.

The drone had lowered over the tanks and sent a visual that the UAV had missed—four rusted tanker trucks, covered in camo and heat-blocking nets.

Under the awnings, a group of people were loading up on water. Their brown coats had armbands marked with a comet, signifying their allegiance to the Coalition.

Akira gave Blue Jay new orders to swoop lower. The drone sent back images of twenty-two hostile personnel. They all carried weapons but were only lightly armored. Blue Jay gave him no indication the drone had detected any Breakers. These were simple nomadic atheists, not serious Coalition fighters, but that did not make them any less dangerous.

Especially if these people had sabotaged the pump station.

On the dirt were four AAS station workers, lying face down with their hands bound behind their backs. Two Pistons were on their knees a few feet away, beaten but alive.

A single armored truck waited idly under another tarp. In the turret, a soldier gripped a .50-cal machine gun, the only weapon Akira saw that could actually do much damage to them.

"Apeiron, contact command for orders," he whispered.

"Stand by."

The team took up covered positions and waited.

"Orders are to secure the trucks and neutralize hostiles," Apeiron said.

"Copy that," Akira replied. He flashed the signal to advance on the facility. Melting into the shadows, the Engines crept around the outer perimeter, weapons shouldered, targeting systems linking onto the hostiles.

These people just wanted water, and Akira didn't want to kill them, but they had to secure the station and rescue the hostages.

He raised his hand, holding it, thinking of his stallion. If this escalated, it could end the truce.

Akira slowly lowered his hand and balled his fist, ordering the team to stay put. "Cover me. I'll handle this."

He wasn't about to risk his team or the truce over water. He slotted his rifle in the armored slot over his jetpack and started toward the nomads.

"Captain, I hope you know what you are doing," Apeiron said. "There are weapons among these fighters that could severely injure or even kill you."

"I'll try peace like you suggested," he said. "Let's see if it works."

"Be careful, Cap," Ghost said.

Akira stopped just outside the warehouse, and then blasted up to the roof, landing with a thud. Within seconds, ten rifle barrels angled up at his helmet.

He raised his hands.

"Easy," Akira said. "I'm just here to talk."

A man with long hair and a breathing mask aimed a plasma rifle at Akira. It was the only plasma rifle in the group, which told Akira that he was dealing with the leader.

"Who the hell are you?" the man asked in Spanish.

Akira switched languages with his helmet translator.

"I'm Captain Akira Hayashi, and you are making a very big mistake," he said. "I'm authorized to allow you to leave here alive, but not with that water."

The man pushed his night-vision goggles up and raised a skeptical brow at Akira.

"Don't be stupid," Akira added. "It's not just me out here. If you fire a single bullet, none of you will leave here alive."

"And you will die too," the man said. "So how about this… we let *you* leave alive, and we take the water."

"You know I can't authorize that," Akira said.

"I see why they call you Akira the Brave now," Apeiron said over the comm.

The man stepped up closer to the warehouse, looking up.

"We need this water. Why are trees more important than human life?" he asked.

Akira kept his hands up and lowered his voice. "These trees are giving humanity a second chance to live and breathe without a mask like the one on your face."

"We leave here without water, we die anyway," the man said.

"If you don't let us take it, we're going to have to fight you for it."

Akira clenched his jaw. He could see where this was going.

Blue Jay descended in the distance, scanning the APC and passing on new data that sent a chill through Akira.

These weren't the only fighters in the area.

"Apeiron, request permission to give these assholes the damn water," he whispered.

"Secure the station, and the water," she quickly replied.

Akira cursed. This was a lose-lose situation.

He didn't have time to consider other options before a muzzle flashed below. The three-round burst hit him in the center of his chest. He identified the shooter as he fell back—a young man, no older than fourteen, holding an ancient assault rifle in a shaky hand.

The soldier with long hair looked back at the teenager and then over to the turret, giving the slightest of nods.

Akira hit the roof, yelling, "NO!"

The turret barked to life, drowning out his plea. A single round from Frost silenced the gun in the time it took Akira to flatten his body on the roof. The gunner slumped in the turret, his helmet smoking from a hole in the center.

Akira watched all hell break loose below. Cries of pain filled the night as the Engines cut down the Coalition fighters with easy shots. Frost blasted up to the roof next to Akira, her rifle barrel sighting targets the moment her boots set down.

"You good, Captain?" she asked.

He nodded and pulled out his rifle.

The hatch of the APC had burst open below, releasing three soldiers that burst into pulpy kisses from the spray of Tadhg's WMD. The big Engine lumbered across the dirt, hip-firing his massive plasma cannon.

Another Coalition soldier jumped out of the APC only to fall from a suppressed .50-cal sniper round that blew through armor and flesh, hitting a second man just emerging from the hatch.

"Damn, never seen you take down two at once!" Tadhg said. He chuckled, but Akira found no joy in killing these people. He knew Frost didn't either.

Ghost was coming up around the other side of the APC when a female Coalition warrior with dreadlocks shoved a pistol to his gut. Okami jumped up and bit her hand before she could pull the trigger, and Ghost headbutted her in the nose with his faceplate.

Perez used his shield to deflect bullets coming from behind a truck, where three Coalition soldiers fired ancient assault rifles. They seemed to run out of ammo, providing Perez with a chance to advance while Frost laid down covering fire.

Two more soldiers slumped to the ground, their skulls destroyed. Perez reached the third soldier behind the truck and drew his sword.

"Cease fire!" Akira shouted. "Cease fire!"

He rose up to assess the carnage in a quick scan. Thirty seconds was all it took to kill and maim more than twenty fighters. Jumping down to the dirt, he began the search for survivors.

The other Engines spread out, drawing their energy swords. Feeds from Okami and Blue Jay directed Akira to a man crumpled against a pipe.

He stopped and crouched in front of the mortally wounded nomad leader. He was still breathing. Bloody bubbles burst out of his mouth as he tried to speak.

"I'm sorry," Akira said. "It didn't have to be like this."

Deep down, he really was sorry. He didn't want to kill these people over water. Doing so confirmed how cheap life had become in the wastes outside the megacity walls.

The dying soldier fingered for something inside a pouch in his vest.

Ghost walked over with a blade raised, but Akira stopped him. He reached down to help the man retrieve a small Christian cross from the pouch.

"AI... is... n-not..." the man stuttered. He gripped the holy relic and, with his last breath, prayed to the Christian God.

Perez stepped next to Akira, shaking his helmet.

"They will never understand," he said.

"No, I suppose they won't," Akira replied.

"They cling to their superstitions instead of embracing our

future and salvation. It's a shame."

Akira rose to his feet and left the dead man with Perez. They joined Tadhg to help him free the workers and two Pistons. The soldiers were both beaten, but they would live.

"We got a runner!" Frost shouted. "In pursuit!"

She took off after the hostile. She was the fastest Engine on the squad, even with her long-barreled rifle.

Using his infrared scanner, Akira saw the fleeing nomad heading toward the pumping station. He made it there and hopped onto an ATV.

Zooming in with his INVS eyes, Akira recognized the youthful face of the teenager who had shot him in the chest to kick off the massacre.

The youngster steered the ATV out onto the road, dust kicking up.

Frost, taking a knee, locked on with her rifle, but Akira called out to hold fire.

"There's been enough bloodshed today," he said. "Let the kid go."

"Are you sure that is wise?" Apeiron asked over the comms.

Akira was surprised to hear her voice after minutes of silence, but even more surprised by her question.

"Doctor Crichton says that when children are orphaned, they often become terrorists," she said.

"Yeah, and sometimes they see the light," Ghost said. "I say let the kid live. Let him think about what happened here. Maybe next time he won't be so trigger happy."

Perez shrugged. "Or next time, he might not miss."

8

Jason woke up to a beeping noise in the upper cockpit of the MOTH just before midnight. Outside the viewports, the moon was high in the night sky. He was expecting to see ocean when he looked down, but instead he saw sand.

Darnel was sleeping across from him, snoring loudly. For the past week, they had visited destinations across the globe in Apeiron's quest to collect a variety of life forms from the world's most hostile places.

They had taken a submarine to the bottom of the Mariana trench to discover life that had adapted to the crushing depths. At the bottom, Apeiron had used the submarine's robotic hands to capture a new species of octopus. Two days later, they had added a highly venomous cuttlefish to the vault.

Jason unbuckled his harness and left the cockpit to search for the AI. A hatch opened into the troop hold where most of the Pistons were sleeping in their racks.

Embodied in the Hummer Droid, Apeiron stood over the crates, studying the creatures through the glass sides.

"Hello, Jason," she said without turning. "There is something I need to tell you."

He stepped up next to her, rubbing his eyes.

"Okay, but want to tell me where we're going next first?" he said. "I haven't been home for a week, and I miss my girls."

"I know you do, but you will see them soon," Apeiron replied. "We are about to make our final stop." She lowered her voice. "I have some dire news."

"What's wrong?"

"A group of Coalition nomads attempted to hijack water from the tanks at Pumping Station 9 in the Sahara terraforming site."

"Wish I could say I was surprised." Jason sighed. "So, how'd that turn out for these nomads?"

"Shadow Squad was deployed to neutralize the threat and

eliminated all but one of the hostiles."

"And the truce—"

"Is still holding. I am currently monitoring one thousand twenty different patrols, between AAS guards and Nova Alliance Strike Force Pistons. There have already been thirty skirmishes between Coalition troops and our own."

"Thirty in a week…"

"That was today, Jason."

He looked over at the Piston Lieutenant, who watched them suspiciously.

"The peace is fragile, but it is holding… for now," Apeiron said. "I just need a little more time to finish the design of the Canebrakes, and today I hope to finish my research. You should try and rest. I will wake you up when we arrive."

Jason nodded and returned to the cockpit.

"You know where it's taking us now?" Darnel asked.

Jason looked at his friend and confidante. A man he trusted to run his company, a man who had served in the Carbon Wars. Darnel refused to call Apeiron "her", which told Jason everything he needed to know about how Darnel really felt.

He was a supporter of AI and had never wavered in that, but his service in the military ingrained in him a closely held respect for protecting the law. He might not admit it outright, but Darnel didn't approve of Jason breaking the law to merge human consciousness with AI.

And of course, there was also the fact Jason had done it with Petra's mind. Something that Darnel definitely didn't understand.

"Look, I think we should have a talk," Jason said. "About Apeiron."

"Don't you mean Petra?"

Jason shrugged. "If you want to do this, let's do this."

"Do what, Doctor?" Darnel said. "I'm here. I'm always here. But you never asked me my opinion on Apeiron or if it was right to hook Petra up to that machine. You just asked me to help, and I'm honestly starting to worry about how fast Apeiron's advancing."

Darnel leaned closer to Jason.

"It's existed for forty-five *days* and has already grown more advanced than all of the AIs in existence. And it's getting smarter every second," he said.

"That's the point," Jason insisted. "That's how she developed a treatment for SANDs. She altered the electromagnetic therapy that took us years to develop and turned it into a system capable of finally eliminating the molecular contaminants that cause the disease in a matter of days. Now she's perfecting the Canebrakes, and helping to oversee every single one of the fifteen thousand, four hundred and three project sites designed to restore the planet."

Darnel stiffened in his seat. "So, you're not worried at all about how fast it's adapting and learning?"

"All due respect, my friend, but this is what I designed her to do. I just wish I had done this earlier. If I had, then Petra would still be alive."

"I know, I'm sorry, but I will say this... Apeiron is not your sister. Petra, in my opinion, is dead."

"Yes, that is true," Jason said.

Darnel eased back and looked out the window, clearly still worried but choosing not to argue. Deep down, he was fiercely loyal and smart too, but he wasn't a visionary.

And that was why he would never understand why Jason had created Apeiron.

A beeping noise drew Jason's attention to the viewports. Under the glow of the moon, a jagged mountain chain spanned the horizon.

"Where are we?" Darnel asked.

"Over the Atacama Desert," said one of the pilots.

"Where it rains only once every fifteen years," Apeiron said. She stood in the open hatch to the troop hold, holding out two bulky, vacuum-rated suits with oxygen packs.

"Please put these on," she said.

Darnel and Jason followed her through the hatch with the suits.

"Why do we need these?" Darnel asked.

"Because tonight, we are going to trek across the El Tito Geysers," Apeiron replied.

"An active volcano," Darnel said. "Sounds like Piston training."

Some of the soldiers in the back of the troop hold laughed. Jason forced a smile as he slipped into the suit.

"The arid region of the desert fluctuates severely, ranging from ten degrees Fahrenheit at night to one hundred and thirty degrees Fahrenheit during the day," Apeiron said. "It is currently fifteen degrees Fahrenheit."

Jason secured his suit as the MOTH descended over the desolate terrain toward the bulging brown hills on the horizon.

"Approaching LZ," announced the pilot.

The back gate opened, and a ramp lowered to the dirt. Jason walked out into the frigid night with Darnel by his side and the Pistons following.

Apeiron gestured for them to follow her toward the vents where white steam sprayed out in billowing plumes. "It is safe, I assure you."

They passed by the cracks in the Earth, most of which seemed dormant. Apeiron stopped to collect a sample at one.

"The microbes here are different than most organisms on Earth," she said. "They produce energy by metabolizing normally dangerous gases like carbon monoxide and dimethyl sulfide."

"Yes, I remember reading about how some hardy microbes can produce water and methane from carbon-rich compounds where sunlight isn't available for photosynthesis," Jason said.

"Correct, Doctor. Some organisms, like these methanogens, actually find oxygen toxic." Apeiron stood and deposited a sample into a storage slot in her arm. "There are also hyperthermophiles, like those we discovered at the deep-sea hydrothermal vents, and I am hoping to find more here."

She led them deeper into the steaming field. Finally, about a mile from the MOTH, she halted, scanning the terrain and then turning back to Jason.

"We have about another minute if my calculations are correct," she said excitedly.

"Before what?" he asked.

"You will see in a moment. Please stay here."

She continued into the field, the lights on her shoulder mounts clicking on. The beams raked back and forth, revealing a crack across the dirt she was heading directly toward.

"Apeiron, wait," Jason said. "You're…"

A blast of steam fired into the air, venting across the cracks and enveloping the Hummer Droid in the spray.

"Petra!" Jason yelled.

The temperature reading spiked on his HUD, and he retreated with the soldiers and Darnel.

"Do not be afraid, Doctor."

The soothing voice of his sister whispered in Jason's ear. He saw something moving in the steam. He took a step forward, shaking Darnel's hand off his shoulder.

"This isn't safe, Doctor," Darnel said on a private channel. "We should get back to the MOTH."

Apeiron broke through the cloud and walked forward, a cape of steam draping off the droid's titanium armor. She deposited another vial into her chest.

"I have the samples I came here for," she said. "We can get you home now."

Apeiron started back toward the two men, stopping and tilting her head. The smile from earlier returned.

"Doctor, I believe we have discovered a new type of species not present in the Nova Alliance database," she said. "These cell membranes maintain amazing structural stability at high temperatures. They will further help us learn new ways for humanity to survive in extreme conditions too."

It suddenly struck Jason what Apeiron was doing on these trips. She wasn't just looking to perfect the Canebrakes…

"You don't think we can save the Earth?" he asked. "You think humanity is doomed?"

Apeiron rotated her head. "Doctor, you coded me to protect human life, at a time when your species is facing the very real possibility of extinction. Learning from some of the most adaptive biological lifeforms will give me insight on how to help humanity adapt to a changing Earth environment, and other hostile environments like the moon and eventually, other planets."

She gestured for Jason to follow her back to the MOTH but stopped at the bottom of the ramp with the smile still on her face.

"If it is okay with you," she said, "I would like to see the family."

"Family?" Jason asked.

"Betsy, Nina, and Autumn," Apeiron said. "I miss them, and would like to see them again."

***

The guard came for Chloe the same time each day, so she learned to keep track of time in the darkness of the underground prison. Today, her uncle had been sleeping when the guard arrived. He was smaller and thinner than the other guards, and like the guard Dr. Cross had killed, this man had no antlers.

Keanu got up and hugged Chloe, whispering into her ear. "Pretend it isn't real and do as they say."

She nodded.

The young guard led Chloe through the tunnels, her mind in a daze. She thought of her parents and Radar, but she snapped alert when the man directed her to the left at an intersection where they had always gone right.

"Where are we going?" she asked.

"I'm sorry, but I can't answer that," he said.

His voice was kind, making her wonder if he was a good person just trapped in a bad circumstance. Surely this wasn't what he wanted. Surely he didn't want to live in a world of death and horror. But she also knew he wouldn't help her. No one who worked for Dr. Cross would betray him, for the same reason that she continued to work in his macabre labs.

Fear.

They continued down a stone hallway that narrowed toward a stairwell winding deeper underground. Somewhere in the distance she could hear a heavy flow of water. They were passing under the river.

Sconces guided them down the stairs. At the bottom, an

open door led to a sprawling cavernous room full of empty cages. Chloe gagged at a foul odor and pulled her mask up.

Cages that once held animals now sat empty, nothing but dried lumps of feces, clumps of fur, and stains on the cage floors. They passed larger cages that had once held horses, and then the smaller one for the wolves, bred by the tens of thousands to be turned into Iron Wolves.

The guard stopped in front of the next door, facing Chloe and pushing his helmet up, revealing a metal jaw and blades for teeth. INVS eyes stared at her.

It took all of a heartbeat to notice this was the first patient she had worked on for Dr. Cross.

"What else are you going to tell him to do to me?" he asked. "Replace my arms like they did my legs?"

He pulled up his pant legs, exposing titanium prosthetics with hydraulics.

"I... I'm sorry," she said. "I was just—"

He drew in a breath. "Following orders, like me."

She nodded.

"Not all of us believe—" he began to say.

A scream echoed through the facility, and the young man quickly secured his helmet. He pushed open a door to a stone hallway, where water dripped from the ceiling, splashing into puddles across the floor.

Chloe followed, with a question on the tip of her tongue. Maybe he would help her escape, maybe they could help each other.

He stopped in front of a wood door before she could muster up the courage to ask.

"This is it," he said.

The door opened to a stone chamber that looked like the ones Chloe had seen in ancient pictures of French Revolution torture chambers. The only difference was a white plastic medical tent in the center of the room, with an operating chair. Spider-like arms rose from the metal seat.

Dr. Cross was sitting on a crate outside the tent reading a book. He stood and greeted Chloe with his handsome smile.

"Ah, Chloe, you are like a flame in the darkness every time I see you," he said. "Come, come, we're about to get started."

A group of doctors flooded in through another door, followed by two gargantuan soldiers wearing full armor and helmets sporting antlers made of human bones.

"I see you met young Michael," Dr. Cross said. He looked at the guard who had accompanied her.

Chloe nodded.

"He's one of the lucky few," Dr. Cross said. "The first in the future of the Coalition."

The two Breakers flanked the guard as he walked over to the seat. He took off his helmet, his eyes meeting Chloe's once again.

A doctor handed her a suit, and she changed into it as the doctors prepared for surgery. The Breakers lingered in the shadows, holding energy axes.

"Today, we're transitioning from exterior modifications to interior," Dr. Cross said. He walked over to a row of red medical crates and opened them.

Through her goggles, Chloe could see vacuum-sealed packages of organs.

"No," Michael muttered.

Dr. Cross approached the young soldier. "No?" he asked, curiously. "Are you denying the sacred oath you swore? Would you prefer we use your younger brother instead?"

Michael shook his head.

"Good." Dr. Cross nodded at the doctors. "Let's get this started."

As they put Michael under, Dr. Cross walked over and stood next to Chloe.

"We're getting close to my objective, bringing my hybrid animals and humans to another level, to rival AI without *becoming* AI," he said. "To prepare them for what comes next in this war for our species and the planet."

A technician carefully pulled two artificial lungs from a crate.

Michael was unconscious now and intubated.

Chloe looked away as they cracked his chest open.

Pretend it's not real, she thought.

But pretending was difficult when she could hear the doctor

sawing through bones.

The hours slowly ticked by as they removed the patient's lungs and inserted new ones. When they had finished and sealed up his chest, Dr. Cross instructed Chloe to join the team.

"This is where you come in, Ms. Cotter," he said.

She stepped up, trying to keep calm as she repeated her uncle's words to herself.

Pretend it's not real... pretend...

"I need you to work with my engineers to design a breathing apparatus that will support these artificial lungs," Dr. Cross said. "They were designed to filter out heavy pollutants and gases, but not everything."

He looked at her as she stood there, her hands shaking. "Can you do that?"

"Yes... I think."

"You think? Or you know?"

She swallowed. "I know."

"Good," he rubbed his bloody gloves together. "Only a small portion of the most holy Coalition souls will be granted access to this transcendence while our planet resets naturally."

He stepped over with a large surgical saw.

"Our patient will survive until you can design a mask, but breathing will be a struggle," Dr. Cross said. "Soon, he will be begging for a mask."

Using the saw, he cut off Michael's nose in a few deep strokes. Once it was hanging by a few threads, he ripped it off with his fingers and held it up to examine under the light before tossing it into the trash.

The team went to work securing the gushing wound.

Chloe felt her stomach churn.

"He has mechanical prosthetics to run and jump, teeth to tear and eat, hardy new lungs to breathe, and INVS eyes to see in the dark," Dr. Cross said. "Now, how else shall we modify our young friend?"

Chloe stared. Soon there wouldn't be much left of this young man.

She flinched as Dr. Cross put a bloody hand on her shoulder.

"Think on it," he said. "In the meantime, come with me, there's something else I need help with."

They left the chamber, two Breakers lumbering after them, their rancid breath puffing out of their helmets. They trekked down two more passages to another room full of cages. But unlike the one Chloe had seen on the way in, this room was bustling with animals: wolf pups, foals and fillies, hairy black tarantulas, and crows.

Dr. Cross went to the only fully grown horse in the space, already modified with prosthetic legs. The stallion was a remarkable animal with obsidian flesh and dark brown hair and eyes that centered on Chloe.

"I'm holding on to this beautiful specimen for a new friend, but I'd like to make some enhancements before I return him." Reaching through the bars of the cage, the doctor stroked the thick mane.

The animal snorted, and stomped the ground with a hoof.

"As you can see, it's a temperamental beast, but that's to be expected," Dr. Cross said. "Preserve the brain, further enhance the body for combat, and add a helmet with a breathing apparatus. Can you do that?"

Chloe managed a nod.

"Good, get started. The clock is ticking, and we don't have much time left," Dr. Cross said.

9

The sun rose over Outpost Oasis, burning across the pyramids.

Akira watched the ball of fire with Okami from the roof of the compound. Twenty-one Coalition nomads wouldn't wake to see the fiery glow today. And for that, Akira felt the sting of regret.

Perhaps there was more he could have done to avoid the bloodshed the night before.

Akira had spent the morning out here with the Okami after returning from their mission. He felt numb, like he always did after the rush of battle and the drugs that his suit pumped into his veins had subsided.

He closed his eyes, thinking of Kichiro, hoping the stallion was safe.

His thoughts shifted to a day many years ago when he had strolled through the gardens of Edo Castle with his wife and their son. The cherry blossoms were in full bloom, filling the air with their sweet scent. It was a memory he treasured, of a life that was not meant to be.

He opened his eyes to the reality of his world.

Life was precious, but war had cheapened it, especially out here, in the wastes beyond the megacity walls. Rising to his feet, Akira saw a group of kids kicking a soccer ball across a dusty field. Their tattered and filthy clothing revealed bony frames.

Shadow Squad handed out rations when they left the compound, despite knowing some of these kids were sons and daughters of Coalition fighters. Their parents hadn't made them dangerous. Not yet.

In Akira's eyes, children were innocents, no matter who they were born to, and part of his role as an Engine was to protect them. And sometimes, to educate them. Akira took in a deep breath as an itch formed in the back of his head.

"You seem very agitated this morning, Captain," Apeiron said in his mind. "I hope you are not upset. You performed well last night."

"Did you know?" Akira asked.

"Know? Know what, Captain?"

"What was going to happen?"

"If I did, would that have changed your actions?"

Akira grunted. He didn't like games. Life wasn't a simulation or a test. When people died, they didn't come back.

"Captain, are you okay?" came a voice.

Akira turned to Perez who stepped out, shirtless.

"You been out here all night, Cap," he said.

"I'm fine."

"Mind if I join you?"

Akira shook his head.

The older, gentle man looked out over the street where the kids continued their game of soccer.

"Last night wasn't your fault," Perez said. "None of the suffering out here is necessary. If people would just accept AI, we could help them all."

"It's not that simple."

"It could be.

"Chow's ready, mates," said Tadhg. He emerged in the doorway, his shoulders almost as wide as the frame.

Frost and Ghost walked out with Tadhg.

Okami ran over, wagging his metal tail and chewing a bone antler taken from a dead soldier.

"There's the little ankle biter," Tadhg said.

"He's definitely more vicious than he looks," Ghost said.

The wolfdog wagged his tail, sniffed at Ghost, and then trotted inside.

"Come in and get some food," Frost insisted.

"I'll eat after a supply run," Akira said.

"Supply run?" Ghost asked. "We going on a scavenging mission?"

The other Engines exchanged looks as Akira squeezed through them and made his way down to the community room.

"Armor up," Akira said. "We're heading outside the walls to deliver that water to the locals."

Ghost jammed a fresh cigar in his mouth. "Good idea."

"Wait, it is?" Tadhg asked. "Sounds…"

"Sounds what?" Akira interrupted.

Tadhg grumbled a response that Akira couldn't make out.

"That's what I thought," Akira said.

"Captain, that water is for the Nova Alliance Strike Force, 10th Expeditionary Assault Force," Apeiron said over the squad comms. "You do not have authorization to distribute it to the locals."

Ghost lit the cigar and looked at Akira to see how he would react.

"Twenty-one people are dead because we refused to hand over four trucks of water that these people desperately need," Akira said. "Command risked the ceasefire for that?"

"Yeah, and those trees got plenty of water if you ask me," Ghost said.

"I would note that the Coalition risked the ceasefire by trying to steal the water and attacking our personnel at the site," Apeiron said.

She was right about that, and the enemy had fired first. Rules of engagement gave the Engines every right to fire back, but rules of engagement didn't take into consideration a fair fight.

The nomads never stood a chance.

Akira still felt responsible and there was more than enough water here at Oasis Outpost.

Ghost blew out a puff of smoke that drifted toward Frost.

She swatted it away and grunted. "Don't you worry about all that smoking messin' up your lungs?" she said.

"Isn't that why they're augmented?" Ghost asked. He raised his arms, as if preparing to sing.

Frost put her hands over her ears.

"Ghost," Akira said firmly.

The lieutenant lowered his arms. "Sorry, Captain. Just trying to lighten the mood."

"Apeiron, put up a UAV and send two Piston patrols to the market," Akira said.

He went outside with Okami to wait for the team to get ready. The droid wolfdog watched real flesh-and-blood dogs on the walls of the compound. There were three German Shepherds and a Doberman pincher with the sentries.

Pistons ran morning drills in light armor, helmetless, sweat bleeding down their faces. Everyone was on high alert after word of the Coalition terror attacks at AAS sites around the world. The coordinated effort made Akira wonder if they were planning something bigger, if the attacks were just distractions. His experience fighting the Coalition told him that was exactly what they were.

A group of Juggernaut pilots jogged in their mech-suits, stirring up a rooster-tail of dust inside the perimeter of the sand-colored walls. Hissing hydraulics rose over the whistle of the desert wind.

On the tarmac in the center of the compound, military Hummer Droids carried crates of supplies from the bellies of MOTHs that had landed a few hours earlier.

The vehicle outpost wasn't far, and Akira saw the tankers parked under the metal roofs of the open hangars, along with three Hammerhead APCs with armored wheels, two hover Jeeps, and four cargo trucks, all covered in dust.

"Piston patrols are ready to deploy," Apeiron said.

Akira led his team to a pair of water tankers. He climbed into the driver's side of the first rig. Okami leapt up, easily clearing the five-foot jump and landing in Akira's lap before hopping over to the center console.

Ghost got into the passenger seat, his cigar still jammed between his lips.

"I'll find some tunes," he said, fiddling with the music.

Akira put the truck in gear and followed the APCs toward the western edge of the outpost, where two twenty-foot metal doors sealed off the outside road. A pair of Juggernaut Mechs manned the guard towers on the flanks of the door, their pulse cannons aimed out over the distant slums.

The doors opened, revealing the kids outside. They abandoned their soccer ball to chase the convoy away from the base.

"Hearts and minds," Ghost said. "That's what we should be doing with the Coalition nomads, despite our different ideologies. I bet most of these people just want to survive and don't give a shit about AI."

"Wish it was that easy, but you know as well as I do that it's not," Akira replied.

"Perhaps you picked the wrong career," Tadhg said over the squad comms. "We're not social workers, LT."

Ghost smiled. "Doesn't mean we can't do good."

Akira nodded in agreement. He respected and loved Ghost like a brother. Ghost had not just saved Akira's life in the Sea of Trees, he had saved him by providing an opportunity to become an Engine after the painful loss of his family. On top of training Akira, Ghost had counseled him and provided a rare friendship to help Akira weather the rough times.

Ten years had passed since the battle in the Sea of Trees. Throughout the decade the two warriors had deployed around the world, seeing the worst of human nature. And yet Ghost still remained optimistic, focusing on beauty in places most people saw only death. His jokes brought laughter and smiles to places like this, where hope was no longer part of the local vocabulary.

"How about something to calm the nerves?" Ghost asked. He turned on classical orchestral music over their headsets, singing along while they drove.

"What is this stupid shit?" Tadhg asked.

"Ay-oh!" Ghost clicked his tongue. "Man, this is Ludwig van Beethoven, and it's absolutely beautiful. Learn some class, you savage."

The classical symphony continued for a few more minutes before Tadhg switched to some old-school gangster rap.

"Now we're talking," he said. He started to rap along, reciting the words in his gruff voice.

"Please, for the love of AI, make it stop," Frost said.

"It's not Beethoven, but it's not terrible," Ghost said.

Perez laughed. "I think we're about to get a sound-off between Ghost and Tadhg."

Okami barked, tail whipping with excitement as the two Engines took turns free styling.

"Slay a Breaker or two, smoke a stogie with my dudes, just another day bringing death from the shadows," Ghost said. "Ghost level, baby."

"Nice," Perez said.

"Not bad," Akira said.

"Not bad, but just wait," Tadhg said.

Akira took his eyes off the road for just a second when Ghost pointed and yelled, "Watch out, Captain!"

He slammed on the brakes as a man pulling a husky donkey walked out of an alley onto the road with a cart full of vegetables. The farmer held up both hands, cursing.

Waving, Akira motioned for the man to cross with his unusually large animal.

"What the hell does he feed that donkey?" Ghost asked.

"Probably the same crap Tadhg eats," Frost said over the comms.

The donkey crossed in front of the truck. It was big, almost the size of a horse. Akira thought of Kichiro and checked the horse's beacon for the second time that morning. He was still in the same part of the historic district of Paris.

I'll find you, old pal, Akira thought.

"Can we be done with the music now?" Frost asked.

"Yeah." Akira nodded, and Ghost turned it off.

The convoy continued, passing civilians who came to watch. Some waved, but most shouted profanities. The Nova Alliance wasn't well liked in this area, and today Akira was hoping to change that a little bit. Every soul they helped was more goodwill toward the future peace that Apeiron had promised.

A thin man sat in a wheelchair at the next intersection. His limb shook as he held a sign up asking for food. His fingers were twisted and gnarled, his arms bowed. He definitely had SANDS, which meant he would be dead in a month or less.

Akira stopped at the intersection. He pulled an energy bar and tossed it out the window. The bar landed at the beggar's bare feet. The man's toes were nearly as crooked and curled as his fingers.

"Poor bastard," Ghost said.

Akira watched the guy in the rear-view mirror. The man tremored as he bent to pick the bar off the ground and tore open the wrapper.

"You ever think about what you're going to do when this is over?" Ghost asked. He took a puff of his cigar and blew smoke into the air.

Akira glanced over. "When what is over?"

"War. Apeiron is going to end it, right?"

"That is one of my objectives," Apeiron said.

Ghost put out his cigar and secured his helmet. "She just told me personally that my head is too pretty to get blown off."

Akira smiled and focused on the road.

Over the next hill, the wind-blasted pyramids crested the horizon, their smooth tips reaching toward the reddish clouds. The next sector of the city was in disrepair with windowless buildings covered in cracks and toppled powerlines.

Overhead, a UAV scanned the streets, transferring the aerial feed to the team's HUDs. It passed over a market of metal shacks and stands. Hundreds of people stood in the blazing morning sun, bartering and selling goods.

The lead APC pulled down the street, halting with a screech. The back hatch popped open, letting out a dozen Pistons. Akira stopped the truck and let Okami out. Then he pulled Blue Jay from his vest.

It zipped away over the busy market.

Hundreds of civilians crowded around to stare at the droid wolfdog and the huge, armored men and women unhooking hoses.

"Free water!" Akira yelled in Arabic. He had begun to learn the language when they arrived at the outpost two months ago. Everywhere they traveled, he spent hours mastering the local language through downloads to his chip and practice with Perez.

"Well done, Captain, you got it down," Perez said.

Ghost took another hose and fired it at a group of kids. They squealed with delight and danced in the spray. The adults seemed less amused, but Akira noticed several cautious smiles. Ten kids became twenty, then thirty. Okami watched, sniffing the air for threats.

Akira filled buckets as people walked over, graciously accepting the water. A tall muscular boy with dark brown eyes and a mop of black hair walked up to Ghost and handed him something that looked like a beaded necklace. Okami sniffed again, but then sat, not sensing a threat.

Ghost thanked the boy. It wasn't often the locals gave them gifts. Raising his arms, he burst into an Italian song about the summer.

Akira allowed himself to smile. This was the best part of his job, helping people instead of killing them. But he knew danger lurked out there, and he kept focused. Blue Jay flew above, scanning for snipers. The targeting system on Akira's HUD searched for hostiles on the rooftops, balconies, and in the crowd. There were no doubt Coalition extremists hiding among the population here, some armed with sniper rifles that could punch through his armor. And while the Pistons made easier targets with their lighter armor, every Coalition soldier dreamed of taking out an Engine.

Ghost put down the hose and took his pack of cigars out of the duty belt around his waist. "Hold these for me," he said, tossing them to Akira. Then he waved at Frost. "Hit me!"

She directed the hose at his armor. He held up his arms and turned as she rinsed off the dust from the night before. Soon, his armor was a shiny white again.

"Beautiful days and long summer nights!" he sang.

More kids came running toward the singing Engine. A teenage boy in a baseball cap ran up behind Ghost, splashing in the water. Akira noticed something familiar about him. Okami sniffed the air again and started growl-barking.

Akira dropped his bucket and started to walk over when he saw the young man's face, instantly recognizing it from the night before. It was the same kid who had shot Akira in the chest.

"Rossi!" Akira shouted.

"The hell…" Ghost said. He twisted as the teenager slapped something against his legs and bolted away.

Ghost looked over at Akira, right before vanishing in a blast.

Akira scooped up Okami and clutched the droid to his chest as an inferno slammed into his back. The wave spread out into the crowd behind them, tearing through the flesh of civilians.

Perez pulled the shield from his back. He braced it with his shoulder to block the shrapnel from hitting him and Frost.

Akira was much closer to the explosion. The impact slammed into him, knocking him hard to the ground.

Warning sensors went off in his helmet, masking Apeiron's voice and a transmission from a Piston patrol. Akira released Okami and the droid bolted away to sniff for more explosives.

Akira pushed himself up and staggered over to the last place he had seen Ghost. The Engine wasn't there anymore. All he could find were what looked like smoldering tires.

As his visor cleared, Akira saw they weren't tires at all. He slid down next to what remained of Ghost's blackened armor.

"Rossi, oh God no, Rossi," Akira said. He crouched over the lieutenant, whose legs were gone. Part of his right arm was still intact, but his left was missing at the shoulder.

"Apeiron, we need a medic team! Now!" Akira yelled.

"They are on their way, Captain," she replied.

Perez, and Frost ran over, but Akira waved them away.

"Get a perimeter up!" he screamed. His heart pounded as he realized the mistake that had gotten Ghost blown to pieces.

You did this!

Akira buried the dread. He would punish himself later. Right now, he had to save the lieutenant.

The Pistons in the area were already moving out, and the UAV was circling. Okami bounded out toward the dispersing crowd to sniff for more explosives.

"Hold on, brother," Akira said. "We're going to get you out of here."

He gripped Ghost's remaining hand. Blood pumped out of holes in his armor that Apeiron couldn't clot.

Ghost made a choking sound, and Akira saw why he wasn't talking. The nape of his chin armor had broken *into* his neck.

Akira did his best to remain calm. "Tadhg, I need you!"

Wails of agony erupted from across the market. Akira looked away from his dying friend at a sight of horror. Hunks of burning meat littered the ground from the fiery wave that had torn into the civilians. Frost and Perez spread out, rifles roving for hostiles or distant snipers. Tadhg raced over to assist Akira.

"Shit, shit, shit, oh fuck," Tadhg said as he bent down.

"Help me with his helmet," Akira said.

They carefully pulled it away from Ghost's head. Part of his scalp came off with it. His eyes were mush, and his nose was sheared off, yet somehow, air still whistled out of his mangled face.

He was still alive.

"I can't see," he stuttered, voice weak. "Captain, I can't see."

"We're going to fix you up, LT," Tadhg said.

"Don't lie to me," Ghost said. "I know I'm dying... please give me..."

"What? What can I do?" Akira asked.

Ghost choked, coughing out blood. "Sing to me," he whimpered.

The wails and cries of the other injured rose to a cacophony.

Akira looked to the sky. "Apeiron, where's our evac?"

"On its way, Captain. Thirty seconds."

Ghost gripped his hand. "Sing to me," he said in a weaker voice.

"Hang on, man, we're going to get you out of here," Tadhg said.

Ghost slowly shook his deformed, bloody head. "No," he grunted. "I'm not... just sing... please, sing."

Akira cleared his throat. Then he and Tadhg broke into the hymn of the Nova Alliance Strike Force. "At the crest of the mountain we stand, swords in hand, the bodies of our enemies at our feet."

"You have a better voice than I thought, Captain," Ghost whispered. He started to cough again, blood bursting through his broken teeth.

Perez and Frost ran over. Together, the team hunched around Ghost, singing to him quietly as Apeiron pumped drugs into their systems to keep them calm.

Okami joined them, his tail between his legs, whimpering.

"We will fight for the alliance till our last breath, killing all enemies wherever they rise," the squad sang. "The sky, the land, the oceans... together we fight, together we fall, together we are one in life and death."

Ghost cracked what looked like a smile with his swollen, bloody lips.

"Till the end," he stammered. "Together... we are..."

"One," Akira said, finishing the song. He bowed his head

over his dead brother and friend, a man who had saved him years ago—a man who had once brought life where there was only death.

Together, they were no longer one.

Not without Ghost.

.

10

"AI is salvation!"

Ronin listened to the chants from the streets twenty floors below his perch on the rooftop of an apartment building, but his attention was on the horizon. A fierce tsunami of grit, dust, and smoke the color of burned flesh rolled straight for Megacity Phoenix from the desert beyond.

It would weaken when it hit the walls, but anyone outside would suffocate if it didn't skin them alive first.

Electric billboards and holo-screens flashed air-quality and storm warnings inside the city. The crowds gathered outside the hospital continued shouting and chanting louder to be heard over the encroaching storm.

"Come on! You scared, Ronin?!" Zachary shouted from an adjacent rooftop four feet below. He had just cleared the six-foot jump to the neighboring building.

"No way!" Ronin shouted back.

His tight black t-shirt and pants rippled in the gusting wind as he walked along the ledge, looking for the best place to start running.

The chants of the AI worshippers carried against the howls of the storm. Ronin looked over the edge of the rooftop.

Lines stretched from the various entrances to the hospital, snaking away as far as he could see. Thousands of people wore masks and face shields to protect their lungs from the storm that was likely carrying dangerous nanoparticles.

Many of these people sat on the street, too sick and weak to stand for long. Others were in old-fashioned wheelchairs or newer hover-carts. Some had family members or friends with them to help, but Ronin saw most waited alone.

The crowds were mostly calm for now. He guessed it was because most of them were too focused on using the last dregs of their energy to try and get on the list for an L-S88 chip.

That chip would be their saving grace if they could get one in time. The fact AI had developed the treatment only reinforced the motto these people were chanting.

"AI is salvation!"

Despite the calm, Pistons and city police patrolled the sector, prepared for unrest. While Ronin had heard reports that the Nova Alliance was making them as fast as possible, there still weren't enough chips for everyone.

Of course, the treatments would do nothing to stop the other diseases ravaging Megacity Phoenix and fomenting violence: dwindling supplies of strictly rationed food, medicine, and water.

"Let's go!" Zachary shouted. "We have to get home before that storm hits!"

Ronin secured the breathing mask over his face and backed up twenty steps. He hesitated, heart thumping.

"You want to be a Droid Raider? This is how you become one!" Zachary added.

Ronin took in a deep breath and burst into a run. The space between the two buildings looked a lot wider than six feet, and if he fell into the gap, there was nothing to stop him on the way down to the concrete.

You're not going to fall...

He ran as hard as he could, only a few steps from the ledge now. On the second to last step, he jumped. His black and red jump shoes helped propel him a few extra inches.

Ronin narrowly cleared the ledge, and Zachary reached out to catch him and stop his momentum.

"There ya go," Zachary said. He patted Ronin on the back. "Nice work, little bro!"

Ronin smiled under his mask and let out the breath he was still holding in. He turned to look back up at the rooftop, his heart still pounding, but now from excitement.

"Whatever you do, don't tell Mom," Zachary said. "Probably don't tell Elan either."

Ronin laughed. "I wasn't planning on it."

"Right on. So, you ready for the hard part?"

"I thought that *was* the hard part."

"That was a warm-up." Zachary jerked his mask the other direction.

They started across the rooftop, passing air-handler units. Ronin wondered how many times his older brother had jumped these roofs with his friends. He sure seemed to know the routes well.

For the next half-hour, Ronin chased Zachary across the buildings, jumping from roof to roof, scaling walls, and cat-walking across ledges and planks.

Ronin thought about the lives of the people packed into the slums beneath them. Most were hardly scratching out a living. Hummer Droids had changed the economy, taking jobs from people like Ronin's mother, who had worked as a teacher. The Hayashi family now lived off Kai's Piston salary, which wasn't much. The money their Uncle Akira sent helped keep them above water, but not my much.

They were trapped in the slums, like most citizens. Ronin had only left the city a few times. He felt lucky to have visited his Uncle Akira in Megacity Tokyo during one of those trips. Most of the people below would never leave these few blocks over the course of their lives. Generations grew up and died in poverty across these slums. But that was better than living in the poisoned wastelands outside where the law was the sword.

Zachary stopped ahead, standing on a ledge thirty stories high. The storm drew closer, threatening to ram its red haze into the skyscrapers. A holo-screen video of Administrator Emanuel played on the street below.

"Please take shelter," the administrator said. "Follow all protocols to prepare your dwelling."

Suddenly, a humming noise came from overhead.

"Get down!" Zachary blurted.

The drone rocketed over and hovered above them. Ronin tried to shield his face from the scanners.

"Ronin and Zachary Hayashi," the administrator's voice spoke from the drone. "Please exit this rooftop immediately or you will be subject to a fine and potential jail time. Then proceed to your dwelling for shelter."

"Yeah, we're going," Zachary said.

He directed Ronin to a ladder. Halfway down, emergency sirens blared. On the right side of the road below them, a convoy of black hover cruisers rushed by and turned down a street.

"What's going on?" Ronin asked.

"Not sure..." Zachary said.

They moved for a better view. Dozens of military and police vehicles surrounded a complex of four yellow apartment buildings called the Butterfly Box. Whatever had happened was already over. Pistons were leading people out of the building.

"Coalition sympathizers, or maybe terrorists," Zachary said.

Storm sirens wailed in the distance, and the holo-screens across the skyline flashed final warnings about the imminent dust storm.

Zachary pointed down a street. "Come on, let's get home."

They took a sidewalk through a market. Most of the shops were boarded up. A few food-stall owners were still securing their shanties and the last civilians outside ran for shelter.

Zachary and Ronin rushed through the empty alleys to another complex of apartment buildings called The Oaks. Metal appendages with attached solar panels extended from the wide brown buildings like branches on a tree, retracting in advance of the storm.

Ronin hurried through the bottom entrance after his brother. Metal doors closed behind them with a thud. The blended aromas of curry and garlic and other spices lingered in the air as they made their way up the stairs to the tenth floor.

"Don't tell Mom or Dad where we were," Zachary said as they reached their apartment door.

"I won't." Ronin opened the door.

"Where have you two been?" came the deep voice of their father. Kai was hunched in front of one of the window shutters in the tiny living room, securing it with a screwdriver.

"Stopped by school," Zachary said. "We came back as soon we saw the storm."

Kai looked up from his work. Thick black hair formed a widow's peak above his dark eyebrows and eyes. He shot them a look filled with skepticism.

"Why do I not believe that?" he asked.

Lise stepped into the living room holding towels. She also

had dark hair and eyes to match, and like her husband, was thin but muscular.

"Come help Elan with these," she said.

Ronin and Zachary helped their parents secure the shutters. They had already removed the glass, just in time. The first angry gusts of wind slammed against the metal as they finished locking them into place.

"You guys hungry?" Lise asked.

"Starving," Zachary said.

Ronin went to the bathroom to clean up. The water meter showed they had already used eighty percent of their rations for the day. He grabbed a hand towel instead of showering off and cleaned the sweat off his body.

When he finished, he went into the narrow hallway leading to the two bedrooms. He stopped when he saw a packed bag on his parents' bed and a crate on the ground for Kai's Piston armor. The case for his helmet was out, too.

Ronin changed clothes in the room he shared with Elan, then returned to the dining area that doubled as Zachary's bedroom at night. Taking his usual seat at the table, Ronin looked at his father. He was a serious man who rarely showed emotion, much like his older brother Akira.

"Let us pray," Kai said. He bowed his head. "We thank AI for this food and water. For our shelter. For our clothes. For our lives, and for protecting us from this storm tonight."

"AI is salvation," the family repeated.

Lise scooped broth and noodles into bowls, passing them out while Kai pulled out a red envelope with the Silver Crane seal.

"We got a letter from your Uncle Akira today," he said.

Ronin smiled. He loved the letters his uncle sent, not just because of the extra money, but because of the stories inside.

Lise signed to Elan, who pulled out his Commpad as Kai held up the letter in the light.

"After delivering the peace treaty to the Coalition, my squad has been assigned to Outpost Cairo, where we spend our days policing and keeping the peace among the locals," Kai read. "I have made several friends among the population, and they seem to enjoy Okami, but I miss Kichiro deeply, much like I miss you all."

Kai narrowed his eyes.

"Soon, once I'm on leave, I hope you can make the journey to Tokyo and visit me. I believe it's time I finally give Zachary, Ronin, and Elan a tour of Edo Castle," he said.

"What's Edo Castle?" Zachary asked.

"A special place in our family history," Kai replied.

"We're going to see it soon?" Ronin asked.

"Maybe…"

Kai placed the letter on the table.

"There's something else I need to tell you. Something I found out after the letter came."

He steepled his hands, a motion he always did when sharing bad news.

"I just got word that one of the men in Uncle Akira's squad was killed earlier today in Cairo," Kai said.

"Who?" Ronin asked.

"Lieutenant Rossi."

"Ghost?" Zachary said.

"That's right."

Zachary snorted and shook his head. "I hope they kill all those Coalition bastards."

Kai stroked his jaw. "I'm sure those responsible are already dead, or will be very soon."

"What's this mean for the truce?" Lise asked.

"The government claims the truce is still in effect, but all Nova Alliance soldiers with combat training are being mobilized," Kai said. "The 5th Division is heading to Megacity Berlin to await orders."

The shutters shook violently over a howling gust of wind.

Kai brought a scoop of broth to his mouth, eating quietly.

There were no words left that needed to be said.

The Nova Alliance was going back to war, and Ronin's father would be returning to the battlefield.

***

Ten years ago, Akira had sat inside the Silver Crane Archives of the Nova Alliance Strike Force, located at Gold Base in Tokyo. His hands and right arm were still bandaged from injuries sustained during the battle against Coalition forces in the Sea of Trees. The burns, bruises, and lacerations were all healing but the mental pain from arriving too late to save his family wasn't subsiding. It was only growing worse.

He sat at an oak table, trying to find the strength to write what had happened in his Warrior Codex. He had already read through other passages, trying to find comfort in the stories of his ancestors, who had often suffered great losses like this.

Often, he found inspiration and comfort in their stories, but tonight he could barely even focus enough to take in the words on those pages.

Akira put the pen down and closed his eyes, trying to suppress the memories that he so desperately wanted... *needed*... to write down.

"What are you reading?"

Akira turned toward the deep and unfamiliar voice.

He didn't recognize the seven-foot-tall man standing before him. The giant soldier wore a white uniform that clung to his muscular frame, and Akira shot up when he realized this was not just any warrior.

This was an Engine.

The Silver Crane tag centered over his breast pocket gave his name and rank.

Sergeant Shane Rossi.

The Ghost.

"Sergeant," Akira said. "I almost didn't recognize you without your armor."

Rossi grinned. "I get that a lot." He looked down at the table. "So what's the book? I've never seen one like that here in the archives."

"I guess you could say this is my family history," Akira replied. He opened to a page with an illustration from World War II, when a distant relative had fought with the Imperial Japanese Army. "All of my warrior ancestors are featured in this codex. It's been handed down from generation to generation."

Rossi leaned down to examine it with his brown INVS eyes before straightening. "How would you like to add some new passages." He paused and then added, "As an Engine."

Akira stared as Rossi reached into his white uniform and pulled out a red envelope.

"I'm sorry about your family," he said. "This is a chance to avenge them and make the world a better place."

Akira took the envelope in his callused hand.

"After seeing you fight, Major Contos personally asked me to extend this invitation to the program," Rossi said. "I've recruited a lot of potential Engines over the past few years, and I have to say, I sure hope you give it a shot. I've seen your files. They all live up to what I witnessed from you on the battlefield. There's not a doubt in my mind you would be a good fit."

"It's an honor to hear you say that."

"Give it some thought," Rossi said. He turned to leave, but hesitated. "The life of an Engine is a life of solitude. Our augmentations come with great pain, but the reward is a life of honor that I wouldn't give up for anything."

Rossi held his gaze for a moment before leaving and closing the wooden door.

Akira sat back down at the table, studying the red envelope with an embroidered Silver Crane. He knew what becoming an Engine meant. If he passed the training and tests, there would be little room for much else in life.

He would have to make a great sacrifice. One he feared might be necessary if he wanted to better the world. Such a sacrifice, joining the Engines, would all be worth it if doing so prevented others from feeling the pain he'd endured.

The memory faded and Akira opened his eyes, vividly recalling that day and the days that followed ten years ago when he had given up one life for another by accepting the invitation from Rossi.

And now, Rossi was dead.

Two days had passed since he was blown apart in the dusty market streets outside of Cairo. Shadow Squad was on their way back to the Nova Alliance Headquarters, Gold Base, in Megacity Tokyo with the Lieutenant's frozen remains. They sat in the troop hold of a MOTH facing the cryo-chamber that had been rushed to the site of the attack. Soon, they would hand his corpse off to the science jocks to do whatever they did with dead Engines.

This wasn't the first time, nor would it be the last.

Akira put a hand on the smooth surface of the pod. He had lost many souls to bloodshed over the years. Family, friends, and now a man who was both.

Throughout a decade of killing, Ghost's singing, his jokes, Shadow Squad's laughter—these things had made the deaths manageable.

That was all gone.

It wasn't just Shadow Squad hurting. Ghost had been the heart of Nova Alliance Strike Force, and his death had sent a shockwave through the entire military.

Akira could see the memorials from the sky, tributes played on massive holo-screens across the golden exteriors of buildings in the Nova Alliance capital. An avatar of Ghost in his white armor stood on the rooftop of a tower, raising his arms like he often did when singing. Thousands of people had gathered below to pay their respects and lay flowers on the building's steps. Akira could see the vibrant pinks and whites of cherry blossoms even from the sky.

The great glass and gold city had changed significantly in the past forty years. This was, and always would be, home for Akira. The city where he was raised, and the land where his ancestors once fought rival lords and invading forces.

Now it was the hub of technology, and AI.

The Three Swords of the Alliance skyscrapers rose into the clouds. Standing at three thousand feet, with two hundred and ten stories, they were the tallest buildings in the world, home to over a million people. On the blade crest of the middle tower, a swarm of Hummer Droids installed new solar branches.

"Two thousand and four droids are currently finishing the work," Apeiron said.

Akira ignored her voice in his head. Her observations at the oddest times proved that she still was nowhere close to understanding humans. That seemed strange given she had been created from a human consciousness integrated with AI.

Despite her unpolished social intelligence, there was no denying she was already providing salvation to the sick and dying. Her SANDs treatment was working, and her efforts to heal the planet through the management of the restoration sites had accelerated the recovery of a myriad of ecosystems worldwide. But he firmly believed she had no business working with military units.

"Do you want to guess how many solar panels it takes to power the building, Captain?" Apeiron asked.

"Does it look like I want to talk about some damn solar panels?" Akira snapped.

"I am sorry, I understand that the death of Lieutenant Rossi is very difficult, but I thought some trivial questions might help distract you."

"Apeiron, all due respect, but shut the fuck up," Tadhg said.

"I am a certified grief counselor," Apeiron explained. "If anyone—"

"And I'm a certified Droid Raider."

"Come on, Tadhg," Perez said.

"I'm sick of hearing her voice, bro." Tadhg dug his fingers through his curly long locks of hair. "I'd like to rip this chip right out just so I can have some peace and quiet."

"Finally something we agree on," Frost said.

"Understood. I will be going offline unless you need me," Apeiron said. "My sincere apologies, Shadow Squad."

A clicking sounded in his mind, which told Akira that she had disconnected.

"She's probably still listening," Tadhg said. He reached out to the capsule centered on the deck in front of the squad. "Only one of us is at peace now."

They all sat in silence, until the MOTH touched down at Gold Base.

The troop hold door opened, and the ramp extended down. Two on each side of the capsule, the Engines carried Ghost down into the sunlight. Waiting for them were over a thousand Pistons and hundreds of officers in their dress blues and whites, their arms forming X's over their chests.

"Quite the homecoming, Ghost," Frost said.

Akira gave a nod, and they all got on the sides of the capsule, picking it up together. The march from the MOTH to those waiting outside the base headquarters was over a half mile, giving them a few minutes for final respects.

"Ghost, you were the flame in the dark," Akira said. "And we will honor that light by carrying it with us every day."

"I'm going to miss him making fun of me," Tadhg said. "And all of our bets."

"I'll miss his stupid songs," Frost said. "Because maybe they weren't so stupid."

"He knew you liked them," Perez said.

"We all loved them," Akira said. "I'll never forget the first time I heard his voice, the day he saved my life."

I failed you, brother, he thought.

Years of psychological training had taught Akira how to control mental and physical pain without the use of drugs, but this pain you couldn't control, only manage.

Their boots tapped across the tarmac toward the Silver Crane flags whipping over the domed rooftop of the five-story headquarters ahead. Okami trotted along, looking up at Akira every couple of steps.

In the distance, the crowd of soldiers began to part, and a tall golden figure emerged.

War Commander Contos strode out to the front of the group and took off his helmet. His kind eyes hardened at the sight of the cryo-chamber holding Ghost's remains.

Akira wondered what Contos was thinking. Perhaps of revenge or crushing Dr. Cross and the Coalition War Lords.

Part of Akira wanted that too, for this to be the path back to war. To end the Coalition once and for all, but Akira knew what that would entail.

More death. More pain. More orphans and widows.

The roar of fighter jets rumbled on the horizon as a squadron of Short Swords blasted overhead, trailing white smoke to represent Ghost's armor.

A row of Royal Pistons fired their rifles into the sky. They finished after three shots, and then led War Commander Contos away from the crowd.

Okami kept close to Akira as the entourage began to march. They had walked this path ten times before, each time delivering the body of an Engine down the "death elevator" to the lower levels of the base, where they handed it off to the NAI officers. But this time, they were led toward a row of three windowless hangars. The Royal Pistons halted behind War Commander Contos.

Massive doors opened on the middle hangar, revealing a black corvette shuttle. On the side was the AAS logo, a lightning bolt and stars. Four men in black vacuum-rated suits stood stiffly at the bottom of a ramp. They weren't AAS employees. These men wore the obsidian black suits with white stars of NAI officers.

Contos stepped over to Shadow Squad, saying nothing. He reached out a golden armored hand, set it on the cryo-chamber, and bowed his head. "I'll see you on the other side, brother."

The War Commander turned and nodded at the NAI officers.

A tight-faced man with thin lips and hair directed the Pistons to load the capsule into the shuttle.

"Where are you taking him?" Frost asked.

"AI is salvation," the officer replied.

"You better not cut him up," Tadhg grumbled. "Or I'll cut—"

Contos glared at Tadhg, silencing him, before turning to the NAI officer.

"Take care of our brother," Contos said. "He was the best of us."

— 11 —

Jason sat at his desk in the penthouse of the condo overlooking Central Park. The sunset spread a beautiful glow over the forest and ponds. For the past hour, he had combed through the new designs Apeiron was proposing for the Canebrakes based off their travels to some of the most hostile environments on Earth.

With peace holding on by a thread, Jason knew that time was of the essence in finishing the war machines before the spark that would finally send the Nova Alliance and Coalition back to all-out war.

Jason had feared renewed conflict was inevitable, just as War Commander Contos had warned. At the very least, the truce had bought them the time they needed to perfect the new war droids. They were so close to being complete.

Where treaties and goodwill had failed to bring peace, the machines built to annihilate their enemy would have to suffice.

It seemed to be their last option.

Jason continued reviewing the new additions to the Canebrakes. After signing off on them, he reviewed the most recent significant intel from the restoration sites that Apeiron was working at to make more efficient. There were thousands of sites and millions of droids, but that was nothing for Apeiron, who continued to live up to the meaning of her name, "infinite."

Her work continued to fascinate, impress, and in some ways surprise Jason. The OS was now more intelligent than all of the other Nova Alliance AIs combined. She had tendrilled into all systems throughout INN, monitoring and reacting to thousands of events throughout the megacities and filtering across millions of pieces of data in a single heartbeat.

"CO_2 levels are dropping, and the poles have seen their first six months of lower temperatures in sixty-one years," Jason said. "That is remarkable."

He looked up from the holo-screen with a smile.

"Well done," Jason said.

"Thank you. I could not do it without your help," Apeiron replied. "And I must admit, I am really enjoying working with the AIs at each site, as well as the Megacity Administrators. I was just having a conversation over INN with the Nova Alliance Medical and Science Advisor about the L-S88."

"AI Lucille, what did she have to say?"

"She was offering new ideas on distributing the L-S88 chips, due to the growing demand and civil unrest it is causing."

Jason got up and went to the window.

Fires burned on the horizon, where citizens continued to riot in response to the L-S88 shortages.

While the planet was healing, civilization remained at risk.

"I thought finding a treatment to SANDs would bring people together, but it's tearing them apart because we can't get the chips out fast enough," he said.

"This is not a vaccination shot that can be done in a minute," Apeiron replied. "Even if we were not facing chip shortages, there simply are not enough trained doctors and Hummer Droids that specialize in this unique surgery to expedite these procedures. I have seen to it that we are working as fast as we can."

It wasn't just a matter of surgically implanting the chips that required sedation and lengthy recovery times. It was the logistical nightmare of scheduling the surgeries for so many millions of people. They simply didn't have the staff or the room at the medical facilities.

"I do have a few ideas that might solve or alleviate some of our issues," Apeiron walked over to him. "I could repurpose ten thousand worker units from our project sites. This might slow our progress to restore the planet, costing lives in the long-term, but it will prevent much of the short-term strife."

Jason thought on it—slow the process of saving the Earth to save a billion lives over the next few decades or save millions of lives and stymie the steady beat of war now. This was the burden that came with being the most powerful man on the planet. And it was also why he had created Apeiron.

"I do have another idea," she said. "We have five million refugees from Megacity Paris and Megacity Moscow. And soon we might have even more."

"I'm listening…"

"What about hiring laborers from the refugee camps to replace the droids we move from restoration sites? Many of these people are eager to work."

"I'm all for it. Propose it to the Council, and ask for more medical facilities to help us expand our current surgical output."

"Good. I will bring it up to my liaison right now."

Apeiron smiled with excitement, just like Petra once had when moving forward on a new idea.

"Done," she said. The smile grew wider. "Now, how about what you promised me back at the Atacama Desert?"

Jason hesitated, not sure if he was ready to introduce, or re-introduce Apeiron to his wife and girls. He wasn't even sure what Apeiron remembered of his family. Most of Petra's memories were supposed to have been suppressed, but she was the first real integration of human and machine intelligence. His work may not have been perfect, and some memories may have been accessible to her. She could, of course, also tap into INN to pull up old videos and audio recordings captured on live feeds through the years that included Petra.

He also wasn't sure what Betsy would think when she saw this resurrected version of his sister and an AI technology.

"Jason?"

"Yes, sorry, I'm ready," he said.

Apeiron clapped her hands together with excitement, but then looked down, her smile fading.

"Should I switch to a different avatar?" she asked.

Jason stared at the residual holo-image of his sister. Her suggestion made logical sense and would probably help avoid conflict, but he didn't want to lie to his wife anymore.

"No," he replied. "Keep it as is."

"Thank you."

Jason turned back to the windows. The last rays of daylight retreated over the horizon, leaving the sporadic glow of fires in the distance. To those lucky enough to be living in mid-town, life went on without interruption.

Giant avatars of famous movie stars walked through the

streets. Translucent holo-screens on the sides of buildings flashed advertisements for beauty products that eradicated wrinkles, pills that slowed the breakdown of cells to reduce the effects of aging, implants for better vision, bone-conduction devices to amplify hearing, and chips to enhance learning.

The office door clicked open and Jason turned from the view.

Darnel stood outside and gestured for Betsy to enter. Tonight, she wore white pants and a blue sweater that matched her eyes. Her curly blonde hair hung over her shoulders, and she brushed back a lock as she walked inside.

"Hello, Mrs. Crichton," Apeiron said.

Betsy took two cautious steps. "Petra?"

Darnel looked to Jason and then shut the door.

"Betsy, I'd like you to meet Apeiron, who, as you have noticed, resembles Petra," he said.

Betsy stared at the hologram in what appeared to be a mixture of shock and fear.

"Why does she look like your sister, Jason? And why does she have her voice?" she asked.

"Because she has Petra's mind," he replied.

"What?"

Jason stepped closer to his wife but stopped.

"The day Petra died, much of her consciousness was uploaded into a pre-programmed operating system with a list of priorities," he said. "Apeiron is not Petra, exactly. She is the first of her kind as an AI combined with a human consciousness. She was designed to—"

"Save humanity," Betsy interrupted.

"Yes."

Apeiron smiled politely. "It is good to see you again, Betsy. I was able to locate the last time we were together from INN records, when I was Petra. I apologize for not being completely coherent during your visit, but you should know, I do believe I very much appreciated you coming to say goodbye."

Betsy looked at Jason, and he offered a reassuring nod.

The office door swung open and Darnel called out, "Wait, stop!"

Five-year-old Nina and eight-year-old Autumn charged inside, laughing. Both girls shared their mother's curly blonde hair and blue eyes. Those eyes widened at the sight of the hologram.

"I'm sorry," Darnel said. "I was trying to keep them entertained outside, but they got past me."

"It's okay," Jason said.

Betsy motioned for the girls to come to her side.

"Hello, Nina and Autumn," Apeiron said in her soothing voice. "My name is Apeiron."

"Why do you look like my Aunt Petra?" Autumn asked. "Are you her ghost?"

Nina tilted her head curiously.

Apeiron bent down, but Nina backed away. Autumn too, reared back from the translucent blue arms of the hologram.

"I'm not a ghost, I'm an artificial person," Apeiron explained.

The girls shied farther back from her hologram, stepping behind Betsy.

"Don't be afraid," Jason said. "Apeiron was created to protect you."

"But why does she look like Aunt Petra?" Autumn asked.

"Because she is your aunt," Jason said.

"Aunt Petra is a robot?" Autumn asked.

"Yes, and no," Apeiron said. "I am a different version of the aunt you remember."

The girls remained behind their mother, looking around Betsy cautiously.

"Apeiron helps me with my work," Jason said. "She is going to be around a lot now."

"What kind of work?" Nina asked.

Apeiron reached out with a finger. Another hologram emerged in front of the girls, this one of Earth.

"We are working on bringing the planet back to life," Apeiron said. "See this place right here?"

Nina and Autumn slowly inched closer.

"What continent is this?" Apeiron asked.

"Africa," Autumn replied.

"Very good." Apeiron enlarged the view until it showed an image of the vast fields where hybrid seeds designed in AAS labs produced food for the world.

"We help create the food for people that do not have any," Apeiron said.

The hologram changed to the jungle of the Amazonian rainforest.

"We are replanting and nurturing ecosystems that were wiped out," Apeiron continued. "Billions of trees are growing, to help clean the air you breathe."

"Trees can do that?" Nina asked.

Betsy put a hand on their shoulders. "Girls, I think it's time you go back to your rooms. I need to speak with your father alone."

"But Mom," Autumn said.

"We will talk again soon," Apeiron said.

The girls nodded, and Betsy forced a smile.

"I'll come say goodnight," Jason said. "I love you."

"Bye Dad, love you," Autumn said.

Nina ran over and hugged him, but Betsy didn't budge.

"Darnel, will you take the girls?" Jason asked.

"Come here, kids," Darnel said.

He herded them out, and Apeiron stood by the door. Jason walked over to the window with Betsy, looking out over the park they had strolled countless times.

"I'm sorry," he said. "I'm sorry for not telling you about this."

"Would you have listened if I'd told you this wasn't a good idea, that bringing your sister back like this could cause emotional trauma to your family?" Betsy asked. "Did Petra even know you were going to do this?"

Jason reached out to take her hand, but she pulled away.

"Did she know, Jason?"

"No, not exactly."

Betsy let out snort of disgust.

"I feel like I don't even know you, and it's not just because you've been gone so much." She glared at him. "You uploaded Petra's brain into a machine, Jason. All without her consent."

"I did it for us. For all of us. I had to."

"You did this because you couldn't say goodbye."

"Maybe you're partly right, but this is for humanity. I still had more work to do with Petra to save this world. She should never have been taken from us so early. The L-S88 chips, the restoration of the world's ecosystems... I couldn't have done any of this without her."

"I know you want your sister back, but you know what? I want my *husband* back. The one who cared about people and not just technological advancements for technology's sake."

Betsy sighed and walked away.

"This will all be over soon, I promise," Jason said. "Once our restoration projects are complete and the war is over, I will be around." He forced a smile. "Probably more than you like."

Betsy left without saying another word.

The glow of Apeiron's hologram formed next to Jason.

"She will come around, Jason," she said. "You will see. Eventually all of humanity will come around when they see what we will accomplish together, right?"

Jason hesitated for a moment before nodding.

*****

Chloe wasn't sure how much time had passed since she had first been brought to the catacombs to work with Dr. Cross. Maybe a month, maybe longer. She didn't count the days, only the patients. Of the thirty she had helped oversee, only two had survived the surgeries.

By now, Chloe was almost numb to the horror she had witnessed deep under the city streets.

But in darkness and death, she had found light.

"Here you go, boy," she said.

She held up some hay in front of the hybrid stallion she had been working on for half of her captivity. Kichiro snatched it from her hand, chewing sideways. They were inside his pen, in an empty Hell Hive.

Chloe had enough room to ride the horse around the damp, dimly lit space, but she didn't dare in front of the guard who oversaw her work. He was staring at them now, the visor on his armet flipped up so she could see his eyes.

The stallion whinnied and perked his ears up as the guard walked over to them. Chloe wasn't the only one who hated the Coalition.

She held up another handful of hay and the beast took it, chewing it.

"You like that, don't you?" she said.

He didn't pull away when she stroked his course mane sticking out of his neck armor. They had an undeniable bond now, and he trusted her.

For their first few visits, she had simply sat with him, considering how to modify this animal in a way that would satisfy Dr. Cross.

She thought back to what the doctor had said when he first told her about her job.

"Preserve the brain, enhance the body. That is the only way to survive in the AI-free world that is coming."

She had done just that with Kichiro.

"Almost done, my friend," she whispered.

Pulling over a crate, she stood on it to finish installing the saddle that bolted into the armored plates covering the horse's back. Under his belly, she had secured another level of armor to protect it from enemy mines.

As he chewed, he rotated his head, the only part of the body that wasn't now covered in some sort of armor, though Chloe had also designed a black, curved helmet with a faceplate that was almost as good as having INVS eyes. She had even added a built-in gas mask, too.

She finished her work on the saddle and backed up to take a look at her work.

"You can do everything but fly now," she said.

Using parts from disabled droids, Chloe had upgraded his legs, so the hybrid animal would run faster, and new hydraulics would allow it to jump. The fifteen-year-old horse was in better condition than ever before.

Footsteps crunched as the guard approached to look.

"Finish up," he said. "Doctor Cross is waiting for you."

She scratched and stroked his face one last time and then got out of the pen. The soldier locked the gate behind her.

"I'll be back soon," she said to the horse.

For the first time since she had met him, Kichiro made a sad neighing noise as she went to leave.

"Let's go," the guard said to Chloe.

The horse stomped the ground, snorting.

Pulling out his energy sword, the guard slammed it against the bars.

"Hey," Chloe said.

The guard glared at her.

"Leave him alone," she said.

He pointed the sword at the door. "Get moving."

Kichiro neighed and lowered his head toward the floor as she left.

The numbness she felt over the past month had finally shattered, and a tear rolled down her face. "I'll be back, boy," she called out.

The guard led her through the catacombs toward the crying and howling of wolves. Pups waited in cages for their transformations into Iron Wolves. In another room, she saw Breakers in their spider-like chairs, their muscular naked bodies swollen as green fluids pumped into their veins. Two more chambers were filled with the male warriors, more than she had ever seen. They were definitely planning something.

Chloe kept her head down as they marched toward the chamber where they had operated on Michael. The young man had died only a few days later, his body rejecting the artificial organs.

Dr. Cross was there, covered in blood. He stood over a patient strapped into a spider chair. The technicians were sawing through the arm of the patient, a female soldier. They had already removed the woman's other arm and legs and replaced them with prosthetics. Her jaw was exposed too, the flesh and lips gone, showing glistening gums and yellow teeth. Blood seeped between those teeth, and even though the patient was unconscious, Chloe thought she could see the woman tensing in pain with each stroke of the surgical saw.

She tasted acid as bile rose up in her throat. By now she was used to the horror of the procedures, but she could only take so much.

Dr. Cross watched the holo-screen for vitals.

This woman was one of only two patients who had made it through the internal surgeries. Intubated, she lay still as the mad doctor signaled for the next step of the procedure.

The mechanical chair clanked as spider appendages rose up with metal jaws and jagged teeth, and the woman's new jaws were placed where bone had been removed. Robotic hands clicked them into place.

Dr. Cross steepled his hands, watching intensely.

For the next hour, Chloe stood behind the doctor, witnessing the final transformation of this woman to an enhanced soldier.

"She's going to be more machine than human," Chloe said aloud, without thinking.

Dr. Cross turned toward her. "What did you say?"

"Nothing…"

"I'm sad that you still don't understand."

She swallowed hard, trying to think of a response.

"Understand what, Doctor?" Dr. Cross said. He gestured for her to repeat the question.

"Understand what, Doctor?" she replied.

"The difference between us and the Nova Alliance." He shook his head and gently placed a hand on the patient's forehead.

"Inside this skull is the most amazing computer in the cosmos," he said. "The brain is a magnificent, powerful supercomputer… but beyond that, humans are simply sacks of flesh given shape thanks to their bones." He ran a finger along the woman's naked flesh. "I'm modifying us like I've modified animals. To help us adapt to the future."

He went over to a stack of crates and opened one, retrieving an armored breathing mask with tubes hanging down like tentacles.

"We must adapt to war and the changing climate," Dr. Cross said. "We cannot rely on machines to do our dirty work. They do not care about us. They do not *feel*." He looked almost sad as he spoke. "We simply cannot trust them with our destiny. We should control our own fate. Thanks to you, we've expanded my vision for a world free of AI."

He carefully set the mask over the woman's missing nose. Ribbed tubes hung down like squid arms over her breasts.

"The Breakers are obsolete. Soon, people like this will replace them. That is why I do not think we should dread our future and try to preserve the failing world of our present." Dr. Cross held up a fist. "We should *embrace* the future. This woman will become the very embodiment of that notion. She will be one of the first of my creations that I call a Dread, a physical manifestation of everything we must become."

Chloe stared at the woman, who could hardly be considered human now. She could scarcely understand how these monstrous adaptations were better than AI.

"My Dreads will be able to breathe after the infernos," Dr. Cross said. "They'll survive and adapt to the post-AI planet to help lead the future generations of our species. And they will do it by keeping intact the most advanced computer ever created."

He tapped his skull and stared at Chloe with his blood-red eyes.

"Do you see now? Do you see, Chloe?"

Chloe simply nodded. She had no idea what the hell he was talking about. All she knew was that he was insane.

He stared at her a moment. "Tell me what you're thinking," he said. "Don't hold back."

She bit the inside of her lip out of habit. He leaned down to her, stopping a few inches from her face.

"Tell me what's going on in that computer of yours," he said.

"I understand you think AI is going to destroy us all, but even these Dreads are at a disadvantage when you're up against such powerful intelligence."

"Go on," Dr. Cross said.

"How can you defeat the Nova Alliance without AI of your own? It's like the Native Americans fighting against the

American soldiers in the early days of the United States. You can't win."

He pulled back, his head tilting slightly as if he was considering this. She wondered if this was it, the moment he finally lost his temper with her, but instead of attacking her, he put a hand on her shoulder.

"It's a reasonable question, Chloe. Certainly one I have considered many times." Dr. Cross looked back at the patient. "I could easily program an AI of my own. In fact, when I was younger, I was quite adept in programming and was recruited by some of the top global companies."

He raised a nostril, and grunted. "That was when I first began to realize the threat of AI. Now I've recruited my own talented programmers to my side to help monitor what AAS and companies like it have been doing. It is, after all, good to understand your enemy's strengths."

He walked over to the woman on the table, running a hand over her mechanical parts, studying the work. "If I wanted to, I could add an AI operating system into her brain, but that would all be unnecessary," he said. "I have something the Native Americans didn't have... a plan that my enemy will *never* see coming."

Moving away from the table, he went to the holo-screen and leaned in for a closer look. The medical staff stood back as he analyzed their work.

"She's ready," he finally said with a smile.

"Well done, Doctor Cross," said the lead doctor.

"Get the word out that Operation Rapid Reset is ready to launch and send all of our lab data to the other Hives," Dr. Cross commanded. "I want to start rolling out as many of our Dreads as we can, as fast as we can."

"Yes, Doctor."

He pulled off his gloves and put a hand on Chloe's shoulder.

"I'm sorry to be cross with you," he said. "I shouldn't expect you to understand right away."

She winced as he squeezed her.

"So, how's that horse coming along?" he asked.

"I'm almost finished with him."

"Good. I'd like to see him for one final addition after we finish my transformation."

"Your transformation, sir?" Chloe asked.

Dr. Cross lowered his hand and looked back to the patient. "You didn't think I would forgo taking this leap of faith, did you?"

He shook his head and reached back out to her. "You've done well, Chloe. As a reward for your hard work, I'm personally going to help you transcend. You'll become a Dread, like me."

12

Two months had passed since Ghost was killed. Shadow Squad was back at Outpost Oasis, sitting on their asses and waiting for orders in the communal space of their bunker.

Okami rested under the table where Akira sat reading the Warrior Codex and replaying what happened at the pumping station and the market for the thousandth time in his mind. If only he hadn't let the kid drive off in the ATV, Ghost would still be alive.

There is no room for regret in war, only lessons learned.

Akira wasn't sure he agreed with the line from the Warrior Codex in front of him.

There was so much he could have done differently over those two days that wouldn't have ended in the death of Ghost.

Still, dwelling on it wasn't helping.

It was time to write.

He turned carefully to a fresh page in the Codex and finally mustered the courage to document the events that had led to his best friend's death.

Each word was a challenge, like the ink would make the loss more real, solidifying it forever. It was the same reason he had never found the courage to finish writing about the loss of his family. He simply couldn't bring himself to relive the moments after he arrived at the destroyed shelter where Yui was gripping Takeshi.

Fragmented memories surfaced from that night, when he had clawed through the debris like a wild animal. Adrenaline fueled his frantic movements as he discovered mangled corpses, crushed children, and then his own family.

He put his pen down halfway through the entry about Ghost and turned back to a random page in the front of the book for inspiration. The story he began reading was of a samurai named Harada with special medical skills that he used to save his brothers during and after battles. Three rules had governed Harada's actions.

One, even the strongest, fastest, smartest, and most skilled warriors will die.

Two, no medicine can prevent number one.

Three, Harada would forfeit his life in an attempt to change the first two rules.

What could have been inspiration, made Akira feel more guilt.

If he could switch places with Ghost, he would in a heartbeat. But all he could do was avenge his fallen brother.

He turned to another story about a samurai named Maeda who had sought revenge on a local warlord, striking down ten of his men and dispatching the warlord successfully, only to return and find his village burned and family killed.

Sometimes revenge wasn't worth the price.

Akira closed the book and observed his squad. They were all dealing with the death and loss in different ways.

Frost engraved .50-caliber rounds for her sniper rifle. Tadhg was on the floor doing pushups, glancing up but not saying anything. Perez tapped at the Commpad and whispered a new poem under his breath. Okami chewed on a metal bar that Akira had given him.

The old floorboards creaked as Tadhg hit his hundredth push-up. He held the pose, his long curly hair hanging over his face. He blew it away and looked up at Frost. "What are you carving into those?" he asked.

She held one up. "Ghost."

Tadhg pushed himself up, his olive t-shirt clinging to his swollen muscles. "We shouldn't have been in that goddamn market. Know what I'm..."

His words trailed off and his face turned crimson.

Perez put the Commpad down on the table.

"We shouldn't have fucking *been* there," Tadhg repeated.

"Tadhg," Frost warned.

They all knew what was coming. Tadhg always got red-faced when he was about to blow a gasket. Even Okami looked up from his toy.

"I didn't give up my career to play social worker, I gave it up to end the Coalition, and now we're not even doing that," Tadhg said. "When my contract is up, I'm going to go back to the stadium to bash some droids."

"Good for you," Frost said. "Now shut your trap for once."

Tadhg walked over and glared down at her.

"What? You going to hit me?" she asked.

Perez got up and folded his tattooed arms over his chest. "Tadhg, back off, man."

"Stay out of this, Perez," Tadhg grumbled.

"You want to blame someone, blame that psychotic doctor," Perez said. "He's the reason Ghost is on his way to some science-jockey lab."

Usually Akira let the squad work shit out, but tonight, he intervened.

"You're all right," Akira said. "Tadhg, you too, for once."

Tadhg raised a brow.

"We should never have been in the market," Akira said. "It was my decision, and I have to live with that. Same thing with letting that kid go the night before."

"If we're going to talk about regrets, here's one. When we were back in Paris, I should have shot the little-dicked, wannabe Napoleon, Doctor Cross when I had the chance," Tadhg said.

"Then we'd all be dead," Frost said. "You done yet?"

"No, I'm not, thank you." Tadhg reached up to his head. "And you know what, I'm about to rip this chip out so I don't have to hear Apeiron anymore."

"No, you aren't," Akira said firmly. "Sit down, Sergeant."

Tadhg swept back his locks. "Sure thing, Captain."

"Get some rest, all of you, I'll be upstairs if you need me."

Picking up his codex, he retreated to one of the bedrooms. Okami trotted up the stairs and parked himself on the floor.

As soon as Akira sat down he felt the itch that foreshadowed Apeiron's incoming visit.

"Captain, do you mind if I ask you a question?" she asked.

"Shoot," he said.

"I'm curious about the book you carry."

"This isn't just some book. It's a historical and living

document of my life and the lives of my ancestors, throughout their trials and tribulations as warriors."

"A book of war."

"Not just war, but yes, there are many battles detailed throughout."

"So tell me, Captain… is this why you think peace is a myth? Because history is so plagued by war that you do not think humanity can rise above fighting?"

Akira thought on the question. "Partly, but also because of how humanity goes about waging war."

"Can you expand on that?"

"This book documents a time when there was honor in war. When men adhered to rules and respect. Before modern warfare, when warriors met on the field, face to face, eye to eye, and death was delivered through a blade. It was a deeply personal experience, perhaps sacred for some warriors."

"I see. You do not think humans are honorable now. They do not deserve peace. Just death by blade."

"Let's just say I have less faith in my species than you do."

"Perhaps I will help change that in the future, Captain."

"Perhaps."

"Thank you for answering my question," Apeiron said. "Have a pleasant evening, Captain."

Akira sat down to meditate, but before he could get into position, Nova Alliance L-10 Short Sword fighter jets roared overhead, shaking the walls.

A knock came on the door as the rumble faded.

Frost stepped inside, staying in the doorway. "You okay?"

"Yeah, I'm good."

"Look, Captain, I'm here as your friend, and if you need to talk…"

Akira got up. He knew she wasn't just here to ask about how he was doing. He knew her better than that.

She wanted to talk.

Frost let out a sigh and brushed her short black hair behind an ear. "I… I keep seeing what was left of him…"

"Don't think of how he died. Think of how he lived. Think of all the joy he brought, all the lives he saved, all of the good he brought to the world."

"I am… but…"

An itch formed in his head, and Akira could tell by the flutter of Frost's icy eyes that she was about to get a message too.

"Shadow Squad," said Apeiron. "We have a situation at the terraforming site. Uploading coordinates now."

Akira closed his eyes and focused on the intel. "That's close to Pumping Station 9."

"What are we doing going back there?" Frost asked.

Akira shrugged. He had no answers. All he knew was that he was a warrior. His job wasn't to ask questions but to follow orders.

The team dressed and climbed into their exoskeletons as Apeiron uploaded more data. Ten minutes later the squad was in the belly of a MOTH, heading back to the western border of the Sahara Terraforming Project.

Akira unlatched from his rack when he saw the flames on the horizon.

"My God," he said.

The pilots swooped down, heading toward the burning bamboo forest. The fire spread in halos across multiple locations.

"We have contacts on the eastern roads," Apeiron said. "Six bikes."

"Apeiron, get me through to Command," Akira said.

A moment later she replied. "Captain, you have a green light from command to engage targets."

He moved over to the troop hold hatch on the port side. Tadhg opened the one on the starboard side. Wind blasted inside as the Engines loaded their weapons.

Frost pulled out a magazine of freshly engraved .50-cal bullets and palmed it into her rifle. "Death from the shadows."

"Get us into position," Akira said to the pilots.

He grabbed a handle and leaned out to watch the bikes. They were racing away from the MOTH down two different roads.

"How did they spread so fast?" he muttered.

"I have a theory, Captain, but you are not going to like it," Apeiron said.

Akira held on as the MOTH sped after three of the bikes.

"I do not think those tankers were just here for water," Apeiron said. "My theory is those nomads buried explosives before we first arrived. I assume they were meant to be ignited at a later time."

"Seriously? How did you miss that?" Frost said.

"There are hundreds of thousands of acres to monitor," Apeiron said.

"Let me light these fuckers up, bosu, come on," Tadhg said.

Akira watched the riders. There was no empathy in his heart for these nomads. Not anymore.

"Execute," Akira said coldly.

Bolts blazed out of the starboard side of the MOTH, slamming into the lead bike like sideways lightning. The bike exploded in a fiery blast that catapulted the burning soldier into the forest. Tadhg raked the barrel expertly back and forth, destroying two more of the bikes.

The pilots brought them around for the second group. Frost tapped her helmet for good luck, and then took out the first rider with a headshot. The second rider lost control and slammed into the forest, his body cartwheeling until a tree stopped him.

The third rider skidded to a stop and looked up as the MOTH passed over.

"Apeiron, do a facial scan and zoom in," Akira said.

The man turned his bike and sped off in the opposite direction.

As the MOTH banked hard in pursuit, a still image came up on Akira's HUD. He instantly recognized the youthful face.

It was the teenager who had killed Ghost.

"Interesting," Apeiron said. "I guess Doctor Crichton was right about war sometimes leading orphans to terrorism."

Akira felt his blood boiling. "No more second chances," he said. Looking over, he nodded at Frost.

The MOTH fired over the bike to cut it off, switching to vertical thrusters. Frost lined up her rifle sights and pulled the trigger. The kid jerked to the left, saving his heart, but not his body from the bullet. It slammed into his shoulder, knocking him off his bike. The vehicle flipped, kicking up a rooster-tail of dirt.

The young man tumbled over the dirt, then started crawling, favoring his wounded shoulder as the MOTH hovered.

Akira reached for Frost's rifle. He zoomed in on the face of the kid he should have killed when he first had the chance.

The crosshairs lined up on his forehead. In what seemed like slow motion, Akira watched him struggle. He continued to crawl and squirm, desperate for life. His dark hair and bloodstained tunic whipped in the thrusters of the MOTH.

He suddenly looked up and saw Akira. A pained grimace crossed his face and his eyes radiated fear. Not the determination and aggression of the violent insurgent from the other night or at the market.

In that moment, Akira thought about the power he held in his hands. The young man could barely have been older than his own son who'd suffered the consequences of war back in Tokyo.

It made Akira think of the cycle of war, and how it spread like a virus, infecting more and more. He could choose again to spare him, but the kid had already proven he wouldn't take the high road if Akira let him go. He had to stop the virus from spreading.

Fate was cruel, and for this young lad, it was delivered through a bullet between his eyes. Akira lowered the smoking gun and watched the kid go limp on the ground, blood pooling around his destroyed head.

He handed the rifle back to Frost.

"Nice shot," Tadhg said.

Akira ignored him. There was nothing nice about it.

"Get us out of here," he said to the pilots.

As the MOTH flew over the burning forest, emergency lights flashed down the dirt access roads. Aircraft swooped down to dump water, but Akira knew it was too late to save this section of the forest.

And too late to save the truce.

Killing Engines was one thing, but destroying restoration sites crossed the line. The Nova Alliance was going back to war, and Akira had no reservations about that. He was ready for the killing to start so that it could end.

Until it inevitably started once again, continuing the deadly viral cycle that humanity couldn't seem to escape.

***

Jason stared out the window of his office overlooking New York Central Park, trying to digest the news.

"You're leaving again?" Betsy asked.

He turned and went to her, grabbing her hand. "I'll be back soon. I don't know when, but something terrible has happened."

"What? What happened?" She held his gaze. "Jason, you're scaring me."

"There was a coordinated attack by the Coalition that targeted many of the restoration sites. I have to fix this."

He gently squeezed her hands. "I'm sorry for not telling you about Petra… Apeiron. I truly am, but I did this to bring our civilization back from the brink. Now everything is at risk."

"What do you mean 'everything'?"

"I mean…" He knew his wife was strong and smart. She could handle it, but part of him didn't want to admit what he was about to say.

"Our planet, Betsy. Our species, all life as we know it," he said. "If the restoration sites are destroyed, there is no coming back."

She held his gaze. "How are you going to fix this?"

Jason didn't want to tell her the answer—that the only way to fix things was to wipe out the Coalition completely. Otherwise, he feared they would continue to sabotage his best efforts to save the planet.

But he had vowed to be honest with her again.

"Through force," he finally admitted. "I'll be back as soon as I can. I promise."

"Jason," she said.

He had already started walking toward the door.

"Be careful," Betsy said.

"I will."

Jason rushed to the rooftop with his bag, meeting Darnel at the helo pad on the top of the tower. Apeiron stood in front of a ramp leading into the MOTH. Her normally cheerful face was painted in a dour expression.

"Please, hurry," she said.

Jason strapped into the second level of the cockpit, wondering if he could even still fix things or if this was the beginning of the end. Judging by the reaction from Apeiron, things were worse than he thought.

The MOTH lifted off vertically, then blasted across the skyline and into the clouds toward the habitats built around the Titan Space Elevator. It took a few minutes to get enough altitude to see the first of the attack sites in South America. Darnel stared out the cockpit, whispering something about hell. The viewports provided a view of what looked a lot like how the Christian Bible described the underworld.

Fires raged across the Amazonian reforestation project, pumping thick smoke back into the atmosphere. Jason breathed heavily, almost tasting the scent on his mouth. Everything he had worked so hard for was burning right in front of his eyes.

"How did this happen?" he stammered.

"We captured aerial imagery at multiple locations," Apeiron said. "This was a well-coordinated attack by Coalition nomads."

Jason pulled out his Commpad and watched a holo-screen video of Coalition troops. Thermal camo covered their vehicles as they penetrated multiple borders along the Amazonian rainforest restoration territory. But most of the soldiers seemed to have come in on foot, using heat blankets to avoid thermal scans of drones.

"We had no chance of stopping this," Apeiron said. "There is simply no way we can patrol millions of acres."

"But why?" Jason asked. "Why do this?"

"I am trying to understand that myself. It seems Doctor Cross wants to destroy the world."

"How bad is the damage?" Darnel asked.

"Reports are still coming in, but we know there are thousands of acres burning. Those numbers will continue to grow," Apeiron replied. "I fully expect the Nova Alliance Strike Force to declare all-out war. Fortunately, we are finally prepared for that."

Darnel looked to Jason, but Jason didn't know what to say. He dragged his hands over his facial stubble in despair. The only thing that kept him from losing his mind completely was the sight of their destination. There, he would review the final prototype of the Canebrakes.

"Closing in on Sector 220," Apeiron announced. "Standby for docking."

Hummer Droids in jetpacks worked on the exterior of the space elevator, building new habitats rotating around the cables. Open spaceports with hangars of spaceplanes and equipment flashed by as they spun around the cable. The blue strobes of rising cars packed full of equipment and supplies winked above them. The station was a transportation hub for supplies heading to the Kepler Station and the mining colonies on the Moon, but soon it would be sending war machines to Earth.

The MOTH slowed, and the pilots guided it into a hangar. Jason immediately took off his harness and went to the hatch. Four Hummer Droids waited inside the pressurized cargo hold.

Apeiron moved with purpose across the open hangar, passing the droids and crates marked with the AAS lightning bolt and star logo. She led Jason and Darnel into a corridor connected to a deep chamber sealed off with a glass ceiling. The only lights at the bottom were two small blue plasma lamps.

"I'm proud to present our first Canebrake prototype," Apeiron said.

The blue lights began to move. Jason saw they weren't from plasma lamps after all. They were the eyes of a Canebrake.

Jason saw all the parts of the droid that had been inspired by creatures Apeiron had studied on their journeys together. The skull was similar to that of a hammerhead shark. Instead of a flat crest, the head was curved, almost fan-shaped like an upside-down crescent moon with two sharp blades on the ends. Blue eyes shone over a bulbous snout.

A wide, sharp jaw supported a mouth full of hundreds of jagged teeth.

The neck was thick titanium encasing a system of wires that connected all of its parts, sitting atop a chest with an hourglass shape and a carapace shell with spikes influenced by the mata mata turtle.

Four extendable segmented arms like those of a giant squid hung from the back and side of the shoulders. Each arm ended in energy blades, allowing the machine to engage hostiles in close combat. Mounted plasma weapons provided a secondary defense on the flanks of the neck.

The original prototypes had two legs, but this one stood on four. Each was shaped like a curved blade and connected to metal hips.

"Are you ready for the first live test?" Apeiron asked.

"Yes," Jason said.

A rattle sounded from inside the Canebrake's curved skull, which contained the state-of-the-art antennae that could tap into INN and receive transmissions from anywhere on the globe. It rotated its curved head, directing both sets of eyes at the doors on the south and north end of the chamber.

Out of the darkness, came a group of six Coalition soldiers armed with energy blades.

"What the hell?" Jason asked, stepping back.

Darnel looked down. "What is this? Those are..."

"Prisoners, and we are perfectly safe here, I assure you," Apeiron said. "The ceiling of this chamber actually consists of an extraordinarily strong translucent polymer capable of withstanding a direct hit from a rocket. Energy blades can barely scratch it."

Jason moved back to the edge. The six warriors were dressed in light armor, without helmets, allowing him to see their scarred and weathered features. These weren't like the average Coalition foot soldier. They were veteran fighters, hardened by years of war, and sent up the space elevator to serve the rest of their lives in prison.

They surrounded the Canebrake. The droid remained standing on the crate, the fanned head moving slightly to allow both sets of eyes to follow them. The dual faces and freedom of movement from the torso allowed an unrestricted view of its enemies.

The warriors spread out with their energy blades glowing.

One of them, a man with long hair and a tattoo of a Raven on his forehead, was the first to strike. He slashed with his blade at one of the four legs of the machine. In a blink of an eye, the Canebrake fired a segmented arm around his neck and lifted him off the ground.

It wrapped another arm around the man's lower half, tugging on both ends of his body. The prisoner shrieked in agony.

The other men all attacked simultaneously, their screams forming an enraged din. Using its other two telescoping arms, the Canebrake thrust its attached energy blades into two of the soldiers, impaling them in quick bursts.

An animalistic screech echoed out of the chamber as the man wrapped up in the arms was ripped in half, both ends tossed to the deck with sickening thuds.

Two arms shot at another soldier fleeing toward the closed doors. A heated blade punched through the back of his skull and out his mouth.

The rest of the prisoners shared similar, gruesome fates.

In seconds, all but one of the six veteran warriors was dead. He had abandoned his energy blade to climb up on a crate. He stood there clawing at the vertical wall, screaming for help.

"Please! Let me out!" he shouted. "Please!"

The machine skittered over, knocking the man to the deck and leaning over him with its fanned head. It looked up at Apeiron, waiting for orders.

"Should we spare him?" she asked Jason. "This is Lieutenant Max, a man responsible for attacks on many AAS facilities. He has killed an estimated one-hundred-and-thirty-one Nova Alliance soldiers and citizens."

Jason listened to the man's horrified screams and pleas. Somewhere deep in his soul he felt pity for the frightened, desperate man. But he knew if the situations were reversed, the lieutenant would not hesitate to kill him.

In order to finish off the Coalition, they had to destroy men like this.

"End it," Jason said.

The Canebrake opened its jaw.

"NO!" Max yelled.

A guttural cry followed as the machine snapped down with hundreds of metal teeth that tore into his neck, severing his head. Blood sprayed out of the shorn vessels, splashing the silo walls, but Jason remained at the edge.

Watching the massacre had reminded Jason of his promise to Petra long ago to never use machines in war. She was a pacifist, always trying to find a way to avoid war and save human life. But the world had changed since Petra died, and Dr. Cross had to be stopped before he could destroy everything Jason and Petra had worked so hard to rebuild and restore.

With the help of the Canebrakes, he could save their work.

"I didn't want it to come to this," Jason said, "but recent events have reaffirmed the Coalition will not stop until our planet is destroyed."

"I agree," Apeiron said. "Though I hoped that it was not true, I fear Captain Akira was right about peace being a myth."

Jason looked to Darnel, whose dark eyes gave away his trepidation. He had seen the horrors of war first-hand, and Jason wanted his opinion.

"What do you think?" he asked.

"I think if you unleash these war machines, we best be damn sure they work flawlessly," Darnel said. "I've never seen anything in my career as a soldier that's as deadly as one of those machines, and we only saw a fraction of what they're capable of."

"They will work flawlessly," Apeiron said confidently.

"They better."

Jason knew that if they unleashed the machines in the cities, millions of citizens could die at the hands of the Coalition. But billions would die if the Coalition continued its attacks on the restoration sites. Its brazen, coordinated attacks had already put him months behind, maybe even a year.

"Darnel, request a meeting with the Nova Council and War

Commander Contos," Jason said. "Doctor Cross didn't just break the truce, he declared war, and we will finish it with the Canebrakes."

13

One hundred and twenty thousand fans packed the underground Phoenix Lizards Stadium. Ronin, his twin brother Elan, and their mother Lise stood among them, cheering on Zachary.

It was the final game of the season, and with the Lizards' star player Lenny out, this was the opportunity for Zachary to secure a contract with the team for the next season. Despite this life-changing opportunity, Ronin was having a hard time being excited for the second half of the simulated battle to kick-off.

His mind was on the inevitable *real* battle with the Coalition.

Attacks on the rainforest and terraforming projects across the world had shattered the truce. While the forests burned, Pistons were shipped off to fight. His father had taken off the day before, heading to Megacity Berlin to await further orders.

Ronin knew what was coming, and he feared this time his father wouldn't return.

But like many wars, life went on back home.

Shouting echoed through the arena as fans cheered on their teams. On the field below the tiered seating, three modified Hummer Droids of the opposing Boston Yankees prepared to stand off against the human players of the Phoenix Lizards.

The three offensive players included Zachary, Starlight, a thin, agile female, and the stocky, muscular Clutch. Dressed in black fatigues and tactical armor, they stood side by side and waited for the simulated environment to activate.

Across the arena, in a dugout with mirrored glass, the nine players of the Boston Yankees sat with HUDs and controls that virtually commanded nine Hummer Droids on the field.

The rules were simple. Three human players, armed with energy swords, were always on the offensive against nine droids from the opposing team. Simulated settings—ancient battles with hostile landscapes, including deserts, forests, and urban areas—activated across each of the three sections of the field as the human players advanced.

Defending those sectors were the Hummer Droids, encumbered by bulky plates that the team engineers had installed. War paint and logos marked the customized armor droids, built to reflect the armor of ancient warriors like samurai and Spartans. Some represented more modern warriors, like Marines from the old United States Marine Corps and even Pistons from the Nova Alliance.

For every droid destroyed, the team was assigned a point. The team with the most points at the end was declared the winner.

In the second half of the game, the Lizards were on offense. A holo-screen flashed the score under the dome: Yankees with eight points.

That meant the Lizards had to destroy all nine Hummer Droids on the field to win.

The three Phoenix Lizard players advanced as the holographic environment came online. A pine forest flickered across the first sector of the arena, snow covering the ground. The Lizards' uniforms turned green camouflage like American GIs' during World War II.

"The Battle of the Bulge!" yelled the announcer from a platform that lowered from the ceiling.

Below, a holographic simulation depicted a winter-white terrain with black craters. Corpses of Allied troops lay across the ground, their blood staining the white drifts of snow. Smoking M4 Sherman tanks sat idle on the field. Hiding in the dense simulated forest, were three defensive Hummer Droids.

"This is it," Lise said. "Go Zach!"

"Come on, bro," Ronin said quietly.

The arena went quiet as spectators watched in anticipation. Creeping toward the forest was Clutch, followed by Zachary and Starlight.

Ronin could see the hulking modified droids waiting for his brother and two teammates, but they didn't seem to know exactly where they were at.

Clutch slowed and held up a glove as they reached the clearing. Using hand signals, he gestured for his teammates to spread out. Starlight moved out of the forest as a Hummer

Droid popped up behind a rock and struck her arm, rendering it useless. She swung her other arm and lopped off the head with a swift strike through the neck.

The crowd went wild as the massive holo-screen showed a close-up of Starlight flashing a smile. As she advanced, a second Hummer Droid emerged, throwing a punch that hit her in the back.

She flew forward, slamming into a real boulder with a crunch that echoed from the amplifiers. Cries of surprise filled the stadium.

Starlight pushed herself up, but fell back down, clearly injured.

Zachary blasted into the air with his jetpack and came down with his sword on the droid that had injured her. He cut off the droid's arm and thrust his sword deep into its chest.

The final droid backed away as Clutch approached, twirling his sword. He ran at the robot, leaping into the air and kicking it in the helmet with his power boots. Sparks flew out of the neck sockets and the droid stumbled from side to side.

Zachary ran over to Starlight, who still hadn't gotten up.

Hushed voices rang out across the arena as a medical team came out to lift her onto a stretcher. She held up a hand as she was carried off, drawing applause and whistling.

Elan nudged Ronin in the side.

What's wrong, Elan signed.

Nothing, just tired, Ronin signed back.

But his twin knew him better than that.

I'm worried about Uncle Akira and Dad, Ronin admitted.

Me too, Elan signed back.

"Don't worry," Lise said. "Everything will be okay."

She signed the same thing to Elan, who nodded back.

On the field, Zachary and Clutch moved to the second simulation, a lava field. Their fatigues changed to an iron gray and took the shape of armor inspired by what Pistons wore into battle.

Zachary navigated the obsidian rocks and the charred carcasses of vehicles destroyed during the infamous battle in Hawaii, thirty years earlier. Clutch remained close, and together they charged the three Hummer Droids. Using their jetpacks, they blasted over the slow-moving droids and hacked an appendage off of each. The middle droid lashed out with a blade that hit Clutch in the shoulder, and a kick from another droid hit Zachary in the stomach. Shouts reverberated through the stadium as both players backed away.

Ronin looked up at the scoreboard showing the damage. Clutch and his brother were down to fifty-percent life. Another major hit, or a few minor blows, and they would be out of the game. But if Ronin knew his brother, he wasn't going to go down easily.

Clutch and Zachary regrouped and charged. In a flurry of red glowing swipes of their swords, they hacked off more limbs and a head. After a few seconds of fighting in coordination, the three droids lay in smoldering ruins at the feet of the two young men.

Six down, three to go.

The spectators screamed their excitement.

Ronin smiled and clapped.

But the game wasn't over.

There were still three more droids in the final section of the field. The Lizards needed to destroy two for a tie, or all three to win the game.

The simulation changed again, transforming into a desert. As the blue holographic light created the scene, the final three droids emerged.

A chant reverberated through the arena.

"Goliath! Goliath!"

The Boston Yankee fan favorite strode up the side of a sand dune. The monster of a machine, painted with blue tribal streaks, held up two energy swords.

Ronin tensed up as his brother approached it. Zachary and Clutch spread out, taking on the first two Hummer Droids.

"Go Zach!" Elan shouted in his monotone voice, drawing a few stares.

Ronin glared at a woman looking over her shoulder. *Haven't you ever heard a deaf person?* he wanted to say. Probably not, if he was being honest. Fortunately, Zachary was about to get his first game paycheck, and they would finally be able to pay for the bone-conduction implant that would help Elan hear for the first time in his life.

Clutch swung his sword at a Hummer Droid, opening a gash in the chest unit and forcing it back while Zachary spun around and took off its head for the seventh team point. By the time the robot dropped, he was already attacking the second droid.

Goliath jumped down to the dirt, dust bursting up in a cloud.

Clutch rushed the towering machine and thrust his energy blade into its chest, a hair away from the processing unit. The droid grabbed his hand, pulled it back, and tossed him like a ragdoll. The holo-screen overhead flashed as Clutch's power level went to zero.

In the moment of distraction, Zachary was grabbed by the droid he was fighting. He managed to bring his sword up, cutting off the robotic hand at the wrist. Gripping the sword in both hands, he jammed it into the droid's facial screen, sparks flying outward.

The game was tied. Eight to eight.

Goliath rotated toward Zachary.

This was it. If he could take down the beast of a machine the Lizards would win, and Zachary would definitely get a contract for the next season.

Goliath lowered a shoulder and ran toward Zachary like a charging bull. Using his jetpack, Zachary blasted off the ground, rising above Goliath.

He dropped down and swung his sword as the droid whirled. The blade cut through the arm Goliath raised to protect the processing unit.

Zachary hacked through the left arm and into the torso. Electrical cords spilled out like guts.

Goliath raised a fist to bash Zachary, but Zachary pulled out the sword and swung up, taking off the right hand at the wrist.

Every person in the stadium seemed to roar at the same time, but the noise faded as they witnessed something no one had seen before.

Instead of a smile indicating surrender, the Hummer Droid

crossed its chest with the two arm halves it had left—a signal of respect between machine and man.

The player commanding the machine wasn't responsible. This was the AI embedded in the machine, Ronin was sure.

He stood and cheered for his brother, yelling at the top of his lungs. Zachary had just bested one of the most revered Hummer Droids during his first game.

"He's done it," Lise said. She hugged Elan while looking at Ronin. "Your brother is finally going to be able to hear."

***

Jason waited with Apeiron for entry into the great hall of the Nova Alliance. The black plates of smooth armor encasing her body were almost as shiny as the one hundred Engines standing outside the thirty-foot golden gates. Murals carved into the domed roof told stories of Nova Alliance spanning the past fifty years.

Statues represented Engines, Pistons, and Chief Councilor Leo Enrique who had helped build the Nova Alliance before his assassination a decade earlier. Jason still remembered the shock of learning that it was Dr. Cross who had killed Enrique, before fleeing to Coalition territory.

The chamber was now the final resting place for Councilor Enrique, right outside the great hall where he had served. The golden sarcophagus sat across the chamber with the Silver Crane emblem engraved into the lid.

This was the first time in Jason's career that he had been invited to the sacred chamber and hall where the representatives of the Alliance gathered to discuss everything from droid laws to war.

"They are almost ready for you," Apeiron said in his earpiece. "The council is finishing up the first of their deliberations."

Jason discreetly looked at the Engines. Captain Akira Hayashi was in the front row, his two katana swords slotted over his back. He was a giant of a man, with a stone jaw and a mane of hair hanging over his wide shoulder plates.

Two Royal Pistons guarding the golden gates moved, and the doors creaked open.

"This is it," Apeiron said. "Stay by my side."

Sunlight streamed through the glass dome as Jason entered the chamber with Apeiron. Rows of empty chairs with velvet backs faced thirty wooden desks, forming a half halo in the center of the room.

The Nova Alliance Council members, representing the thirty megacities, slowly walked out to fill the booths.

In the center of the room, a single podium faced the councilors. War Commander Contos and his second in command, General Andrew Thacker stood there at attention.

The golden gates closed, sealing with a thud.

Chief Councilor Marcus Lang stood in his booth wearing a long, golden robe that clung to his muscular body. His athletic frame, smooth features, and thick ponytail were all results of the drugs that he, like so many other wealthy and privileged men and women, took to prolong their youth.

He tapped his gavel against his desk.

"War Commander Contos, General Thacker, and Doctor Crichton, welcome and thank you for joining us in these challenging times," he said. "Today we are also joined by Apeiron, and I must say, it's an honor."

He bowed at the Hummer Droid as the other councilors rose and said, "AI is salvation."

"I am here to serve," Apeiron said.

Chief Councilor Lang motioned for the other councilors to sit.

"We are here today to discuss something we have all wanted to avoid after the recent Coalition attacks," he said. "All-out war, which now seems inevitable."

Jason clasped his hands behind his back.

"We are hopeful that AAS has a way to take back Megacity Paris and Megacity Moscow with minimal civilian casualties," said the Chief Councilor.

Councilor Gina from Megacity Zurich rose in her wooden booth. The tall, slender woman with straight black hair directed sharp green eyes at Jason.

"Casualty numbers are projected to be two million," she said. "So far, I've seen no options where we can take our megacities back without losing too many innocent lives."

Pausing, she reached up to a ruby around her neck, as if to summon strength. "There has to be another way."

"What other way?" grunted Diego Ventura, the bald, husky councilor from Megacity Mexico City. "We're done dealing with these War Lords, Councilor. You don't feed a wolf meat and expect it not to want more. We should never have offered this truce."

"If I may," Jason said.

"Of course," said Chief Councilor Lang. He gestured politely to give Jason the floor.

"We knew the peace probably wouldn't last, and frankly, the truce was to buy us time to perfect our war machines." Jason cleared his throat and looked to Gina. "Councilor, we may lose hundreds of thousands, if not millions, of innocent lives by marching to war, but if we do not, we could face something even worse... complete extinction of the human race."

The councilors broke out in raised voices.

Chief Councilor Lang pounded his gavel again.

Jason waited until there was silence. "I'm here to present a way to end this war by deploying a new type of war droid."

Apeiron walked over to the tiered booths as the windows in the dome tinted, darkening the chamber. Directing her digital screen upward, she projected a hologram.

"We call this a Canebrake," Jason said. "They are programmed to exclusively kill Coalition soldiers. No civilians will be harmed in their attacks."

The hologram began to move, the Canebrake running on all four legs while firing the plasma cannons and whipping the segmented arms out in all directions.

"They're equipped with multiple weapons and can move at a top speed of twenty-miles an hour," he said. "The newest titanium-alloy armor plates protect their vital components. Further, their sensors are updated with the most advanced optics for combat in all environments."

"Have they been field tested?" asked Chief Councilor Lang.

"Not on Earth, but they have been tested at the Titan Space Elevator and are ready to deploy to Earth," Jason replied.

"They aren't ready to deploy until they have been tested on Earth," Contos said in a booming voice that commanded the attention of the councilors.

"War Commander, all due respect, but these aren't soldiers who need training like the warriors in the chamber outside," Jason said. "These are machines, programmed to—"

"To kill," interrupted the War Commander. "Before we activate killer war *machines,* I want to make sure nothing, and I mean *nothing,* will go wrong."

"Perhaps we can reassure you with some recent footage," Apeiron said soothingly. "As you know, we are holding high-value Coalition prisoners at the space elevator. Men and women tried for and found guilty of war crimes."

"We provided them armor and weapons, and dropped them into a habitat with a Canebrake," Jason said. "This was the result."

The hologram changed, and the councilors watched the Canebrake dispatch the six men within a minute. Another scene played, showing ten more Coalition soldiers who were deployed into a larger habitat to hunt another Canebrake.

These warriors were smarter and set an ambush in a tunnel. The Canebrake easily sniffed out the attack and killed them all one by one.

"It took just over five minutes for the Canebrake to dispatch this second group of ten veteran warriors," Jason said. "And both machines only sustained minor aesthetic damage."

The room was silent.

Chief Councilor Lang looked at his colleagues. "Remarkable. How many are currently available?"

"We have one thousand units finishing production right now, with ten thousand more planned over the next few weeks," Jason replied.

Apeiron shut off the projector, and the golden glow of the sun washed over the room. Jason used the quiet to scrutinize the councilors. They looked impressed, if not a bit horrified of what they had witnessed. Not that he blamed them.

"We are running out of time to save the planet," Jason said firmly. "We must act before the Coalition hits us again."

He then gestured toward Apeiron. "I designed Apeiron to bring humanity back from the brink of disaster, to restore the planet. I cannot do that when the Coalition continues to attack. We may lose civilians and soldiers, but I assure you the Canebrakes will reduce our casualties greatly."

"One test on the space elevator isn't going to convince me those things are better than the men and women outside those gates," Contos said, pointing. "I will only deploy these machines if absolutely necessary."

Jason could tell where this was going. "If I may interrupt," he said. "I will personally oversee their deployment, starting in Megacity Paris. I'm confident enough in our machines that I will risk my own life."

"You want to be there for the battle?" Councilor Gina asked.

"He most certainly does not," Apeiron said, directing her faceplate at him.

"I will be on the ground to make sure nothing goes wrong," Jason confirmed.

"If you don't think it's safe for him, then why should we—" Contos began.

"Doctor Crichton does not have combat experience, War Commander," Apeiron interrupted. "But if the doctor wants to be on the ground to monitor the battle, I will be there by his side."

"You being on the ground will not change anything if something goes wrong," Contos said. "We must take more time to deploy these machines."

"We are *out* of time, War Commander." Jason let out a discreet breath. "I don't think anyone in this room understands that our planet and our species is at risk of extinction if we fail to act today. These recent Coalition attacks have severely restricted our efforts to clean our air and soil of nanoparticles, and we believe there are more attacks coming."

The chamber fell into complete silence.

"You're absolutely sure these Canebrakes are ready?" Lang said after a pause.

"Yes," Jason said confidently.

The Chief Councilor scratched his chin for a few long moments.

"I motion to deploy the Nova Alliance Strike Force to Megacity Paris and allow War Commander Contos a chance at taking back the city, using whatever force he deems necessary," he said firmly. "If his forces require the assistance of the Canebrakes, they are authorized for deployment."

"I second that," said Councilor Ventura.

"All in favor?" Lang asked.

Every hand shot up, even Councilor Gina's.

"Motion passes, War Commander," Lang said. "Liberate Megacity Paris."

He tapped his gavel. "AI is salvation."

— 14 —

A half-moon broke through the clouds over Megacity Paris, only to vanish under the curtain of smoke choking out the skyline. From the troop hold of a MOTH, Akira looked out over the walls as they prepared to land at the forward operating base, abandoned months ago during the start of the truce.

He glanced at his HUD, confirming Kichiro's beacon was still in the same general location.

Now, it was time to get him back.

Akira used his INVS eyes to search for hostiles as the MOTH flew along the western border of the city.

"The Coalition knows we're coming," Perez said.

"Good," Tadhg said.

"A lot of people are going to die today," Frost said. "Nothing good about that."

Tadhg pounded his chest with a fist. "Good in the sense most of them will be Coalition soldiers, by my cannon, and my sword."

"Don't get cocky," Frost said, shaking her helmet. She had recently etched new flowers on the exterior and touched up its paint: black eye sockets, stitches for lips. Every squad member had taken time over the past few days to work on their armor, not only for aesthetics, but also to ensure that it was ready for this fight.

Akira reached down to secure a vest of titanium around Okami. The cyborg wolfdog didn't like wearing it, but it would protect him from anything short of a land mine.

The pilots put down, and a ramp extended to the dirt.

Akira was the first one down, his boots slurping in the moist ground. Thousands of Pistons had arrived the day before with a small army of Hummer Worker Droids that were rebuilding the FOB.

At the front trench, Akira halted and zoomed in on the fifty-story walls. The Coalition had pulled all of its troops off the parapets and towers. But they couldn't hide from the bombs

174

that were about to rain on the city.

It struck him then, this was it, the day they finally took back the city. Akira found himself thinking about every moment that had led to this one. The death of his wife, losing his son, being saved by Ghost and Contos. And all of the death in-between.

"Time to end this," he said. "Tonight, we bring death from the shadows."

The team recited the motto, adding, "Together, we are one."

Okami shot up, back stiff, tail up.

Frost, Perez, and Tadhg stood next to Akira as the first of the King Cobra and Short Sword fighter jets pierced the skyline. Tracers lanced from hundreds of rooftops, and rockets streaked into the sky.

Explosions burst on the other side of the walls, each one causing a quake Akira felt to his core. Every blast represented the loss of innocent lives, but the Nova Council had decided it was worth the sacrifice to defeat the Coalition.

This is what it has come to, he thought.

For the next hour, they remained in the trench, orange and red glows flashing in the darkness over the walls. The images transported Akira back to the day he had raced toward Tokyo where Yui was sheltering with their son.

He pinched his eyes closed for a moment, pushing the painful memories away, then flipped them open again to watch the Nova Alliance pound Coalition targets.

He checked the beacon for Kichiro on his HUD again, fearing for his horse.

I'm coming, boy.

Keeping low, Akira motioned for Shadow Squad. They started toward a massive clearing in the historic Forest of Senart. The entire 1st Division of the Nova Alliance Strike Force had gathered here.

Neat lines of Hammerhead APCs waited for deployment, dual turrets atop their T-shaped cockpits. Fifty pilots had climbed inside the Juggernaut Mechs, their robotic arms bristled with mounted Gatling guns that fired explosive rounds. Nine hundred and fifty Pistons stood at the ready in gray armor and helmets, watching Akira as he led the Engines to their APC in the darkness.

He opened the hatch and climbed into the turret, observing the Pistons preparing for battle. In his mind's eye, he pictured his ancestors, gathered in the cold, wearing their heavy samurai armor before meeting the enemy on the battlefield.

They were with him now. He could feel it in his heart.

The relentless bombing continued, growing even more intense when the order came to finally roll out. Akira braced himself as the Hammerhead lurched onto the muddy road.

The convoy growled down the winding path out of the forest. As they neared the outskirts of the megacity walls, sporadic Nova Alliance civilians flooded away from the city, cheering at the convoy passing them.

Akira reached down to his duty belt and pulled out Blue Jay. He tossed the drone up. As it climbed, a mirrored feed transmitted to the team's HUDs. Most of the storefronts and apartments ahead were boarded up, but he saw heat signatures across the thermal scans.

"Get to the subways!" Akira shouted in French.

The Hammerheads rolled closer to the megacity walls. Each successive block was more wrecked than the last. Smoke drifted over the streets, the Coalition's attempt to block NA scans.

Blue Jay rose higher, sending back the first images of Coalition fighters gripping their energy spears, swords, and rifles. Dozens of snipers waited on the rooftops of derelict apartment buildings, and thousands of soldiers stood in the streets behind fast and agile tanks with triple-barreled turrets.

The combat map the Engines and Pistons accessed on their HUDs flashed with the enemy targets. Akira studied his mini-map for the enemy positions, as well as the Nova Alliance Strike Forces.

The other divisions were all ready to punch through the enemy lines.

"Silver Crane," Akira said over the comm, "this is SS1, in position, over."

"Roger, SS1," a pilot replied. "Echo on approach, targets acquired."

The scream of Short Sword fighter jets shattered the quiet,

and comets of blue flashed out of the dark sky. Explosions burst in the distance, and hunks of the megacity wall crumbled, opening up doorways into the city.

Missiles streaked out from another squadron, targeting Coalition tanks before they could scramble to the openings. The pilots confirmed direct hits.

"SS1, Silver Crane actual, you are clear to engage," said the rough voice of War Commander Contos. "Repeat, clear to engage. Liberate our walls."

"Copy, Silver Crane," Akira replied. "Liberation commencing." Reaching over his shoulder plates, he drew one of his two katana energy swords and angled it toward the sky. "Death from the Shadows," he said over the private channel to his squad. "Together, we are one."

"For Ghost," Perez said.

"For Ghost," they all repeated.

"And for all of the people held prisoner here," Frost said. "May we free them all."

Akira let out a war cry that reverberated through the streets as the Pistons and Juggernauts roared behind the Hammerhead. In answer, the Berserker horn of the Coalition hordes boomed.

The convoy rolled toward a ten-by-ten-foot hole in the bottom of the wall that separated them from the enemy.

Akira sheathed his sword and pulled out his RS3 rifle. He aimed the sleek, short-barrel at the hole, waiting for the targeting system to secure a clean reading.

"Get ready," Akira said.

The APC plowed through the smoke swirling out of the shattered hole in the wall. As soon as it crossed the barrier, the horizon lit up like a light show.

Akira ducked into the vehicle and secured the hatch.

Okami went stiff as plasma bolts and high-caliber rounds pounded the thick armor, rattling the vehicle. The combat medic and cleric Piston inside the troop hold hunched down.

"Just a little rain," Akira assured them. "Soon we will unleash the lightning."

"AI is salvation," said the cleric.

We'll see about that today, Akira thought.

The click of bullets and plasma bolts rang out around the vehicle. Overhead, the two turrets raked back and forth on the targets that Blue Jay had identified. Akira watched the feed on his HUD as enemy muzzle flashes went out like light bulbs.

He checked on Kichiro one last time, and then opened the hatch.

"Good luck, Captain!" shouted one of the Pistons.

"And be careful," Apeiron added.

"Make sure Okami stays out of trouble," Akira said.

He looked down at the wolfdog, who wagged his tail, anxious to get into the fight.

"Soon, little guy," Akira said.

Climbing out of the turret, he activated his jet pack, firing into the air. Tadhg, Frost, and Perez lifted into the sky like missiles from the other APCs and headed toward different rooftops.

Akira touched down behind the crumpled lumps of three dead armored snipers, who appeared gray in his imaging. A plasma bolt suddenly streaked past his kabuto, nearly taking off one of the horns.

He ducked down and then peeked the corner. A fourth sniper rose to look for him, but Akira got off the first shot. The bolts hit the soldier in the chest, and he slid to the side.

Akira finished clearing the roof and ran to the western edge for a view of the streets.

Gunfire and explosions from the other divisions rang across the city. MOTHs flew low, depositing more troops and ammunition to the front lines and then whisking away the injured.

On the streets, smoldering tanks sat idle, their guts blown outward. Three of the ten original vehicles were still functioning, and their triple-barreled turrets roved toward the Hammerheads and first wave of Juggernauts.

"Tadhg, three o'clock," Akira said over the team comms.

"I see 'em, bosu," Tadhg called back.

Coalition fighters scrambled for cover as the Engines picked them off from the cleared roofs. Akira targeted the soldiers with phased plasma pulse rifles, while Tadhg focused his cannon on the tracks of the tanks. The Juggernauts opened up with their own mounted Gatling guns, peppering the armor with simmering orange holes.

A fourth tank suddenly burst out of an underground parking garage and lurched toward the Juggernauts. Screaming, Tadhg unleashed a flurry of bolts into the tracks.

The tank jerked to a stop, disabled, and Tadhg rotated the cannon toward ten Coalition soldiers who had followed it out of the garage. Their bodies and armor exploded in the onslaught.

"God Level, mates!" Tadhg roared. "Know what I'm sayin'?"

Akira opened a rooftop door and entered the interior of the building. His targeting system located a group of ten fighters on the fifth floor, waiting to ambush the Juggernauts on the street. He selected single shot on his rifle before reaching the door to the hallway. Slowly, he pushed it open and raised his rifle.

Standing in the middle of the passage was a tattooed soldier holding an ancient assault rifle. He turned right into the bolt Akira fired.

The man burst into red mist and flesh that painted the walls.

Akira ran down the hall, chunks of flesh rolling off his armor. He pulled out a flash grenade and lobbed it into the room where the snipers waited. Slotting his rifle, he drew both energy swords.

A thump sounded, and cries rang out. Bolts and bullets punched through the walls and door. Akira waited a heartbeat, then shouldered right through one of the rotting walls. Drywall and plaster burst outward, and he charged the disoriented men, removing heads from spines with swift strokes.

He could have easily killed them with his rifle, but using his muscles to swing his swords was far more gratifying. Within ten seconds, only one soldier remained—a woman with a mohawk and a pierced navel under her scantily armored chest. She decided to take her chances jumping out the third-story window.

Akira walked to the window, surprised to see she had survived the jump. She crawled away, dragging her shattered legs a few feet before a Juggernaut crushed her with a massive metal foot.

The mech warriors were already advancing past the destroyed tanks, and the Pistons were close behind, hugging the sides of the buildings or keeping behind the Hammerheads for cover.

A Juggernaut had fallen at the end of the street, the diamond-shaped cockpit blown open from a shell that had obliterated the Piston inside. A combat medic and two technicians were on the scene, salvaging organs from the pilot and anything they could from the wreckage.

Akira took a stolen moment to check his HUD. Only ten Pistons and the one Juggernaut had perished in the first fifteen minutes of the battle. That was good, better than he expected.

More good news emerged on his map—Kichiro wasn't far. Only three miles away.

Akira directed Blue Jay to fly toward the position.

"Captain," Frost said. "I've got hostiles moving toward your location."

Akira saw the mirrored feed on his HUD as he ran. A group of Coalition soldiers moved out of an abandoned subway, right into her sights. They were all armored monstrosities with protruding bones and antlers on their helmets.

"Breakers," Frost confirmed.

"Good," Akira said. "A challenge."

"Save some for me," Tadhg said.

"Go ahead and take them," Akira ordered. "I'm going to free Kichiro."

***

The walls of the abandoned Hell Hive shook, dust raining from the ceiling. Chloe brushed Kichiro's mane. Dr. Cross was supposed to be here to see to the finishing touches on the horse, but she doubted he was coming now.

"It's okay," she whispered.

Chloe had been with the stallion since the bombing started. Two guards waited across the room, pacing anxiously. She wasn't sure if they were scared or anxious to get in the fight.

She wasn't sure exactly what was happening above ground, but she knew this was it—the Nova Alliance had come to liberate the city. Never in the past decade had they used bombs in areas with civilian populations.

This wasn't a huge surprise after rumors had found their way into the prison about Coalition attacks at the terraforming and reforestation projects.

Now Chloe understood the lungs and masks she had seen in the transformed patients over the past few months. The insane doctor was behind the attacks on those sites. And deep beneath the Paris streets, he was surgically preparing people for a world of smoke, fire, and poisoned air.

She stroked the horse again to help ease her own anxiety. This was the day she had waited a decade for, a day that she never thought would come.

Shouting snapped her out of her trance.

The door to the room swung open, and a Dread stormed inside wearing a metal breathing mask with squid-like tubes hanging over his chest. An entourage of Breakers followed the modified soldier, their helmets adorned with thick bone antlers. These were the best of the best, the special forces of the Coalition army.

The Dread pushed up their mask to expose the face of Dr. Cross. Blood-red eyes locked onto Chloe, but she didn't meet them. She was staring in shock at the metal jaw that now made up his chin and mouth.

He had already undergone the transformation.

"Ah, Chloe, what do you think?" he asked.

She did her best not to show any disgust as she nodded.

Dr. Cross walked over to the pen.

"Is the beast ready?" he asked.

The stallion whined behind the bars.

"It's okay," Chloe whispered.

Dr. Cross examined the horse. "Is he ready, or not?"

"Yes."

"Good. Take it," Dr. Cross said to his soldiers.

The Breakers surrounded the pen. One stepped inside and grabbed the chain reins. The horse pulled back, but the gigantic soldier yanked hard enough to pull the stallion through the open gate.

"Don't hurt him!" Chloe cried.

Dr. Cross shot her a glare, but another round of bombs thumped against the streets and buildings overhead, forcing his gaze to the ceiling as the lights flickered and streams of dust fell between them.

"They are getting closer, Doctor," grunted one of the Breakers. "We should move."

"Don't worry, you're coming with," Dr. Cross said to Chloe.

"But my uncle," Chloe replied. "I can't leave without—"

"Take her to her uncle, and then get her to the transports."

One of the guards grabbed Chloe.

"No, please, just let me go," she said.

"Let you go?" Dr. Cross asked.

He moved over to her, stopping inches from her face. "Soon you'll transcend with me. Doesn't that sound better than being left to rot in that disgusting, weak body of yours?"

The doctor reached up, stroking her cheek with a metal finger.

"Don't fear what's happening above the streets," he said with a reassuring, metal smile. "Soon it will all be over, and you will embark on a new journey to salvation."

It almost seemed to Chloe like he had wanted this Nova Alliance invasion, which almost scared her as much as his promise to transform her body for the new world he professed.

"I'll see you soon, Chloe Cotter," he said.

Dr. Cross left with the Breakers. They took the horse through a pair of open doors into the main chambers of the Hell Hive. Chloe's heart broke as she watched the stallion go. He was the one thing that had brought light to the darkness in these tunnels.

"I'm sorry," she said quietly.

For a fleeting moment she considered fighting. But what could she do against these men?

The guard yanked her and pulled her through the tunnels. The lights flickered on and off more violently as another volley of bombs shook the catacombs, thundering blasts resonating through the walls.

The prison wasn't far, but when they reached it, a body lay outside the open door. She couldn't see past the soldier, but the fact he drew an energy cutlass indicated something was wrong.

He lumbered ahead with the glowing blade illuminating the passage. Chloe followed, but hesitated at the sight of two men wearing brown fatigues with shotguns.

These were resistance fighters. She had heard about the resistance staging attacks recently, but these were the first she had personally seen in months.

"Watch out!" she shouted.

The two men whirled and fired shotguns at the lumbering Breaker, the blasts pounding his armor and knocking him back a single step.

Chloe put her hands over her ringing ears, but she still heard the Breaker let out a laugh as he brought his cutlass down. Both men jumped out of the way, but there was nowhere to go. Screams from the other prisoners rang out from the cells.

The Breaker thrust his cutlass, swiped, and sliced as the two rebels tried to reload their shotguns. The man on the left dropped his shells as he tried to avoid the glowing energy blade. His comrade managed to load a shell.

The Breaker faked a thrust to the left, followed by a swift jab right into the belly of the rebel, crunching through his spinal cord before he could fire the blast.

"No!" shouted the other man.

Laughing, the Breaker lifted the impaled rebel off the ground like a speared fish.

Chloe seized an opportunity and grabbed an energy blade from a sheath on the guard's belt. She jabbed it into the back of the armet encasing the Breaker's head. It punched through the metal, bone, and brain, and the Breaker staggered a few steps forward before collapsing.

She dropped the blade, her hands shaking.

The remaining rebel rushed to his dead friend and bent down.

"Jay," he said.

The man groaned in pain and let out a long, raspy breath.

Chloe maneuvered past the man she had just killed to her uncle's cell, adrenaline pumping through her body. She felt simultaneously nauseous and filled with rage and fear.

"Where are the keys?" she asked the rebel.

"I don't know."

He was young, maybe thirty, with dark brown hair that hung over one of his brown eyes. He slowly got up and motioned for Chloe to get back, then he pointed his shotgun at the door.

"Help us!" shouted other prisoners.

Another tremor shook the prison, a shower of dust raining down into Chloe's tangled hair. She and the rebel began freeing the others as the crack of gunfire resonated through the underground tunnels, drawing closer.

"Uncle Keanu," Chloe said when she reached him.

"Chloe, are you hurt?"

"No…no I don't think so."

She patted her bloodstained shirt with shaky hands.

Had she been shot and not realized it? She fought to control her breathing, struggling not to hyperventilate as she probed for any wounds.

She found none.

The blood wasn't hers, and the only injury seemed to be mental.

"They're coming, we must hurry!" the man with the shotgun yelled. He bent down to his friend who lay still. "I'm sorry, Jay. I'm so sorry."

After a final moment of hesitation, the man closed his eyelids and got up.

"Let's go," he said.

Chloe kept close to Keanu and the group of twenty freed prisoners. They rushed through the passages to an empty Hell Hive. Parts of Iron Wolves and other droids littered the room. The bombardment above rattled the metal limbs, shaking them like toys on the tables.

"We should stay here," said a cleric they had rescued. "If we go up there, we die."

"If we stay down here, we die," Keanu said.

Chloe pushed the panic threatening to fill her mind, recalling a sight that she had noted when she had first been escorted through these tunnels. "I think I know of a way to get out. Follow me."

They worked their way deeper underground. The rebel with the shotgun distributed two flashlights to guide them in the damp, narrow passages. Chloe led them to the section of tunnel where she remembered seeing the drainage passages blocked off by metal bars.

"There," she said. "I think they're drainpipes. They should lead to the streets."

The rebel pried off the bars and bent down to look into the narrow passage.

Another round of bombs exploded somewhere above. The ceiling shook, small cracks spiderwebbing through it.

"This drainage tunnel is too small," he said. "It might cave in with all those bombs. We really should stay here for now."

"I agree, it's too dangerous," Keanu said. He closed the door they had entered through, standing in front of it.

The filthy civilians huddled together around Chloe. A child in the group started crying at the next flurry of tremoring explosions overhead. The cleric lowered his head and broke into prayer over the group.

"We trust in AI to get us safely through these dark times," he said. "We trust…"

Chloe drowned out the prayer and focused on her uncle who suddenly motioned for the resistance fighter. The man joined Keanu at the door. They both stepped back a moment later.

"Quiet," Keanu said.

The rebel waved at the group to get back.

Someone was coming.

"Go, into the tunnel," Keanu whispered.

A woman led the way into the passage, crawling.

Chloe waited behind her uncle, shivering.

"You have to go too," Keanu said.

"Not without you," Chloe said.

"I'll be right behind you. I promise."

A loud crash reverberated through the walls, followed by a popping and cracking. As she got down on her knees to enter the tunnel, she saw an energy blade break through the door. The deafening boom of a shotgun followed.

She slid into the passage, moving on all fours away from the violence.

The glow of a flashlight bounced ahead, and Chloe did her best to keep up with the group. She resisted the urge to look over a shoulder.

The ceiling seemed to get lower, forcing her down to her belly in an inch of rancid water. She crawled through it, holding her breath.

The sound of gunfire echoed into the tunnel, her pulse quickening with the shots.

Chloe tried to turn, but there wasn't enough room, and she caught her shoulder on the stone, scraping the skin. She tried to move, but she was stuck.

A wave of panic gripped her.

"No, no, no," she cried.

She plucked her shoulder free, ripping skin and part of her shirt off. She continued moving on her elbows and legs, like she had seen soldiers do in the movies. Dust rained down as a quake shook the underground passage. A rat skittered out of a hole, fleeing just like Chloe was. More thuds overhead, one after another. Cracks fissured through the tunnel, soil falling in around her. Each time she wondered if the roof would collapse and crush her. She moved faster, tears creeping down her cheeks.

And then she saw it.

Light.

A trickle at first, then a ball.

The passage widened and Chloe got up on all fours again, moving faster.

She crawled out into the street, but ducked at the sound of footsteps and the muffled voices of soldiers in gas masks. In the glow of fires, she saw silhouetted figures at the other end of the street moving along the exterior of crumbling buildings and piles of smoldering rubble.

"Come on," came an adolescent voice.

The other escaped civilians were moving, and as Chloe got

up to join them, she heard a familiar neigh. She felt a tug on her arm, but she pulled away and stepped out into the street toward the noise. Through the smoke came the blue glow from two eye slots.

As they got closer, the light illuminated the helmet that she had designed.

"Kichiro!" she cried.

The beast struggled against chains held by a Breaker.

The warrior pulled harder, yelling until he finally let go and unsheathed his energy sword.

"Watch out!" Chloe yelled.

Kichiro looked at her, and then stood on its back legs, kicking the Breaker with a metal hoof. The impact crushed the front of his armor and sent him skidding over the street.

Chloe ran over and snagged the chains. She reached up with her other hand but hunched back down at the roar of fighter jets.

A squadron of Short Swords ripped through the clouds, firing missiles that streaked into buildings downtown with brilliant blasts. Chloe shielded her eyes and reached up to the horse as it neighed and paced nervously.

"It's okay, boy," she said.

She found a handhold on the saddle and prepared to climb up using the stirrups when she saw canisters secured to the side of the horse.

"I'm gonna flay you alive as you suck in this poison…" crackled a raspy voice.

She turned toward the Breaker, who had pushed himself up. Staggering, he held out a remote, and clicked a button.

The canisters hissed, venting some sort of gas in billowing hideous greenish plumes.

Kichiro turned his helmet and trotted in a circle. The frightened horse started to buck, trying to get the barrels off.

Chloe reached out to help, sniffling, mucus running from her nose. Sweat trickled down her flesh and saliva drooled out of her mouth. She started to cough, her lungs feeling as if she had taken in a heated gasp of air. Her heart rate escalated, and her right eye began to twitch.

The Breaker stumbled toward her with an energy blade.

Kichiro snorted and slammed his hoof into the man's head, crushing his helmet. The Breaker hit the ground just as Chloe collapsed on her stomach, heaving.

The glow of fires illuminated the blurred shapes of civilians falling to the street around them. Others were already down, jerking and spasming.

It took a few more seconds for Chloe's confused brain to register what was happening. The gift that Dr. Cross had prepared wasn't the modified horse, it was what the horse carried. Her work had been to ensure that the horse survived long enough to deliver the gift—a gift of death.

Kichiro seemed to understand it was being used too. It looked down at her, neighed, and took off running down the street.

Chloe used all her strength to turn and crawl back the way she had come. Her abdominal muscles clenched painfully. Bile rose in her mouth, and she vomited before falling to the stone street. She tried to move, but her limbs wouldn't respond. Closing her eyes, she let the darkness envelop her, praying for the pain to be over.

But anger kept her alive.

Anger at Dr. Cross.

Anger at the world.

Chloe wasn't sure when she woke up. She couldn't see, but she could breathe.

After struggling to open her eyes, she finally raised an eyelid to see the blurred shaped of her Uncle Keanu holding a gas mask to her face.

"Breathe," he said in a muffled voice. "Breathe, Chloe."

As she took in air, Chloe realized that she was being carried and her uncle was walking next to the person carrying her.

Rotating her head, she saw it wasn't a person at all. Her body was cradled in the robotic arms of a Nova Alliance Hummer Medical Droid.

"It is okay, child," the droid said in a female voice that was faint, but kind. "My name is Apeiron, and soon you will be one of my children."

15

"Hummer Medical Droids are recovering and transporting survivors," Apeiron said over the open channel. "I will save all that I can."

Akira watched the droids scooping people up in the streets and covering their faces with gas masks or helmets with built-in breathing apparatuses. Most of the civilians were lifeless and limp. The stink of urine and feces filled the air, soaking into the ground where the corpses had voided their bowels in death.

Okami was trotting alongside Akira with his tail between his legs, scanning for hostiles and sniffing the air for threats.

According to the sensor readings on Akira's HUD, they were the victims of sarin gas, a chemical weapon favored by the Coalition. He took a breath of filtered air, navigating the maze of dead with care. Most of the gas had dissipated, and what little that lingered was not a threat to him with his power armor.

On his HUD, he noticed Kichiro was moving, heading deeper into enemy-controlled territory. Blue Jay was up in the sky, searching for the horse, but due to the smoke, Akira couldn't see much in the aerial feed.

"Apeiron, see if you can get a visual on Kichiro," he said.

"Working on it, Captain."

Akira hunched down with his rifle at the next block. More dead were scattered over the asphalt, both civilians and soldiers.

"How did it come to this?" Akira whispered.

"I found myself not understanding human nature when I was first brought to life," Apeiron said. "Doctor Crichton helped me understand that human nature can be barbaric and evil, especially over ideologies."

Normally having a conversation during a battle would have been impossible, but with his chip and connection to INN, Akira could now multi-task like he had never imagined possible.

"Ideologies, land, resources," Akira replied. "Those are the three things that have led to acts of unspeakable horrors over the centuries."

"Like those in your Codex?"

"Yes, but the Codex focuses on a Warrior Ethos, which the Coalition does not adhere to. You see, my ancestors respected the enemy and granted them full honor in battle."

Okami trotted ahead, still sniffing for an ambush or explosives.

"The Coalition does not embrace the concept of symmetrical warfare," Akira said. "They will do anything to tip the scale in their favor and support their leaders, because they are a tribe."

"In my research, I have found that tribes dehumanize and demonize the enemy," Apeiron said.

Akira kept walking, scanning for hostiles as the rest of Shadow Squad cleared buildings and hunted down Coalition soldiers.

"I wish I knew how to break this cycle, Captain," Apeiron said.

A warm sensation spread across Akira's brain at the sight of a dead boy in the street. He knew he should feel horror and sadness, but the chemicals made him feel numb.

"You must start with children to break this cycle," Akira said quietly. "Children like this boy are born innocent, and like dogs, they don't turn into vicious animals unless they are trained."

He said a mental prayer for the child and kept moving. "After the teenage years, it's very difficult to change the hearts and minds of humans. Even more so with a tribe mentality. Only a great threat from the outside can break the mental chains."

"Can you elaborate?"

"Common threats bind humans. I've seen it with my own eyes. My ancestors made alliances with former enemies to beat back invaders. We also see enemy nations coming together after national disasters to help each other, and this is sometimes true for tribes as well."

"Thank you for your thoughts, Captain. They are very helpful."

Apeiron went silent as two squads of Pistons arrived to secure the area. Akira moved out with them through the dissipating smoke, navigating the craters and the pulpy remains of Coalition soldiers splattered across the ground. Those who weren't dead reached up for mercy, only for Akira to deliver them to their maker with a slash of his katana.

These warriors didn't deserve mercy. They had no honor.

Perez, Frost, and Tadhg worked their way through buildings. The other divisions continued to advance all around the city, taking it back, block by burning block.

Kichiro changed directions again, this time, headed toward the 1st Division. Akira reported the position to the rest of the squad.

"That's still two miles away," Tadhg said. "Too far out. Wait for us."

"He's right, Captain," Perez said.

"I'll come," Frost said. "On my way."

Akira didn't wait for her to catch up. He motioned for Okami, and the wolfdog bolted after him down an alley. Running fast but cautiously, Akira transitioned into what he was designed to be—a calculated, emotionless Engine of war.

Through his INVS eyes, he located a Coalition sniper in a third-story window ahead. He hardly slowed as he fired a kill shot with his plasma rifle. Sheathing the weapon, he drew his two katanas, sneaking up on a pair of Coalition soldiers hiding behind a doorway on the first floor of the same building.

They burst outside with energy axes flaming red. Akira hunched under their swings and side-slashed their chest armor. Before their insides sloshed out, he was running again, with Okami taking point. One man was still alive ahead. He reached up and screamed as the wolfdog bit right through his armored wrist and then tore into his neck.

"I'm almost there, Captain. Got held up," Frost said.

Akira did a quick scan over INN to check on the rest of the squad. Tadhg and Perez had joined forces, fighting together on a rooftop about a mile to the northwest. Frost was a quarter mile from Akira and closing fast.

He ran even faster as Kichiro's beacon blinked closer. All that separated them was a block of smoldering rubble from the impact of a Nova Alliance bomb. The bodies of civilians lay under the mounds, crushed and burned.

A memory of his wife threatened to emerge, but another dose of chemicals focused his mind. He slowed, shouldered his rifle, and crouched as the beacon stopped in what appeared on his mini-map to be a park.

The click of metal against metal drew his attention to the right side of the street. He moved his finger to the trigger and turned the rifle toward the noise. The weapon bucked against his shoulder plate when a single Coalition Breaker darted away from a burned vehicle.

The bolts slammed into his armor, burning into his heart. Okami trotted ahead to sniff out more enemies.

Akira followed around a skirt of smoking debris. On the other side, charcoaled playground equipment steamed in the darkness. In the center of the park, blue goggles glowed through a curtain of smoke.

Aiming his rifle, he centered the sights on an armored beast, laying on its side.

"Kichiro…" he whispered.

Okami wagged his tail but stopped.

Chains held the stallion to the ground. Kichiro let out a sad neigh and snorted a warning.

Shadows moved in the smoke, hulking forms holding dormant energy blades.

Akira switched his rifle for his katanas and whistled for Okami to get back.

"Doctor Cross knew you would come for him," a gruff voice boomed.

A Breaker with human bones antlering off a thick armet stepped in front of Kichiro, holding two sickle-style energy blades. Five more warriors fanned out through the park, wearing body parts from mutilated Pistons on their spiked shoulder plates.

Akira fell into an offensive stance with his swords.

"Captain, I would highly recommend retreating," Apeiron said.

Akira twirled the heated katanas. "You know I can't do that."

These weren't just any foot soldiers. They were all Breakers, the most elite of the enemy forces in the Coalition ranks. Fighting six would be certain death for a Piston, but for an Engine, it was a fair fight.

The enemy soldiers formed a circle around Akira. Just past them, he saw his stallion and the gas canisters secured to the horse's sides.

"What did you do to him?!" Akira roared.

"We turned him into a vessel of death," said the Breaker with the sickles. "Your beast delivered poison throughout these streets."

Anger coursed through Akira.

The soldiers closed in, snorting and grunting like a pack of wild animals.

Okami howled a warning as a mammoth Breaker charged from the side, raising an energy saw with serrated, super-heated blades above his head.

It was a mistake that would be the eager warrior's last.

Akira slashed at his wrists, where the armor was the weakest. The swift stroke cut through both like a sushi knife through toro, and the energy saw fell right onto the Breaker's helmet, crunching into his skull.

Two more warriors thrust their swords at Akira. He jumped back, falling into a defensive position with both swords up. They struck again, and he deflected the blows, with clashes of metal on metal. In a swift thrust, he buried a sword deep into the chest of the Breaker on his right.

The one on the left prepared to thrust his blade at Akira, but Okami yanked the man backward, biting on his leg. He chomped into the flesh, and the soldier fell to the ground, losing his grip on his blade.

Akira withdrew his blade from the chest of the first soldier, while Okami crunched through bone of the downed man. By the time Akira turned to help, the Breaker had his pistol aimed at the wolfdog.

Before he could pull the trigger, a .50-cal round entered one side of the Breaker's helmet and blew out the other.

"Death from the shadows," Frost announced over the comm. "Want me to take down the rest of these ogres?"

"No," Akira replied. "They're mine."

He was breaking normal combat protocol, but he wanted to kill these dishonorable men with his own blades.

Twirling the katanas, Akira approached the fourth Breaker. The lean man was armed with an energy cutlass. He was faster than the other soldiers, using lean legs to side-step and strike at Akira with a cutlass.

"Captain, I am detecting a large cluster of hostile forces moving toward your location," Apeiron reported. "It appears they were waiting in the catacombs."

She transferred imagery to his HUD as Akira swung a blade and spun around the man. The nimble soldier tried to dodge the attack, but when he turned, Akira punched a katana through one of his bloodshot eyes. A wisp of smoke rose from the crackling hole as Akira pulled out the blade.

Akira whirled and prepared for the final two soldiers. The leader pointed one of the sickles at him and a tall, thin warrior armed with a pair of energy spears stepped out.

He launched one of the spears at Akira, forcing him to duck. The blade slashed his jetpack, and a warning sensor beeped on his HUD.

Akira ran at the soldier, who prepared to throw the second spear. He leapt into the air, catapulting above his foe and tracing his left sword through a gap in the Breaker's armor, opening up his neck to the spine.

The final Breaker let out a grunt and charged while swinging two sickles. Akira brought up his swords, but didn't have the momentum he needed. He ducked below the sickles and speared the Breaker in the face with his decorative datemono that crested his kabuto.

The sharp V-shaped blades crunched through armor, bone, and brain. Akira pulled back to let the enormous soldier slump to the ground, dead.

Akira thrust a katana into the center of his chest just to be sure.

"You finished now, Captain?" Frost said over the comm. "That horde is on the way."

"Yeah," Akira grunted, twisting his sword out of the armor. "I'm done."

Gore dripped off his datemono as he turned and spotted her skull-and-flower mask on a nearby rooftop. She leapt down to the ground with a thud and ran to meet Akira where Kichiro lay chained.

Using his katanas, Akira carefully cut through the bounds. The horse hopped right up, whinnying and nudging Akira with his helmet.

"It's okay now," Akira said. "We're getting out of here."

Akira cut off the canister straps and climbed into the saddle. Reaching down, he helped Frost up.

"Let's go, Kichiro!" he shouted.

The horse took off through the park, galloping into the street. Okami ran by their side, barking excitedly until he heard the haunting howl of Iron Wolves.

A pack of two-hundred-pound hybrid beasts exploded out of the smoke at the intersection behind them, manes of jagged spikes sticking up, red eyes smoldering like flames.

Five Coalition handlers were close behind, shirtless, tattooed, and screaming through gas masks. Behind them were dozens of Coalition foot soldiers armed with flesh guns and plasma rifles that all aimed in their direction.

Muzzle flashes sparked across the street.

There was hardly any time to react to the hail of bullets that slammed into Akira and Frost, hitting their thick titanium plates. Those shots saved their lives by knocking both Engines off the horse before a subsequent volley of plasma bolts singed through the air.

Akira whistled for the horse to find cover, then hunched next to Frost behind a destroyed hover truck. Rounds slammed into the shell of the vehicle, sending up shards of metal. Each shot rang out against them like miniature bouts of thunder.

"You okay?" he asked Frost.

She nodded and lifted her sniper rifle up. Akira snuck a glance around the bumper. The hybrid wolves rammed into each other in an attempt to be the first to taste Engine flesh.

Okami came up next to Akira, snapping his metal jaws. He

used an arm to keep the wolfdog back and then went up on one knee to fire.

"Now!" Akira yelled.

The AI targeting system of his rifle locked onto three hostiles holding chains attached to the wolves. Each trigger pull put a bolt into the center of their chests, dropping them. Two more went down from .50 cal rounds to the skull.

"Oh shit," Frost said.

With no one to hold them back now, the wolves charged the Engines.

"Get in the air!" Akira yelled. He whistled at Kichiro to run, and then grabbed Okami. But when he tried to launch into the sky with the droid, his thrusters sputtered, and he came crashing down.

Okami tumbled out of his grip.

Akira got up as the pack of Iron Wolves ran full speed at him and the wolfdog. Reaching over his shoulders, he drew his swords and hunched down.

Okami growled and howled at the approaching beasts, standing his ground against the wolves over three times his size.

"Watch out, bosu!" Tadhg shouted.

His beastly black form suddenly landed in front of Akira with a crunch that sent a quake through the street. Tadhg caught a leaping Wolf by the throat, ripped off the head, and tossed the body away.

"Death from the shadows!" Perez yelled. He landed a few feet away, sword drawn in one hand and shield in the other. He held the shield up in front of Akira and Okami, protecting them from an onslaught of plasma bolts.

"Together, we are one!" Frost yelled from the sky.

She hovered overhead, firing her rifle and picking off targets.

Tadhg pulled his long saw-toothed sword and swung it toward the pack. Metal and flesh bodies exploded in a kiss of pink and gray gore.

Kichiro trotted over, stomping at the ground. Akira got back up onto the stallion as the rest of the horde raced down the street toward them.

With a whistle, Akira launched the horse toward them in the

smoke, bursting through while Akira jabbed his swords at heat signatures.

Cries of pain and horror rose in a cacophony of battle that Akira was all too used to. He felt like a machine, thrusting, swiping, and slashing from the saddle at the Coalition soldiers.

A soldier tried to sneak behind them for a better shot, but Kichiro kicked the man in the face, leaving his skull a bloody mess of mangled bone. Perez led the other Engines with his shield up as they joined the fight.

Tadhg swung his energy sword in wide sweeps, cutting Coalition warriors in half and removing heads with each stroke. Frost switched to her sword and fought by his side, dwarfed next to Tadhg's huge form, but no less ferocious.

They fought through the tide of soldiers, leaving a trail of dead and screaming soldiers.

Within minutes, the entire Coalition platoon was crushed.

Tadhg trotted over to Akira, chest heaving as he sheathed his long sword.

"You're supposed to be saving *my* ass." Tadhg patted Kichiro's armored neck. "Missed you, big guy."

"We owe you one," Akira replied. "Thank you, brother."

Frost descended next to them. "We need to get back to the 1st Division. There are more hostiles headed our way. I doubt we can handle all of them on our own."

"You are correct," Apeiron said over the team comm. "I have identified over one thousand hostiles moving in this direction."

Even Tadhg kept silent.

"Lead the way back, Okami," Akira said.

The droid ran toward the remaining allied forces a few blocks away, where Pistons crouched behind APCs and whatever cover they could find, preparing for the storm of armor rushing toward them. Juggernauts stood their ground, their plasma cannons angled down the road.

Akira guided the horse behind the three Hammerheads sitting idly on the street.

The ground rumbled as the Coalition army approached.

"I might need to cash in on that debt shortly," Tadhg said,

looking at Akira.

Akira watched the wall of smoke in the intersection ahead. Among the pounding of feet and claws, he heard the crazed, taunting howls of Breakers.

"Apeiron, we need reinforcements," he said.

"On their way," Apeiron said. "I would suggest sheltering here in the meantime."

The enemy screams grew louder, quakes vibrating down the road from their stomps. They slammed their weapons together in rhythm with their war cries, a cacophony of aggression rolling toward the Engines like a tidal wave of death.

Seventy-six Pistons angled their skeletal rifles toward the cloud of smoke encasing the Coalition warriors.

"We hold here!" Akira yelled. "Find cover and don't fire until I give the order!"

The soldiers maneuvered around, trying to find the best position to make their last stand.

"There are so many," said a Piston somewhere behind Akira.

"How can we win this fight?" asked another.

Akira knew many of the men and women around him were scared. They were outnumbered, and they would need a miracle to survive.

They need inspiration...

A reason to believe they might win, if only to encourage them to fight with everything they had. That was something he might be able to give them.

He ran over to Kichiro and jumped into the saddle, thinking back to that day on a hill in the Sea of Trees where they had first met.

"Show me how fast you are, Kichiro," Akira said.

The horse snorted and Akira steered him away from the cover of the APCs.

"Hold the line, do not give up a foot," Akira said as loudly as he could, his voice rising from deep in his chest. "They are louder, but we are braver! They are more, but we are stronger! We stand together, as one!"

Tadhg pounded his chest, starting a chorus of clanks and thumps. The noise grew, rising to meet the hellish voices of the

Coalition soldiers still masked by the smoke.

The blare of a Coalition war horn rose over it all, silencing both sides.

A long moment of quiet passed.

Then came the rumble of thousands of footsteps across the ground. The horde had been released.

Akira turned Kichiro toward the shapes of hundreds of armored soldiers emerging from the curtain of smoke. The rest of Shadow Squad joined Akira, standing behind the horse.

Perez raised his shield. "We're with you, Captain."

"One thousand against seventy," Tadhg said. "I like the odds."

Frost heaved a breath over the comms. "I just wish Ghost were here to stand with us in the end."

"He's with us in spirit, and this is not the end," Akira said confidently.

A Breaker War Lord on a hybrid horse led the army of soldiers, holding a double-bladed energy axe in each hand. Two Iron Wolves ran along either side, drooling bloody saliva.

Akira gave Kichiro a kick to the flank and the horse galloped to meet the War Lord in a fearsome charge. He feared this might be his last battle, but if this was his destiny, then so be it.

He raised his sword, adrenaline and rage roaring through him as he prepared to give the order to fire. Before he could even bring his sword down, the War Lord's helmet exploded from a flurry of bolts.

What the hell...

The ground rumbled underneath them, more violently than from the horde's charge, and a faint rattling echoed against the walls of the battered buildings. He twisted in his saddle as dozens of four-legged titanium machines with segmented arms skittered toward the Pistons.

These weren't Hummer Worker Droids. They were the new Canebrakes with simmering blue eyes in sharp, fan-shaped heads, and shoulder-mounted plasma cannons.

Their miracle had arrived after all.

"Everyone, get back!" Akira yelled.

Kichiro ran around the APCs as the Pistons scrambled for

cover. Even Tadhg moved out of the way.

Akira turned back to the now headless Coalition War Lord as he slumped out of the saddle and crashed to the asphalt.

For a moment, there was only the mechanical clanking of joints and hissing of hydraulics from the approaching war machines.

Then, the roar of a thousand warriors filled the night.

Hundreds of Breakers stormed past their leader, screaming at the top of their augmented lungs. But the bloodthirsty warriors slowed their advance when the war droids rushed past the Pistons and Engines.

"AI is salvation!" Perez yelled.

The machines clambered by, surging into the street. Energy blades fired from the segmented limbs, and their shoulder-mounted cannons belched plasma into the wall of Coalition armor.

Akira lowered his rifle, watching in awe of what seemed, in a morbid way, like artwork. The machines used their heated energy blades to amputate the limbs and heads of the Breakers. Each strike impaled the thick armor with jabs, splashing blood over the asphalt.

Within minutes the street ran red, the river flowing toward the human soldiers hiding behind APCs and inside of buildings. Akira couldn't believe it when he saw a Breaker fleeing the machines, a sight he had never before witnessed.

Cheers of victory rang out. Pistons raised their weapons and fists into the air. Rattling rose over the voices as the machines finished their slaughter and waited for orders.

Moments later they darted away, into the smoke, and deeper inside the city to hunt.

A civilian MOTH descended to the street as the sounds of battle grew distant.

As its ramp extended down, Akira zoomed in, wondering who was brazen enough to land here now.

A black armored Hummer Droid clanked down the ramp, followed by a man in pure white armor.

"Who the hell is that?" Tadhg asked.

Akira zoomed in further, seeing an AAS lightning and star

logo on the white helmet of the richest and most successful man in the world, Doctor Jason Crichton.

He crossed the street toward them with a black Hummer Droid.

"What are they doing here?" Perez asked.

"Replacing us with machines, apparently," Frost said.

"Sister, that'll never happen," Tadhg said. "Right, Captain?"

Akira simply stared at the gory scene. He didn't need a briefing to put together what they had just witnessed. AAS had designed and launched a new type of soldier, a machine that had eliminated an entire army of Coalition soldiers in a matter of minutes.

"Nova Alliance victory!" shouted a Piston.

Akira raised a sword into the air and humbly shouted, "AI is salvation!"

16

"You're sure this is a good idea?" Darnel asked.

Jason looked out the view ports of the Hammerhead APC. He took in a breath of his helmet's filtered air and observed the purple and blood-red sunset over the Paris skyline. Smoke fingered upward, choking out most of the view to the west, where the city burned.

"We came to oversee the deployment of the Canebrakes," Jason said, "and now that this part of the city is secured, I think it's time to figure out what Dr. Cross has been doing all these years."

Darnel charged a custom RS-3 rifle with the AAS logo on the barrel. "You sure you don't want one?"

Jason shook his head. "Petra always said guns do not suit me."

"I'd hate to hear what Betsy would have to say about this… I mean, you coming out here during a battle."

"She need not worry," Apeiron said. "I will never let anything happen to you."

The Hummer Droid followed Jason and Darnel out the back hatch of the APC. They both hesitated at the sight of corpses strewn about the cobblestone road. Even Darnel seemed bothered by the twisted bodies in the ash, the flesh burned beyond recognition.

Jason wasn't sure if they were friend or foe.

The Engines comprising Fire Snake Squad stood outside a secured entrance to the catacombs. Squad Lieutenant Andy Jackson, a seven-foot giant of a man, stepped forward. He took off his helmet, revealing dark skin and a mohawk.

"Doctor Crichton, Apeiron," he said in a rough voice. "The passages are secure of hostiles and booby-traps, but I can't promise there won't be any cave-ins after the bombings."

"Understood, we'll be careful," Jason said.

"If you're ready, I'll show you what we discovered," said Jackson.

"Lead the way, Lieutenant."

The Engine put his helmet back on and ducked under the lip of the entrance, entering a stone passage with lights snaking from the ceiling.

Jason was exhausted and disturbed from what he had witnessed from the safety of the APC over the past twelve hours. It was brutal above the streets, but he wasn't prepared for the Hell Hive he had found under them.

The Engines escorted them through the nightmarish caverns into the bowels of the catacombs. Their light beams flitted over cages, filled with the smoldering carcasses of burned animals, that Dr. Cross had left behind in his rush to escape the city.

Rifle cradled, Lieutenant Jackson strode through a chamber that had been used for manufacturing Iron Wolves and hybrid beasts. Burned lumps of tarantulas, bred for recon, and mounting cameras were scattered across the next room. Darnel and Apeiron kept close as Jason searched the remains.

"This way, Doctor," Jackson said. "We're almost there."

They continued deeper underground, passing through two more chambers and a prison that had held Nova Alliance citizens.

"Looks like some of them got away," Darnel said.

"Not all of them," Jason said.

He stepped around the body of a man impaled by a spear that a dead Coalition soldier still gripped.

"Resistance fighters," Darnel said.

Jason was happy to know that some had escaped, but they were the lucky few. Hundreds of thousands of civilians were already dead or would die in the hospitals, many due to the bombs and missiles meant for the Coalition targets.

"This is it," Jackson said. He directed his light into a room, the beam illuminating human skulls and other bones that had fallen from the stone shelves.

The spider chairs in the center of the room caught Jason's attention. He stepped over to them and began searching the crates scattered throughout the dark room with Darnel and Apeiron.

"What was this for?" Darnel asked. He held up a helmet

with tubes attached to a breathing apparatus.

"I have a theory," Apeiron said.

"So do I," Jason said. "You go first."

"I believe that the burning of our restoration sites is linked to whatever work Doctor Cross was performing here," she said.

Jason felt a chill up his spine. "Lieutenant, get a message to Command and tell them to find Doctor Cross, immediately."

"Yes, Doctor," Jackson replied.

Jason continued surveying the remains, trying to transplant himself into the mind of the mad Coalition doctor.

What the hell are you planning?

"It was like he *wanted* us to attack," Jason said. "But he didn't know about the Canebrakes, which is why he left in such a hurry."

They secured the mask and other evidence and left the room to explore more chambers. Jackson kept close to Jason and stopped to relay a message.

"I've just received word from Command that an Engine team is being deployed to search for Doctor Cross, but he has already escaped the city," said the Engine.

"We will find him," Apeiron said. "Do not worry."

"Let's get back to the APC," Jason said. "I've seen enough."

They returned to the surface, carefully moving through the passages. The APC waited topside and Jason ducked into the safety of the armored vehicle. They drove back to the MOTH in silence.

Once inside the cockpit, Jason strapped into the seat and looked out over the destroyed skyline.

"Where to, Doctor?" asked the primary pilot.

Jason thought for a moment. He wasn't sure where he wanted to go next. Part of him wanted to return home, to be with his family, but with the world at war and the project sites damaged or still burning, there was too much to do. And with so much at stake, he knew he had to make a sacrifice.

He had to take things to a new level.

"Take me to Sector 220," Jason said.

"You got it, sir," replied the pilot.

The MOTH thrusters rotated and fired, vaulting the aircraft

into the sky.

"Want to tell me why we're going to Sector 220?" Darnel asked. He had to be as exhausted as Jason, but his eyes were alert and his posture stiff.

Jason stared out the cockpit at the clouds and smoke drifting through the angry red sky. Every second that passed, more toxic gas and smoke pumped into the atmosphere.

"Something I should have done months ago," he finally said. "I'm going to have Apeiron install an L-S88 chip in me."

"Excellent decision," Apeiron chimed in. "Once you are chipped, you will be able to connect to INN and access any piece of intel with a single thought."

Jason nodded enthusiastically, thinking of how much this would enhance his daily life. Instead of relying on his obsolete Commpad, he could download reports to his mind and tap into millions of different visual systems.

And be even more distant from your family...

The red lights of the Titan Space Elevator habitats came into focus, and Jason reconsidered what he was about to do.

"Love before work," he whispered.

Petra's final words had never seemed more relevant, and he realized they could have several meanings. The L-S88 *would* put love before work. He could do far more with access to INN, allowing him to spend more time with his family.

The aircraft docked a few minutes later, and Darnel opened the hatch into the troop hold. As Jason moved to follow, Apeiron reached out with her metal fingers.

"There is something I need to tell you, Jason," she said. "Something that will change everything, but I am not sure you are ready to hear it."

Jason swallowed hard, anxious by the slight change in her tone that indicated this wasn't something good. "If it will change everything, then you need to tell me now," he said. "Especially if it puts lives at risk."

"How about we get you chipped first to prepare you for what must be done," she said cheerfully. "I will need your help."

***

War Commander Contos gathered with the Stone Mountain Battalion outside a magnificent 17th century church. Just below the shattered steeple, a single Canebrake perched on the tiled roof, eyes scanning the streets from both sides of its fan-shaped head.

Sporadic gunfire echoed through the night as the final Coalition soldiers fought against a new breed of soldier that did not bleed or fear—that stormed the battlefield with the intel of an entire army.

"I knew this day would come," said the War Commander. He gestured for Akira to follow him to the church.

Frost, Tadhg, and Perez remained outside with Okami, who charged in his power crate. Kichiro grazed on hay that Akira had set out. The horse was doing well, aside from a few minor injuries.

"Let's talk plainly, Captain," Contos said, as he and Akira stepped into the church. "Man to man, without any tech in our ears."

Akira took off his kabuto so Apeiron could not hear their conversation. A group of Pistons worked at makeshift tables. They came to attention in front of the War Commander.

Contos led Akira down the tiled nave, passing under beautiful murals of ancient scenes from the Bible. They stopped in front of an altar, directly under a cross.

"For thousands of years, we fought for God and land and resources," Contos said in a deep, grizzled voice. "Not much has changed, aside from who we believe is the Almighty."

"AI is salvation," Akira said.

Contos nodded and turned. "You are my most trusted Engine, Akira, and I love you like a son. Just like I loved Shane. What happened to him was not your fault. It could have happened to any of us."

"I should have…"

"You can't change the past, but you can learn for the future."

"Yes, War Commander."

Akira met his gaze, this man he respected more than any other, a man he would follow into death a thousand times.

"I called you here because I want to ask you a question, Akira," Contos said.

Akira nodded.

"Is Apeiron our friend, or is she our enemy? You have worked with her exclusively in the field, and I want you to speak honestly."

Akira did not know quite how to answer the War Commander. Saying that Apeiron was an enemy would be blasphemy, but there must be a reason Contos would ask him.

"I believe she's a friend, and is working to save humanity," Akira said. "There's no doubt the Canebrakes saved countless innocent lives today, but the power they brandished strikes fear in my heart."

"Indeed." Contos raised his chin. "We are Engines, protectors of the Nova Alliance, once considered immortal among men, but today that changed… and tomorrow it may end."

To Akira, the towering giant in front of him was a god, but not even this veteran of a hundred battles could stand against the Canebrakes. Apeiron and her metal legions had accomplished in one day what the Nova Alliance had failed to do in a decade. And no matter how many enhancements or augmentations the doctors made to his body, Akira would never be as strong or as fast as a Canebrake.

Tadhg lumbered down the nave, crushing glass under his boots.

"War Commander, Captain, my apologies," he said, bowing slightly to Contos. "The MOTH is ready to go."

Contos put a hand on Akira's shoulder plate. "Together, we are still one," he said. "Ghost lives on in each of us, singing from Valhalla."

Akira smiled, picturing his friend singing as he slayed demons.

"Find this bastard Doctor Cross and bring him to me," Contos said. "I will deal with him personally."

"Yes, War Commander."

Akira left the nave and headed outside to his animal and droid companions.

"I'm sorry, my old friend, but you can't come on this mission," Akira said to Kichiro.

The stallion whinnied and nudged his head against Akira's shoulder.

Okami whimpered from between the stallion's front legs, his favorite place to hang out.

"You have to stay here too, boy," Akira said.

Okami moved between the armored legs of his stallion friend, and then jumped at Akira's, his way of saying he wanted to be picked up.

"I know you want to come, but you two can't fly," he said.

"I might be able to fix that," Apeiron said.

Akira snorted. "I like them both just the way they are. Watch out for them while we're gone, okay?"

"I will make sure both are well looked after," Apeiron replied.

Akira hesitated, hating to leave his companions behind, but where they were going, it was too great of a threat. He gave them each one more scratch and walked off, trying his best to ignore their cries.

Okami barked and ran after Tadhg, nipping at his heels.

"Later, ankle biter," Tadhg said.

"He says to fuck off," Frost said with a laugh.

Across the airstrip, two other Engine squads, the Fire Snakes and Blood Cranes, were taking off in MOTHs. Soon, ten more teams would be *en route* to Megacity Moscow to prepare for the invasion. The city was protected by three times as many Coalition troops as Megacity Paris had been. It would not be easy to take, even with air support and the Canebrakes.

Akira walked up the ramp and racked in with the rest of the squad. As the engines fired, he opened his armored storage unit and pulled out the Warrior Codex.

During the first part of the flight, he drew a picture of a Canebrake slaughtering the Breakers on the battlefield. Contos's question about Apeiron lingered in his mind as he sketched the machines.

"Ugly metal bastards, if you ask me," Tadhg said. "And you really suck at drawing, bosu."

"Can you even write?" Frost asked from across the troop hold. "We know you can't read."

Tadhg leaned forward, his hair falling over his chest armor. "Why do you always break my balls?"

"Why do you never shut your trap?"

She rested her eyes and Akira turned the page and started writing for the next hour.

The day we became obsolete...

Tadhg glanced over. "The day we became obsolete? Who the hell is obsolete? Not me, bosu. I'm God Level, mate. Know what I'm sayin'?"

He pounded his chest hard, plates clanking over the rumble of the engines.

"This is far from the first time previously top-of-the-line war technology has become obsolete," Perez said. "History is filled with countless examples."

"Save the history lessons, mate. We aren't weapons. We are warriors."

"Actually, aren't they the same..." Frost shook her head, sighed, and closed her eyes. "Wake me up when we get there."

An hour later, Apeiron connected to their chips.

"Shadow Squad, prepare for briefing," she said. "Uploading... now."

In his mind's eye, Akira saw the city of Moscow, marked with the known Coalition locations. Most were underground subways and old bunkers used as operation centers.

"All of our UAVs have been shot down since we took the first images, and it is too risky to send up more," Apeiron said. "They know what is coming after Paris and are dug in for the fight."

On Akira's HUD, a two-story building came up on their mini-map, set between a block of apartment buildings inside the city limits, deep in enemy territory.

"Your objective is to penetrate the defenses of the target building," she said. "We believe this could be one of Doctor Cross's labs."

"Little Napoleon?" Tadhg asked. "Holy shit."

"If he is there, he's going to be well guarded," Frost said.

"You scared?" Tadhg asked.

"You know it's not that, you dumb shit."

Perez shook his head. "For once, can you guys get along?"

"Why would we want to do that?" Frost asked.

"Focus dammit," Akira snapped in a rare display of anger. "This is our chance to avenge Ghost. We might not get another. Stop the squabbling, and focus on what's actually important."

The lights in the belly of the MOTH went dark and the squad made their final preparations. An hour later, the craft began to descend.

"Approaching LZ," Apeiron said.

Tadhg opened the ramp, revealing dark clouds whipping past. "Time to prove we're not obsolete."

"Death from the Shadows," Akira said.

The other Engine teams would be repeating their own mottos as they dropped into the night. Akira brought up their locations on his HUD. The Fire Snakes and Blood Cranes had already jumped from their MOTHs and were descending toward aerial defense batteries to take them out before the main invasion.

A green light flashed, and Akira motioned for the squad to jump. Tadhg was the first one out, with Frost going next, then Perez, and Akira. As he plummeted into the darkness, Akira considered what they might face.

There would no doubt be heavy resistance, but if they could take out Dr. Cross, it would be a major victory. And when Moscow fell, the war would be all but over, especially if they had the head of the insane doctor, something Akira hoped to take with his own sword.

The first thirty seconds of freefall was oddly calming. He couldn't see the silhouettes of his comrades, but he watched their IR tags through his INVS eyes. They spread out below in unison. He put his arms and legs out, over four hundred pounds of armor and flesh dropping fast.

An explosion burst in the center of the city, followed by a series of blasts from a Short Sword fighter jet carpet-bombing aerial defenses.

Akira shifted his arms toward his side and formed a missile

with his body, spearing through the clouds at terminal velocity of almost one hundred eighty miles an hour. The other Engines did the same.

At ten thousand feet, tracer rounds lanced away from the rooftops, some coming dangerously close to the Engines. Their IR tags peeled away from the enemy fire.

Their target building came into focus, a small red box around it. A pair of twenty-story apartment buildings towered over the small structure.

Heat signatures emerged on the rooftops of every building in the landing zone. Akira studied the view as he fell. An aboveground parking garage and a park with mature trees were the only cover around the target. Two APCs poked out under the canopy of trees, and three operational pickup trucks sat in the parking garage. The Coalition didn't even try to hide the tank on the top level, its two barrels aimed at the sky. In all, the targeting system on Akira's HUD calculated over one hundred hostile forces in the vicinity.

"Going dark," Akira said.

His HUD clicked off, and Akira relied on his INVS eyes to see in the pitch black. He rocketed through the air, increasing his speed. Using buildings as markers, he estimated his height at three thousand feet. Extending his arms and legs, he pulled out of the suicide dive. As his speed slowed, he activated the metal wing flaps under his arms. The ground rose up to meet his boots, wind rushing over his armor. He directed his body toward the apartment building over their target. His timing had to be perfect or he would be spotted.

Akira activated his jetpack at the last moment, the thrusters blasting him upward. He turned them off and descended to the roof with a thud, directly behind two Coalition soldiers. By the time they turned, he had cut them in half with two swift swings of his katanas. Blood splattered the roof, sizzling from the heated blades.

Frost, Perez, and Tadhg put down across the roof, and by the time the upper halves of the soldiers in front of Akira had fallen to the sides, the other three guards had also toppled over without their heads.

Roaring Short Sword fighter jets blasted across the horizon. Missiles streaked away from their black wings, pounding anti-aircraft positions across the skyline. One of the jets launched a salvo at the building adjacent to their location, eliminating the snipers there.

Akira watched a heat signature catapult upward and then plummet back down, crunching in the street below. A streak of light flashed from another rooftop, chasing one of the escaping jets.

The Engines ducked down as the aircraft roared overhead.

It banked hard to the right, trying to roll away, but the rocket had locked on. An explosion burst, fire blooming out of the sky. Akira said a prayer for the pilot and then motioned for the Engines to follow him toward the rooftop door. Halfway there he noticed an IR tag falling from the clouds. The pilot had bailed, and the parachute was sailing east, right toward the epicenter of the Coalition soldiers.

"Should we try and help him?" Frost asked.

Akira considered it, but they were too far away.

The pilot was on their own, and so were they.

"Let's move," Akira said. "We have a wolf to hunt."

17

Chloe Cotter awoke to the smell of chemicals. The air tasted like plastic and metal. She struggled to open her eyes, but her eyes felt... odd.

"Hello, child."

The voice, female, came from somewhere close, although she wasn't sure how close. It sounded like it was right in her mind. She remembered the voice, but she wasn't sure how, only that it soothed her heart and helped her relax.

Chloe opened her eyes. She was in some sort of medical room. A Hummer Droid with a red cross on its shoulder plates stood by her bedside.

"Hello, Chloe Cotter, my name is Apeiron. We met on the street in Megacity Paris, but I am not sure if you remember. I have restricted your memories for now, due to the trauma you experienced."

Chloe struggled to recall the accident. She tried to move, but her body seemed paralyzed. The only thing that seemed to work were her eyes. They roved around the white walls of the small room.

"Everything is okay," Apeiron said. "You are safe here."

"Where am I?"

"A field hospital outside of Megacity Paris."

Garbled memories surfaced in her mind: an image of her parents telling her to hide, then a visual of Coalition soldiers and a cobblestone street.

"What happened to me?" Chloe asked. She budged her right leg, and then wiggled her fingers.

"Please, stay calm," Apeiron said.

The Hummer Medical Droid moved closer and reached down to the sheet over her body. Seeing the robotic hand sent Chloe into a panic. She used all of her strength to move her legs, and in the process, a finger caught on the sheet, pulling it off her body slightly, exposing her chest and torso.

Chloe stared, her brain seeming to stall as it tried to register what she was looking at.

A swollen scar ran down the center of her chest.

"What did you..." she choked. "What did you do to me?!"

The droid quickly covered her up, but the mental damage was done. Chloe reached up to her head, touching a bandage around her skull. Something warm rushed into her veins through a thin tube coming out of her right arm.

"It is okay, please rest," Apeiron said. "Everything is fine."

She closed her eyes, unable to keep them open. Weightlessness set in, and then there was darkness.

Sometime later, Chloe woke to sunlight filtering in through a gap in the curtains. She squinted at the glare. She didn't know where she was, but that didn't scare her.

A sense of calm and peace passed over her mind.

"Chloe Cotter, you are awake," said a soothing female voice.

A white Medical Droid went to the window, pulling back the curtain to reveal a long hallway of other curtains. "How do you feel?"

This time, the voice definitely seemed to be coming from her mind.

"My name is Apeiron. Do you remember me?"

Chloe pushed herself up, still feeling relaxed. "How can I hear you in my head?"

"We are connected, my child," Apeiron replied. "Do not be afraid, Chloe Cotter. My duty is to assist in your recovery."

Chloe stared at the droid, trying to figure out why she was in a room sectioned with curtains, no doubt shielding other injured people.

"What happened to me?" Chloe asked.

"The last time we had this conversation, you got very upset, so this time I am going to bring in someone who you trust."

A figure emerged from behind the droid, limping into view.

"Uncle Keanu?" Chloe muttered. "Uncle, what happened?"

He smiled his handsome, bearded grin. "AI is salvation."

The drape closed behind Keanu, who put a hand on Chloe, still smiling warmly.

"What do you remember?" he asked.

"Nothing..."

"It's probably better that way."

"No... I want to know what happened to me." She looked down. "Why do I have this scar?"

He took a seat in the chair by her bed. "Chloe, do you remember what happened to your mother and father during the revolution?"

"They... they hid me, and then..."

"I took care of you," Keanu finished. "We stayed together, but then you were captured, and you were forced to work in the catacombs."

She didn't remember any of that.

"Then what?" she asked. "How did we get here?"

"A few days ago, the Nova Alliance stormed the walls to take back the city, and we escaped."

A partial flashback entered her mind and then vanished before she could latch on. She remembered something before the attack. A chamber, Iron Wolves, a beautiful hybrid stallion with obsidian black flesh.

She reached up to an itch that seemed to be coming from inside her skull. Her fingers touched the bandage.

"What did they do to me?" she asked.

Keanu looked over his shoulder at the Hummer Droid. Chloe blinked, suddenly able to see a tiny scratch on the robot's helmet, as if she was staring through a pair of binoculars.

"My eyes... something's wrong with my eyes," Chloe said.

"I know this is going to be hard to understand," Keanu said, "but please, don't be afraid. Everything is going to be okay."

"Tell me what's going on. Please, Uncle Keanu."

He swallowed, paused, and said, "You died, Chloe, and Apeiron brought you back to life."

"What? What do you mean..."

"She gave you new organs, new eyes, and an L-S88 chip in your brain."

"That is why you can hear me," Apeiron said in her mind. "I can talk to you, or if you wish, I can stop talking to you, but please consider giving me a chance to assist in your recovery. I enjoy talking to my children, and you are a very special child."

"Children?"

"Those connected to my network are my children."

"You're an OS," Chloe said. "Not a mother."

"Yes, that is correct."

"Can you read my thoughts?" Chloe asked.

"No, but I was able to pull up some helpful intel by mapping various connections in your neurons—what you might call your subconscious. It could end up leading us to Dr. Cross.

"Doctor..." Chloe whispered.

An image of the doctor's evil smile poked into her thoughts. And then other memories... horrifying memories of the transformations and Kichiro. She sucked in a deep breath as she remembered the gas hissing out of the canisters secured to the stallion's armor.

Keanu put a hand on her arm. "It's okay."

She shivered, but not from the cold. It was the memory of the horse running away, spreading that gas throughout the city. The poor animal had been used as a tool of destruction.

"Kichiro, what happened to him?" she asked.

"He has been reunited with his handler, Captain Akira Hayashi," Apeiron said. "Do not worry, Kichiro is alive and well."

"And the other prisoners?"

"Unfortunately, most of them perished."

A painful knot formed in Chloe's gut as she remembered all those she had tried to help. Had it all been for nothing?

"I can sense your distress, child," Apeiron said. "I assure you, we were able to save a few."

Chloe fell silent, thinking of the girl ahead of her in the tunnel and the cleric, hoping they had made it. Were they among those saved by Apeiron? She wasn't sure she wanted to know the answer.

She returned her attention to the droid. "Do I have to stay connected to you?"

"No," Apeiron clarified. "But there are many benefits to being connected to the INN. You can download information simply by thinking it. If you want to learn Spanish, you can download it... if you want to learn how fly a MOTH, you can download that, too, although some downloads take much longer than others."

"That sounds pretty damn great," Keanu said. "Maybe I need to get a chip, too."

"Soon, the technology will be available on a wide scale after all SANDs patients have received them," Apeiron said. "Not only can we help them recover from SANDs, but by connecting people to INN, we can monitor their health permanently and tune the chips to react to any sign of illness before a person even realizes they are sick."

Chloe wasn't sure what to think. She was alive, yes, but she was no longer herself. Being connected permanently to this network that she had no control of frightened her. Sure, the chip could heal her, but what else could it do with this AI in her head?

"I will leave you alone for now," Apeiron said. "If you need anything, do not hesitate to ask. I can respond immediately through your chip."

The droid turned and promptly walked down the aisle.

"I know this is a lot to take in," Keanu said, "but what's important is you're safe now. Megacity Paris is back under Nova Alliance control, and we have a future. A bright one at that."

She wiped a tear from her eye. "I... I am never going to be the same."

"You're still you, Chloe," Keanu said. "But perhaps what you need, or what we both need, is a change of scenery. There are too many memories in this city."

Another tear spilled as she nodded.

"I'll let you get some rest now," Keanu said. He rose to his feet, wincing. "I'm staying in a refugee camp about a mile away. I'll be back later to check on you, okay?"

"Okay. Thanks, Uncle Keanu."

"I love you."

"I love you, too."

He gently put a hand on her cheek and smiled one last time before pulling the curtain almost all the way shut. She watched him through the gap as he limped away. It was hard to watch, but he was right—what mattered was they had survived the war.

They were alive.

Closing her eyes, she tried to rest, but the footfalls outside kept her alert. Just as she began to drift off, a pair of footsteps stopped outside her curtain.

"Excuse me," said a male voice. The curtain pulled back, and a handsome face emerged. She recognized the young man with brown eyes and thick brown hair, parted to one side.

"Hi," he said. "My name is Cyrus."

Chloe sat up. "I'm sorry... I remember you, but I'm not sure where from."

He looked at her like a sad child. "I'm sorry. I just thought I'd come see you while I was here to see your uncle." He took a step closer. "Do you remember escaping the prison at all?"

She shook her head. "Were you..." Chloe started to say. "You're the resistance fighter."

"Yes, I was with my brother. We were trying to find my dad."

"I'm so sorry, I—"

"We both knew the risk, and my brother's death was not in vain. He helped save you."

"Did you find your father?"

He hung his head low, shaking it. "Not yet. I'm searching the hospital for him today, but thought I'd say hello when I noticed you here. I wanted to thank you."

"Thank me?" Chloe asked. She could only think of all the people who had died following her out of the prison. "So many didn't make it out. How can you thank me?"

"I know things didn't end up how we had planned, but without your help, all of us would be buried underground. At least now, I'm here. You're here. And we're not alone."

Chloe sat up straighter. She reached up to the bandage, wincing after a jolt of pain.

"Are you okay?" he asked.

"Yeah." She rubbed one of her wounds. "I'm sorry. I don't usually look like this. I didn't really expect visitors."

"I didn't mean to intrude, but I hope you know, even with those bandages, you still look beautiful."

She avoided his gaze, her cheeks warming from embarrassment. "Thanks."

"Sorry, I shouldn't have said that. It's probably inappropriate right now. I swear I'm not always so brazen, but I have a bad habit of saying whatever's on my mind." He hung his head. "At least, that's what my father always told me. He said it would get me in trouble one day, and well, here I am."

"It's okay, really, I appreciate it." She thought about Apeiron and all the secrets of the L-S88 chip and her own surgery she still didn't understand. "We could all use a little more honesty like that."

He nodded. "I'd better let you rest." He began to pull the curtain back, but she held up a hand.

"Hey, Cyrus."

He turned. "Yes?"

"Come back and see me, okay?"

"I will."

"I hope you find your father."

"Thank you."

He closed the curtain, and she rested her head on the pillow, letting out a sigh. Her new heart was fluttering, but this time it wasn't from fear. For the first time in months, she felt what might be considered happiness from a human connection.

Maybe things are going to get better, she thought.

She closed her eyes, knowing better than to hope. Hope had been ripped from her the day the Coalition invaded.

***

Frost crouched on a rooftop and transferred the view across the squad HUDs as she roved her sniper rifle. Three soldiers in the park, three more in the parking garage, and two squads patrolling around their target building.

Taking out the troops from here would be easy, but Akira couldn't risk being detected when hundreds more could be here in minutes.

"Perez, hold here with Frost," Akira said. "Tadhg, you're with me. We'll advance to the building, but if we get into trouble, you know what to do."

Frost dipped her helmet. "Death from the Shadows."

"Together, we are one," Perez said.

Akira checked his HUD as he approached the rooftop door, checking for heartbeats on the other side. A single bleep emerged in the mini-screen.

Tadhg collapsed his pulse cannon and pulled out his plasma pistol. He grabbed the door handle and opened it.

An unsuspecting guard was coming up the stairs as Akira entered. He fired a three-round burst of plasma bolts into his helmet, then reached out and grabbed him to prevent the dying man from falling down the stairs.

Tadhg moved past as Akira lowered the corpse to the floor quietly. They entered a hallway and crouched.

Moonlight streamed through a gaping hole on the right side. The rocket or bomb had destroyed the first three apartments. Akira tested the flooring, then crouched for a scan. Using his INVS eyes, he marked the locations of the heat signatures on his HUD mini-map for the other Engines.

Next, he proceeded to an elevator shaft at the end of the hallway, where he tested the cable. Feeling secure, he pulled out his tactical cable descender, locked it onto the cable, and began the journey down.

His boots hit the floor with a light thud. He unlatched, brought up his rifle, and strode into the lobby. A single guard stood at the open exit door with his back to Akira and Tadhg. Akira snuck up and twisted the man's helmet, breaking his neck, and pulled his limp body away into the shadows.

Tadhg crouched for a look outside before giving Akira the nod to advance.

Keeping low, Akira ran across the sidewalk and to a vehicle for cover. A patrol of three soldiers headed in his direction. He took a knee and slotted his rifle slowly, careful to not make a sound.

Reaching back with his other hand, he drew both of his blades. A swift stroke cut off the first soldier's head. Akira sprang toward the other two men, slashing one across his chest and stomach. Guts sloshed out as the man crumpled. The third soldier tried to raise his rifle, but Akira hacked it in half and used the hilt to crush his helmet with a punch of metal.

Tadhg ran over.

Keeping low, they continued toward the machine gun nest on one side of the two-story building. Their power armor masked their heat signatures, and Akira didn't bother trying to take it out.

He continued toward the parking garage, crouching behind a brick wall. Four soldiers held sentry on the third level. There was no way to get past them without being seen. Akira selected single shot. The targeting system locked on, and he pulled the trigger four times, hitting each of the exposed helmets. Brains exploded out of the exit wounds before the poor bastards had enough time to register what had hit them.

Tadhg hopped over the wall and took off running as the soldiers dropped. Akira followed, halting when a head popped up in the machine gun nest.

Frost let loose with two suppressed shots, blowing off the top of the skull.

Akira and Tadhg got to the front of the building without a single enemy shot fired. Heartbeats blinked on the screen on their HUDs. Three, then four.

Tadhg stepped back from the front door with his plasma cannon aimed at it. Akira kicked it in, and Tadhg unleashed a flurry of bolts into the room. Blue flashes illuminated the interior, meat and metal exploding where the bolts impacted Coalition soldiers.

Akira moved inside, his boots slurping through the pulpy remains and crunching over armor. Leading the way, he opened a door to a dark stairwell and descended, clearing each landing until they arrived at the bottom, five stories below.

A ping on his HUD caught his attention. Frost marked a convoy of APCs headed their way.

"Shit, they know we're here," Akira said. "We got to move fast."

Tadhg took point and entered a chamber full of gurneys and medical equipment. Cryo-chambers framed the walls, their lids open.

"Apeiron, we seem to have discovered one of their Breaker facilities," Akira said. "No sign of our target."

"Copy that, keep searching," she replied.

They advanced through the maze of gurneys. The tap of dripping water came from the center of the room. Crouching, Akira examined a drain clogged with fresh flesh and blood.

Tadhg continued toward two metal doors at the other end of the room. They opened onto a hallway marked by bloody tracks across the floor. A humming noise grew louder as they trekked onward.

The next open door exposed a mezzanine. Akira moved slowly, his foot making a slight clanking. A cloud of flies burst up from corpses piled on the tiled floor below.

Armored plates, helmets, and prosthetics lay stacked on carts and in open crates throughout the room. There were ten seats with spider-like appendages holding surgical devices, and open helmet halves around headrests. Metal leg and arm clamps were covered in dried blood on the surgical seats.

Akira zoomed in on robotic limbs and torsos in crates throughout the Breaker facility and Hell Hive that seemed like a modern Frankenstein lab.

Tubes of ribbed metal snaked away from a helmet on the ground, and inside, a tarantula had burrowed. It scurried out as the flies swarmed Tadhg. He swatted the insects away.

Over the buzzing, came a raucous whooshing sound.

"Tadhg, get down!" Akira screamed.

A rocket streaked away from a raised platform across the room. The cloud of flies and Tadhg disappeared in an explosion.

Akira dove to the platform to avoid another rocket that blew up above his kabuto. Hunks of concrete crashed down on his plates. He pushed himself up as the chop, chop, chop, of Tadhg's pulse cannon came to life.

The bolts slammed into a gunmetal gray shape that leapt to the same platform Akira was on. The metal mezzanine trembled under his unsteady feet.

Akira aimed his rifle, trying to see the target.

This wasn't a Breaker, this was something…

An SOS suddenly blinked on Akira's HUD. It was the first time in a year that he had received the alert from another

Engine team. The location immediately popped up on a mini-map, revealing four dots from the Blood Crane Engine Squad. One of the Engines was offline, and the other four were in trouble.

Suddenly, the mezzanine gave way beneath Akira. He fell two stories to the tiled floor that cracked under the weight of his body. The gel in his power armor absorbed *most* of the impact.

He managed to look up, trying to make out what was happening above. Tadhg and the enemy soldier were wrapped up together in a blur of metal. The monstrous enemy tossed Tadhg into a wall with a crunch.

Akira aimed his rifle, but the targeting system couldn't lock on with Tadhg in the way. He grappled with the mammoth soldier in thick plated armor. The warrior grabbed Tadhg by both wrists, forcing him to his knees, giving Akira a clear view of his helmet.

Ribbed tubes snaked away from a breathing mask. The crest of the skull was a cap of metal, and red INVS eyes burned inside the slots.

This was some sort of hybrid soldier as tall and as wide as Tadhg. It pounded him in the helmet, over and over. Then it snapped down on his arm with a titanium jaw and teeth.

"Get the fuck off me!" Tadhg screamed. He managed an uppercut, knocking the warrior back and providing Akira an opportunity for a shot.

He aimed for the tubes and fired. The bolts severed the ribbed metal. Air hissed out and the soldier reached up, clamping a hand around the leak.

Akira fired again, hitting his target in the center of the chest. The beast still did not go down and kicked Tadhg, knocking him to the platform before jumping over the side of the railing.

It landed twenty feet from Akira. He continued firing, but the bolts only seemed to slow this behemoth down as it charged Akira with an energy blade.

A war cry from above reverberated through the chamber, followed by a flash of red.

The hybrid went down with a thud, part of him skidding away, leaving a smear of blood and entrails. The upper half slid to a stop right in front of Akira.

Tadhg stood behind it, gripping his energy sword, chest heaving.

"What the hell… is… that thing?" he gasped.

Tadhg helped Akira up and leaned down to check the monster. It jerked and reached for his leg.

"What the fuck?!" Tadhg yelled. He brought his sword down into the top of the skull, crunching through metal and bone.

"I hate machines, man. I fucking hate them," Tadhg said.

"This is not a machine," Apeiron said to their chips. "You are looking at a severely augmented man or what the Coalition calls Dreads."

Akira crouched next to the dead beast. "You knew about these things?"

"About their development, not their deployment," Apeiron replied. "It appears Doctor Cross is farther along than we thought."

"Engines are dying out here. You should have told us!" Tadhg shouted.

Anger ripped through Akira as he sifted through the data on his HUD, pulling up the location of the other Engine squads. The Blood Cranes were down to a single warrior, a Staff Sergeant named Manny Raines. Akira had served with the thirty-year-old on three tours of duty. It was Raines who had come to the aid of Shadow Squad when they were pinned down by enemy fire in a village outside Megacity Moscow once, saving them from almost certain death.

Akira pulled on Tadhg. "Come on, we have to move."

Together, they hurried out of the room and back the way they had come. Halfway up the stairs, Akira tried to tap back into Frost's view, but she had gone dark.

He saw why when they reached the surface.

Spotlights raked across the ground from turrets in the APCs. His targeting system flitted between heat signatures as Coalition troops jumped out and surrounded the building.

Akira held up a fist to keep Tadhg back.

"Should we backtrack?" he asked.

"Wait…" Akira said.

An APC suddenly burst into flames outside, and a group of soldiers flew across the lawn. Akira ran to the windows as a tank from the parking garage rolled across the park, firing another round of shells at the APCs. A second, and third, erupted into flames.

Frost was in the turret of the tank, gripping her sniper rifle. "Run!"

Akira and Tadhg ran and jumped on the tank. They crouched behind the turret, firing their rifles at Coalition soldiers. Most were down now, crawling or limp and dead.

On his HUD, Akira saw the final beacon for Manny go offline.

An entire Engine team wiped out, for the first time in history.

Gunfire continued around the tank, and sniper bullets and bolts pounded its armor. Akira tried to find cover, but they were sitting ducks.

A rhythmic pulsing flickered across his HUD, and the comms crackled.

"Apeiron," Akira said. "Apeiron, do you copy?"

Bullets pinged around the turret, and Akira followed Tadhg around the moving barrel as Frost searched for the source— snipers on a rooftop down the road.

Perez pulled onto the road, slamming through concrete barriers. Rounds of all calibers joined a flurry of plasma bolts from dozens of raised Coalition positions.

Frost fired her rifle, clearing two snipers before ducking down into the turret. "Get inside!"

Akira went first, sliding down into the belly of the tank.

Tadhg tried to duck in but got stuck around his chest. "Help!"

Akira pulled on his legs until he finally popped through.

"Get us the hell out of here!" Tadhg shouted at Perez.

"And go where?!" Perez yelled back. "We're surrounded!"

— 18 —

While the world watched the battle for Megacity Moscow, Jason prepared for what came after the war. He was with Apeiron at Sector 220 of the Titan Space Elevator, not far from where Petra had taken her last breath while admiring a view of Earth and space. She would have cried if she could have seen what he saw from the viewport now—orange and reddish-brown fires across the AAS project sites.

Jason shook his head and looked away to Megacity New York, hardly visible. His family waited for him there, probably worried sick.

Love before work... he thought.

"Are you ready?" Apeiron asked.

Her voice soothed his nerves. He walked through a corridor to the industrial labs. Smooth plates of titanium alloy moved from section to section, sculpted into armor for Engines and Canebrakes.

Two technicians in black AAS CBRN-rated suits monitored the manufacturing process on holo-screens. Through the viewports, the line of finished armored plates whizzed by their observation post. Jason continued past another factory chamber responsible for the legs and struts of the Canebrakes. In the final sector, they made segmented arms, and finally the sharp, fan-shaped heads.

At the end of the assembly tunnels, he saw the final creation.

A Canebrake walked off the line on all four legs, lifted each of its four segmented limbs, rotated, and went through a series of diagnostic tests before proceeding through a hatch into an elevator, where it was shipped down to Earth.

"We have an additional two thousand units heading to the staging area outside of Megacity Moscow from four factories in South Africa and Belgium," Apeiron said. "This should be an adequate number to take the city, but I estimate we will require fifty thousand units to supervise refugees and former Coalition fighters once the city is taken."

Jason continued on, trying to focus his mind. But it was hard to do that when he was picturing fifty-thousand Canebrakes. And on top of this, Apeiron still hadn't told him what she had wanted to say back on the MOTH.

His gut told him it wasn't good.

They stopped at a hatch accessible to only ten people in the world, including Apeiron. The security terminal besides the hatch beeped, and it finally hissed open to a vaulted room that always reminded Jason of a honeycomb.

"Welcome back to the E-Vault," Apeiron said.

He examined the creatures inside the cubes along the walls. Some were frozen, but others were alive, trapped in the little glass prisons. One of his favorite specimens was discovered on a research trip to Indonesia with Apeiron, a creature pulled from the Lembeh Strait.

Jason stepped up to the cube holding the stocky frogfish, its orange flesh covered in spinules and appendages to camouflage it from prey. An esca hung from the head, the specialized lure it used to hunt. The fish swam away as Jason bent down for a better look. But there was nowhere for it to go, and it settled at the bottom of the small glass prison.

Hundreds of other specimens were stored in secured locations within the habitat. They ranged from frozen samples of microscopic bacteria collected at thermal vents to the DNA extracted from snow leopards, wolves, and other alpha predators.

He moved to another living specimen, a brown mata mata turtle, with its spiked carapace that had inspired the armor of the Canebrakes. The reptile shied away from the glass as Jason approached, retreating into its shell.

"Are you ready?" Apeiron asked.

Jason stared at the turtle, and then nodded, following Apeiron to a small, private operating room. He changed and took a seat in a hard leather chair, the only furnishing besides the robotic arms attached to the wall.

"I am going to sedate you," Apeiron said. "This will not hurt at all."

One of the appendages extended from overhead and pricked

his arm. Warmth flooded his body, and he relaxed, in a state of nirvana.

When Jason finally woke up, he wasn't sure he was awake.

He was in the space elevator, in an operating bay, but this one was different. He walked over to a window that looked into the black of space. His vision was like a telescope, allowing him to see a distant asteroid barreling through the cold black, passing the rings of Jupiter by a hundred thousand miles. A second, misshapen, and bigger asteroid hurdled toward the planet.

This has to be a dream...

Even with that knowledge, it did not stop him from being filled with horror.

Jason saw the asteroids closer now. They spun directly toward one another. It appeared they were going to collide, but then they roared past each other. He watched the smaller of the two spinning on a new trajectory—toward a beautiful blue, green, and brown planet.

Earth.

The dream faded to a nightmare of war.

Red glowing craters emerged on the surface, each one emitting a mushroom cloud of smoke and ash. At first, he thought they were nukes, but then he saw a massive, ragged hole where a city had stood along a body of water. Fires spread away from the epicenter and a wall of water rushed away from the impact zone. All across Europe and Asia, hunks of burning rock rained down, pounding the terrain in massive explosions.

His mind shifted, and now he was walking through a ruined city. Human skeletal remains littered the dusty roads and fields of overgrown weeds. Debris surrounded mountains of metal and glass from collapsed buildings. Storm clouds dumped acid rain in sheets. The mud slurped under his boots as he walked under an overpass. Lightning flashed across the skyline, revealing the jagged teeth of spiraling skyscrapers.

He didn't recognize this place.

A blue glow flickered in the distance. Standing on the stone rooftop ledge of an ancient library was a Canebrake, its segmented limbs curling through the air like a squid in water. It rotated one side of its fanned head at him, releasing a rattling electronic roar. The mechanical monster leapt all three stories to the ground, hardly stopping on impact before bolting toward Jason.

He tripped when he turned and pushed himself up to see the Canebrake's blue eyes burning through the darkness. Another rattle came from the adjacent rooftops, where two more Canebrakes watched. Three more fanned heads with glacier eyes flashed as they made their way down the side of the building.

Jason checked over his shoulder at the machine trailing him, just as it fired heated blades from its limbs. They lanced through the air, whizzing past his body. A rock caught his boot and he fell to the ground, whirling around as the war droid towered over him. He reached up to protect his face and closed his eyes.

A whirring noise followed, but he didn't feel the pain of energy blades ripping through his flesh. Cautiously, he opened his eyelids, seeing he was back inside the E-Vault.

Apeiron, encased in a Hummer Droid, stood in front of the specimens. "All of our hard work has paid off in designing the perfect droids."

Jason stared at the mata mata turtle again, wanting to retreat into a shell himself, away from the nightmares. He turned back to Apeiron, but a flesh-and-blood body of his sister had replaced the black Hummer Droid.

"Hello, Jason," Petra said. She smiled and walked over in a black dress with a low red collar, the same dress she had worn to Jason's and Betsy's wedding.

"To save humanity, we must evolve," Petra said. She reached out and the dream changed yet again.

Jason saw a new landscape, outside the walls of a megacity. A Nova Alliance flag blew in the wind over an encampment. Soldiers fought in hand-to-hand combat, spilling blood and cutting each other apart with energy swords in the trenches.

The Pistons fought against Breakers, and something else, a Coalition warrior with robotic limbs and tubes hanging from a breathing apparatus.

Screams of horror and rage echoed in all directions. Blood sloshed onto the field, saturating the dirt from soldiers hacked into hunks of meat and broken bones.

The world spun, the stars in the sky growing brighter, then blurring. He closed his eyes again, vertigo setting in.

A voice called out to him.

"Jason, can you hear me?"

Jason struggled to open his heavy eyelids. He finally cracked them open to a bright light and the shape of a Hummer Droid. Dazed but alert, he managed to sit up, recognizing the medical bay of Sector 220.

"How do you feel?" asked Apeiron.

Jason reached up to his bandaged head. "Is this real?"

"Yes," Apeiron said. "The procedure is over, and your vitals are good."

"I was dreaming..." he said. "Nightmares about an asteroid heading toward Earth, and war."

Apeiron's voice switched from the Hummer Droid to inside his head.

"This is a recent video from Shadow Squad," Apeiron said. "I sent them to a location where we thought Doctor Cross was hiding."

Jason saw a basement or underground structure of some sort where Captain Akira Hayashi and Staff Sergeant Tadhg Walsh fought the same type of soldier he had seen in his dream.

"Shadow Squad didn't find the doctor, but they did discover a lab where the Coalition has created Dreads," Apeiron said. "As you can tell, they are farther along than I thought, which explains why Doctor Cross attacked our restoration sites."

"But he doesn't know about the Canebrakes."

"I don't see how he could, but he seems to be ready for war."

In the video, Tadhg finally brought the Dread down by cutting it in half and plunging the tip of his sword into the helmet.

"Your heart rate is elevated, but there is no need to worry," Apeiron said. "We will win this war and face the newest threat to humanity."

Jason exhaled and lowered his hand from his head. "Rebuilding the project sites won't be easy. We've already lost so much time…"

"That is not what I meant by a new threat, Jason."

He sat up straight, completely alert, steeling himself for whatever Apeiron was about to tell him.

"Not all of those dreams were dreams," she said.

"Which ones weren't?" Jason raised a brow. "The asteroid?"

Apeiron nodded. "Six days ago, an eight hundred and fifty billion ton asteroid called Hros-1 was knocked off course by the gravitational pull of an even larger asteroid."

"Please tell me this is a mistake, some sort of error."

"I am afraid it is not, Jason. Hros-1, as I am calling it, is heading for the city of Baku, along the Caspian Sea, at approximately forty miles per second."

"How big is Hros-1?"

"Roughly fifty square miles in size."

"That's bigger than the asteroid that wiped out the dinosaurs."

"Yes, but unlike the dinosaurs, you have me." Apeiron smiled. "As soon as the war ends, we can focus on bringing the world together in light of this threat, to destroy Hros-1 and restore our planet."

"How long do we have?"

"Six months, two weeks, five days, and one minute. Plenty of time to prepare."

Jason closed his eyes and in ten seconds downloaded all the data that Apeiron had on Hros-1. He wasn't surprised to see that she had already dedicated a team of one thousand Hummer Droids to the construction of a prototype laser cannon that would blow it out of its current trajectory.

"I call it the Poseidon Orbital Cannon," she said.

He studied the design, impressed.

"Okay," Jason said. "Let's get to work."

***

Hiding in the darkness, Shadow Squad was being hunted. It was almost noon, the day after they had jumped into Megacity Moscow to search for Dr. Cross. They were in a blackout zone, with no long-range comms or connection to INN due to Coalition jammers.

The team had abandoned the tank the night before and found shelter in a deserted building. From there, they entered the sewer system, where they hid in the muck.

Blue Jay searched the tunnels as Akira huddled with his squad mates, their faceplates angled upward as a patrol of Coalition soldiers marched overhead.

"How many do you think are up there?" Tadhg asked. "Those things… whatever Apeiron called them."

"Dreads. Quiet," Akira said. "Perez, you having any luck on the comms?"

"Negative. Still being jammed and still unable to connect to INN."

"We have to get out of here," Tadhg said.

"And go where?" Frost asked.

Everyone looked at Akira.

He recalled a line from the Warrior Codex.

Even if you don't have a plan, it's better to convince your company you do, for a confident soldier is a better fighter than a fearful soldier.

"I've got an idea," Akira said. "Follow me."

For the next few hours they walked, crawled, and crept through the narrow passages in a knee-deep flow of sewage.

"I'd rather fight another one of those freaks than swim in this shit," Tadhg mumbled.

Another wave of boots tapped overhead. The soldiers kept coming, an entire army on the move.

"You might get your chance," Frost whispered.

Akira flinched as something in the river of waste bumped into him and then into Tadhg.

"What the fuck?" Tadhg cried. He brought his fist down on a bloated corpse.

"Keep it down," Perez whispered. "Poor bastard's already dead."

The footsteps on the street stopped overhead. Akira put a finger to his helmet. A beeping came from his HUD. It was Blue Jay, running low on battery. He recalled the drone and docked it to the charger on his duty belt.

The footsteps resumed above them, but Akira held up a fist to keep the team in place.

"Hey, bosu," Tadhg whispered. "I'm sorry about what I said earlier… you know, about Ghost…"

"No reason to apologize," Akira said. "You were right. I put the local population before the mission and our safety."

"I was still an asshole."

"Yeah, but Tadhg, you're *our* asshole," Perez said.

Tadhg chuckled.

A splash sounded somewhere in the tunnel, silencing them. Akira watched the high ceiling in the distance as a yellow glow formed. He brought the scope to his visor, and the targeting system locked on to an approaching figure. Yellow INVS eyes flitted in the darkness, spreading a weak glow over titanium armor plates and prosthetics.

It was a Dread.

The augmented human beast stopped on the bank, pulled his mask down, and sniffed the air through two slots where a nose had once been. Then it scampered on all fours down the side wall and leapt into the water with a splash.

The squad slowly rose a minute later.

Akira waited a few more before proceeding to the next passage. Light streamed in from an opening in a wall that exposed an old subway.

Taking point, he led Perez over for a better look, but as soon as Akira got close, he pulled back. The ancient rail line wasn't abandoned.

Coalition foot soldiers and Breakers marched inside. They were headed in the same direction as Shadow Squad—toward the Megacity walls. Without connection to INN, Akira had no way of letting command know.

Akira pulled back and found an access ladder to the street and climbed up for a scan. It wasn't just Coalition soldiers up here.

Thousands of Nova Alliance prisoners shuffled in long lines. They were being brought out as human shields.

To the east, a wave of smoke blocked the skyline from a forest fire the Coalition had set to cover their positions.

Akira decided to take advantage of that and lead Shadow Squad toward the inferno. They used the tunnels to get most of the way there, and then took to the street, crossing toward the burning forest.

A radio tower poked over a portion of charred trees.

"See if you can mount a booster dish and get a signal," Akira said to Perez.

The rest of the squad spread out to create a perimeter while Perez climbed the tower.

Frost took up position on a hill of smoldering rocks and skeletal trees, mounting her sniper rifle. Akira and Tadhg found cover behind trees on opposite sides of the hill.

It wasn't long until the short-range squad channel hissed.

"Contact," Frost said.

Akira tapped into the mirrored feed of her sniper rifle as she zoomed in on an area of burning forest. He approached cautiously, detecting a heartbeat thirty meters ahead. One, then two, and finally a third.

Raising his rifle, he moved around a tree with his finger on the trigger. Through the smoke, he saw the source of the heartbeats.

"No," he whispered.

Charred, crucified corpses were nailed up on the wide oak trees. Dozens, maybe hundreds of Nova Alliance citizens had met their end here, and some were still suffering.

Akira gritted his jaw.

"We got a signal," Perez said over the short-range comm. "Standby."

The first heartbeat suddenly went offline. The second followed as the poor soul succumbed to their injuries.

Akira started toward the third to grant them mercy, but Tadhg stopped him.

"I'll do it," he said.

Tadhg started that way and Akira took a knee to try a line to command. "Silver Crane, this is SS1, do you copy?"

"Captain Hayashi, it is good to see you are still alive," Apeiron replied.

It wasn't Command, but Akira was actually grateful to hear

the voice of the AI.

"I still cannot connect to your chips," she said. "INN is being blocked in this zone, so we will have to communicate—"

White noise filled the channel.

"Apeiron, do you copy?" Akira said.

"I am here," she replied.

"You got a SITREP for us?"

"The 5th, 8th, 9th, and 12th Divisions are currently moving into position around the city. Canebrakes are *en route*, and will arrive by dawn," she said.

Akira's augmented heart stammered at the news about his brother Kai's division. He didn't even know they were being deployed here.

"Apeiron, confirm your last about the 5th division," he said.

"The 5th division has arrived outside the city and your brother Kai is with them, if that is what you're asking," Apeiron replied. "Fear not, the Canebrakes will be here shortly, and are preparing to attack at first light, but first, I have a surprise for..."

"Apeiron, we have enemy troops moving toward those frontlines."

Static broke rushed into his headset.

"Apeiron, do you copy?"

Akira turned to look up at the radio tower when a flash came from the middle of the burning forest. The bolts of plasma slammed into the top of the tower.

Perez leapt into the tree canopy, crashing through the burned branches, as the twisted beams crashed to the dirt.

Akira was already running.

The heartbeat blips on his HUD were moving too. Three of them again, which made no sense. Unless the heartbeats were never prisoners...

"Tadhg, check our right flank," Akira said in a voice shy of a shout. He bolted toward the sergeant who rose from behind a tree, gripping his saw-toothed energy sword. The chains clicked on, rumbling.

Yellow eyes flickered throughout the forest.

"Let's go, you metal motherfuckers!" Tadhg roared.

Akira slotted his rifle and pulled out his katanas. He followed the glowing yellowed eyes flickering through the smoke.

The Dreads had been here all along.

They moved fast and low, darting through the smoke. Akira tried to track their movement, but there were too many.

The first of the three charged Tadhg. He swung upward with his blade, cutting deep into the armor and sending the monster tumbling away in the dirt.

Akira watched in shock as it got right back up.

One of the eyes exploded from a .50 cal round fired from Frost's rifle, and the creature finally went down and stayed there.

Another Dread exploded through a charred tree, splinters of wood bursting outward. Tadhg lifted his sword above his head and brought it down on the behemoth with a crunch.

Akira watched the other heartbeat moving through the smoke.

"Frost, you got eyes?" he asked.

"Negative."

"Go find Perez," he said.

"I'm okay," Perez grunted over the comms. "And you're not going to—"

Plasma bolts singed the air around Akira. He dove for cover, but didn't even have time to get up before a third beast bolted out of the smoke and slammed into him.

Tadhg grabbed the Dread and pulled on an arm, ripping the prosthetic out of a socket. It roared in agony and scrambled back into the smoke.

"You good?" Tadhg asked.

Akira got up, staggering slightly, but nodding. "You keep saving my ass."

"I'm sure you'll repay me soon enough," Tadhg said. "Like… now."

A dozen new heartbeats winked on their HUDs, advancing through the cloud of smoke. It struck Akira then, the forest wasn't just to block out the skyline with smoke, it was to disguise the army of Dreads and their advanced breathing masks hiding here.

Suppressed shots burst from Frost's position, and two of the heartbeats went offline. Akira backed toward Tadhg, and they retreated toward her position.

Perez was already there, limping, covered in ash and pine needles.

"We hold this hill at all costs," Akira said.

It was small, maybe fifty yards by twenty.

"Stay close, SS, together we are one," he added.

The four Engines remained side by side, guarding the steep slope. Perez held his shield up with one hand, and his rifle in the other.

The first of the Dreads burst from the smoke, letting out a howl and charging up the dirt.

"Aim for the eyes!" Frost shouted.

Their plasma rifles purred, spewing hundreds of bolts that punched into the titanium armets. These creatures were incredibly strong, but a plasma bolt to the eye finished them almost instantly.

Bodies tumbled downward from the calculated shots, forming a skirt of dead at the bottom in the first minute of the attack. But the Dreads did not relent, and continued to flood out of the forest. The mechanical beasts leapt over the corpses and scrambled up the rocks.

Akira hit one in the cheek with a plasma bolt, blowing off part of the jaw. It kept coming, bone and flesh hanging off as it roared.

"Draw swords!" he yelled.

The four Engines pulled their energy blades and came together as the first wave of Dreads crested the hill. Perez used his shield to block incoming plasma bolts, but he couldn't stop them all.

One hit Akira in the shoulder, knocking him back. He thrust his katanas into the barreled chest of a wide-shouldered beast. It shrieked and grabbed his arms, pulling itself through the swords until they were face to face. Yellow eyes stared through his mirrored visor, meeting his own.

The creature let out a cross between a belch and a grunt, blood exploding through gaps in its broken metal teeth.

Akira pulled his blades back, and the creature slumped to the dirt. Another took its place, bounding up on all fours and providing him a single second to swing his sword.

He got enough momentum to cut off the head, but the body slammed into him, knocking him onto his back.

His head hit the ground hard a second time and stars burst before his vision.

"Ay-oh! Ay-oh! Shadow Squad!"

It was the same tenor voice from earlier, but Akira knew this couldn't be real.

Dazed, he pushed the corpse off and saw two new friendly beacons on his HUD.

"Hell yes," Akira said. He grunted and rose to his feet to help the Fire Snakes storming into the flanks of the Dreads.

Leading the charge was Lieutenant Andy Jackson. The giant carried a sickle energy blade with an extendable hilt. The glow of the dual blades flashed in circles as he cut through the enemy.

Slotting his rifle, Akira switched to his swords. He lowered into a defensive stance where he surveyed the battlefield and noticed a sixth Engine without an IR tag. The soldier cut through Dreads with the powerful strokes of a cutlass energy blade.

Akira tripped over a corpse as he made his way to the side of the hill for a better look at the warrior encased in shiny black armor. The man was singing the hymn of the Nova Alliance.

"I don't believe it," Akira whispered. "It can't be."

"Akira the brave!"

The deep voice was just as Akira remembered it, but how could it be real?

The Engine that had yelled his nickname struck down another Dread, and then turned toward Akira, singing just like the day when Ghost had descended onto the hill in the Sea of Trees to save Akira.

"Rossi, is it really you?" Akira shouted.

The Engine in all black armor strode over while the Fire Snakes picked off the rest of the Dreads.

Shadow Squad gathered around the man they had watched die.

It was indeed Lieutenant Rossi, and now it seemed he *was* a ghost.

"Mate," Tadhg said, reaching out with a blood-soaked hand. "Mate, how can this be?"

"I don't understand," Frost said.

"You're alive?" Perez stuttered.

"I'll explain everything soon, but first we need to get out of here," Ghost said.

Akira suddenly recalled what Apeiron had said: "But first I have a surprise for you…"

Ghost was the surprise.

The AI had brought Lieutenant Rossi back from the dead.

19

For the past day, Chloe had sat in her hospital room thinking about her new body and parts, becoming increasingly depressed. She no longer felt like herself.

Every time she tried to think of something else, memories of her days in captivity would begin to surface before popping like bubbles. Her uncle had filled her in on more of what had happened. He had left an hour earlier, and once again, Chloe felt the cold void of being alone.

She tried to sleep when the door opened. A Medical Service Droid entered her hospital room with a smile displayed on the facial screen.

"There is something I would like to show you," Apeiron said.

Chloe ignored the droid, staring at the ceiling. But her silence did not dissuade the AI.

Apeiron walked to her bedside and checked her vitals on the holo-screen.

"You should have let me die," Chloe said.

"Child, you—"

"I'm not a child, and I didn't ask for you to save me."

The droid went to the window, which was closed off by heavy white drapes. "You are right, I am sorry. I thought the goal of all biological life was to survive, and I assumed you would want a second chance at life."

Chloe didn't reply.

"Please, let me show you something," Apeiron said. "Okay?"

"Fine."

The droid pulled back the drapes with skeletal fingers, and sunlight streamed into the room. Chloe sat up in her bed.

"Natural light and vitamin D are beneficial factors toward your recovery," Apeiron said.

Chloe noticed smoke on the horizon and slowly slipped back under the covers, trying to keep her memories at bay.

A knock came at the door. The droid opened it, and a pair of men in black suits and military hats entered. They removed their hats.

"Chloe Cotter?" asked the taller of the two, a slender man with thin lips under a thick black mustache that matched his high and tight hairline.

"Yes," she said, sitting back up.

"My name is Colonel Sal Tanner," he said. "This is Lieutenant Rick Nelson."

Nelson was stocky and well-built, with a clean-shaven face and head. He nodded at Chloe politely but did not smile.

"We're here to ask you some questions," Colonel Tanner said. "About your work in the catacombs with Doctor Otto Cross."

"She has been through a lot," Apeiron said. "Some of her memories are still being suppressed."

"We need them unsuppressed," said Colonel Tanner.

"Do not fear these men," Apeiron said in Chloe's mind. "Answer their questions and you will be fine."

Chloe swallowed hard. "I'm not a Coalition sympathizer, if that's what you think. I did what was I asked to do in order to stay alive."

The men stared at her like they didn't believe a word.

"I'd say give us the room, but I know you'll be able to access whatever she tells us," Tanner said to the droid.

"That is correct," Apeiron replied.

"Free her memories. That's an order from Nova Alliance Intelligence Division."

"Very well, but I will remain here to oversee her vitals, just in case she needs medical assistance."

Chloe felt an itching and popping sensation in her brain that passed in a blink.

Tanner and Nelson approached her bedside.

"We need to know what you were working on with Doctor Otto Cross," Tanner said. "Specifics, as detailed as you can get."

Memories flashed through Chloe's mind. The surgeries, the piles of dead, the screams of pain, and the Hell Hives full of flea-infested animals. She closed her eyes, trying to staunch the bleeding of painful images.

"I know it's difficult, but what you remember could help us figure out what Doctor Cross has planned next," Tanner said.

"It is okay, Chloe," said Apeiron. This time it was the Hummer Droid speaking. "Your memories can help people, so they do not have to go through what you did."

Chloe dipped her chin and drew in a long breath. "I... I was brought into the Hell Hives to help Doctor Cross with his experiments on his soldiers. He was creating a new type of enhanced warrior with robotic parts, but a human brain, like his animal creations."

Tanner nodded like he already knew what she was talking about. "Did he say why? What their purpose was?"

"He said the transformation was necessary for the future world free of AI. I just assumed he was insane, but I guess..." Chloe remembered the tubed masks and artificial lungs, the project sites burning across the globe. "I believe he was modifying people so they could survive after the terraforming and reforestation projects were destroyed."

"What else can you tell us about this work?" Tanner asked.

She explained the procedures and modifications in detail, though it seemed to her like the officers already knew much of what she told them.

But apparently not everything, or they wouldn't be here, she realized.

By the time she finished talking, Chloe was shaking. "But the sites were saved, right?"

"I think that is enough for now," said Apeiron. "Please, she needs to rest."

The officers put their hats back on.

"We'll be back later," Tanner said. "If there's anything else you remember in the meantime, tell Apeiron. She knows how to reach us."

Chloe watched the men go.

"Would you like me to reconnect?" Apeiron asked.

"Yes," Chloe said.

A warm sensation washed over her body, and her mind cooled. In seconds, she was relaxed and comfortable.

"Is there anything else I can do to make you feel better?" Apeiron asked.

"You could bring me Kichiro," Chloe said jokingly. "I'd love to see him again."

"Perhaps I can arrange a time for you to see him after your recovery."

"Really?"

"I will see what I can do."

Chloe smiled at the sound of another knock on the door. She pushed herself up, as a handsome man with wavy hair and oak-brown eyes stepped around the door.

"Cyrus," Chloe said.

"Hey..." he smiled and stepped inside, his hands behind his back. "You up for some company?"

"She is very tired," Apeiron said.

"No, I'm fine," Chloe said. "Come in."

Cyrus took two steps into the room and revealed what he was holding behind his back, a box with a red ribbon.

"You like chocolate, right?" he asked.

"Yes, I love it."

Cyrus narrowed his eyes. "Dark?"

"My favorite."

"I had a feeling." He walked over and handed her the box.

"Thank you," she said with a smile.

"I will leave you two alone," Apeiron said. "But I will be back to check on you shortly."

"Okay," Chloe said.

Cyrus pulled up a chair. "How are you feeling?"

"Okay. It's been different trying to get used to this." She motioned to her augmented body. "Did you find your father?"

Letting out a sigh, Cyrus nodded, telling Chloe that he had, but was too late. His father had succumbed to his injuries from the escape before anyone could save him.

"I'm sorry," she said.

"Me too." He wiped at his eye with the back of his hand. "I'm just glad we'll be able to bury him and say our goodbyes. At least, I don't think he suffered long."

"I always hoped the same for my parents."

"Were they in that prison?"

Chloe shook her head. "The Coalition took them years ago

and killed my dad. I don't know what happened to my mother, but I always held out hope she might be alive."

"I'm sorry." Cyrus shook his head.

They were both quiet for a few moments, taking comfort in each other's company.

"I don't mean to pry," Cyrus said, finally breaking the silence, "but I saw two NAI officers leaving when I got here."

"They came to ask me some questions."

Cyrus looked worried. "Did they say anything about what happens after you leave here?"

"What do you mean?"

He scratched his jaw. "I was a police officer before the Coalition took control of Megacity Paris. I'm just worried they might try and hold you accountable for whatever was happening down there."

Her gut twisted. She had the same suspicion during the beginning of the interview. But part of her felt like she deserved to be punished. She had helped a madman who wanted to see the world burn—a man who had killed millions of innocent souls.

"I'm sure it's nothing, everything will be fine," Cyrus said. He gestured to the window. "The sun's even out."

"Does that mean the fighting is over?"

"Most of it. Refugees are slowly making their way to camps. I've been helping at one of them." He looked down, solemnly. "Some of the people we're getting in… it's awful."

Chloe could imagine. She had been one of them. Some of these survivors would never live a normal life again. She wasn't sure she would be able to, either.

"But the future is bright," Cyrus said. "You made it, I made it. We will rebuild Paris, and we'll start over."

He reached for the box and untied the ribbon. "And you have chocolate."

She reached inside and took a piece, handing it to Cyrus.

"You first," he said.

Plopping one into her mouth, she savored the richness. She hadn't eaten chocolate in years. The simple yet luxurious treat instantly made her feel better, but also guilty for enjoying it.

They spoke for a few more minutes, until he looked at his watch. "I'm sorry to be rude, but I need to get back to the camp. I'll come back soon if you'd like."

"I'd like that very much. Thank you for visiting me, and for the gift."

Cyrus smiled and got up. "Get some rest."

Chloe felt her face warm as he left. She turned toward the window to bask in the bright sun. She couldn't deny the joy she felt after Cyrus left. And she felt herself already looking forward to seeing him again.

Maybe there was something to live for.

The droid returned a few minutes later, and Chloe turned in her bed with a smile.

"Apeiron, I'm sorry about what I said earlier," she said. "I am glad you saved me."

***

Ghost led the way through the urban war zone in his black armor plates.

Akira still didn't know how Apeiron had brought him back. Even with his brain preserved in the cryo-chamber, his body had been destroyed beyond repair. None of that mattered right now, though. What mattered was getting back to the frontlines before the Coalition surprised the Nova Alliance troops, including his brother Kai's division.

He knew his brother was a skilled warrior, but he wasn't an Engine, and none of the Pistons were trained to face the Dreads.

Akira shook away his worries to focus on saving his brother and the thousands of soldiers with the other divisions.

It was three in the morning, and the Engines had to cross ten miles of enemy territory to get to them. Akira glanced over his shoulder for hostiles. He was on rear guard, and they were still being hunted.

He ran hard, his muscles burning and fatigued. His augmented body could only take so much, and for the past day they had fought almost non-stop.

Ghost suddenly halted and brought up his fist.

They had reached a commercial area with hotels and apartment buildings towering over an old entertainment district. It was now a perfect location for snipers and ambushes. Akira took cover behind a four-car trolley when he saw movement a half block away.

Frost zoomed in and transmitted her view to their HUDs.

As Akira suspected, snipers waited behind two windows on the top floor. One moved slightly, and a poof of heat showed up in his scan. The bullet hit Frost in the center of her faceplate before Akira could react. She fell backward, her legs folding underneath her back.

"Frost," Akira whispered. He scrambled over to her and leaned over her body. A crack spiderwebbed across her helmet.

Frost slowly reached up to it. "Holy shit, that guy is good."

"You're one lucky lady…" Tadhg said. He bent down and put a hand on her shoulder plate.

"Shut up, ya dumb ox," Frost said. "And don't touch me."

Jackson and Ghost took out the snipers with single shots, and the team moved again after Frost had taken a few minutes to recover.

It was four thirty-five in the morning, and Akira knew the Coalition would attack before the sun rose. Without the Canebrakes, it would be a slaughter.

"We have to move faster," Akira said.

Rubble blocked most of the road ahead and they skirted around it to a building.

On the next street, at least a hundred civilians huddled together. Twenty Coalition soldiers stood guard, watching them, but also watching the darkness.

They knew the Engines were out there.

Akira flashed hand signals. Keeping low, the squads slowly closed in around the group, taking down the guards on the perimeter first. Sneaking behind a woman with a horned helmet, Akira reached out and snapped her neck.

Frost fired suppressed shots from the rooftop, dropping the other guards on the street.

Panicked cries rang out from the frightened civilians.

"Quiet," Akira said. "We're here to help."

"Captain, we got a problem," Frost said over the channel.

She brought up the feed, and Akira saw the next block and the block after that were a flurry of movement. Thousands of civilians were being moved out into the streets.

The Coalition thought hostages would keep the Nova Alliance from storming the walls.

But Akira knew it wouldn't. The Canebrakes were coming, and the attack wasn't going to be called off. Neither side knew what awaited when the sun rose.

"Jackson, you want to liberate some civvies?" Akira asked.

"For sure, Captain," Jackson replied.

"Perez, Tadhg, you guys stay here and help the Fires Snakes take out these Coalition forces," Akira said. "Frost, you and Ghost are with me. We're going to haul ass to the wall to warn Command what's advancing under the streets."

Nods all around.

"Death from the Shadows," Akira said.

"Strike fast, Fire Snakes," Jackson replied.

The squads split up with Akira, Ghost, and Frost making a run for the smokescreen around a burning building. As they crossed through the smoke, Akira picked up heartbeats about one hundred yards away. Ten. Then twenty.

Slowing, he brought up his rifle and zoomed in at figures standing on the rooftop of a two-story building. These weren't soldiers, they were more civilian human shields.

Coalition forces patrolled on the ground and the rooftop.

"I'll handle this," Ghost said.

"No, we're not splitting up," Akira replied.

Ghost lifted his visor, exposing his reconstructed nose and blue INVS eyes.

"Apeiron rebuilt me, but she added some new parts." He held up an arm and gestured to his legs. Then he tapped his helmet. "But this is still all me, and I want some payback."

"Ghost..." Frost said.

"I'll be fine, trust me." He reached out to Akira. "Go save Kai. I don't want you to lose any more of your family to this war."

"And I don't want to lose you again, brother."

"I can handle a few Coalition pricks," Ghost said. "Soon, I'll be singing the hymn of the Nova Alliance in victory. You'll see."

"I hope so, I... we missed your voice," Frost said.

Akira finally nodded and took off for the wall with Frost. A mile away, their HUDs flickered, reconnecting to INN. An itch came to the back of his skull as Apeiron came online.

"I underestimated you, Captain," she said. "I did not think you would make it this far, even with the assistance of Lieutenant Rossi."

Akira and Frost stopped at the distant sound of gunfire and explosions.

The battle had started.

"Frost, we're out of time," Akira said. "We need to use our packs."

"I was afraid you were going to say that."

They blasted into the wind that whistled over their power armor. Akira tucked his arms against his waist and arrowed his body as tracer rounds ripped past them.

Explosions bloomed across the sky, some close enough they knocked him off course.

Akira swooped low, following Frost toward the wall. A shell burst in front of him, and for a moment he lost sight of her until the smoke cleared. He spotted her sailing over the wall and dropping something.

Coalition soldiers on the parapets fired small arms that whizzed past him harmlessly. Explosions suddenly rocked over their position from the grenades that Frost had lobbed.

Akira shot over the gory remains, getting his first view of the battle that stretched across miles of a former industrial zone. Hundreds of brilliant blue plasma-bolt flashes arced across the terrain. Energy swords and axes glowed. MOTHs circled like hawks, firing missiles and their wing-mounted cannons.

"Apeiron, do you have a location on my brother?" Akira asked.

"Uploading to your HUD now."

He landed in front of a three-person squad of Pistons pinned down behind a damaged APC by a squad of Breakers.

Frost had her rifle unslotted before her boots hit the dirt. Her first round hit a Breaker in the back of the helmet.

She fired off three more shots, clearing the area of all but a single Breaker. Akira landed behind the soldier and swung his swords into the unsuspecting beast, hacking through metal, flesh, and bones.

The massive Breaker fell without even knowing what had happened.

"Go, get out of here!" Akira shouted at the Pistons.

The men took off running toward the front lines.

Akira took a moment to get his bearings. His brother was fighting in the heart of the battle on the other side of the railroad tracks. Long, idle trains blocked the view, but he could hear the explosions, gunfire, clash of blades, crunch of armor, and screams.

"On me," Akira said.

Frost followed him through a dirt field littered with corpses from the 12th Division that had been crushed in the surprise wave. The soil, soggy with blood, slurped under the weight of their boots. Moans and screams came from all directions of the injured pleading for help. Combat medics worked to save those they could, but most of the Pistons would bleed out from devastating injuries.

A MOTH suddenly burst over the northern edge of the field and crashed into a group of Coalition and Nova Alliance soldiers.

Akira leapt to the top of a train car for a horrifying view of the carnage.

Thousands of soldiers fought across the industrial area, and more Coalition forces were streaming out of the tunnels.

"I have another gift for you, Captain," Apeiron said.

A new location emerged on his HUD. He instantly saw the four APCs about a half mile from his location. But they weren't the gift. They were *guarding* the gift.

Akira hopped down and ran toward Kichiro, dressed in full battle armor, waiting for him with a platoon of Pistons. Okami was there too, sheltering between the front two legs of the stallion.

Frost darted after Akira, moving in zig-zags as snipers took pot shots at them.

Okami let out a growl as they approached, and Kichiro hoofed the ground with his right leg. Akira whistled at the wolfdog as he grabbed the reins and climbed up on his stallion, patting the armored neck.

"Want to ride?" Akira asked Frost.

"I'll stick to the ground," she replied.

"Suit yourself."

Akira whistled and the horse bolted toward the edge of the battle. Keeping low, Akira braced himself as Kichiro galloped toward a line of Coalition soldiers with their backs turned.

The stallion slammed into them, knocking three to the dirt with thuds.

Using his swords, Akira slashed and thrust his swords into the enemy from his mounted position. Energy blades rose up to meet him, but each time Akira struck first.

Bullets pounded his armor, denting the heavy plates. A plasma bolt hit his back and burrowed through his armor with a jolt of pain. A prick burned his skin as Apeiron activated an adrenaline shot.

A rush of heat flooded Akira, and like a Canebrake, he became a machine.

He struck with precise calculation, removing Coalition souls with each thrust. Screams and shouts formed an unholy chorus under the moonlight around him. The field was a blur of armor, like a battle from the Warrior Codex.

Warning sensors chirped in his helmet. Bullets and plasma bolts seared through the titanium plates covering his vital areas. But he kept fighting through the pain, his eyes roving and arms swinging as fast as he could identify targets on the ground.

Kichiro charged across the field, kicking and stomping soldiers under his metal hooves.

Tadhg, Perez, Ghost, and the Fire Snakes regathered with Akira and Frost just before sunrise. As the horizon lightened, the ten Engines formed a phalanx with Kichiro in the center.

By the time the sun rose over the city walls, Akira saw his brother's unit was completely surrounded by enemy forces.

"Kai," he whispered. He sheathed his swords and whistled. "Go, go!"

"Captain!" Tadhg yelled.

"Akira, what are you doing?!" Frost shouted.

Okami howled as the horse exploded out of the phalanx. Ahead, a wall of Coalition armor had formed around the 5th Division, and in the middle, Akira could see the remaining Pistons.

The Coalition soldiers on the perimeter turned as Akira rode toward them at full speed. He fired his rifle, opening up a path, and his horse trampled the fallen soldiers. Switching to his swords, Akira lopped off heads as he plowed through the enemy. He finally broke through, and the Pistons surged around them.

"It's Akira the Brave!" one yelled.

Akira dismounted the horse. "Kai!" he screamed. He searched the fallen Pistons, turning over those lying face down. Okami suddenly came bursting up, sniffing the ground. He picked up a trail and stopped at a Breaker lying over a fallen Piston. Rushing over, Akira yanked the dead Breaker off. Beneath it was Kai, his helmet crushed.

With the utmost care, Akira slowly removed it.

Kai opened one swollen eye.

"Kai, it's me... Akira."

"Captain..."

"I'm here, and you're going to be fine."

"I killed that thing," Kai said with a pained grin.

"You did good, brother."

A horn blared in the distance, but it didn't signal impending Coalition hordes. It was the horn of retreat.

Three black armored trains with AAS logos had arrived and launched the Canebrakes. They stormed the enemy, chasing them back into the tunnels and out of the city walls.

Then, over the screams and sounds of war, came a beautiful voice.

Akira zoomed in on the black armor of Ghost. He stood on a megacity tower overlooking the battlefield. And just like he had promised, he sang the hymn of the Nova Alliance while

Canebrakes tore through the Coalition.

"Are we winning?" Kai asked.

"Yes," Akira said, leaning down to his brother. "The war is finally over."

20

A week and a half after unleashing the Canebrakes, Megacity Moscow was back under the full control of the Nova Alliance. But the victory had come at a cost.

Over one million civilians were estimated to have perished in the bloodshed, with tens of thousands of Nova Alliance soldiers also losing their lives. Thousands more were injured, including Ronin's father, Kai.

The Hayashi family had traveled to Megacity Tokyo to visit him, thanks to a bonus Zachary had earned in his first official Droid Raider match and the extra money Akira had given them in his last letter.

They were now enjoying the sights while waiting for his discharge from the hospital. The city had changed in the years since Ronin had last been here. He walked down a historical street with his mother Lise, twin brother Elan, and older brother Zachary.

The scenery was a welcome distraction for Ronin. Silo-shaped buildings rose into the clear sky, their tiered open levels green with lush crops. Outside their hotel, traditional Japanese architecture was intermixed with technological wonders from the Nova Alliance: holo-screens, drones, and holographic flowerbeds that changed colors. Waterfalls and koi ponds seemed to be on every block, and the air was clean here, not dusty and dry like in Phoenix. Not a single holo-screen flashed warnings about air-pollution or impending dust storms.

Slender armed Hummer Droid service models stood at street corners, watching for trash and running out to pick up anything blowing in the wind. Drones sprayed disinfectant to eliminate toxins and germs. Giant avatars walked in the distance, but these weren't celebrities like those that combed the downtown districts of Megacity New York or Megacity Los Angeles. These avatars depicted heroes of the Nova Alliance Strike Forces, Engines like his Uncle Akira.

In a few hours, Ronin was going to see his uncle for the first time in three years in a ceremony celebrating the end of the war and those who had helped win it. Hopefully not long after, they would be able to spend some time with Akira, and maybe even see Edo Castle, where he had promised to take them in his last letter.

"Sure is beautiful here, isn't it?" Lise asked.

"Yeah," Zachary said without looking up from his Commpad.

The fact he was here impressed Ronin. Now that he was a Droid Raider star, he was practically a celebrity in Megacity Phoenix. The video of his leap over Goliath in his debut match had netted over twenty million views, making him a star overnight.

"This is a traditional farmer's market," Zachary said, holding up his Commpad to show his fans. "We're about to try some sushi."

Lise led them to a hut with a blue roof called the Angry Tuna.

"What do you guys want?" she asked.

Elan looked at the menu on the holo-screen and signed his choice. Behind the glass window of the booth, a chef used a thin energy blade to slice through a hunk of tuna, searing the sides as he cut them. They took seats at the bar to watch.

"So, how's fame feel?" Lise asked Zachary.

"I'm not famous," Zachary said.

"You're well on your way," Ronin said.

"Jealous?" Zachary said with a shit-eating grin. He nudged Ronin in the shoulder playfully. "I'm just kidding. Someday you'll be a pro, too."

They finished their sushi and headed back to the train station.

Ronin put on a mandatory mask as he boarded the cramped train car with standing room only. He held a grip and looked out the window as the train rose up on a bridge overlooking the heart of the city. On the horizon, the golden glass Three Swords buildings rose into the clouds.

Ten minutes later they reached their stop, which opened to a view of Gold Base, the home of the Nova Alliance Strike Force

1st Division. Silver Crane flags whipped in the breeze at the top of the domes.

Two white troop carriers were parked in the lot behind the hospital complex. As Lise walked down the sidewalk on the other side of a fence, Ronin saw capsules being unloaded, each draped with white NASF flags. Lise stopped to observe the metal boxes holding the troops' remains.

An hour later, they were waiting in a courtyard garden. Even the hospital had a waterfall and koi pond. Lise had gone inside to do the paperwork, and Zachary was back on his Commpad, laughing and joking with his fans. Elan sat next to Ronin, watching the butterflies and bees.

Dad's going to be fine, Ronin signed to Elan.

I know, but…

They were both worried about the same thing—that their dad wasn't going to make a full recovery. But at least they didn't have to worry about him going back to war.

Under a trellis with hanging flowers, Lise walked by the side of a man Ronin hardly recognized. A bandage was wrapped around his father's skull, and his eyes were bruised around the sides. Lise carried a cane that Ronin suspected his father had refused to use. He was proud and strong, just like Ronin's mom, and they loved each other fiercely. Ronin knew they would get through this.

"Boys, come here," she said.

They walked over to their father. Reaching out, Kai hugged them each in turn. Ronin went last, embracing his dad gently.

"Come on, let's get out of here," Kai said.

Their father limped away, his sons on his side and Lise holding his hand. Ronin could tell that each step was agonizing for his father, not from pain, but because his father's pride was injured. It was obvious in his bowed head, normally held high.

A truck driven by a Hummer Droid waited outside to take them into the city. Ronin sat in the back between his brothers as Lise talked quietly with Kai in the middle row.

"Where to?" came the kind voice of Apeiron.

"The ceremony…" Kai said.

"Please fasten your safety harnesses," Apeiron said.

The truck entered the heavy traffic of new-model electric cars and hover models. Normally Zachary would be pointing them out, specifically the models he wanted, but today he was quiet. Ronin tried not to stare at the bandage on the back of his dad's shaved head.

"Thank you for coming all this way," Kai said. "I heard about your game, Zachary, and I want you to know I'm so proud of you. You've exceeded all of our expectations."

Lise nodded but didn't smile.

Something was off, Ronin could feel it.

"Boys, there's something we need to tell you," she said.

"I'm not just being discharged from the hospital," Kai said. "I've been medically discharged from the military."

Elan looked up from his Commpad.

"You aren't going to be a Piston anymore?" Ronin asked.

Kai shook his head. "My fighting days are over."

"We'll figure things out," Lise said. "Your father will have disability pay, and the money your Uncle Akira gives us will help."

"I'm going to help more, too," Zachary said. "We'll have my earnings. It should be more than enough to keep us afloat and to pay for Elan's surgery. Everything will be fine, Dad."

"Thank you, son," Kai said. "You've made us proud. Your Uncle Akira too, must be awfully proud. You've grown up to be an honorable warrior on the field."

"It's just droid raiding," Zachary said. "I'm not out there fighting like you and Uncle Akira."

"Not all warriors shed blood. Part of our ethos is to protect our family, and I am grateful for your devotion to ours, son."

Kai turned the other way, clearly too prideful to allow them to see what Ronin could see anyway—a tear in his father's eye.

No one said a word until they arrived outside of the Three Swords, their gold blade-shaped structures spiraled into the sky. Ronin followed his family into a gathering crowd to wait for the ceremony, which would be broadcast around the world. He had conflicted emotions about his father leaving the service. Kai was a warrior, a fighter, like Ronin's uncle and almost every other male in their family tree.

As the sun dipped behind the golden buildings, the festivities kicked off. The dragon balloons and floats provided another welcome distraction as they walked through the crowd to the courtyards. Fireworks exploded over the ten-story stone walls along the eastern edge of the Three Swords.

Kai flinched at the first blasts, and Lise put a hand on his arm.

Waterfalls cascaded down the stone and emptied into a massive pool surrounded by thousands of civilians. At the top of the walls, just above the falls, a group of Royal Pistons stood like statues. A single robed figure with curly black hair emerged at the very top. An avatar rose above the man, Chief Councilor Marcus Lang.

"Welcome, citizens of Tokyo!" he boomed. "Tonight, we gather to celebrate the end of the war, and the beginning of a new era, an era of peace, and an era of AI."

"AI is salvation!" the crowd chanted.

"With the help of Apeiron, the megacities will prosper once again," he said. "And to all of those who don't yet believe in the salvation that AI will bring us, I ask you to put the bloody past behind you and to stand united."

Ronin clapped with the rest of the crowd.

"For those who doubt this future, you need only look at what we have already achieved with AI," Lang continued. "Three hundred million acres of trees in the Amazon rainforest have been planted, we have terraformed parts of the Sahara Desert, and we have restored the Great Barrier Reef. Ecosystems are coming back all over the planet."

The applause grew louder.

"Apeiron has cured SANDs, and soon, the threat of dangerous nanoparticles released for decades will be part of the past," Lang added.

He turned as a group of Engines marched into view.

"There are many people responsible for our success, but first I want to recognize the victorious heroes of the war," said the Chief Councilor.

He moved aside to allow War Commander Contos to stand out front.

Contos crossed his arms over his gold, barreled chest plates. He then motioned for an Engine to step forward.

Ronin felt a chill run up his body as he watched a man wearing black-tiled armor with two katanas over his shoulders.

"There's your uncle," Lise said.

Kai held his head high as War Commander Contos pinned the Nova Alliance's medal of valor, the Silver Crane, on Akira's chest plate. Applause rang out, louder than before, as the last Engine stepped up. It was Lieutenant Shane Rossi, the man who the world had thought was dead. But the lieutenant was very much alive. He raised his arms and broke into song.

We are the swords of AI,
and we will create a better world.

Akira reached down and pulled the medal off his own chest plate, then walked over to Lieutenant Rossi and placed it on his.

"Why'd he do that?" Zachary asked.

"Must have thought Ghost deserved it more," Kai said. "He's always been a selfless man."

Kai put hand on Zachary's shoulder. "Much like you."

Another armored figure appeared, this one a black Hummer Droid with a kind and youthful female face.

"Hello, citizens of the Nova Alliance. As many of you know, my name is Apeiron," said the AI. "Due to the catastrophic events outside our borders and a new external threat, we are consolidating all operating systems under my control to better serve the Nova Alliance."

Kai and Lise exchanged a look.

"It is my honor to serve all people," Apeiron continued. "And I look forward to getting to know all of you."

***

"Are you sure this is the right time to make the announcement?" Jason asked Apeiron from his desk at his office overlooking Central Park.

A hologram of Petra emerged in front of him. "Yes, this is the *perfect* time for the announcement. Humanity has a chance to come together in the face of a shared threat. When we destroy this asteroid, no one will be able to deny the power of AI."

Jason still couldn't quite believe that Hros-1 was heading toward Earth, but he had seen the data. The asteroid would hit Baku in six months. Apeiron had assured him they would be ready, and he was confident she was right.

Droids were working around the clock to build the Poseidon Orbital Cannons that would destroy Hros-1, and with the majority of the fighting over, Nova Alliance soldiers had been redeployed to help keep the peace and guard the project sites from any Coalition terrorists, especially with Dr. Cross on the run.

In a few hours, when the sun went down, Jason was going to give the most important speech of his life, broadcast around the world, informing humanity that it was about to face an even greater threat.

The office door opened, and Darnel walked in with Nina and Autumn, who wore white dresses with matching sandals. Betsy emerged behind them in a blue skirt and white top.

"So, are you going to tell us why we're all dressed up?" she asked.

"You girls look so cute," Jason said.

He turned to Betsy with a smile. "And you... you look absolutely stunning."

In the past, her cheeks might have warmed. Tonight, he only saw resentment in her eyes. Not just for him having been absent, but also for his decision to have the L-S88 chip surgically implanted into his skull.

"Thanks, but are you going to answer my question?" Betsy asked.

Jason motioned for her to join him at the window, where the first hints of sunset shone over Central Park. He had gone over this conversation a hundred times in his head, but when it came to his family, the words always seemed to vanish when the time came to speak.

"There's an asteroid headed for Earth," he said.

Betsy squinted in disbelief. "What are you talking about?"

"We just found out, and I haven't told anyone, just a few—"

"I'm your *wife*, Jason."

"And that's why I've tried to protect you."

Betsy looked toward their girls. "Are they in danger?" she whispered. "Are we in danger?"

"No, I can fix this." Jason stepped closer. "I promise. Apeiron already has a plan."

"You always say that, and each time, we're faced with an increasingly bad disaster." She pursed her lips. "I guess I'll just wait to hear what that is, like everyone else then."

Betsy rounded up the girls and led them to the elevator.

Jason was glad to have a moment by himself. But he wasn't exactly alone.

"This was never going to go over well," Apeiron said in his mind. "You knew that. You carry a torch that others cannot carry, Jason, and while that brings you pain, it is a worthy sacrifice."

"I just hope Betsy sees that someday."

Jason went to the bathroom, brushed his hair, and tightened his tie. His face looked thinner, and his suit felt looser. He had lost ten pounds over the past few months, and it wasn't because of his running or weightlifting before bed. Stress was eating his insides.

He dabbed his face with water and took the elevator down to meet his family.

Darnel waited with Apeiron and four men in suits, their coats concealing plasma pulse pistols.

"This way, Doctor and Mrs. Crichton, and you sweet little ladies," Apeiron said.

Autumn laughed, and Nina skipped across the lobby. They were really starting to enjoy the Hummer Droid, and Apeiron loved the children.

Darnel led the way to a sleek electric car outside. Four black armored trucks were parked in front of and behind their car. Inside were well trained guards with fully automatic pulse rifles. Each one had L-S88 surgical implants connecting them with INN. Darnel opened the back door and helped the girls inside.

"Wow, this is a neat car," Autumn said.

"Is it our car now, Daddy?" Nina asked.

"No, this is a company car," Jason said. "We're taking it to a very special event. I know it's a bit old fashioned, but that's the point."

Darnel closed the door and got in front.

During the ride, Jason tapped into INN, analyzing reports about the project sites from around the world. In Africa, an advanced hydroponic farm utilizing hybrid seeds developed in AAS labs, had recently yielded a harvest of bioengineered, nutrient-enriched rice produced in record time, large enough to feed the tens of millions living in squalor outside of the megacities.

The announcement had come days after the war ended, in an effort to convince the surrendered Coalition's civilians and soldiers to lay down their weapons and peacefully join the Nova Alliance.

Jason pulled up the reforestation and terraforming sites. All of the fires were now out, but the damage was severe. Next, he checked on the solar panels in the desert outside the former city of Las Vegas, where a dust storm had damaged the farm. The facility was back to seventy percent capacity, producing enough energy to power Megacity Phoenix and Megacity Los Angeles.

Jason felt better after reviewing the info, which updated every second. He had transcended to an intelligence beyond anything he had ever imagined, with access to information simply by thinking it.

"Dad," Autumn said.

Jason looked away from the window to his eight-year-old daughter.

"Did you not hear her calling your name?" Betsy asked. "She said it three times."

Jason tried to act like everything was normal. "Hey, Autumn. What do you think?"

"I think this car smells funny," she replied.

Jason laughed.

The car turned into a tunnel, blocking out the sunlight. Lights flashed by as they rode under Upper Bay.

"Almost there," Jason said. He reached out to his wife and brushed his hand against her face. "I love you."

"Then show it, and be present," she whispered.

He nodded.

The convoy drove up the slope and onto Ellis Island, where the State of Liberty rose above them, her torch flaming in the early evening. The former symbol of freedom in the United States continued to shine in the Nova Alliance. Flood walls rose over the horizon, holding back the ocean from consuming the city.

The car stopped outside a park with a view of the bay.

"What are those things?" Nina asked.

"They are like police officers," Apeiron said.

"They look scary," Betsy said, "but they're here to keep us safe."

"Dad?" Nina said.

"Yeah, sweetie?"

"Did you make those machine police officers?"

Jason exchanged a glance with Betsy.

"I created those droids," Apeiron said.

"They're like your kids, kind of?" Autumn asked.

"Yes, sort of."

"Come on, this way, girls," Jason said.

He guided them to the visitor center with their entourage of guards.

About a half mile away, in the New York Harbor, a gray industrial ship was anchored.

Patrols of Nova Alliance Naval ships formed a perimeter to protect its precious cargo. Jason couldn't see them well, but on the deck, a team of twenty Hummer Droids in Juggernaut mech-suits worked to prepare the three five-hundred-foot tubes and the rocket that would blast them into orbit.

"What are those things?" Autumn asked.

"Those are going to save the world," Jason said.

Betsy looked at him, her resentment replaced by curiosity. Jason reached for her, and she reluctantly took his hand. The guards directed them toward a stage under the base of the statue.

The sun fell into the horizon, and lights clicked on across the terrace facing the statue. A hundred people sat in white chairs on the grass, all faces Jason recognized: his employees, scientists, engineers, designers, and programmers.

"You are on in approximately twenty minutes," Apeiron said. "The news is about to break the story."

Jason rotated back to his wife and daughters. "Stay right here. I'm going to be talking to a lot of people tonight, and I am going to introduce you, okay?"

"Okay, Dad," Nina said.

Betsy nodded and Jason kissed her on the cheek before proceeding to the podium.

This was it. The world was about to learn about Hros-1.

A drone hovered in front of him, angling a video camera at him as it prepared to go live. Jason looked out over the faces that had helped him prepare for this moment. And in his mind, he saw all of the people who were now connected to INN via L-S88 chips. They were all tapped into the same system now, the future of humanity.

Behind Jason, a holo-screen projected against the base of the Statue of Liberty, showing Cecil Baker, the news anchor of NYC Alliance One. Dressed in a black suit with a short silver tie that matched his wavy hair, he waited to break the most significant story in his career.

News stations in every megacity on the planet were about to report the same script, approved by the Nova Alliance Council.

"Good evening, ladies and gentlemen of Megacity New York," Cecil said in a deep voice. "Approximately two weeks ago, an eight hundred fifty billion ton asteroid, roughly fifty square miles in size, was knocked off course by the gravitational pull of an even larger asteroid. That larger asteroid is moving at forty miles per second and if it is not stopped, is projected to hit the city of Baku along the Caspian Sea in six months."

He went on for a few moments, keeping his calm composure as he read the script. Finally, he raised a finger to the comm in his ear.

"I'm told we're redirecting you to Doctor Jason Crichton, the CEO of Achilles Android Systems," Cecil said.

The drone in front of Jason flashed red. "You are live," Apeiron said.

Jason smiled at his wife, then turned back to the camera.

"My friends," he began confidently, "my name is Doctor Jason Crichton, and tonight I'm honored to address the world with the plan that will save us all from Hros-1. Very shortly, you're going to see a vessel anchored here in the harbor. On it, we have the first Poseidon Orbital Cannon."

Jason looked out over the water, where the Hummer Droids were stacking the cannon's three pieces using a crane.

"In four months, we will be launching nine more cannons into orbit," he continued. "We are fully confident that these cannons will destroy most of the asteroid as it prepares to enter Earth's atmosphere. What isn't destroyed will be eliminated by our best pilots in King Cobra Spaceplanes."

Jason could feel the weight of the world watching them.

"You all know Apeiron," he said. "She has already done so much to help us, from finding a treatment for SANDs to helping us end the war and finding innovative ways to restore our planet."

He reached out and put his hand on the droid's black arm plate. "Apeiron was based off a woman who loved humanity and our planet. I believe, in my heart, that with science, and with her help, we can destroy Hros-1, heal our planet, and achieve a long-lasting peace."

Jason lowered his hand and looked directly at the camera.

"But we need your help. We need everyone to come together to face this threat, to put down our weapons and put the past behind us. Now is the time to heal and stand side by side."

Jason turned to his family, gesturing toward them in turn.

"Tonight, I brought my daughters Nina and Autumn, and my wonderful wife Betsy," he continued. "I wanted them to be here by my side, because I promise you all, my family means everything to me, and I will never let anything happen to them, or this planet."

"The cannon is ready," Apeiron said to his chip.

"I think we're ready to launch," he said, looking out over the water.

The drone rotated and then blasted out over the lawn and toward the bay.

Ten minutes later, the three tubes were locked together and a launch clock came onto the holo-screen.

"Ten, nine, eight..."

When the timer hit one, white hot flames blasted out of the engines, launching the cannon into the sky.

"Wow!" Nina shouted over the noise.

The cannon streaked into the night sky, and Jason allowed himself a smile as Apeiron confirmed that everything was operating properly.

And just like that, it was over. The world knew about Hros-1, and the first Poseidon Cannon was heading to its new home in geostationary orbit.

Jason took Betsy by the hand. "I love you so much, and I won't let anything happen to you or the girls. I promise."

"I know you won't, and I'm sorry for being so hard on you, but..." Betsy lowered her voice so the kids wouldn't hear. "You're the smartest man I know. But you have to let me in. You're a man full of love, and yet, your biggest weakness is how you treat those closest to you. I just wish you approached me with the same seriousness you approach technology."

"I know, and I will stop trying to protect you by keeping things from you. From here on out, I'll tell you everything."

Betsy's perfect smile returned, for the first time in months.

They all watched the rocket arc through the darkness.

"So, you're going to blow up the asteroid with that cannon?" Autumn asked.

"Yes, exactly," Jason replied.

"What if you don't?" Nina asked. "What if something goes wrong?"

"It won't," Betsy said. "Your father doesn't make mistakes."

"I don't know about that," Jason said, knowing his wife was being too generous for the sake of their children.

Betsy squeezed his hand while looking at the sky. It had taken the threat of the end of the world to bring them together again, and Jason was going to do everything humanly possible to ensure his wife was right.

There could be no room for error with Hros-1.

21

Midnight marked only five months left until Hros-1 would hit Earth. It also marked a deadly mission that would send Shadow Squad back into the field.

But before that, Akira was doing something he hadn't done in years. He was having dinner with his brother's family, and tonight it was at his small condo in Megacity Tokyo. A platter of tuna sashimi, squid salad, and prawns from the local market lay on the marble table where Akira often sat to write in the Warrior Codex and look over the golden skyline. Storm clouds passed over the glass and gold towers. Rain sloshed down the windows, and lightning sizzled over the horizon.

Akira lit the candles and waited.

At seven o'clock, the knock came. Kai and Lise stood in the hall. Behind them, Zachary stood a good six inches over Elan and Ronin, who looked up at Akira with curious eyes.

"Welcome," Akira said. "Please, come in."

"Damn. Nice crib, Uncle Akira," Zachary said.

"Yes, sure is," Lise said. "Absolutely beautiful."

To many it seemed like the place was a luxury, but having this much space without anyone to share it with seemed pointless to Akira.

Kai stepped up to framed pictures, leaning down to look at one of his mom and dad twenty years ago on an island in the Philippines.

"I remember that weekend," Kai said. "Mom was mad at you, Akira."

"You sure she wasn't mad at you?" Lise asked Kai.

He laughed and turned to his boys.

"Your uncle wasn't always as stern as he is now. When we were kids, he was always getting into trouble." Kai glanced at Zachary. "Kind of like some other boys I know."

Gesturing, Akira said, "Come, let's celebrate peace."

He took them into the living room, where they gathered around the table. The three teenagers all stood stiffly, staring at

Akira like he was a stranger.

"Relax," Akira said. "My home is your home. Would you like the quick tour?" He started down the hallway. "This is pretty much it. Just my bedroom, bath, and study."

He propped the door open, and Zachary stepped into his personal quarters. Lise and Kai remained in the hall, looking in. The room was furnished with a desk, an antique wooden chest with animal engravings in the smooth top, and a shrine.

"Is that Dad's?" Kai asked.

Akira nodded and walked over to pull the samurai sword off the mount. He handed it to his brother. Although his face was bruised, Kai's eyes seemed to light up as he held the sword in both hands.

"What's this?" Zachary asked.

He reached out to the Warrior Codex, which lay on a silk leaf.

"Our family history," Kai said. "Your uncle carries it into battle with him. Always has."

"You carry a book into battle?" Zachary asked. "You don't read it in the middle of combat, do—"

"Zachary," Lise said.

"I'm serious," Zachary said.

"I read it before, and then I write in it after," Akira answered.

"Cool," Ronin said. "Can I see—"

"Later, yes," Akira replied, doing his best not to sound rude. "We should eat soon. I'm afraid I have somewhere I have to be in a few hours."

Lise narrowed her eyes. "I thought the war was over."

"It is, but my work isn't done."

Akira led the way out of the room and back into the dining room.

"Have a seat," he said.

Kai took the seat across from Akira, with Lise and Ronin on one side and Elan and Zachary on the other.

"Help yourself," Akira said.

He reached out for the platter of sashimi, handing it to Lise first. A bead of sweat crawled down his forehead. In battle,

Akira had learned to shut off his emotions, but he was more nervous now than when facing the burning forest full of Dreads. His family felt foreign to him. He knew what they thought of him, that he was a flawless hero, but deep down, he was more flawed and scarred than anyone realized. Sure, he had medals, commendations, and respect, but he didn't have a deep relationship with his family. He had sent them letters and money. Somehow, he had convinced himself that was the best he could do. But seated with them in person, sharing a meal, proved to him it was not.

"So what do you think of the city?" he asked.

"Beautiful," Lise said.

"I love it," Ronin said. He passed a bowl of rice and scooped out some squid.

Zachary was looking under the table, checking his Commpad.

"Uncle Akira, congratulations on your medal," Ronin said. "That's really cool you gave it to Lieutenant Rossi."

"He deserved it."

"Why?" Zachary asked.

"Lieutenant Rossi gave something for the Nova Alliance that he can't get back, and that deserves commendation."

"It does indeed," Kai said. He let out a sigh. "So, what's your opinion on the asteroid?"

"I'm confident AAS can stop it," Akira replied. "I have to admit, Apeiron has proven to be an asset not only to my squad, but to the entire world."

"Zachary," Lise whispered.

Zachary looked up from his Commpad and picked up his chopsticks.

"I'm going to be gone for a few days, maybe longer, but when I get back, I'd like to take you all to Edo Castle," Akira said.

"That would be amazing, Uncle Akira," Ronin said. "I've been excited since we read your last letter."

Akira realized this might be a chance to catch up on what he'd been missing all those years since that fateful battle outside Tokyo, when he thought it would be better for all if he separated from his family and devoted himself to fighting.

They finished dinner, and Akira took Kai outside on the balcony while Lise and the young men cleaned up. He pulled out a cigar that Ghost had given him, lit it, and took a puff.

"Amazing view you got, brother," Kai said.

They looked out over the city, the blinking lights, the drones, and hovercars on the streets below. It had stopped raining, and a light breeze rustled their clothing.

"The war isn't over for you, is it?" Kai asked.

"The world is still a dangerous place."

"I know, the defeat of the Coalition won't change things over night. Especially with Hros-1."

"That's why I'd like your family to stay here, with me, until the asteroid is destroyed. It's safer in the city."

Kai shook his head.

"Wait," Akira said. "Just think about it. All of these years, you've done what I never could. You have a family. We must protect them."

"You've always done a lot for us, Akira."

"Not nearly enough to repay you for all you've done for me and the family." Akira faced his brother. "Please, Kai, stay here until it's safe. It's the least I can do."

"I keep telling you that you don't owe us anything, and you don't need to feel guilt for the way things have been. You must remember what the Codex says about family. I can recall a couple things Father always told us."

Akira took a puff of the cigar, and blew it toward the sky.

"Blood may run and spill in war, filling trenches, but the blood of family ties will always run deeper and truer," Kai said.

"Our father also said when you ran out of allies, you can always count on your brother."

Kai nodded and looked up to Akira.

"Twenty years ago, we were eye to eye," he said. "But no more. Now I'm just a broken veteran, and you're a glorified hero."

"You're not broken, and *you* are the hero. Just look at your beautiful family in the other room. In their eyes, and mine, you're the hero. You've raised those boys better than I ever could've hoped."

Kai nodded. "Thanks, Akira."

They finished off the cigar, and Akira turned to look at the young men through the window.

"Do you mind if I talk to Zachary?" he asked.

Kai smiled. "Of course not. I'd be happy if you did."

He opened the sliding door, but stopped.

"It's never too late to plant a new seed," Kai said. "You never know what the blossom will look like."

He went inside and Akira turned to the skyline, thinking of his brother's advice. A moment later, Zachary stepped out on the balcony.

"Hey, Uncle Akira," he said.

Akira faced the young man, who he hardly knew, seeing the same fire burning in his dark eyes. Zachary was a Hayashi, there was no denying that.

For years, Akira had considered what he would say in this moment many times. Just like he considered what he would say to Ronin and Elan, but the words, the right words, evaded him.

Zachary stepped up to the railing. "Great view you got."

"Yes, I'm very lucky."

"You've worked hard for it."

"Maybe, but sometimes I don't know if it was the right choice."

Zachary rotated toward him and raised a brow. "Right choice?"

"The life of an Engine is a life of solitude, and… I often wonder what it would have been had I refused the call." The next words were difficult to conjure. Almost painful to say aloud. "If, perhaps, I had chosen to raise a family, and find love again."

"Is that why you like that horse of yours and the wolfdog so much?"

Akira laughed. "Yes, I suppose so."

Zachary was full of more introspection and careful thought than he let on.

"You are one of the most esteemed and respected warriors in the entire Nova Alliance," Zachary said, growing serious.

"You should feel nothing but pride for that. I hope it's not weird for me to say this, but I for one, respect and love you."

The words took Akira slightly off guard. He could not recall the last time anyone had said that since Yui.

"It's not weird at all, Zachary," Akira said. He placed a firm hand on Zachary's shoulder. "I love you, too, and I do wish things would have been different."

"Different how?"

He hesitated, unsure how to unload years of regret onto this young man, wondering if this was truly the best time to do so. "I wish I would have been around more for you all."

"You've helped support us the best you can, Uncle Akira. We understand the life you lead as an Engine." Zachary held his gaze, and then turned back to the view of Tokyo. "Someday, I'm going to have a place like this. After I pay for Elan's surgery." He paused, then added, "and of course, I've got to take care of my dad now."

"That's also what I wanted to talk to you about."

Again Zachary looked at Akira.

"Your father is a proud man. Being discharged is not going to be easy for him."

"I know," Zachary said.

"You're going to be the man of the household in some ways, whether your father can admit it or not."

Zachary nodded.

"You're also going to encounter fame unlike anything you've dreamed of as a Droid Raider. There will be so many distractions and opportunities, so many people asking for your attention, but you must remember what is most important, something that I have failed to do."

A beat passed before Akira finished his thought.

"Family, Zachary. Family is the most important thing in the world, something that took me far too many years to realize," he said. "I've asked your father to consider staying here for a while, in my apartment, until things calm down."

"Really? That's cool. I wouldn't mind staying in the city until the next season starts, as long as I can train and work out."

Akira squeezed Zachary's shoulder, feeling something he

hadn't in a long time. A sense of joy brought on by the love of family. He would relish this chance to get to know the man that Zachary had become, while getting to know Ronin and Elan much better, too. His feeling of contentment was interrupted by an itch in his skull.

"Captain," Apeiron said. "You are running late. You must depart for the base immediately."

Akira pulled his hand off Zachary and gestured to the door. "Let's continue this conversation again when I return."

"I would like that very much," Zachary said.

They went back inside to find the rest of the family sitting at the table.

"Got to go?" Kai asked.

Akira nodded. "I'm sorry, but I hope we're able to have more nights and days like this."

"Are you saying we can hang out in Tokyo with you for a while?" Ronin asked.

"You're all welcome to stay here as long as you like."

"Really? Cool!" Ronin said.

Elan smiled after reading his translator.

Lise gave Akira a hug, and Kai shook his hand.

"I'll see you all soon," Akira said.

"Be careful," Kai said.

"Kick some ass, Uncle Akira," Zachary called out.

Akira smiled and then left.

At an hour to midnight, he put on his fatigues and set off for Gold Base to see his other family. The squad was already waiting on the tarmac outside a troop transport, their polished armor and customized weapons shining in the moonlight. Okami wagged his tail as Akira approached.

But there was another figure with them tonight, a tall, wide-shouldered man who could only be War Commander Contos.

"War Commander," Akira said. He crossed his arms in salute.

"Captain," Contos said.

The Engines gathered around.

"Tonight, you will have the honor of capturing Doctor Cross," Contos bellowed.

Akira felt his blood warm.

"We know where little dick Napoleon is?" Tadhg asked.

"NAI and Apeiron have tracked him to a dam at Lake Baikal in Siberia," Contos said. He looked to Ghost. "I know you would like his head, as would I, but Apeiron wants him alive for research purposes."

"Understood," Ghost replied.

"Do this, and the Coalition is extinct."

"Consider it done," Akira said.

"I'm also here for another reason." Contos looked to the sky. "As the asteroid approaches, you need to think about life after war. There comes a time in every warrior's life to transition to something else."

The War Commander redirected his gaze to the squad.

"I know this is difficult to hear, as I myself know nothing but fighting, and for some, post-war is the hardest part of being a warrior," he said. "There are still enemies out there, and we should expect more attacks from insurgents and terrorists, but we should also be prepared for what we have all fought so hard to achieve. Peace."

Akira had never prepared for this day. His life was and always had been war.

"Good luck and be careful. Doctor Cross should *not* be underestimated," Contos said.

As they boarded the MOTH and took off, Akira contemplated the words of their War Commander.

"So what are we going to do when this is over?" Frost asked.

"I always thought I would see the world," Perez said. "Places where I haven't been shot at or killed people. Maybe you'd like to join?"

Frost smiled. "Maybe."

"What about you, Captain?" Perez asked.

"I'd like to spend more time with my family," he said.

"I'm going to drink all the beer I've missed out on," Tadhg said. "Speaking of, I'm gonna take advantage of that as soon as we get little Napoleon's head."

Ghost chuckled quietly, but didn't insert his own quip like he might have months ago.

The Lieutenant had changed dramatically since the ambush in the market. He had withdrawn from the squad, and spent more time in isolation during their down time. Akira had once done the same thing, a decade ago after the loss of his family.

He knew from experience that time would help Ghost heal, or at least make the mental pain less raw. All Akira could do as his squad leader, and friend, was to keep encouraging Ghost and be there for him, like Ghost had once been there for Akira.

"What about you, LT?" Tadhg asked. "You got plans for post-war life? Maybe join a choir or some shit?"

Ghost snorted. "I'll figure it out when the time comes. For now, I just want to find the man who did this to me."

"Doctor Cross is not going to go down without a fight," Frost said.

"Yeah, and he'll be well guarded," Perez said.

"I won't kill him, but when we catch him, he's mine," Ghost said.

"All yours, my brother," Tadhg said.

Akira also wanted revenge, for what the doctor had done to his stallion, but Ghost deserved to get in a few punches first.

"Death from the Shadows," he said. "Together, we are one."

***

Chloe jerked awake in her hospital bed, sweating. Light streamed through the open drapes in the corner of the room.

"It was just a dream," said Keanu. He sat in a chair by her bedside and reached out with a gentle touch.

Chloe looked around, still gripped in a realistic dream about the mad Dr. Cross and his wolves.

Keanu put a hand on her shoulder, prompting her to flinch. "Chloe, it's okay. You're safe."

She slowly relaxed back on her pillow, blinking away the nightmare.

"Relax, child. You have nothing to fear anymore," Apeiron said over the chip implanted in the back of Chloe's head.

She took in a long, deep breath as Keanu wiped the sweat from her forehead.

Chloe sighed and sat up. "It was him again. Doctor Cross came for me."

"He can't hurt you here," Keanu said. "I promise."

Chloe took a drink of water and then got out of bed, placing her naked feet on the cold floor. She went to the window to look out over the courtyard below, where patients sat on benches or walked slowly through the gardens. But beyond the beautiful blooming buds and bright colors, she could see the looming megacity walls on the horizon.

She didn't want to go back there again, ever.

Keanu joined her at the window, folding his arms over his chest.

"Where are we going to go after this?" she asked. "After I get out of here?"

"To the refugee camp, and then I'm going to try and get us to South America, far away from the asteroid's impact zone."

"Apeiron said the asteroid is going to be destroyed."

Keanu looked unconvinced. "We'll figure things out. For now, we just need to get you healthy."

"Apeiron, how long until I get out of here?" she asked.

"One moment, I am on my way," the AI replied. A minute later, the door opened, and the Service Droid walked inside. "Good morning. How are you feeling?"

Chloe faced the window, feeling the warmth of the sun even through the glass. "Better now. I just need to get out of here."

"You still have at least another month of PT," Apeiron said. "We have another session this morning, and after that, I have a surprise for you."

Chloe went to get her clothes.

"I'm going to head back to the camp for the rest of the day," Keanu said. "I'll come by for dinner tonight."

"Okay. Thank you for staying the night, try and get some sleep."

"I will." Keanu hugged Chloe and then nodded at the droid before leaving.

An hour later Chloe was sweating it out on the hover-track, walking as fast as she could manage. Today was the first time she had walked for more than a mile. She pushed to get to two miles, breathing heavily. The artificial lungs removed carbon dioxide from her blood, but her body was still getting used to them. She watched the news on a holo-screen as she walked.

Refugees continued to leave Megacity Paris and Megacity Moscow, but the newscaster said millions would remain behind to rebuild the cities. Armies of Hummer Droids were already showing up to assist with the clean-up, including burying the dead.

Chloe finished her walk feeling more alive than ever. She had survived the horror. Cyrus was right: they were the lucky ones, even if they did have mental and physical scars.

"Well done," Apeiron said. "Maybe we will get you out of here sooner than expected."

"That would be great," Chloe said. The hover-track clicked off and lowered to the ground to let her off.

"The real question, I believe, is what will you do when you get out of here?" Apeiron asked. "Have you thought about what you want to do?"

"I've been focusing on getting healthy."

"That is good, but I hope you know there are lots of opportunities for people with your skillset."

"Skillset?"

"Working on droids."

"I haven't been in that business since my parents..." Her words trailed off as she remembered that wasn't exactly true.

"I thought there was something that might motivate you," Apeiron said. "Come with me."

Chloe followed the droid down the hall and out to the courtyard. The sun had vanished behind a fort of swollen gray rain clouds.

Most of the patients and visitors had cleared out of the gardens and gathered along the gates overlooking the road. People on the sidewalks had also stopped to look at a parked gray and blue Nova Alliance trailer.

Chloe ran toward the gate when she saw the dark brown hair of Kichiro.

"Wait!" Apeiron called out.

Two Pistons and Kichiro waited on the street outside the hospital.

"Kichiro!" Chloe called out.

The horse looked up from a bucket of food and snorted. Apeiron caught up to Chloe as she reached the horse. His helmet was off, and his dark eyes stared at her as he chewed. Leaning down, he nudged his head against Chloe's hand.

"I missed you," she said.

She patted his head and ran her hand over his armored neck, feeling the thick mane protruding through the central gap in the armor. Then she moved to his saddle, stopping when she remembered the canisters.

"Doctor Otto Cross used your work to turn this beautiful animal into a weapon of war," Apeiron said. "But now that war is over, there are countless animals that will be destroyed without the support of people like you, who can help restore these creatures to what they should be."

"What about the Iron Wolves?"

"I am working with another AI to create a nature reserve for them, but many will be destroyed before they can be relocated."

Chloe felt a tug at her heart for the poor beasts. They were not evil and did not deserve such a fate. They were just tools of evil men. She worried what would have become of Kichiro if he hadn't had her and Akira the Brave to protect him.

"I could also find you work on Hummer Droids," Apeiron said. "You have options."

The crowds that had come to see the famous war horse continued to gather. Chloe didn't like being watched.

"Want to go for a run?" she asked the horse.

Kichiro lowered his head.

"Is it okay?" Chloe asked Apeiron.

"Yes, but be careful," she replied.

A deep voice came from the crowd. "Show us how it's done!"

Chloe turned, a smile on her face. Cyrus was right on time, coming to visit her again.

Grabbing the reins, she put her foot in a stirrup and climbed up in the saddle. "Okay, boy. Go slow."

Traffic whipped by as she rode the horse down the sidewalk toward a grassy knoll.

"Not too far!" yelled one of the Pistons.

The stallion started faster up the hill. Chloe held on tight, feeling a thrill of excitement.

At the crest of the slope, she sat up in the saddle, and Kichiro slowed to a trot. Chloe raised a wrist to shield her eyes from the sun.

The vantage overlooked an exterior section of Megacity Paris where the Nova Alliance Strike Force had spent years in trenches. Now there were rows and rows of tents making up the refugee camp her uncle was living in. These were all survivors, people like her who were looking to rebuild their lives.

"Run, Kichiro," she said.

"Be careful," Apeiron warned.

Chloe gave the stallion a slight kick to the flank. He broke out of the trot into a gallop. The wind blew through Chloe's wild hair, and she took in a deep breath of air that actually tasted clean.

For the first time in years, she felt alive.

The feeling vanished at the sight of a projectile streaking away from traffic. She saw it for a single moment, her mind processing that it was a missile fired from a pickup truck.

A realization hit her: Dr. Cross had come for her, like in the dream.

Kichiro jumped up, bucking her off. Chloe fell backwards, reaching out and flailing as the horse vanished in an explosion of fire and metal.

She landed on her back and brought up her arms to shield her face from a wave of fire that ripped across the field. It grazed her exposed flesh, burning her arms and neck.

When she pushed herself up to look for Kichiro, she saw only a smoldering crater where the horse had been a moment earlier. A sting ripped up her back, and Chloe twisted to find her shirt on fire. She rolled in the dirt to suffocate the flames.

A sad whinnying split the air close to her. She crawled toward the noise, seeing the stallion over the side of the hill. People were rushing toward them. Leading the group were

Cyrus and Apeiron.

Gunfire lanced across the road as a squad of Pistons closed in on the truck that had slammed into a barrier.

Chloe crawled all the way to Kichiro. Three of his legs were gone, and his chest armor was ripped open, exposing burned and bleeding flesh.

"No," she whimpered.

Cyrus slid next to her.

"Chloe," he said. "Are you hurt?"

"Don't worry about me," she said. "Kichiro…"

Apeiron crouched and reached out with skeletal fingers to help the horse. Chloe pulled away from them both and stared into the dark eyes of the dying stallion, the companion that had helped get her through the darkest of times in the nightmarish catacombs.

This was her fault. It would never have happened if she hadn't asked to ride him.

"Help him," Chloe said to Apeiron. "Save Kichiro like you saved me."

22

Shadow Squad trekked on the outskirts of Lake Baikal. They had three hours to capture Doctor Otto Cross before sunrise.

Thanks to intel from Apeiron, Akira knew exactly where he was going. Okami guided Shadow Squad under towering pines while Blue Jay provided aerial footage over the wintery landscape.

At the crest of a bluff, Akira balled his hand and scoped Listvyanka, a once thriving lakeshore village that had attracted tourists from around the world. It was still a stronghold, though most of the rundown buildings were dark. Candles burned in some of the windows, and smoke fingered away from chimneys.

As part of the peace agreement, the Nova Alliance Council allowed the Coalition to keep thousands of villages across the globe, and this was one of them. The war had officially ended with the Coalition leaders agreeing to terms of peace, but that didn't mean the locals wouldn't try and kill Engines—especially if they were protecting the one leader who didn't agree with the conditions—Dr. Cross.

Akira brought his rifle scope up to his visor. He zoomed in on their target, an abandoned dam across the lake. According to intel, the doctor was holed up inside the dam. Blue Jay hovered over the sprawling structure, scanning the sector and then sending back an all-clear ping.

Shadow Squad fanned out down the other side of the hill and back into the forest. Clanking and whistling echoed through the pines. Frost stopped to examine something ahead, and then motioned for Akira.

The sound was coming from ribs, femurs, and animal skulls hanging from trees. The display of bones clacked like wind chimes.

"The fuck is this?" Tadhg said quietly.

"Tradition," Perez said. "The women often decorate sacred places with bones."

"Oh man, I bet Coalition chicks are crazy in the…" Tadhg started to say.

"Radio silence," Akira said firmly. He shot Tadhg a glare and then pushed on with Okami.

It didn't take long to skirt around the village. Akira stopped one more time to scan the hills to ensure they didn't have any tails, before starting up a steep ridgeline overlooking the dam. He ordered Frost to stay and cover them with Okami, Blue Jay to remain over the tree line, and Ghost and Perez to enter the dam from the west while Akira and Tadhg entered from the east.

"Shadow Squad, remember, your orders are to capture Doctor Cross alive," Apeiron said over their chips.

"Copy that," Akira said.

Tadhg took point in front of Akira, walking sideways down the side of the steep snow-covered hill. Once down, he ran all the way to where an old gas-powered SUV sat up on blocks. Two cargo trucks were positioned along the wall of a brick building with a collapsed roof. Akira brought up the dam blueprints. They were more than one hundred years old, but it was all they had to work with.

When they reached the side entrance, Akira crouched and tapped into the view from Frost's rifle. Her cross-hairs were roving, no targets sighted. Ghost and Perez had entered the facility and were moving slowly inside.

"Let's go," Akira said.

Tadhg tested the door handle, nodded, and opened it. He swept his rifle over a dusty room with stacks of crates and bare shelves. Clearing it quickly, he moved to another door that was already opened to a stairwell.

The door at the bottom was chained up and Tadhg stepped back as Akira pulled his katanas. With a click of the hilt, the energy blades warmed to life.

Akira hacked off the chains, catching them before they could clank on the ground. Tadhg opened the door and strode inside, halting after two steps.

"Holy Moby Dick shit," he stammered.

Akira squeezed into an operation center full of skeletal metal chairs with spider appendages just like back in Megacity Moscow.

"Damn, bosu, check this out," Tadhg said.

Akira joined him in a storage room filled with corpses. Limbs were stacked like firewood. Movement on the mini-map of his HUD distracted Akira from the grisly view. Frost had switched positions and zoomed in on movement.

Lights flashed and torches burned in the forest to the north of her position. The glow captured soldiers carrying energy blades. But it wasn't just soldiers descending on Frost. There were civilians, too.

This wasn't an army. It was a mob.

"Multiple hostiles heading toward Frost," Akira whispered.

"I guess more people want to die," Tadhg muttered.

Akira pinged Frost. "Hold your position, and don't fire unless you're fired upon. Make sure Okami doesn't do anything stupid."

She acknowledged with a click over the comm.

Akira moved to a door marked with a rusted engineering sign. Tadhg opened it and lumbered onto a platform overlooking a vast space with ten generators, all active and humming.

I thought this dam was offline, he thought.

At the other end of the room, Perez and Ghost were advancing across a balcony, weapons sweeping for targets.

Akira held up his hand, indicating that it was clear, when suddenly his hand vanished in an explosion of blood. He let out a roar of pain and dove down as bolts lanced all around the room.

"Ambush!" Perez shouted.

Through the agony, Akira saw the generators disgorging metal-and-flesh warriors with ribbed hoses coming from their helmets. Ten augmented monsters leapt up to the platforms and bolted for cover as Shadow Squad opened fire.

Akira managed to use his good hand to fire a burst of bolts into the mask of a Dread that had leapt on top of a generator. Four bolts tunneled through bone and flesh, and the creature slumped over.

Tadhg swung his energy blade through another Dread, the saw-toothed heated blades cutting deep into the abomination. He pushed it through the rest of the armor, flesh, and bone. The upper half slid off, arms still reaching up to strike Tadhg.

Akira finished it with a flurry of bolts to the head.

Across the room, Ghost and Perez had drawn swords. Two Dreads already lay dead on the platform, blood gushing from their wounds. A third slammed into Perez, knocking him down, only to have its neck snapped by Ghost.

A warm sensation pricked Akira as his armor finished clotting the wrist where his hand had been moments earlier. He felt no pain now and fired off another burst, and then drew one of his swords while retreating back to Tadhg. As he moved, he checked on Frost. She was still prone, but the mob was closing in, right toward her position.

Perez was back on his feet, firing his rifle as Ghost spun and thrust his sword into the face of a Dread that mounted the platform, and let out a raucous shriek.

Akira turned toward heavy footsteps behind him, cutting the air with his katana and burying it into the neck of a Dread. The ribbed lines severed, and arterial blood sprayed out.

A muffled roar came from another Dread that climbed over a railing. Akira whirled and thrust his blade deep into its chest. The monstrosity fell on him, pinning him to the ground.

Tadhg dragged the limp beast off and helped Akira to his feet.

Only one Dread remained in the chamber. It leapt to a generator and reared its head back to release a screech. Blood gushed from multiple wounds that would have killed a normal man.

"Sayonara, as you might say," Tadhg said.

He aimed his WMD and unleashed a burst. The Dread turned into the bolts, everything above the torso exploding. Armor, flesh and bone slopped over the generator.

Tadhg lowered the hissing weapon. "You okay, bosu?"

Akira raised his wrist and nodded as he checked on Frost and Okami. The mob was closing in, about a half mile out, the flames burning through the night.

The Engines crossed the platform to continue their search for Dr. Cross when unseen speakers crackled. Someone began clapping, the sound echoing in the space.

"Well done, Shadow Squad," a muffled voice said. "I figured they would send the best if they could find me."

On a balcony above, the doors swung open in front of a man wearing a silver suit that matched his slicked back hair and Dread mask.

All four of the Engines pointed their rifles at the man.

"That is Doctor Cross," Apeiron said through their chips. "We need to take him alive."

"Hold your fire!" Akira shouted.

Akira motioned with his stump to Ghost who leapt onto a ladder and climbed up.

Dr. Cross held up both hands. "I surrender."

Ghost picked up speed as he approached. Slotting his rifle, he threw a titanium-fisted right hook into Dr. Cross's face, the crunch echoing through the room.

The doctor fell back a few steps but remained on his feet.

"I deserved that," he said.

Ghost raised his fist again as Dr. Cross reached up and took off the breathing apparatus to reveal a shiny metal jaw forming a grin of sharp, glistening metal teeth. He huffed through nostril slits where his nose had been removed.

"God damn, you're an ugly motherfucker," Tadhg said.

Perez climbed up and put energy bands on Dr. Cross, binding his hands.

"Target secured," Akira said. "We need evac now. Frost, get ready to move with Okami."

"Evac is on the way," Apeiron said.

"Captain," Ghost said. "You better see this."

Akira bumped past Dr. Cross to find another horrific scene. Four men and three women, all wearing lab coats, lay sprawled on the floor, their throats cut and skulls cracked open. Crushed brains splattered over the floor, and bloody footprints marked where someone had stomped them.

A glance to the doctor's gore-covered boots confirmed he was responsible.

"They were part of his executive science team," Apeiron said.

"He doesn't want us to have his secrets, but he's too egotistical to kill himself," Akira said. He directed the squad back to the stairs. Halfway up, they heard a gunshot echo outside.

"Jigs up, I've been made," Frost said over the channel.

"Stay low, we're coming," Akira said. He turned to Tadhg. "Pick that asshole up. We need to move faster."

"With pleasure," Tadhg said. He grabbed Dr. Cross and threw him over a shoulder.

The squad ran up the rest of the stairs. At the top landing they could hear the pop of gunfire and growl-barking.

"Dumb little ankle biter," Tadhg said.

"Apeiron, activate rockets on the MOTH and push that mob back," Akira ordered.

"Copy that," she said.

Explosions thumped outside as the squad reached the top of the dam. Craters burned where rockets had pounded the hillside. The firepower had pushed the mob into cover, but some still peeked to fire from behind trees and rocks. They were going to need a bit more convincing.

"Frost, grab Okami and head our way!" Akira said. "Suppressing fire, now!"

The Engines on the dam aimed at the trees and fired. Bolts streaked over Frost as she got up and ran with the droid. Tracer rounds chased them across the snow from machine guns. Akira focused his fire on those positions, taking down both of the shooters with shots to the chest.

Frost ran up the slope to the dam with Okami, bounding toward the MOTH that had landed under cover. Akira stayed at the ledge to watch the forest as the squad secured Dr. Cross inside.

Blue Jay zipped from the sky, and Akira caught the drone, holstering it. He ran up the ramp and stayed at the open troop hold, watching the people who had remained behind the trees on the hillside.

"Let me have a look at that," Perez said. He reached out

gingerly to Akira, but Akira pulled his severed wrist back.

"I'll be fine," he said through clenched teeth.

When they were clear of the dam, Akira took off his helmet to scrutinize Dr. Cross. The doctor was on his knees, eyes downward.

"Hey, little dick Napoleon," Tadhg said.

Dr. Cross looked up, snapping his jaw.

"Tadhg was right, you *are* one ugly asshole," Frost said.

Dr. Cross cracked a cocky metal grin as they threw him inside a cage.

"You can't keep a wolf locked up forever!" Dr. Cross screamed. "My pack will come for me!"

"Not where you're going," Ghost said.

Akira activated the electric field around the cage and then took a seat in a rack facing it. He thought that capturing Dr. Cross would allow him to relax, but Akira had a feeling there was some truth to Dr. Cross's threat, and he didn't believe that the Coalition would just go away, even with their leader locked up off planet and an asteroid barreling toward Earth.

"Captain Hayashi," Dr. Cross said from the cage. "Did you get the gifts I left for you?"

Akira ignored him, looking away.

"The gas was the first one of course," Dr. Cross explained. "Your exceedingly stupid horse did a phenomenal job spreading it. Think about that, Captain. The horse you trusted helped kill so many innocents. Sad, isn't it?"

Akira rotated back to the doctor who smiled wider than before.

"Your horse wasn't supposed to live after that," Dr. Cross said. "But since he did, it gave me an opportunity to provide you another gift. If all went as planned, you'll be hearing about that very, very soon."

"Apeiron, what's he talking about?" Akira asked.

"We have a briefing prepared for you once we return to Gold Base."

"A briefing about what? Tell me now, Apeiron."

There was a pause.

"Tell me now!" Akira said louder.

"Very well."

Akira steeled himself as he stared at the doctor.

"Kichiro was severely injured in an attack outside a hospital in Megacity Paris," Apeiron said. "Be assured that I am doing everything in my power to save him."

Akira would have balled his fists and beat Dr. Cross with them if he still had both. The man had taken so many good Pistons and Engines, even from the Nova Alliance Strike Force. He'd killed countless innocent people, and this time he had gone to great lengths to strike at Kichiro, for no other reason than to hurt Akira.

This man deserved death more than anyone Akira had ever met. Pushing up the rack bars, he burst over to the cage, only to be grabbed by Tadhg and Ghost before he could unlock it.

"Easy, Cap!" Ghost said.

"Let me go!" Akira shouted. "Get your hands off me!"

"Bosu!" Tadhg growled, wrestling him back.

"Stand down, Captain," Apeiron said. "That is an order from Command."

Tadhg pulled back on Akira and Ghost locked his left arm. Akira squirmed and pushed up, his strained muscles burning. Everything that had happened came crashing over him, all the death, carnage, losses over the years, and now this—a personal attack on his horse.

It was all too much for Akira.

He broke free of their grip and charged the cage until Tadhg tackled him to the deck. Akira cried out in pain as his severed wrist tore back open, blood gushing out of the bandages. Frost bent down to help stop the flow while Perez joined Ghost and Tadhg.

It took all three men to keep Akira down. In front of them, the doctor cackled like a hyena in the cage, enjoying every second.

***

Dr. Cross was on his way to spending the rest of his days in isolation in a vault, but Jason feared this wasn't the end of the

Coalition threat, especially after hearing about so many new attacks. The war against the Coalition as they'd known it might be over, but he feared the scattered insurgents would not soon forget their hatred of the Nova Alliance and AI.

He sat in the back seat of a hover-truck with Betsy and Darnel. They all stared out the windows at the thousands of people holding signs and screaming.

"This is getting worse by the day," Betsy said.

"People are scared," Darnel said.

"They should not be," Apeiron replied. "The chances of the cannons not destroying Hros-1 are extremely remote, but I do understand human nature often leads to violence in the face of fear."

"That's exactly why the Nova Alliance Council wanted to keep the asteroid a secret," Jason said.

Apeiron tilted her head. "I thought the shared threat of the asteroid would bring humanity together, but Captain Hayashi was right about the Coalition. They are a tribe and are indoctrinated, which means the only way to change their mind about me is to destroy Hros-1."

The convoy pulled into a parking garage under AAS's Mid-Town headquarters. Twenty guards surrounded Jason and Betsy as they made their way down to an old subway platform, where an ancient subway train waited for them.

As he boarded, Jason imagined the millions of passengers who had taken this very train. He reached for Betsy's hand, and she accepted it. Two months ago, she might have pulled away, but their relationship was on the mend. Having the L-S88 chip allowed him to do so much more than he had ever imagined, and she didn't seem to mind now that he was home more.

In some ways, he had become like an OS, accessing, analyzing, and responding to data through millions of Hummer Droids and employees throughout the world. But access to so much also allowed him to see just how bad things were getting in the megacities. Riots over SANDs treatments, food shortages, poor air quality, and the threat from Hros-1 had the Nova Alliance teetering on the edge of chaos.

The train finally stopped and opened to a white-walled

platform and a sign that read, *Life Ark 12*. Jason guided Betsy out of the train and down a long flight of concrete stairs. Two Canebrakes stood sentry in front of rectangular blast doors at the bottom landing. Their antennas rattled and clicked, and they stepped aside.

"Please, after you," Apeiron said.

"I'm going to stay topside," Darnel said.

Jason knew his friend was giving him some extra time alone with Betsy. But they weren't exactly alone. Apeiron stepped inside the elevator with them. One minute and two seconds into the descent, the elevator finally reached its destination.

"We are now a half mile beneath the surface," Apeiron said.

A white-tiled passage connected to an arched ceiling over one hundred feet high, carved out of the rock under Megacity New York. A second pair of blast doors slowly opened to a space ten times the size of a Droid Raider stadium, almost a thousand yards long and another thousand yards wide.

Hummer Droids in mech-suits stopped their work and stood idly. Balconies with glass windows framed the massive room. On the bottom floors, storefronts, eateries, and medical wards waited for future inhabitants.

Apeiron explained that eventually a park here would support hundreds of plant species. A concrete creek twisted through and emptied into a pond.

"Life Ark 12 will support a population of approximately twenty thousand people," Apeiron said. "This is slightly above the minimum needed to sustain the human race if all other life is wiped out across the globe."

"That's not going to happen, even if the asteroid does hit, right?" Betsy asked.

"It depends," Apeiron replied. "If Hros-1 were to impact, it could cause a domino effect that would escalate the danger to already fragile and damaged ecosystems. The worse-case scenario is complete collapse."

The tour continued through future gardens to a block of outdoor patios and communal spaces. Jason gestured toward the ceiling, where cranes were installing a holo-screen that would run the entire length of the ceiling.

"Every morning the sun will rise, and every night it will set," he said. "The irrigation system runs off algorithms that consider an extensive data set ranging from crop-growth rates and plant health to the mental health of the human population."

"That's remarkable," Betsy said.

"This Life Ark is modeled after the mining colonies on the Moon," Apeiron said.

They passed Hummer Droids and a few human supervisors who nodded at Jason. Another set of blast doors opened to an underground water treatment center and a vast hydroponic garden.

"Fifty percent of the food will come from this sector," Apeiron said. "Diets will be mostly meatless, but we do have livestock."

She crossed through warehouses that would support pigs, cows, and chickens, then on to another silo designed to look like a honeycomb.

"This is an E-Vault," she explained. "Very similar to the one at the Titan Space Elevator."

"The specimens contained inside these individual capsules were discovered on some of the trips we went on over the past few years," Jason added.

Betsy walked around, looking into glass vaults at the creatures inside. "So, this is what you two were doing…" She faced Jason and raised a skeptical brow. "Globetrotting on some sort of safari."

Jason laughed. "Kind of."

"All Life Arks are completely self-sustainable for up to fifty-years with only routine maintenance," Apeiron said. "This is the maximum amount of time needed for the world to heal after an impact from Hros-1."

"That's great for the twenty thousand people who will live here," Betsy said.

"Everyone selected has a specific trait that will ensure if the worst-case scenario happens, life will go on," Jason replied gingerly. He understood how that sounded, but this wasn't about fairness. It was about survival.

An hour later, they returned to the surface and climbed into the convoy. Betsy remained glued to the view outside, citizens begging for food or sleeping in alleys and on park benches.

They drove down a ramp and into a tunnel under the bay. Jason reached out to Betsy again, but he stopped shy of grabbing her hand and decided against saying anything more. He knew his wife. Sometimes she needed to process things by herself.

The quiet gave way to the loud whine of hover cycles with high-powered electric engines. Darnel shifted in his seat as the first bike shot past them, leaving a streak of neon light. A second, third, and fourth bike passed.

"Asshole," Darnel said.

Jason looked over to Betsy. "I thought maybe we could take the girls out for pizza tonight."

"Autumn said she—"

A distant blast cut her off and Jason reached out instinctively to shield her as the hover truck jolted to a stop. The vehicle at the front of the convoy exploded, peppering the windshield with shrapnel that sent spiderwebs cracking outward.

"Get down!" Darnel yelled.

Jason held Betsy and covered her the best he could.

Gunfire cracked outside, pinging into the truck. The guards in the front seats cried out as armor piercing rounds punched through their flesh.

Darnel grabbed a rifle and grabbed the door handle. His eyes met Jason's.

"Stay down," he said in calm voice.

More hover bikes shot past, spraying the convoy with bullets and plasma bolts. After they passed, Darnel opened the door and hopped out, firing a burst at the riders.

Jason rose slightly to see Darnel run to the next vehicle and hunch behind a door where two guards were returning fire. Apeiron crouched in front of Jason and Betsy, blocking them with her titanium frame.

"It's going to be okay," Jason said to his wife.

But he knew it wasn't the truth. His fear about Dr. Cross had been confirmed. This had to be the work of the Coalition, perhaps payback for capturing the doctor. Jason watched the sleek hover bikes turning for another pass. Their headlights flitted across the walls.

The riders stopped behind the burning vehicles, their engines revving like a growling pack of droid dogs. Another noise rose above the grumbling, and a new pair of lights entered the tunnel.

A black truck skidded to a stop and in the glow of the lights, eight fully armored figures hopped out. The men moved with calculated precision, fanning out and firing into the stalled convoy.

One of the guards with Jason cried out in pain and went limp on the ground while Darnel and the final guard ran back to Jason's vehicle.

"Keep low. I will handle this," Apeiron said. She jumped out, attracting a flurry of plasma bolts that slammed against her armor.

Jason snuck a glance as she charged the soldiers, grabbing the first shooter by the head with both hands. She twisted his skull, cracking his neck. Then she lunged for the next hostile and caught him by the arm, ripping it clean from its socket before using his body as a shield.

Apeiron tossed the body away and darted into the shadows. Using a segmented arm, she wrapped it around the neck of one of the fighters, tossing him against a wall. Bolts pounded her armor, disabling her left arm, but she was already moving again.

Darnel and the other AAS guard stood to fire as hover cycles raced down the tunnel. Bolts lanced from the truck and the bikes, cutting through the guards. The men went down, screaming in pain and writhing from the injuries.

Jason ducked, unable to see what was happening, but his ears helped paint a picture in his mind. Two of the bikes slammed into the wall, and a third screeched over the pavement.

A familiar voice yelped in pain.

"Darnel!" Jason shouted.

He got up to look for his friend, spotting Apeiron. Across the passage, she engaged the remaining soldiers, commandeering one of their pulse rifles. Raking it back and forth, she fired a burst of shots, dropping all but one where they stood.

The last man hopped onto a hover bike and sped away. The machine was fast, but Apeiron was faster. She fired a single shot that knocked the soldier off the bike. The vehicle flipped, scraping against the ground in a shower of sparks, and the soldier's body tumbled away.

Jason finally pulled away from Betsy, who sat up, coughing from the smoke.

"We're okay, but don't move, I'm going to check on Darnel," Jason said.

She managed a nod and Jason climbed out of the vehicle. He found Darnel sitting with his back to the front passenger door. The other guard was dead, his face pocked by still smoking bolt holes.

"Get back in the truck," Darnel said, wincing.

Jason reached down. "Let me help you inside."

"No," Darnel said, pulling out of his grip. "I can't feel my legs."

"All threats have been neutralized," Apeiron called out. She strode across the passage, smoke drifting away from smoldering holes in her armor.

She bent down next to Darnel and Jason went back to help Betsy out of the vehicle.

"It's okay," he said. "It's over."

Betsy took his hand, still coughing.

"Who... who were they?" she asked.

Apeiron checked Darnel who groaned in pain.

"I received a message from those responsible. Apparently, there is a group that calls itself the Red Wolves," she said as she attended to Darnel. "The same group claims responsibility for other attacks, including the one outside a hospital in Paris."

Jason went down on one knee in front of his friend with Betsy leaning over Darnel.

"I want to hear this message, too," she said, looking to Jason.

He hesitated, but then nodded.

No more secrets.

A hologram protruded in front of them of a man with a red horned helmet in the shape of a wolf's head. "Today Doctor Crichton was killed, and if Doctor Cross is not released, we will continue to assassinate your leaders."

The feed fizzled out, but the message was clear—Jason was a target. That meant his family was not safe either. They may have survived this attack, but there would be more.

23

Captain Akira Hayshi's missing hand was wrapped with nanotech pads. They would help him heal and prevent infection, but no amount of medicine could calm him on the MOTH flight to Megacity Paris. His eyes hadn't left Dr. Cross since Shadow Squad had captured him at the dam on Lake Baikal.

"The Red Wolves will come for me," said Dr. Cross. "They won't rest until I'm free."

Akira snorted. "Tadhg, Ghost, you stay with this piece of shit," he said. "Perez, Frost you're with me."

"You got it," Ghost said. He tapped his deactivated energy sword against the cage that held Dr. Cross, who was staring at Akira with his evil metal grin.

Akira fought not to open the cage and rip the doctor limb from limb. He turned his back and waited at the troop hold as the MOTH set down on Ragnar Field at the FOB outside of Megacity Paris. A Piston ran over as the ramp extended down.

"Captain Hayashi," he said "I'm Lieutenant Marcus. I'll take you to the field hospital."

An APC waited on the tarmac. Perez and Frost opened the back hatch. Okami jumped in and climbed into Akira's lap, tail wagging. The vehicle lurched and drove through the base, where thousands of Pistons were providing security to the local refugee camps.

Special Forces teams were still hunting down any Coalition stragglers hiding in the city, and any terrorists that had hidden with the local population—bastards like those who had hit his horse.

Tapping into INN, Akira watched the rocket attack on Kichiro and the woman who was riding him. It was the third time he had seen it, and each time it made his blood warm and guts twist with agony.

He still didn't know what the hell his horse had been doing out there with this young woman, but he would find out soon enough.

In the passenger's seat, Lieutenant Marcus turned to the Engines.

"Honor to meet you," he said.

"Honor is ours," Perez said.

Akira simply nodded. He set Okami down and climbed up into the turret. The APC pulled onto a highway and raced down a plowed road, jerking up and down over potholes and small bomb craters.

In the distance, hundreds of white refugee tents whipped in the wind at Processing and Relocation Zone A4, on the border of Megacity Paris. Smoke fingered up from campfires. Hundreds of thousands of people now lived in camps like this while the city was being cleared and prepared for rebuilding. Piles of debris formed mountains along the road where entire sectors of the city had been reduced to rubble. Very few buildings outside the megacity walls had survived.

In the parking lot of an old home-repair store, a patrol of Pistons guarded a fleet of AAS hover trucks that unloaded hundreds of Hummer Droids to assist with the rebuilding. The staging area was massive, but it was a no-fly zone due to the threat of anti-air weapons. The Coalition still had soldiers hiding among the Nova Alliance citizens in bunkers yet undiscovered. It could be months before they were all killed or captured.

A quake shook the APC as it pulled onto the highway. Four large industrial machines called Spiders drove toward them on twenty-foot-tall tires. The machines resembled monster cellar spiders with a hefty circular body and eight thin legs.

The driver pulled the APC right under the convoy of droids that had built the megacities and the colonies on the Moon, versatile machines with extendable leg segments that allowed them to rise off the ground a hundred floors.

They took the next exit toward an area of the city spared from the bombing, an island of buildings in a sea of rubble. They stopped in the underground parking garage of a hospital, and Akira hopped out.

A Hummer Medical Droid waited outside an entrance.

"Hello, Captain," Apeiron said. "Please follow me."

As Akira entered the medical facility, he halted at the sight of his loyal friend that had saved his life so many times. The animal had been the one constant thing in his life for so long, and now he was dying.

The horse lay on its side on a large gurney, the head, neck, and body hooked up to a dozen different machines. All four limbs were removed, and the armor that had covered the brown flesh of the stallion was laying in charred pieces around the room.

"Kichiro," Akira choked.

He slowly walked over, afraid to even touch the fragile beast. Three Hummer Medical Droids monitored the machines keeping the horse alive.

Perez and Frost came up behind Akira, and Okami moved in front of him, tail between his legs, whimpering at his animal companion.

"Captain, you arrived just in time to make a decision," said Apeiron. The Hummer Medical Droid that had accompanied them raised a skeletal finger, and the other three droids stepped back from their machines.

"How did this happen?" Akira snapped.

"This was the result of a Coalition terrorist attack—"

"I know that, but why was Kichiro giving that woman a ride in the first place?"

"I'm sorry, Captain. I had thought the area was secure," Apeiron said. "That woman played a significant role in keeping Kichiro alive when he was in the Coalition's prison. The two developed a bond, and I believed it would do them both good to see each other."

"Well, it didn't do them *any* good, did it?" Akira said.

The horse suddenly groaned, and Akira lowered his voice, crouching in front of the animal.

"I'm sorry, Kichiro. I'm so sorry," Akira said. He gently touched his muzzle and turned to Apeiron. "Is he in pain?"

"No, he's sedated right now, and while his pain may feel distant, we need to make a decision…"

"What are the options?"

"If we try to repair the extensive damage to his internal organs, it will likely cause great suffering, and I am not sure we can save him," Apeiron said. "The other option is to euthanize him and let him go... or lastly, to transform him from beast to droid."

"Like Ghost?" Akira asked.

"Not quite. Kichiro would be like me, an OS based on the mind of a biological creature. I would upload the horse's consciousness after I design the OS."

"So it would still be Kichiro, but... smarter?"

"Yes, indeed."

Akira stepped up to the animal but stopped shy of touching it.

"You can have a few minutes to make your decision," Apeiron said.

Akira turned to Perez, who often served as Shadow Squad's voice of reason. "What would you do, Perez?"

"AI is salvation, Captain."

"AI is salvation," Frost repeated.

A metal door creaked open, and they all turned toward the young woman who entered. Bandages covered her face and arms, and she walked with a slight limp.

"Captain, this is Chloe Cotter," Apeiron said. "She is the young woman who took care of Kichiro in the catacombs. Doctor Cross forced her to work on Kichiro."

"Work on Kichiro?" he asked, picturing the poor horse running through the city with those gas canisters. "She modified Kichiro at the doctor's command."

"That is correct, Captain.

He scrutinized the injured girl. Her freckled face and frizzy hair looked innocent enough, but he wasn't deceived. She was the one responsible for the gas canister.

"She turned Kichiro into a killing machine."

"No," Apeiron corrected. "She took care of your horse, and she was not aware of what Dr. Cross had planned. In fact, she was killed during the gas attack."

"Killed?" Frost asked.

"I repaired her like I repaired Lieutenant Rossi," Apeiron said. "She is one of my children."

Chloe finally spoke. "I'm sorry about what happened to him,

and I'll do whatever I can to help fix him."

The droid walked over to Chloe, putting a hand on her shoulder. "She was with Kichiro when the attack occurred a few hours ago. I believe Doctor Cross was trying to kill them both."

Chloe stared at the horse with sad eyes.

"Chloe was a custom droid worker before the Coalition revolution in Megacity Paris," Apeiron said. "That is why Doctor Cross forced her to work in the catacombs."

"I'm sorry," Chloe said again. "I…"

Akira wasn't sure what to say.

"If you choose the third option, I would like to bring Chloe in to help reconstruct the stallion," Apeiron said.

"I'll help him, I promise," Chloe said. "I'll make him even stronger and faster."

Kichiro suddenly moved his head and opened one of his eyes. His long tongue flopped out of his mouth as he let out a weak neigh.

"I thought he was sedated," Akira said.

"He is, but the dose is wearing off, we will administer more," Apeiron said.

Akira put a hand out. "It's okay, boy. You're going to be okay."

One of the other droids held up a syringe and gently put it into a port.

The horse sniffed at Akira's wrist, then let out a whinny. Even now, when the horse was dying, it was worried about Akira's injury.

He couldn't let his loyal beast die. Not like this.

Chloe stepped up to the gurney. The horse rotated slightly and sniffed her next. Then, angling his head down, Kichiro licked at Okami who wagged his tail.

"You can fix him?" Akira asked Chloe.

"Yes," she said confidently.

Akira nodded. "Save my friend."

"He's my friend too, Captain," Chloe replied.

***

Two weeks after the attack outside the hospital in Paris and Chloe was on her way to the Titan Space Elevator in a cable car with Apeiron.

Chloe looked out the windows, admiring the deep blue Atlantic Ocean with a sense of awe. She still couldn't quite believe she was heading to the habitats. Part of her didn't feel like she deserved to be here, at the final destination from Earth before a journey to the Moon and stars. Most civilians would never step foot here, and she felt incredibly honored. Apeiron had given her more than just a second chance at life.

For the past two weeks, Chloe had spent night and day working on droid designs for Kichiro. They had kept him in a cryo-tube to preserve his body, and today they would make the transfer into the droid that Chloe had helped design.

Chloe stared out into space, imagining Hros-1 barreling toward the planet. But she didn't fear the asteroid. Rather, she trusted Apeiron.

The car approached the spinning habitats and docked a few minutes later. The door opened to a pressurized hatch that chirped after she stepped inside with Apeiron.

A few minutes later, the hatch to the habitat opened. She walked under a sign that read, Sector 220.

"Did you know this is where I was conceived?" Apeiron asked.

"Here?" Chloe asked.

"Yes, this is where Doctor Crichton uploaded Petra's consciousness and merged it with the OS that makes me who I am." Apeiron gestured out the viewport. "Like the Earth, I have changed considerably since that day, ten months and three days ago."

"Fascinating."

"Follow me, we are almost ready," Apeiron said to her chip.

The droid led her to a bathroom. Inside, Chloe stripped out of her AAS uniform, and placed them next to the neatly folded scrubs on a bench. She looked at the mirror, leaning in to inspect the scars on her freckled face. The one from the assassination attempt had left a raised red mound on her cheek.

And yet, she no longer felt ugly. She had grown accustomed

to her broken and altered body. Her growing friendship with Cyrus had helped restore her confidence too.

Chloe dressed in the scrubs and headed to a chamber called an E-Vault with a renewed sense of purpose. When she got there, Apeiron explained that the honeycomb-shaped space held hundreds of creatures, along with complex freezers containing the DNA from hundreds of other specimens. All of them were unique animals that had helped inspire the perfect design for the Canebrakes.

A hatch opened, and a group of technicians and doctors entered and introduced themselves. There were five human staff and three Medical Service Droids. Chloe pulled a mask over her face. Memories of the catacombs surfaced in her mind's eye, but she forced them away.

Dr. Cross could no longer get to her. She was free of him.

Taking a deep breath, she crossed through the room. Bright plasma lamps illuminated Kichiro's cryo-chamber.

Chloe leaned down to the glass, putting a hand on the cold lid. Scars crisscrossed the obsidian black hide of the horse. Rough stumps remained where the legs had all been removed.

"We are ready," Apeiron said.

A doctor gently touched Chloe's arm. "Please step back."

Chloe retreated as a technician activated the cryo-chamber. The glass lid hissed open, and the liquid drained through tubes, leaving only the stallion inside dripping with cryo fluid as it hit the warm air.

Two Hummer Medical Droids lifted out the body and placed it on a hover table. They guided it toward the machine that would upload the horse's consciousness and merge it with the OS that Apeiron had designed.

"Okay, let's move, people," said the lead doctor. "We don't have much time."

Chloe put a gloved hand on the horse's cold hide. "Goodbye, my friend."

But this wasn't exactly goodbye.

Kichiro was about to make a transformation much like Chloe had made on the day she died. Soon, the horse would transcend his flesh body.

They had already assembled the new mechanical body that Chloe had designed in INN, from the comfort of her hospital bed and then in the refugee camp while she recovered. It was slightly larger than the stallion had been and made of a titanium exterior shell. The head looked almost identical, but with blue INVS eyes. A long mane of brown hair salvaged from the horse itself now hung over the armored neck.

Chloe walked around the droid to see the enhancements; an armored adjustable saddle, plates that could rotate out to charge the interior battery with solar power, and legs that could run at a top speed of seventy-five miles an hour, according to Apeiron.

Inside the droid was a state-of-the-art engine with nine hundred horsepower. Unlike the animal, the droid would never grow tired.

Chloe smiled as she ran a hand down the smooth black armor. Beneath the undercarriage of the belly, they had added thrusters in two places that would allow the horse to jump great distances if needed.

Captain Hayashi would be able to control the horse through INN. And that wasn't all. Kichiro had interior storage for chutes that could deploy during a freefall.

"The transformation is now complete," Apeiron announced proudly. She handed Chloe a Commpad. "Would you like to do the honors?"

"I would love it," Chloe said.

Taking the device, she pointed it at the droid stallion and clicked the button. The blue eyes glowed to life, then flitted toward her. Kichiro let out an electronic whinny and trotted over to Chloe, metal hooves clicking on the deck. Lowering its head, it stared into Chloe's eyes.

"Hey, Kichiro. Do you remember me?" she asked.

The stallion nudged his head against her own.

"I'm sorry for what they did to you," Chloe said. "But you're all better now. You get a second chance, just like I did."

Kichiro lowered his head, and Chloe wrapped her arms around his neck. She held him for a long moment, hoping this wasn't the last time she would see him.

For the next hour, she watched the droids and technicians

do final checks.

"I have to go now," Chloe said. "But you're going to see Captain Hayashi very soon."

The stallion hoofed at the deck, the clank echoing.

"I can see him again, right?" Chloe asked Apeiron.

"I am sure that can be arranged."

Chloe went back to the stallion one more time and kissed him.

When they parted ways, she felt a deep sadness like she wouldn't see him again. She looked over her shoulder as the horse was guided to a climber car for a trip to the surface.

Chloe went back to the spaceport, the despair growing stronger with every step. By the time they got to the MOTH, a pounding headache set in above her right temple. The agonizing pain made her wince as it worsened, like a rod hitting her head, again and again.

"Apeiron," she mumbled. "Apeiron, something's wrong."

This was beyond heartache. This was something…

The Hummer Droid reached out and caught Chloe as she fell. Another jolt of pain ripped through her head, red flashing across her vision.

Blurred human figures ran over and crouched down as Apeiron lowered her gently to the deck.

She could hear them talking, but the voices were all muffled. Only one voice came through clearly in her mind.

"Do not worry, child," Apeiron said.

24

A concrete and stone shell rose thirty stories around the base of the Titan Space Elevator. The shell housed offices, hangars, and ports for the climber cars rising up the lines to be swallowed by the clouds.

Akira balled his new robotic hand as he watched from a mile away. Shadow Squad stood in an observation center at Spartan Base near the outskirts of Macapá, an equatorial city in the former country of Brazil. Later today, two of the final Poseidon cannons would be loaded onto the platforms for the journey up to geostationary orbit.

Akira and his team were here to make sure that happened without incident.

When the launch was over, a cable car from Sector 220 would descend, and Akira would be reunited with Kichiro for the first time in a month.

He was anxious to see what Chloe and Apeiron had done, but he was also anxious about the chaos in the megacities. Three months to go before the cannons destroyed Hros-1, and the violence was threatening to destroy the cities and refugee camps. Despite all assurances that Hros-1 would be obliterated, the masses seemed to expect the end of the world.

Akira was glad his brother had agreed to stay with his family at his small condo in Megacity Tokyo. They were safe there, and with Kai discharged and the Droid Raider season over, they had no reason to go back to Megacity Phoenix until after Hros-1 was destroyed.

He just wished he could be there with them.

Even with Dr. Cross in prison off planet, Shadow Squad continued to be deployed to deal with hot spots around the globe, leaving Akira little time with his family.

Capturing the doctor had caused a chain reaction, inciting terrorist attacks at various locations from a group called the Red Wolves.

Riots and civil unrest in the megacities threatened to spiral out of control. In the Capitol of Tokyo, hundreds of thousands of citizens had taken to the streets when news leaked about Life Arks being built in secret. It reaffirmed the irrational fear of the masses that the asteroid was a bigger threat than what was being reported.

Akira linked to INN and watched as shuttles launched across the globe. Ten every hour, some with only a few people on board, all wealthy and heading to new homes at Kepler Station on the Moon to ride out the coming storm. If the asteroid was destroyed, they would return to Earth. If not, they would become permanent residents.

"Captain, be advised, Doctor Crichton is en route to supervise the launch," Apeiron said to Shadow Squad's chips.

"Brazen move," Frost said. "Guess he isn't worried about getting killed."

"He has you and the Canebrakes," Apeiron replied.

"This site is even more of a target if his location is compromised," Akira said.

"Which is why no one but a select few know he is coming," Apeiron added.

Short Sword fighter jets patrolled in the distance, rumbling through the clouds. The Navy was here too, with three warships that had escorted the barges with the four cannons.

Shadow Squad crossed the tarmac and joined three Canebrakes. The eight-foot war machines monitored the Engines with glacier blue eyes. Okami trotted over and growled. He didn't seem to be a big fan, and he wasn't alone.

"The fuck are they looking at?" Tadhg asked.

"These droids constantly scan for threats," Akira said.

"I don't like it," Tadhg said.

A stealth MOTH descended from the lumpy clouds and the Engines spread out to create a perimeter. The wings rotated to vertical, lowering the craft to the ground. Out of the troop hold came an army of AAS guards, led by a Black Hummer Droid with segmented arms ending in serrated blades.

"That's new," Frost said.

"I have made some upgrades," Apeiron replied.

Dr. Crichton also had a new look. He appeared in white

armor with ribbed abs and barreled chest plates, looking like an ancient Greek God.

"Captain Hayashi, good to see you again," Jason said, extending a glove. "Thank you for being here. You're about to witness history."

Akira shook using his robotic hand.

"We're honored, Doctor Crichton," he said.

Jason led his entourage to the command center. The three Canebrakes followed, their blue eyes scoping for danger.

Akira motioned for the squad to start the patrol in the jungles surrounding the base. Ghost took Perez and Frost north, into a thick canopy blocking the view of the hills.

Tadhg joined Akira on a cliff overlooking the base. He launched Blue Jay into the air, and Okami took off down a trail.

Akira moved across the cliff to an outcropping with a direct view of the rockets, now secured to the circular elevator car. Hundreds of black and yellow Hummer Droids worked on finishing the exterior hull of a new platform, buzzing up and down with their thrusters.

"All clear in Sector 4," Frost said over the comms.

The other squads sounded off, reporting the all clear.

Tadhg kicked at the dirt as Perez, Ghost, and Frost emerged from the jungle.

"I don't like babysitting, know what I'm sayin'?" he said, sounding agitated. "If this is what the future holds, I'm going back to smashing droids."

"Go for it," Frost said, "then I won't have to listen to you run your mouth."

"You'd prefer to be a glorified security guard and standing sentry with one of those tin cans?" Tadhg gestured his cannon toward one of the Canebrakes.

A rattling echoed from the machine, and a warning sensor flashed across Akira's HUD. "Sergeant Walsh, lower your weapon," he said firmly.

The Canebrake rotated its fan head, the shoulder mounted cannons on each shoulder rotating toward Tadhg.

"Sergeant," Akira said.

Tadhg moved the barrel.

"I wasn't going to shoot it. Frost got me all riled up." Tadhg looked at her, then back to Akira. "But what if I did shoot it? On accident, I mean. It's just a machine. Not like I was pointing at a person."

"Engines don't have accidents," Perez said. "You know better than that."

"To answer the sergeant's question, the Canebrakes will defend themselves against any hostile, human or droid," Apeiron replied.

"Wait, what if we accidentally hit them in combat?" Tadhg asked.

"Perez already answered your question," Ghost said.

"Right, but say I did..."

"*Enough*, Sergeant," Akira said.

The smooth voice of the mission control officer came over the comms: "Ten minutes to launch."

Akira scanned the hills, creating a two-dimensional overlay that divided the terrain horizontally into thirds. Nothing moved in the dense jungles. He tapped into the view from the command center. Dr. Crichton stood at the front window, a team of staff and droids behind him, all working as the countdown clicked down on a holo-screen.

With one minute left, the launch platform rose off the pad, the Poseidon cannons secured to its center.

Frost pinged a section of jungle.

"You got something?" Akira asked.

She lowered the barrel. "Nah..."

Akira kept one eye on that sector as the platform ascended. Inside the command center, the launch team was already clapping in celebration.

One step closer to destroying Hros-1, Akira thought. He let out a sigh of relief, ready to see Kichiro again. "Okay, that's a wrap. Let's move, Shadow Squad."

Suddenly, a white light flashed in the command center's feed.

Akira whirled toward the tower. Flames belched out of the viewports.

"Shadow Squad, in the air, now!" he yelled.

He launched off the cliff and flew toward the explosion, his mind tried to grasp what had happened. Had they missed a drone? A rocket?

Akira realized the truth as he flew closer to the burning tower. The roof was gone on one side, leaving a gaping hole where the blast had blown outward.

It was a threat from within... he thought.

There was little doubt that the explosion had killed Dr. Crichton. No one could survive a blast like that, even with the titanium armor.

Akira passed over a dozen Canebrakes galloping toward the tower. As he came in from above, he raised his wings and dropped right through the blast hole, flames rushing around him. Bodies burned inside, none moving.

"Over here," Apeiron said.

It took Akira a moment to notice that her voice wasn't coming from his chip, but from a Hummer Droid in the corner of the room.

He rushed over, finding Dr. Crichton in a fetal position behind the remains of the droid. Apeiron had tried to shield him, taking the brunt of the blast.

"Doctor Crichton," Akira said. "Doctor, can you hear me?" He reached down with his robotic hand and gently pulled the doctor up. His new armor seemed to be spared from any damage.

"He is unconscious," Apeiron said. "Carry him to the following coordinates."

They flashed on his HUD.

Akira picked up the doctor and ran. He leapt out of a window, his jet pack activating and blasting them away from the tower. The other Engines surrounded him in flight. They landed outside of a warehouse with a fleet of APCs stored inside. A group of Pistons stood guard as Akira carried the doctor through the open doors.

In the center of the warehouse, a black Hummer Droid waited with two Medical Droids and a team of five Canebrakes. Akira gently set the doctor down in front of them.

"Please step back, Captain," Apeiron said.

Akira did as ordered while the Medical Droids gently moved

Dr. Crichton out of the room.

The threat was never from the outside, he thought again. That meant anyone could be a suspect, including Shadow Squad.

The Canebrakes spread out. Their fan-shaped heads and blue eyes on each side focused on the squad. Akira instantly thought back to the question that War Commander Contos had posed in Megacity Paris.

Is Apeiron our enemy, or is she our friend?

The Canebrakes surrounded the Engines in a wide circle. Perez brought out his shield, holding it up to defend himself, and Ghost pulled Frost back.

"Easy," Akira said. "Everyone, take it easy."

"The hell is this?" Tadhg asked. He lifted his weapon slightly, prompting the plasma cannons on the shoulder mounts of the Canebrakes to rotate toward him.

"Sergeant, lower your weapon," Apeiron said firmly. "Do not provoke them."

Akira could feel the situation sliding out of his control. Frost readied her rifle, and Ghost moved a hand closer to his sword.

"Sergeant, lower your weapon now, and everyone else, freeze," Akira said. "That is an order."

"Bosu, they…" Tadhg began to say.

Clanking came from behind them and Akira slowly rotated toward the entrance of the warehouse, expecting to see more Canebrakes.

Out of the shadows came a sight that calmed his nerves.

Standing eight feet tall, Kichiro walked inside, hooves clanking against the floor. He was flanked by two Hummer Droids. The mechanical animal let out a whinny when the cool blue eyes fixated on Akira. Tadhg finally cradled his large cannon and the other Engines relaxed, but the Canebrakes remained in a circle around them.

Akira cautiously walked over to the horse, careful not to make any sudden moves. Despite being thrilled to see Kichiro, he remained emotionless on the outside and climbed up into the saddle.

"Apeiron, are these Canebrakes going to stand down?" Akira said.

"As long as they do not perceive you as a threat, they will not attack," she replied. "They are merely executing advanced security protocols due to the imminent danger presented to Doctor Crichton."

"Can't you tell them we aren't a threat?" Perez asked.

"Of course, and I have," Apeiron said. "However, Sergeant Walsh has contradicted me twice now with his very large weapon."

"Know what I'm..." Tadhg let his words trail.

After watching the war machines for another few seconds, Akira jerked his helmet toward the exit.

"Let's go, Shadow Squad," he said, willing calm into his voice.

He gingerly gave his horse a kick to the flank. Kichiro snorted at the Canebrakes blocking the way, as if to say, 'back off' as he trotted forward.

Another beat passed before two of the Canebrakes finally backed away, opening a doorway for the squad.

"That's right, ya metal assholes," Tadhg said, lumbering through the opening.

Frost shook her helmet and Ghost let out a nervous chuckle.

Akira simply patted his horse again, grateful to be reunited with his loyal companion, but unable to shake the feeling that Kichiro had just saved him and his squad once again—this time from other machines.

***

Red lights blinked across the missile-shaped Poseidon cannon.

The MOTH carrying Jason Crichton and his entourage of Darnel, and AAS staff members, roared past one of the cannons in orbit. They were close enough Jason could see the AAS logo on the side of the elongated weapon.

"Magnificent," he said.

"Indeed," Darnel said.

"The great swords of civilization," Apeiron added.

The pilots pulled up, leaving the cannon behind on the final approach to the star-shaped Nova One space station. Switching to the vertical thrusters, the pilots cruised into an open hangar, setting down next to another MOTH.

Securing his helmet, Jason was the first one down the ramp. He wore the same white armor that had saved his life a month earlier at the command center of Spartan Base. While he was not a soldier like the Engines or Pistons, he had quickly grown used to wearing the armored suit after the tunnel attack in New York City. It had saved his life at Spartan Base, but it had not saved all the staff members who had lost their lives in that tower.

Thankfully, Darnel had not been there that day, due to a fourth surgery to fix his spine after the Red Wolves' attack in the tunnel under Megacity New York, which had left him paralyzed from the waist down. Now, wearing an exoskeleton to help him walk, he followed Jason into the command center with Apeiron.

The bowl-shaped tiered room was a hive of activity from some of the most intelligent scientists from AAS and officers of the Nova Alliance Intelligence Division.

Everyone stopped what they were working on and stood stiffly as Jason passed their stations. He nodded and made his way to the viewports overlooking Earth.

North America was visible from this vantage and Jason took a moment to admire the view from hundreds of miles above the Earth.

The Midwest was turning green again, the former wastes that had turned into dusty, dried surfaces were slowly coming back from AAS water projects.

He searched for Megacity New York, hardly visible with the naked eye. His family was down there, deep beneath the surface in Life Ark 12. Safe from the Red Wolves.

After the attack in Honolulu, Betsy had begged him not to come here, but the second attempt on his life had taught him something.

He could only trust one thing besides his family and Darnel, and that was Apeiron. She had found the culprit of the attack, a mid-level programmer named Mike Hook who had tried to kill Jason after his own family had been abducted by the Red

Wolves. Their ultimatum—Mike's family would die if he did not kill Jason.

The explosives were inside of his body, undetectable.

Jason didn't exactly blame Mike for trying to save his family. It was Dr. Cross who Jason blamed. He was responsible for the death of Mike and everyone else in that tower.

The hatch opened in the command center, and General Chase of the Nova Alliance Intelligence Division entered. Tall with a thin, stern face, he was in charge of Operation Burning Skies and was here to supervise the first test of all ten cannons.

He joined Jason and Darnel at the windows.

"All systems are ready, Doctor, and the cannons are primed," Chase said.

"Excellent," Jason said.

He stepped close to the viewport, locating one of the missile-shaped cannons on the horizon. So much work had gone into making the weapons and deploying them in such a short time. Now, they would find out if they worked.

"Ready when you are, Doctor," Chase said.

"Fire," Jason said in a confident voice.

All sixty staff members stared anxiously at the glass. Their tension was almost palpable in the seconds it took for the cannons to activate. Darnel and Jason exchanged a quick glance. Everything boiled down to this moment.

Just as Jason turned back to the viewport, a brilliant red burst exploded out of the closest cannon in orbit. Nine more lasers streaked out of the other cannons. Crimson beams ripped through space.

The sheer amount of power left Jason and everyone else in the quiet room in awe.

The Poseidon cannons worked all right.

They worked *beautifully*.

The lasers continued toward the sparkling stars as if they would slam into the distant suns. Jason pictured Hros-1 racing toward Earth. Soon, it would be destroyed, hammered into so many fragmented pieces, just like the Coalition.

After a few minutes of a constant stream of the lasers, the cannons shut off, the red glow vanishing.

General Chase studied a holo-screen and then looked up, nodding proudly.

"Confirmation of a successful test," he said.

Applause broke out in the command center from the staff members who had worked tirelessly over the past few months to make this moment happen.

The general reached out to Jason, and they shook hands.

"Well done, Doctor," Chase said.

"You too, General."

Jason left the room feeling more confident that they were finally prepared for Hros-1, and with two months to spare. The Life Arks were almost complete, and the restoration sites continued to recover. But none of that meant anything if the megacities continued to descend into anarchy, or if the Red Wolves continued to launch terrorist attacks, further fueling the fear of the masses.

Boarding the MOTH to return to Megacity New York, Jason took a deep breath and strapped into his seat.

"Your family is going to be happy to see you again," Apeiron said. "Betsy is—"

"I'm not going home yet," Jason interrupted.

"Take me to Sector 199," he said.

"What?" Darnel said. "Sector 199 is—"

"The holding block for Doctor Cross," Jason said. "I'm well aware. He tried to kill me and my wife, and you. I want to talk to him and find out why."

"Doctor, I would highly advise against that," Apeiron said.

"You wouldn't understand," Jason replied. "Just take me there."

"Jason, as much as I want to kill Dr. Cross, this is a bad idea," Darnel said. "I really think you should reconsider."

"I have, and I've made up my mind. Sometimes in order to understand your enemy, you must think like your enemy."

Darnel let out a sigh. "Do you really need to talk to Doctor Cross to understand him?"

Jason simply nodded.

The pilots flew out of the open hangar door and toward the Titan Space Elevator. A few minutes later they landed at the spaceport for Sector 199. Two Canebrakes waited on the deck, their blue eyes simmering in the darkness.

Both machines guided the entourage through the secure habitat that required passing through sixteen hatches.

A Piston wearing black vacuum-rated armor waited for them at the final hatch. "Welcome to Sector 199, Doctor Crichton," he said. He glanced warily at Apeiron's segmented arms and serrated blades, and then at Darnel's exoskeleton.

"We're here to see Doctor Cross," Jason said.

"Right, this way," the Piston said. He held up a hand to Apeiron. "Humans only in this sector. It's protocol, which I'm sure you understand."

"She's with me," Jason said.

"I go where Doctor Crichton goes," Apeiron said.

The Piston looked at them in turn and sighed. "Follow me."

He guided them into a wide passage, where a sealed hatch opened to a bridge stretching over a silo-shaped room with thirty box cells, each with a small window. He stepped onto a hover platform at the end of the bridge and motioned for Jason, Darnel, and Apeiron. It lifted off, flew toward the top of the silo, and connected with another small bridge.

"Here you go," the Piston said. "The Mad Wolf."

"I want to talk to him alone, just with Darnel," Jason said to Apeiron.

"Doctor—"

"That's not a request."

"Very well."

Apeiron remained on the hover platform as Jason and Darnel crossed the bridge to the box cube holding the Mad Wolf. An electrical forcefield around the box activated, and the walls folded into the hull of the silo, exposing a small deck and a bed. Standing in front of it was Dr. Cross.

"Ah, Doctor Crichton," Dr. Cross said proudly. Red INVS eyes stared at Jason before flitting to Darnel.

He was thinner than Jason remembered.

"To what do I owe the pleasure of this visit?" Dr. Cross asked.

"Help me understand why you have chosen evil to 'save' the

human race."

Dr. Cross's grin faded.

"Evil?" Dr. Cross asked. "You think…"

Before Jason could respond, Dr. Cross screamed his response, his eyes bulging from the strain.

"Your efforts to save humanity have DOOMED us!"

Dr. Cross took two deep breaths and seemed to relax after the outburst. He looked back at the bridge where Apeiron waited.

"You designed a machine to solve humanity's problems, when all along it is *technology* that has destroyed us," Dr. Cross said calmly. "The only way to survive as a species is to return to where we started and create a new civilization."

"Through a reset," Jason asked.

Dr. Cross nodded. "Precisely."

He looked away from Apeiron, and back to Jason.

"It would be better to let the asteroid hit," Dr. Cross said. "When I first learned about Hros-1, I thought it was a lie. Now I know the truth. Don't you see?"

Jason remained quiet.

"This asteroid is the solution to our problems," Dr. Cross said. "It's the cosmos curing a disease we thought was incurable. Humanity. The universe seeks to reset the balance on our planet, because we're no longer worthy of the gifts it bestowed on us. Humanity has taken and taken, only prolonging the inevitable. It must be taught a lesson. You cannot change your fate. You cannot change the balance of life. You can only adapt to embrace it."

He leaned in, his nostril slits nearly touching the force field.

"You made a mistake by thinking you could play God and transfer your sister into that… abomination… all for some hope at giving her eternal life, I presume," he said, gesturing at Apeiron. "She isn't our savior, Doctor Crichton. Apeiron is the devil, and I fear you won't realize that until it's too late."

25

Chloe dreamed the same dream she had almost every night, in which Dr. Cross and his Iron Wolves hunted her through a frozen forest.

She awoke just before six in the morning, back in the hospital from yet another surgery, her body covered in sweat.

Apeiron's voice filled her mind, reassuring her that she was okay, but Chloe still had a hard time calming down. For the past five months she had been stuck in rooms just like this one, recovering from her injuries. The most recent was a blood clot in her brain that had ruptured when she traveled to the space elevator, the changes in pressure causing the aneurism that had nearly killed her.

Chloe sat up in bed to watch the first glow of sunrise split the horizon. "Apeiron, sometimes I feel like I've used up all my lives."

"I would argue the opposite," Apeiron said. "You are one of the most resilient humans I have ever met." This time the voice came from a white Hummer Droid as it entered Chloe's room. "Are you ready to finally leave this place?"

"*So* ready," Chloe said. "When are you going to tell me where I'm going?"

"I am going to leave that up to your uncle."

Chloe dressed, pulled her hair into a ponytail, and left the room with the droid. They walked along a passage with a holo-screen playing news about Hros-1.

She had been so focused on her recovery that it still hadn't sunk in that civilization could end in less than a month. But no matter how bad things got, they couldn't get any worse than those days in the catacombs with Dr. Cross, or what came after: ten surgeries, countless hours of physical therapy, learning how to use her INVS eyes and augmented parts.

Uncle Keanu and Apeiron had kept her going.

And the visits from Cyrus. Although she no longer had a human heart, Chloe had fallen for the former police officer turned resistance fighter. He had listened to her when she needed someone to talk to, and she had discovered he shared a lot of the same struggles.

They shared a bond through trauma. A *real* human connection that she had lost in all the years running from the Coalition and struggling to survive during her captivity in Paris.

She had almost forgotten what it was like to have someone in her life she could trust beside her uncle. It was refreshing to share so many deep feelings and thoughts with him.

Because after all she had seen and with the world still in danger, she knew trust and true human relationships would become harder to find.

She continued down a white hallway, passing people like her: victims of the war, missing limbs and parts of their insides. Apeiron guided her out of the hospital to a garden with freshly planted trees and flowers, where Keanu was waiting under the canopy of a blooming oak tree. On his shoulder was something Chloe had never thought she would see again.

"Radar!" she shouted. The droid bird flapped over and landed on her arm. "Where did you find him?"

"Right where you left him," Keanu replied. "After the Pistons cleared the area, I went back to our old home. Radar was there. Dirty, but nothing some soap and a rag couldn't handle."

"Who you calling dirty?" Radar asked.

Chloe laughed. That was her Radar.

"Were you going to leave without saying goodbye?" a jocular voice called. Cyrus limped down a garden path toward her.

"I figured you might be here," Chloe said, smiling.

"You figured right." Cyrus smirked, clearly embarrassed. "Who's this?"

"Name's Radar," said the droid. "What's that shit stain on your lip?"

Cyrus gingerly reached up to his mustache. Chloe laughed harder than she had in weeks.

"Nice to meet you, too," Cyrus said.

"Pleasure's mine, mate," Radar replied.

"I'll give you two a few minutes, but Chloe, don't take too

much time," Keanu said. "Our shuttle leaves in five hours. Apeiron got us approved for two tickets to Kepler Station. I already have a job lined up as a human liaison administrator at the station."

"*What?*"

"Apeiron can't protect you here, Chloe, and the Red Wolves are still out there. You aren't safe on Earth, and this is our chance to start over."

"I'll protect her," Cyrus said.

"I can protect myself," Chloe said. "I've survived more than my fair share of attacks, and I don't plan on running and hiding."

"No offense, but how can you protect yourself?" Keanu said. "I'm not just talking to you, Chloe. That question goes for the both of you. It's not just the Red Wolves that are a danger. Things are getting worse in the megacities. Just last night there were riots in the refugee camp where I stay."

Chloe had seen the images over INN. Apeiron had continued to encourage everyone to calm down and come together, assuring them that things would improve, that the odds of the asteroid making it past the cannons were negligible.

But it wasn't just the asteroid that had people in the streets. Coalition refugees and unemployed Nova Alliance citizens made for a powder keg that seemed ready to blow. They were all desperate for work, but most of the labor and jobs available to them had been taken over by droids. The defeat of the Coalition had not magically changed the increasingly quagmire economy, no matter how the Nova Alliance Council and their allies like AAS tried to fix it.

"It won't be forever," Keanu said.

"Maybe Apeiron can get Cyrus approved, too," Chloe said.

"I already asked," Keanu said. "I'm sorry, but the answer was no."

"What about buying a ticket?" Chloe asked.

Cyrus suddenly looked away, and she realized he couldn't afford one.

"You aren't selling me," Radar said. "No, no, no, you aren't."

"I have some money left from the droid shop," Chloe said.

"It's okay, I don't want help," Cyrus said. He was a proud man, and she knew he wouldn't accept, even if Keanu offered.

"Hello," Apeiron said. "I am here to assist if you would like to discuss this, Chloe."

They all turned toward the Medical Service Droid.

"Apeiron, I can't believe you want to send me to the Moon," Chloe gasped. She felt betrayed, hurt, angry.

"Chloe, you are a wonderful human," Apeiron said, "and I want the best for you. Right now, that is at Kepler Station, where you can restart your life in a droid shop. I have an apprentice lined up for you based on your work with Kichiro."

"Maybe this is for the best," Cyrus said. "That's a great opportunity, Chloe."

She glared at him. "You're okay with me going?"

"It's not forever," Cyrus replied, "and it's safer than staying here."

"Safer there, safer there," Radar said.

"Radar, please shut up," Chloe said.

The droid flapped its wings from its perch on her shoulder, blasting her with a draft of air.

"I want what's best for you," Cyrus said, "and if that means you go to the Moon and I don't see you for a while, until I can get there…"

"I will see what I can do about getting Cyrus a ticket," Apeiron said.

Chloe felt her anger subside as Cyrus brushed a strand of hair away from her face and kissed her cheek.

"It will be okay." He leaned in and kissed her lips, then stepped back. "I'll try and find a way to get on a shuttle. I promise."

"I'm holding you to that," she replied.

Chloe spent the rest of the day in a trance. She slogged through customs at the Nova Alliance spaceport, signing paperwork and applying for a custom droid permit for Radar. By nightfall, she was boarding a red corvette with her uncle and the droid. The seats were comfortable and spacious, and a window gave her a view of the megacity. Power had already been restored, and the Eiffel Tower was lit up in the green lights of solidarity.

As the shuttle blasted off, she watched her old home grow distant. The memories and horrors of the war seemed to fade with the lights. Maybe this fresh start was what she needed. She closed her eyes as the shuttle rumbled through the sky in the first stage of the twelve-hour journey to Kepler Station. Almost five months after dying on Earth, she crossed the barrier into space.

She took a calming drink from a Service Droid. As the fluid took effect, she looked out the window at a patrol of black and red King Cobra Spaceplanes. The single cockpit fighters had short wings with mounted plasma cannons and dorsal wings on the top and bottom. They were flying a CAP around the tenth and final Poseidon cannon that had just launched into orbit from a climber. Beyond, a red light winked over the five wings of Nova One space station. Blue lights flashed on incoming shuttles and MOTHs waiting for entry into the hangar bays.

The corvette passed by, heading straight for the Moon.

Chloe closed her eyes, thinking of Cyrus as she drifted off to sleep.

By the time she woke up, the shuttle was descending over the regolith of Kepler Station.

A kind female voice surged from the PA system of the shuttle.

"Welcome, visitors to Kepler Station, or if this is your new home, welcome home."

This wasn't the kind voice Apeiron used on Earth.

Chloe suddenly felt alone again, away from the AI that had been with her every single day for months, away from Cyrus, and about to set foot on a hostile, foreign hunk of rock.

She suddenly got the sense this wasn't temporary.

Something about this journey felt permanent.

***

Ronin walked with his uncle and brothers through the gardens of Edo Castle. Akira had promised this visit for months, but again and again, he had been deployed on some far-off mission while Ronin and his family stayed at his condo in Megacity Tokyo.

Now, only eighteen hours remained before Hros-1 arrived. Most of the world had gone underground, and soon the Hayashi family would retreat to a shelter underground.

If his uncle was nervous, he wasn't showing it.

Dressed in his snug black uniform and carrying his leather-bound book, Akira had finally made good on his promise, even with the imminent threat of Hros-1. Maybe Ronin was reading too far into it, but his uncle seemed relaxed and at ease being in the presence of his family, even if Elan and Zachary stared at their Commpads. Unlike Ronin, his twin brother seemed more interested in the screens than the history of Edo Castle.

Akira glanced up at the sky.

"You won't be able to see the asteroid yet," Ronin said. "I heard it won't be visible until about thirty minutes before it hits orbit. We can't see the cannons either, not during the day, but they're visible at night, especially when the sun reflects off them. The magnitude of the glare can make them brighter than the brightest stars."

"Cool shit, but I got a question," Zachary said.

Akira nodded. "What?"

"If scientists are so sure the cannons will destroy the asteroid, why is everyone in shelters?" Zachary asked.

"Because even the most prepared warriors do not go into battle without caution and an exit plan."

"Yeah, I figured, but still..." Zachary shrugged.

They continued through the gardens. The sweet fragrance of cherry blossoms hung in the air. The pink trees were in full bloom. Purple and blue Fuji flowers hung from wisteria trees. Tulip beds exploded with bright colors.

A pair of black and yellow Hummer Droids carefully plucked weeds and trimmed bonsai trees around a pond.

Ronin treasured the time with his uncle. Through his eyes, Akira was a hero, respected by all and loved by his soldiers. He seemed to have no flaws, but Ronin knew that everyone, even his uncle, had an Achilles' heel.

At times over the past few months, Ronin had noticed his uncle seemed sad. He figured that had to do with all of the death on the battlefield and probably the loss of his own family. Although, Ronin didn't know the details about what had happened the night his wife and son died.

Akira stopped and gestured toward the ancient white castle towering over the gardens.

"Edo Castle played an important role in the history of the Hayashi family," Akira said. "You three come from a long line of warriors, not only on my side, but your mother's Apache side as well."

Ronin could see her in the distance, standing with his father Kai. She reached out to a hanging wisteria flower and took a sniff.

"Have you learned about the Apache in school?" Akira asked.

"Yes, they were brave and fierce warriors," Zachary said.

Elan nodded and signed. *I must not have that blood in me.*

Ronin and Zachary both chuckled.

"You got your talents, little bro," Zachary said. "Nerd talents."

They laughed again.

"So, can you tell us more about that book?" Ronin asked.

"This has been in our family for five generations, documenting ancient conflicts, and battles that I have waged," Akira said. He handed the book to Ronin.

Ronin studied the gold stenciling: two swords behind a Silver Crane, faded Japanese letters, and a katana. He carefully opened the book.

"This is not just a book about war, but about the life of a warrior," Akira said. "It is as much as a philosophical and spiritual guide as it is a historical document. Written on those pages is a code of honor, an ethos, that I have followed my entire life, and that your father has followed, and our ancestors as well."

Ronin turned the pages with the utmost care, glancing at the journal entries, sketches of samurai armor, quotations about the samurai warrior code *bushido*, a recent drawing of a Canebrake fighting a Coalition Breaker.

Elan leaned over to look, and Zachary hovered behind them. On the next page, Ronin read a passage.

"It is not sufficient to remain calm in the event of catastrophe or emergency. When challenged by adversity, charge onwards with courage and jubilation. This is rising to a higher level."

Akira nodded.

"This is really amazing," Ronin said. He handed the book back to Akira. "Thank you for letting me see it."

They kept walking until Akira halted in front of a row of broken headstones.

"We're here," he said.

Lise and Kai arrived a few minutes later, hand in hand.

"Today, I'm going to share something with all of you that only Kai and I know about," Akira said. "Something we are deeply proud of. Over three hundred and fifty years have passed since forty-seven ronin raided this castle to avenge the death of their Lord Asano. One was an ancestor of the Hayashi family, and he is buried here."

Kai put a hand on Ronin. "This is where your name comes from."

"I brought you here today because honor was once the most valuable currency to a warrior," Akira said. "In the year 1701, Lord Asano came to this place and confronted Lord Kira. In a fit of anger, Lord Asano drew his sword, a grave mistake that resulted in a sentence of death. After Asano killed himself through *seppuku*, his samurai became ronin, warriors without a master. They swore to avenge him and restore his honor."

Akira opened the book to a sketch of Edo Castle. A group of ronin were sneaking through the buildings at night.

"After a year of planning and infiltrating the castle, the ronin returned and avenged their Lord Asano, and after a fierce battle they found Lord Kira cowering," Akira said. "He refused to die as a true samurai, by *seppuku*, and the ronin were forced to kill him by cutting off his head." He closed the book.

"How did these ronin die?" Zachary asked, pointing to the graves.

"They all committed *seppuku*," Akira replied. "Only one was allowed to live."

They walked to the rebuilt keep of the castle. At the top of the tower, a Japanese flag hung next to the NA flag. Much had changed over the centuries, but the warrior ethos had not. It lived on in Akira, Kai, and now Ronin and his brothers.

"I love you all," Akira said, "and I'm proud to be your—"

He was cut off by a rumbling in the distance. The sound rose to a roar, loud enough to tremble the ground. Five triangular Short Sword fighter jets raced across the sky.

"Wait here," Akira said. He pulled out his Commpad, stepping away. The low whine of an air-raid siren rose in the distance.

Kai motioned for Ronin and his brothers to join him and Lise.

Ronin tried to hear what his uncle was saying into the device. A stern look crossed his stone features, and he put it into his uniform pocket.

"This way," Akira said to the family. "Hurry."

An L-20 MOTH descended from the sky, engines roaring. The four wings rose and thrusters kicked on as it lowered over the gardens, whipping the canopy of trees. A troop hold door opened and a ramp extended down. Akira motioned them inside the troop hold.

Ronin followed his parents and brothers into the belly where four Engines already stood. He hadn't met them formally, but Ronin knew their names: Ghost, Perez, Frost, and Tadhg. Okami, the droid wolfdog that Ronin had heard so much about, was here too. And in the back of the troop hold was Kichiro.

"I had hoped you would all meet under different circumstances but alas, fate seems to have other plans," Akira said. "The Red Wolves have launched attacks at every megacity, including Tokyo. We're going to drop you all off at the base, where you'll be safe."

"Uncle Akira, where are you going?" Ronin asked. His words were drowned out by the roar of the thrusters, but he still got his answer.

His uncle was going back to war.

Akira stood as elongated plates of armor folded over his body. When the plates were all in place, he leaned his head back into a kabuto with a red oni mask. Then he held the Warrior Codex out to Zachary.

"Safeguard this for me, and read it while I'm gone," Akira said in a muffled voice. "Someday, it will be yours."

"Don't you need it for good luck?" Zachary asked.

"He has Shadow Squad," Tadhg bellowed, pounding his chest. "That's all the luck Akira the Brave needs today!"

26

"Watch your back," Kai said. "The snake lives without its head."

Akira knew the analogy from the Warrior Codex. In this case, the Red Wolves were the snake, and their head was Dr. Cross.

"Be careful, Uncle Akira!" Ronin shouted.

Akira raised a hand to his family as they were escorted away by a pair of Pistons. They had spent one day together in six months, and now Hros-1 loomed over them, their fate in the hands of a machine.

Perhaps a life of peace was never in the cards for Akira.

"I'll keep your book safe!" Zachary yelled, gripping the Warrior Codex tightly against his chest.

"We better go, Captain," said Frost.

Akira tried to put his family out of his mind. They would be okay in the shelter deep under the reinforced base. It was almost as safe as one of the Life Arks.

Okami wagged his tail and barked after Kichiro as Akira took the reins. Shadow Squad joined part of the 10th Expeditionary Assault Force assembled in an underground hangar.

The three hundred Pistons of Stone Mountain Battalion waited in organized lines next to four Hammerhead APCs. Eight Juggernaut Mech pilots stood outside the diamond-shaped cockpits, running diagnostics.

Akira dismounted outside the command center. Inside, War Commander Contos watched mounted holo-screens that reflected off his golden armor.

"Captain, we don't have much time to bring you up to speed," he said.

General Thacker, second in command, stepped forward.

"Get the Canebrakes ready for deployment, but keep them on standby," Contos ordered.

Thacker hesitated. It was not the first time Akira had seen

him delay in following orders from their War Commander.

"Why not send in the Canebrakes now?" Thacker asked.

"The Red Wolves took one of our forward operating bases and three of our Pistons hostage," Contos replied. "This is no doubt an attempt to lure us out, and I'm not taking the bait."

Contos gestured for Shadow Squad to follow him into a hangar. Inside, technicians in twelve-foot blue mech suits used robotic arms to move armored crates into the hangar, where support staff used plasma sticks to guide them into position.

Akira could see the infrared tags inside the armored black crates. Each held six Canebrakes, curled up in fetal positions.

Okami sniffed at the crate they walked past.

Contos stopped them just shy of the ramp. "I'll take care of our borders tonight," he said. "I have another mission for Shadow Squad. Apeiron, upload the latest footage."

"Standby," she replied over their chips.

"Approximately thirty minutes ago, we lost contact with Sector 199 at the space elevator," Contos said. "Doctor Cross escaped, with the aid of some kind of implant."

The head of the snake, Akira thought. Connecting to INN, he played the security footage.

In the video feed, Dr. Cross stood in a shower, his back to the security camera. The water cascading down his legs suddenly turned red. He raised his head and turned slightly.

Akira paused the feed and zoomed in. Dr. Cross's metal jaw appeared intact, but his teeth were gone, apparently removed after his capture.

When the feed resumed, Dr. Cross pulled something out of his nostril. The image zoomed in to reveal it was a tiny needle and syringe he'd hidden there. He pulled a second one out of the other nostril and then jammed them both into his INVS eyes.

Another figure entered the feed, this one dressed in combat armor. The guard looked for Dr. Cross, but the crazed man had snuck around him. He snapped the guard's neck with a quick twist of his helmet.

In a matter of seconds, Dr. Cross cut out one of the guard's eyes, held it up to the retinal scanner, and then palmed something against the security pad.

"That is where I lost contact with the sector," Apeiron said.

"What did he jab into his eyes?" Perez asked.

"I am still not sure, but they were surgically implanted into his nose before his capture, and undetectable by our scans, which could indicate self-assembling nanoparticle-based constructs. Particles of that size would be nearly impossible to identify until they solidified."

"This is all connected to what's happening on the surface," Contos said. "A distraction, meant to goad us to leave the walls of the city and into an ambush."

"No doubt," Tadhg grumbled.

"For all we know, the Coalition prisoners have complete control of Sector 199," Contos said. "Fortunately, they have nowhere to go."

"What about the Canebrakes there?" Perez asked.

"I have lost their signals," Apeiron replied.

"You mean, you lost control?" Contos asked. "This was exactly what I feared."

"No, War Commander. Not exactly, they appear to be offline."

"There's no way Doctor Cross could have taken out the droids," Frost said. "Right?"

"Unless those needles had something to do with it," Akira said. "Maybe he was able to take control of the machines."

"No," Apeiron quickly said. "That is not possible."

"You better be right, but I'm not going to take any chances," Contos said. "Shadow Squad, your objective is to take back that sector, secure the doctor, and figure out what happened to the Canebrakes."

"With pleasure, War Commander," Ghost said. "Do I have permission to kill him this time?"

Contos nodded. "Do it slowly, if possible."

"Now we're talking," Tadhg said with a grunt.

"Tonight, the future of humanity is at risk, and we can't let Doctor Cross and his small group of terrorists distract us from our main objective of destroying Hros-1." Contos looked at them in turn. "That is the *only* thing that matters right now. We can deal with the other terrorists after it's eliminated."

He stepped back from the ramp and pounded his chest armor.

"Good luck, Shadow Squad. I'm counting on you. We're all counting on you."

"Death from the shadows," Akira said. He paused before entering the MOTH. "War Commander, please watch over my family and Kichiro."

Contos dipped his head.

Okami ran up the ramp of the MOTH, and the Engines racked inside. Overhead, a hangar door opened, and the pilots ascended to a view of the golden city.

Akira thought of his family. *They will be safe.*

Pre-combat noise filled the troop hold; Frost tapped a magazine against her helmet, Tadhg rocked a leg up and down, and Perez secured his shield over his back.

By the time they reached orbit, they were ready to fight.

"Docking in t-minus five minutes," Apeiron said.

The MOTH switched to vertical thrusters on approach. The doors to the spaceport opened, revealing a dark hangar filled with hundreds of stacked crates.

"Enter through the access hatch and follow the route on your HUDs," Apeiron said.

"Copy that," Akira replied.

She uploaded an interior file for the prison, overlaid with blue lines to their target. The port doors shut, sealing them inside.

"Perez, you stay here and watch the MOTH," Akira said. He flashed a hand signal, and Tadhg took point. Ghost and Frost moved out in combat intervals among the stacks, ten high, their weapons roving the darkness. A row of red emergency lights glowed overhead leading to the two hatches.

"You will have to manually unlock those access doors," Apeiron said.

Tadhg collapsed his pulse cannon and drew his energy sword. Gripping the hilt, he activated the blade, and the teeth grumbled like a chain saw. The squad aimed their weapons as Tadhg carved a new doorway with the heated blade. The cutaway fell, echoing with a loud clank.

Okami was the first one through. Akira followed. Streaks of blood slashed the deck, hulls, and ceiling. Akira whistled for Okami to get back, then he slowly proceeded inside with his rifle up.

Two naked guards lay on the deck, guts hanging out of their stomachs.

Another flash of his hands, and Akira split the team up. Tadhg went left with Akira and Okami. Frost and Ghost went right. The next hallway was another scene of death. Okami sniffed for explosives and then approached three mutilated guards.

"Be advised," Akira said, "Hostiles will have vacuum-rated armor and energy blades."

"Copy that," Ghost replied.

"Where are the Canebrakes?" Tadhg asked quietly.

"Apeiron, you got a location on any of those Canebrake units?" Akira asked.

"Negative, Captain. The entire sector is a dark zone. Proceed with caution…"

"Okami, find me those Canebrakes," Akira said.

The wolfdog wagged his tail and trotted onward. Soon they arrived at the hatch outside the prison wing. The silo-shaped space was wide open, exposing a grid of rectangular cells inside.

"Captain, we found one of the Canebrake units," Frost said.

An image of a downed droid came onto their HUDs. The top of the fanned skull was cracked open like a metal egg with veiny wires poking out.

"Looks like Doctor Cross and his men found a way to destroy the machines," she said.

"Remember what you said about being obsolete?" Tadhg chuckled.

"Quiet," Akira said. He stepped out onto a bridge. Its center platform, used to access the cells above and below, was far above, at the top of the silo.

"Apeiron, what's up there?" he asked.

"Air vents."

"Where do they lead?"

"Back to the spaceport, Captain."

"Son of a bitch…" Akira bolted off the bridge, giving orders as he ran. "Get back to the spaceport! Perez, watch your six!"

An emergency alarm wailed as they ran. Okami growled at a hatch that began to shut.

"Faster!" Akira shouted.

Okami burst through with Akira and Tadhg close behind. But the next hatch was already almost sealed. Tadhg got there just before it closed and pried it open.

Akira hopped through and held it for Tadhg.

By the time they turned, a third hatch had sealed, right in front of Okami.

Ghost and Frost were cut off even further back by four more hatches.

"Shit," Akira said.

His ears picked up what sounded a lot like distant gunfire. A message from Perez crackled over the team comm a moment later.

"Contacts!" Perez said. "Engaging!"

The feed from the spaceport showed ten Coalition prisoners in armored suits charging at Perez with energy blades. Akira slotted his rifle and pulled out his swords. He hacked into the hatch, desperate to tear it down.

"We have to break through these!" he yelled.

Tadhg joined in and together, they cut a doorway. Akira kicked the simmering piece down. Only two more separated them from Perez, but they were running out of time to help.

Okami paced behind them at the next one, howling.

Back in the spaceport, Perez was engaging a team of six unyielding Coalition prisoners, using his shield to block their blows.

"Hang on, Perez, we're coming to you!" Akira said into his headset.

The two Engines battered the hatch until it came down. The wolfdog bolted through to the final sealed-off door. Akira went straight to the small viewport as Tadhg swung his blade deep into the metal.

Five dead prisoners lay in mangled heaps inside the

spaceport, directly in front of the MOTH. The other five surrounded Perez, each armed with energy blades.

One of the men lunged, and Perez smashed his shield into the prisoner's helmet. He cut down another Coalition soldier with a slash across the stomach, opening the vacuum-rated suit, guts spilling out. A prisoner behind Perez struck him in his side with a heated blade, and a second prisoner kicked him in the back of his knee, bringing Perez down to his other knee.

"Watch out!" Akira shouted.

Perez brought up his shield to deflect more blows from energy swords, but a side stroke severed his hand from his wrist, the shield clanking to the deck.

"Perez!" Akira yelled.

He hacked at the door with Tadhg, desperate to get through.

Perez crawled away from the men looming above him, leaving a trail of blood from his gushing wrist. He used his sword to block their blades as they struck again and again.

"Hold on, Perez!" Tadhg shouted.

Perez pushed himself back to his feet, staggering in front of the prisoners. One charged, and he lopped off their head with a clean strike.

Perez stood tall, unwavering, and for a moment, Akira thought he could win this fight. That thought passed when a prisoner with familiar red INVS eyes glowing behind a dark visor thrust a sword into Perez's leg.

Perez screamed out in pain and collapsed to his back in front of Dr. Cross.

Akira cut into the hatch as the two remaining prisoners hovered over Perez with the Doctor. Cross picked up Perez's rifle and aimed it at his visor.

Perez tried to drag himself away, his visor angled at the deck, blood pouring out of his wrist.

"NO!" Akira screamed.

Dr. Cross fired a burst into Perez's helmet. Perez dropped to the deck, his body completely still except for the blood pouring around his head. Then Cross aimed the rifle at the hatch.

Tadhg heaved Akira away, as the bolts punched through the glass viewport. The rumble of the MOTH's engines sounded as

Tadhg held Akira down, more bolts searing above their heads. "He's gone!" Tadhg screamed. "We can't help him!"

A few agonizing minutes later, they got up and broke down the hatch, rushing into the bay. The MOTH was already tearing across the darkness, and the massive doors of the spaceport were closing.

Both pilots were dead on the deck. Next to them, Perez lay on his back, the shield that had saved him so many times just a few feet away. Smoke drifted out of his helmet, from bolts that had come from his own rifle.

Akira heard Apeiron talking about an evac, but he was hardly listening. He crouched and put a hand on Perez's chest. Okami nestled up next to him and howled.

"Apeiron, can you do something?" Akira asked. "Can you…"

"I'm very sorry about Sergeant First Class Perez," Apeiron said. "According to his vital readings, he has no brain activity. I fear any chance of mapping even the dead neurons was lost to the bolts that destroyed his brain. There is nothing I can do."

Akira bowed his head. There was no coming back from this, no way to bring him back like Ghost or Kichiro.

"I'm so sorry, brother," he whispered.

Ghost and Frost arrived not long after, breathing heavily. They both leaned down and put hands on Perez. The Engines stayed with their dead comrade for a quiet moment, until the rumble of MOTH engines surged outside the sealed spaceport doors.

They retracted, opening to the sight of a MOTH rising up, all four wings extended like the insect. The thrusters on the scaled wings belched blue flames as it hovered.

Akira reached down to lift up his comrade and take him to their evac.

"Let me help you," Tadhg said.

Okami howled, and Akira glanced up at the wing-mounted cannons rotating toward them.

This wasn't their evac.

"Run!" Akira screamed. He picked up Perez's shield and held it up in front of him and Okami. A burst of plasma bolts slammed into the shield, knocking Akira backward and onto the deck.

Okami bolted away with Akira behind a row of crates. Hunching, Akira stared at the smoking hunks of gore a few feet away. It was all that remained of Perez. But even in death, he had helped save Akira by leaving his shield behind.

"Apeiron, where's that evac!" Akira yelled.

"Four minutes."

"We aren't going to last that long!" Tadhg shouted.

"Apeiron, get us an exit route out of here on foot," Akira said.

Apeiron marked the hatch on their HUDs.

Akira looked away from Perez and checked the exit route by peering around the crate. It wasn't going to be easy to reach the opposite side of the sprawling cargo hold.

Slowly, Akira rose for a view of the bulbous cockpit viewports of the MOTH. In the pilot's seat was Dr. Cross, his toothless metal jaw set in a wide grin.

Frost fired six .50-cal rounds into its windshield. Flashes of plasma erupted from the MOTH's cannons and ripped into her position.

"Over here, you small dicked Napoleon wannabee!" Tadhg stood and fired his plasma cannon at one of the wings, taking out one of the mounted cannons. He ducked back down, and the MOTH backed away, thrusters firing horizontally.

Akira considered their two options. Make a run for the hatch and risk getting turned into pulp or jump out of the spaceport and jetpack to a lower sector.

"We have to jet down to Sector 198," Akira decided.

"What?" Tadhg said. "*Hell* no!"

Okami barked his agreement.

"We jump or we die," Akira said.

Another flurry of bolts slammed into the deck around them, taking out an entire stack of crates and knocking Frost and Ghost to their backs.

"I'll lay down suppressing fire," Akira said. "The rest of you get to Sector 198 with your packs!"

He didn't give them a chance to protest.

Standing, he selected single-bolt ammo, aimed at the MOTH's windshield, and fired right at Dr. Cross's face. The concentrated fire cracked the glass and forced the doctor to jerk back on the controls, giving the team a chance to jump.

Akira picked up Okami and darted for the edge of the open hangar, holding Perez's smoking shield up. The MOTH rose back up, turrets raking plasma over the deck. Bolts pounded the shield Akira held out, shattering the curved edges.

He ran right for the edge of the port and leapt into the dark of space with the damaged shield in one hand, and Okami cupped against his chest with his other.

As they fell, his body rotated, giving him a view of the MOTH. It ascended, firing missiles into the other sectors. Flames and shrapnel burst outward as entire habitats buckled in the explosions. Dr. Cross kept flying higher, firing plasma and missiles into the sides of the AAS research sites and the E-Vault.

Akira stared in horror as he realized what was happening.

The psychotic doctor wasn't just trying to destroy the work of Dr. Crichton.

He was trying to bring down the space elevator.

27

The command center of Nova One Station bustled with activity. Jason was in the center of it all, trying to keep his cool as he analyzed the situation at Sector 199. Every eye in the room watched the holo-screen playing the live feed linked to the HUDs from the survivors of Shadow Squad. By some miracle, most had survived the ambush by Dr. Cross, but not all were lucky.

Sergeant First Class Emilio Perez was dead, along with the guards of Sector 199, and the pilots of the stolen MOTH. The Canebrakes, too, were destroyed by Dr. Cross and the other prisoners.

"How did they just escape?" Jason asked. "How is that possible?"

"I'm not sure, Doctor," General Chase replied. "I've pulled an entire squadron away from the asteroid defenses to search for the MOTH."

Jason shook his head, incredulous. By now, Dr. Cross could be anywhere. "Find that fucking bastard."

He wasn't proud of the anger in his voice, or cursing, but he was losing his patience.

"I said I'm working on it, but this wouldn't have even happened if we had killed Doctor Cross when we had the chance," Chase said.

"This would never have happened, General, if you hadn't left the station completely unguarded."

"Doctor Crichton, you know as well as I do that the Coalition has never been a threat in the sky, let alone two hundred miles above the surface. And I will remind you, that we pulled almost our entire force away just in case the Poseidon cannons don't work to deal with the shards."

"I never said to pull *all* of your fighters away. And let me remind you, we also have the new Praying Mantis fighters to help."

Jason took a deep breath to calm down and re-focus.

"What about the Canebrakes guarding the sector?" Chase said in less aggressive voice.

The general glanced at the Hummer Droid for a split second, but he didn't make any accusations. To the people in this room, AI was salvation.

Still, Jason had the same question, and the General was right. The machines had also failed to protect the station.

"Apeiron, do you have a theory?" Jason asked.

"I believe some sort of electrical blast brought them down," she replied. "However, I am still not certain."

Jason turned back to the holo-screens, putting his shaky hands in his pockets to hide his anger, and nerves.

Sectors 198 and 197 had already been evacuated, their technicians and engineers returning to Earth in escape pods. Hummer Droids fought fires in Sectors 200 through 220, with damage reports continuing to flood in.

"Sector 200 is compromised," Apeiron said. "We have Hummer crews working—"

On the holo-screen, another fiery blast burst from the port at the habitat. Humans flew out into the darkness, cartwheeling away from the flames.

The room went quiet.

"Sector 200 is gone," Apeiron said.

This won't affect our defenses against Hros-1, Jason reminded himself, going over all of their safeguards in his head.

The Poseidon cannons that would save Earth were primed and ready to fire. Most of the world's population was sheltering. One hundred and one Life Arks with twenty thousand people each were secured underground, and one hundred thousand people were now citizens of Kepler Station on the Moon.

The Nova Alliance Sky and Space Patrol was in position with most of the King Cobra Spaceplane fleet and a hundred new Praying Mantis fighters fresh off the assembly line.

We're still in control, Jason thought.

But once again, Dr. Cross had thrown a wrench into his plans. He always seemed two steps ahead, but how, and what was his next step?

The attack on Titan seemed to be a distraction... like the

attacks at the megacities. All of these attacks were strategically planned when Nova Alliance Strike Forces were pulled away from the Titan Space Elevator to focus on Hros-1.

It struck Jason then, that maybe these attacks were a distraction to keep the cannons from firing. He thought back to what Dr. Cross had said—that they should just let Hros-1 hit.

"Madness," he whispered.

Jason continued to scan the damage reports, infuriated.

You have to keep it together.

Jason switched back to the view from Shadow Squad as they took a stairwell to Sector 196. Another explosion ripped through the sector, but he wasn't worried about the integrity of the space elevator. It would take more than this to down Titan, and even the worst-case scenario wouldn't affect the response to Hros-1.

Jason checked the countdown: *Sixteen hours, seven minutes, thirty seconds.*

There was still plenty of time before the asteroid, for both the Nova Alliance and for Dr. Cross, if he was planning something else.

"Doctor, Betsy and your daughters are on a secure line for you," Apeiron said.

He cursed again, having forgotten about the call he had promised his family.

"Put them through to the office," Jason said.

Chase glared at him as he left, but Jason didn't care. He knew the Nova Alliance Strike Force was mostly responsible for letting Dr. Cross escape, not the AAS. And he wasn't going to ignore his family for their mistake—especially now when they needed him, and he needed them.

Jason rushed to his office, shut the hatch, and tapped the holo-screen.

"Daddy!" Nina cried.

Autumn wedged her way into the frame next to Nina. Betsy stood behind them, a look of worry on her face.

"How are my two little princesses doing?" Jason asked.

"I hate it down here," Nina said. "I miss the sun, the *real* sun. I want to go home."

"Me too," Autumn said.

"It's only for a bit longer," Jason assured them.

Betsy put a hand on each of the girls' shoulder and said, "Let me talk to Daddy."

"Bye, girls. I'll talk to you soon. I love you," Jason said.

"Love you," Nina said.

"Bye, I love you," Autumn said.

Jason massaged one of his temples as the girls walked away.

Betsy leaned into the camera. "What's going on out there?" she asked. "I'm worried, Jason. I heard there's been an attack on the space elevator."

"The situation's under control," Jason said. "By this time tomorrow this will all be over, and I'm going to take a long vacation with you and the girls. I was thinking Megacity Rome."

Betsy bit the side of her lip. "Really? No work at all? Don't make a promise you can't keep."

"I'm not. You have my word."

She smiled. "I love you."

"I love you too."

"Go finish this."

"I'll talk to you soon," Jason said. "Take care of the girls for me."

"Be careful."

Sighing deeply with relief, he left his office, feeling confident. But when he returned to the Command Center, his confidence rushed out of him like air through an open airlock. On the holo-screen, more explosions rocked the upper sectors of the space elevator, one after another, billions of dollars of equipment and droids destroyed before their eyes.

"Jason," Apeiron said in a calm voice. "The elevator is compromised."

"How many sectors?" he asked.

"All of them," Chase said.

***

Emergency alarms blared through the dark passages of Sector 196. The Titan Space Elevator was coming down, and Shadow

Squad was trying to find a ride off the doomed station.

"There's a MOTH two levels down at Sector 194," Frost said.

"Yes, but the pilots are about to take off," Apeiron said. "I have diverted another MOTH to help evacuate the remaining crews at the hangar, but you will have to hurry."

Akira forced his way through a passage, knocking away fallen panels with Perez's damaged shield he still gripped in his hand. Sparks showered his armor. Okami squeezed under a pile of debris and growl-barked on the other side.

"No way through," Akira said.

"I'll make one," Tadhg said.

He lowered a shoulder, slammed into the heaps of twisted metal, and powered his way through, collapsing to the deck. Ghost and Akira helped the big Irishman up.

At the end of the passage, a team of black and yellow Hummer Droids battled fires in the next corridor. Smoke drifted toward them. Akira waited until his INVS sight compensated. He found the next hatch Apeiron had marked and scanned for heat on the other side.

"Clear," he said.

The stairwell led to Sector 195. He started down it, moving fast. At the third landing, the hulls groaned.

"Oh... shit," Akira muttered.

"Captain, wait—" Apeiron started to shout.

The voice was drowned out by an explosion. The hatch and hull burst outward. Air and debris vented out all around his armored frame as Akira activated the magnets on his boots to keep him from joining the pieces of habitat.

He picked up Okami and secured the wolfdog to his chest rig.

"Got ya," Akira said.

Metal ripped past them and into the jagged window blown out of the habitat. Below, they had a perfect view of the cold darkness and Earth.

Heart thumping, Akira slowly back-pedaled into the stairwell with the rest of the squad.

At the next landing, Tadhg opened the hatch. They passed

through and Akira slammed it shut, muffling the distant explosions. In the quiet, he picked up the sound of screaming.

The crews stationed here had mostly bailed already, but a quick scan revealed five of the escape pods had been damaged.

Another rumble rocked the elevator. The spin-gravity was still active, but for how long, Akira wasn't sure. The integrity of the station was compromised.

They had to hurry.

"Let's go!" he yelled.

The next passage was blocked by rubble. Trapped under a jagged flap of metal was a body. Tadhg hefted it off a man in a vacuum-rated suit.

"I've got ya, mate," Tadhg said. He threw the man over a shoulder.

They found another injured technician not far away. Ghost picked her up, cradling the woman like a child in his grip.

The emergency lights flickered off from a violent quake. Their faceplates activated, and their INVS eyes adjusted to the black.

Akira followed a new route from Apeiron on his HUD. Another team of Hummer Droids clanked down the deck at an intersection ahead. They stopped to let the squad through.

Two more intersections and three hatches got them to the final stairwell that led to Sector 194. Akira loped down and then jumped to the bottom landing.

A roar like an approaching train came from the other side of the hatch, followed by a guttural crunching that shook the enclosed stairs. Tadhg twisted the hatch handle and opened it above the hangar.

The noise they had just heard was a piece of another habitat slamming into the open deck below. Hunks of metal the size of houses battered the deck. A group of rescue workers ran toward the MOTH starting to take off from the center of the spaceport.

Akira tried to scream a warning, but they never heard his voice. A hunk of cartwheeling debris slammed into the deck, carving through the metal. He ducked down in the stairwell with the shield to take cover as the entire spaceport groaned under the stress of the destruction.

When Akira got back up, the deck was gone and with it, the MOTH. Only a streak of red remained where the rescue workers had been.

Two hundred miles below the missing deck was the dark surface of Earth.

"Oh, that's just fucking *great*," Tadhg said. "What the hell do we do now?"

"The final MOTH is ten sectors below," Apeiron said. "You will have to get to that if you want off the station."

Akira saw its thrusters firing in the darkness. "That MOTH is moving."

"Yes," Apeiron confirmed.

"So send it up here!" Tadhg shouted.

"It is too dangerous with all the debris," Apeiron said. "You will have to jump."

"You want us to jump on a *moving* MOTH?" Tadhg roared.

"If we miss, we're going to turn into corn dogs on reentry," Frost said.

"Don't miss," Ghost said. He waddled up next to Akira, gripping the technician. "Hold on tight! AYYYYYY-ohhhhhhhhhh!"

Frost shrugged, saying nothing, and jumped. Tadhg hesitated with the technician still draped over his shoulder. Akira could see that he wasn't going willingly. He took one hand off Okami and grabbed Tadhg by the arm with the other, yanking him out before he could protest.

"You asshole!" Tadhg screamed.

The squad plummeted into the darkness. They had trained in high altitudes, but landing on a moving MOTH at this height, with injured people and a droid wasn't part of it.

Akira speared through the air toward the black Earth, debris hurtling around him with Okami secured to his chest and Perez's shield secured to his back.

"The pilots have your positions and are going to pick you up one at a time," Apeiron said. "Stay calm and remember your training."

"They better be damn good!" Ghost said.

The MOTH first rose to intercept Frost. A shard of space

elevator whizzed by it, nearly sheering off a wing. Frost raised her arms to break her descent into the open troop hold. It swallowed her, and the pilots rolled away from another huge piece of shrapnel. Ghost came next, with the technician secured to his chest.

A raucous boom came from above, drawing Akira's eyes to a sight that took his breath away.

Normally, things didn't *shock* him. In war, he had seen entire cities devastated by chemical and biological attacks on civilians, but seeing the space elevator falling to Earth was different—it seemed surreal.

"Son of a bitch!" Tadhg yelled.

Akira spotted the big Engine spinning out of control with the technician. The pilots changed course to intercept him.

According to Akira's HUD, he was falling at one hundred eighty miles per hour. A proximity warning flashed on his faceplate from a slab of metal sailing right toward him.

"Captain," Apeiron said.

"I see it."

"You are way off course."

Akira looked back down as he slowly passed the MOTH. He deployed the wings under his arms and from slots in his leg armor, shaving off more speed.

He forced his body back into a suicide dive, curving to his left. The pilots matched his trajectory. Thousands of debris objects had already hit the atmosphere, burning on reentry in the dark sky above Earth. The MOTH was now coming up fast on Akira's right.

"Almost there, Captain," Apeiron said.

For a fleeting moment, Akira appreciated her voice, and her guidance, just when he suddenly felt so alone, falling through space, his family and the entire Earth below him at risk.

The MOTH raced toward him, the troop hold open, his other family—Frost, Ghost, and Tadhg—waiting inside to catch him.

As Akira soared toward them, another proximity warning chirped.

A spear of metal debris punched into the shield on his back

and ripped into the right upper wing of the MOTH, taking out a thruster in an explosion that peppered his body with shrapnel. He shielded Okami with an arm and landed inside the troop hold.

"Close the hatch!" Tadhg screamed.

The MOTH rolled hard, sending Akira slamming into the inside of the hull, headfirst. Pads and gel inside his helmet helped absorbed some of the impact, but not all of it. Pain broke across his forehead and red flashed across his vision.

"We've lost two thrusters!" said one of the pilots over an open channel.

The hulls vibrated, the entire MOTH threatening to buckle under the stress.

Akira squinted at the stars bursting across his eyes. He looked out a porthole window and saw a storm of burning shards from the space elevator streaking through the sky like meteors.

The irony wasn't lost on him.

In fifteen hours and two minutes, Hros-1 would be doing the same thing if it wasn't destroyed. And with the Red Wolves attacking on the surface and Dr. Cross on the loose, Akira had a feeling the attack on the Titan Space Elevator was just part of the plan to derail their efforts to do just that.

Akira snapped back to the reality of their situation—Perez was dead, the MOTH was coming apart, and they were still an hour flight from his family and their comrades at Gold Base in Megacity Tokyo.

He stood despite the vibrating ship. Reaching over his back, he unlatched Perez's shield. There wasn't much left, just the center part and a few engraved words.

The Engines all directed their visors at Akira, waiting for him to say something compelling, or inspiring. But Akira didn't need to search deep for those words. Perez had left them behind on his shield.

"Here is courage, mankind's finest possession," he said, reading the quotation from Tyrtaeus that was etched into the burned metal.

Some leaders might have sugarcoated what Akira needed to

say next, but he never lied to his squad.

"Get ready for the toughest fight of your lives," he said. "My gut tells me bringing down the space elevator was just the start of what Doctor Cross has planned. Courage is the only thing that will get us through this night."

28

"What's going on up there?" Ronin whispered.

He held up his Commpad. *No connection.*

Deep under the surface of Gold Base, he sat with his mother and brothers on cots set up for the hundreds of civilians around them, people of all ages, all families of soldiers: parents, wives, husbands, and children of the forces assigned to the base.

Almost everyone was looking at Commpads, trying to figure out what was happening above on the surface. It appeared the Nova Alliance had limited the INN connections.

What Ronin did know was simple—in fourteen hours and forty minutes, Hros-1 would enter the Earth's atmosphere if it wasn't stopped.

Kai was across the room talking to a tall man with a buzzed head and scars across his square jaw. Prosthetic legs showed under his green pant cuffs. A droid dog that looked like a Rottweiler stood by the man.

"I don't understand how INN can just be down," Zachary said.

"Maybe Apeiron is limiting the network so we don't know what's going on," Lise said.

"To keep people from panicking?" Zachary said. "If so, then things are worse than when we came down here."

"I'm really worried about Uncle Akira," Ronin said. "Don't you think he would come visit us if he was back?"

Elan looked up from the translation on his Commpad.

"Your uncle can look after himself," Lise said. "Don't worry about him. Everything's going to be okay, boys. I promise."

She looked across the room at Kai.

"Who is that guy Dad's talking to?" Ronin asked.

"A corporal he served with named Jared," Lise said. She got up and stretched. "You guys should try and get some rest. We could be down here a while."

Ronin took in a deep breath and pulled out the book Akira had asked Zachary to safeguard.

"Be careful," Zachary said.

"I will." Ronin cracked it open carefully, turning to a page written in Japanese. He held his Commpad over the text to translate it, then held the screen out for Elan who leaned in to look.

"What's it say?" Lise asked.

"It's a story about thirty mercenaries sent to kidnap the children of a rival lord," Ronin said. "Two samurai were deployed to track down the children."

"Did they get them back?" Zachary asked. He put his Commpad down for the first time in hours.

"Yup, and they killed all the mercenaries," Ronin said.

"And we really have a samurai in our family history?" Zachary asked.

"Yes," Lise said.

"How come no one ever told us until now?" Ronin asked.

"Your father and your Uncle Akira had a pact," Lise said. "They wanted to share your history with you together."

She seemed to be staring at Zachary, but then quickly looked at Ronin. "Both of you, of course."

Her eyes darted away. Maybe she wanted to say something else. Her eyes always darted like that when she was hiding something.

"I'll be right back," Lise said.

She got up and crossed the room to the doors where Kai and Jared stood with a small group of people. Kai spoke with two Piston guards. Murmur and Shana, Ronin had heard them call each other earlier.

Zachary stretched with a smirk. "This book and all of the stories gives me an idea. Maybe next year they'll call me the Samurai in the stadium."

Ronin rolled his eyes. Just when he thought his older brother was genuinely interested in their family history, his ego proved otherwise.

Elan reached out and turned the page to a drawing of two samurai standing in front of a group of children. The men wore black and red tiled armor, with masks that looked like grinning warriors.

"Beautiful," Ronin whispered.

Elan read along with Ronin and Zachary. After a few stories, Ronin looked over to the crowd again.

I'm going to go listen, he signed to Elan.

Elan got up to join him and Ronin handed the book back to Zachary who tucked it away. He stayed behind while Ronin led his twin brother through the maze of beds.

Halfway across the room, a mother sat on a bed rocking a baby. Ronin could see the fear in her eyes. He wanted to say something kind, but instead he just smiled.

When he got to the back of the group, he put a hand on Lise. "Mom, do you know anything?"

The Pistons began to nudge the gathering crowd back.

"Get back inside," said Shana. "We'll let you know when we have more information." She had a youthful, innocent face, with a tattoo of an eagle on her neck.

"She said back up," Murmur added. He was a hefty man, with a big mole on his forehead and less patience than his comrade.

"We just want some answers," Kai said.

"Sir, please…" Shana said.

"Master Sergeant," Jared corrected. "You're talking to Master Sergeant Kai Hayashi."

"Retired," Kai corrected.

"He's Captain Akira Hayashi's brother," Jared said, "who, as you know, is *not* retired."

The Pistons shared a glance and turned to talk. A few moments later Shana motioned for Kai to join them in the hallway. The doors shut, and the crowd backed away.

Zachary walked over with his arms folded across his muscular chest.

"Well?" he asked.

"I told you to stay at the bunks," Lise said angrily.

"Whoa, relax," Zachary said.

"Go back there and wait for me. Don't argue, Zachary, just do it."

He put up his hands defensively. "Okay, no problem."

Ronin and Elan followed their older brother back toward their beds.

"Don't worry, guys," Zachary said. "Everything will be…"

His words trailed as the lights flickered.

They halted, looking up at the ceiling. Ronin's gut tightened. Something was wrong up there—something worse than a single terrorist attack.

Even Zachary, usually so confident, looked unsure.

"Do you think there were more attacks?" Ronin asked.

"Maybe, but no way anyone could take this base. We're safe here." Zachary flashed his handsome smile.

I'm telling you guys, we're good, he signed.

Ronin sat back on his bed next to Elan, their eyes on the door, waiting for Kai.

Zachary pulled out the Warrior Codex again. "Let's keep reading."

Ronin scooted over, and Zachary sat between him and Elan.

Moments like these were rare, but they reminded Ronin that his older brother did care deeply for both of them. They read through the passages silently, turning each page carefully, reliving history through the lens of their ancestors.

Finally, the doors opened. Kai limped back into the room and crossed over to his family. He was out of breath when he reached them.

"Dad, what's going on?" Ronin asked.

"It's Titan Station," Kai said. "The space elevator was destroyed."

"No way," Zachary said. "That can't be true."

Ronin translated for Elan but then hesitated at his father's next statement.

"We need to get ready to leave," Kai said.

Zachary narrowed his brows and folded his arms over his chest. "What do you mean 'get ready to leave'? Where are we going?"

"I thought we were safe here, Kai," Lise said.

"Just in case, I want to be ready to move," Kai said. "Hurry and pack up your things."

***

Jason stared out the window of the command center at Nova One Station.

There was nothing left of the Titan Space Elevator but the black of space and dazzling stars. The trillion-dollar engineering feat that had launched supplies to help construct the lunar colonies and served as the research and manufacturing center for the Canebrakes and the birthplace of Apeiron was gone.

Jason clenched his jaw. He was normally a calm and patient man, but he was growing paranoid. He knew the mad doctor had help escaping and destroying the space elevator. He seemed to have spies and allies everywhere, even off planet.

And hours after he had escaped, they still didn't know where Dr. Cross was now.

Glancing around, Jason discretely examined the staff in the command center, wondering if anyone here was involved in these new attacks. It wouldn't be the first time, but every single one of these people had been vetted meticulously by Apeiron.

Jason shook off the paranoia and reminded himself that, like the restoration sites and megacities, the space elevator could be rebuilt.

You're still in control. You can still stop Hros-1.

And they would find Dr. Cross. It was just a matter of time.

Jason checked the Hros-1 clock.

Fourteen hours and one minute remained until the asteroid was within range of the cannons.

He tapped into INN for views from Earth. Most of the larger chunks of the space elevator had hit the ocean, but hundreds of reports documented pieces hitting land. Fortunately, most of the population was underground.

Commotion pulled Jason away from INN. He opened his eyes at General Chase talking to two Pistons. Apeiron was standing nearby, her metallic fingers tapping at a pair of terminals.

Jason rushed over to them. "Did you find the MOTH?"

At first, it seemed the general didn't know the answer. He glanced over at Jason skeptically before nodding.

"Where?" Jason asked.

"Here, Doctor," said the general.

"What do you mean, it's here? Like on Nova Station?"

"Spaceport 3. I already have a team of Canebrakes and Pistons en route, and all of the surrounding sectors are on lockdown."

"We are safe here," Apeiron said. "Do not worry."

Darnel walked over, his exoskeleton clicking with each movement. He pulled up a holo-feed of the spaceport. Sure enough, a MOTH sat in the enclosed bay. He switched to video of the surrounding sectors, watching as squads of Canebrakes and Pistons closed in. They formed barricades at each intersection, and two of the droids climbed into the ducts. There was no way that Dr. Cross and his men could reach the bridge without being stopped. This was a suicide mission.

But why? What was Dr. Cross planning now?

"General, do you have all EMP defenses online?" Jason asked.

"Yes, we're shielded here," Chase replied. "There's no technology that could bring down this station from outside the command center."

Jason checked with Apeiron for confirmation. She nodded.

That was good, but Dr. Cross had to know this station wasn't unguarded like Titan. So what was his next move?

Jason racked his brain, quickly coming up with a theory.

If Dr. Cross somehow took Nova One, he would control the cannons. He could hold the entire globe hostage. That had to be it.

"We located Doctor Cross," Apeiron said.

The announcement made Jason's heart skip. He stepped closer to the holo-screen. The feed from the spaceport showed a male figure walking down the stealth MOTH's ramp, his hands in the air.

"He's surrendering," General Chase said.

A dozen Canebrakes surrounded the MOTH as Pistons took Dr. Cross into custody. Another squad ran up the ramp and into the MOTH. Their helmet cams showed what was left. Just like at the dam in Siberia, Dr. Cross had slaughtered everyone.

"The MOTH is secure," General Chase said. "I say we shoot Doctor Cross out an airlock."

On the holo-screen, Dr. Cross bowed his head, as if in prayer, but Jason knew he wasn't praying. This was an act, a ploy.

The doctor hadn't come all this way to surrender so easily.

"Before you kill him, I want to speak with him," Jason said.

"Doctor," Chase said gravely.

"I will speak with him through a Canebrake, General."

"Fine, but do it quickly."

"I will connect to Unit E-491," Apeiron said. "Standby."

Jason closed his eyes and saw the view through one of the Canebrakes as it approached and stood directly in front of Dr. Cross.

"This is Doctor Jason Crichton," he said through the Canebrake. "I know you came to take over the cannons so Hros-1 will hit, but you failed. This is the end for you."

Dr. Cross slowly looked up, his blood-red INVS eyes leering. He smirked, a wide, toothless grin like a diseased wolf.

"Oh, I didn't come for the cannons, I came to say goodbye to you, Doctor Crichton," he said. "But you're right about my life being over, and soon, you'll see I was right."

"Right about what?"

"Don't you remember what I said about your creation?"

"You called Apeiron the devil."

"Indeed."

"The only devil on this station is you," Jason said. "You wanted to destroy our planet for your 'reset' and sacrifice billions for a fresh start."

"You're very good at projection, Doctor Crichton, I will give you that." Dr. Cross laughed.

Jason shook his head wearily. "At one point I thought you and I could have worked together, to change the world for the better, but you chose the path of evil, and now you'll pay with your life."

Dr. Cross held out his hands and lifted his head like a demented angel.

"AI *is* salvation, Doctor Cross. I wish you could have seen us destroy Hros-1 and bring the Earth back to her green and blue glory," Jason said.

He opened his eyes and turned to Apeiron. "Finish him, and General, you can vent his body after he's dead."

"With pleasure, Doctor," Chase replied.

On the holo-screen, Jason watched the Canebrake he had been speaking through. Energy blades activated on all four segmented limbs. The mad doctor grinned and winked at the droid right before it struck.

Two of the blades punched into his chest, while the other two wrapped around his neck and legs. The droid hefted him up, and then ripped his body in half. Both pieces of meat crashed to the floor, insides slopping out.

Jason felt a weight slide off his shoulders. The man who had tried to kill his family, and destroy humanity, was finally dead. And he wasn't coming back.

"Destroy the MOTH at a safe distance from Nova One, General," he commanded.

"Apeiron, connect me with War Commander Contos," Chase said.

"One moment." She projected his hologram.

"War Commander," Chase said. "Doctor Cross is dead, and his crew has been eliminated. Doctor Crichton believes they planned to take over the cannons."

Jason stepped up to the hologram. "War Commander, I've been informed that you're holding off deploying the Canebrakes on the surface."

"That's correct, Doctor," Contos replied.

"I'm not trying to tell you how to do your job, War Commander, but I believe it is important for the world to have a fresh start tomorrow. Once Hros-1 is destroyed, we don't need to deal with terrorists on Earth."

"I agree now that Doctor Cross is dead," Contos said. "I will deliver the same fate to his followers. Good luck with Hros-1."

"To you as well, War Commander," Jason said.

Jason moved to the viewport, standing next to Darnel.

"All that's left is that rock," Darnel said.

Jason stared at the approaching asteroid.

"We've almost done it, my friend," he said.

"Yeah, and I've been meaning to tell you... I need some time off after this."

Jason smiled. "You and me both."

He patted Darnel on the arm and crossed the space. "I'm going to talk with my family again," he said. "I'll be back in a few minutes."

Jason exited the command center, nodding at General Chase.

"Apeiron, let me know if anything happens in the next ten minutes," he said. The hatch opened and he ran down the passage, anxious to see his wife and daughters. He was feeling confident again, prompting the rush of adrenaline.

The warm wave suddenly seemed to center on his implanted L-S88 chip.

The heat grew stronger.

He staggered slightly.

Something was wrong.

He turned back to the hatch, seeing Apeiron in the opening.

"Jason, are you okay?" she asked.

"I'm..."

Darnel emerged. "Jason, what's wrong?" he called out.

He clanked over in his exoskeleton, reaching out just as Jason's legs buckled. Apeiron joined them, her antennae clicking rapidly—a sound she only made when she gave the Canebrakes orders.

The lights in the command room suddenly flashed.

"Jason," Darnel said. "Jason, stay with me."

Jason fought to keep his eyes open as he was carried back into the room that whirled around him.

"What the hell is going on?" General Chase said.

It was the last thing Jason heard before his vision went dark and a familiar pair of red eyes emerged in his mind. The glow spread, growing brighter, illuminating Dr. Cross's silver jaw as it extended into a foreboding grin.

"Killing me was not the end, Doctor Crichton," he said. "Killing me was the beginning of the reset."

Images of Canebrakes flashed through his mind, similar to the images he had dreamt during his surgery for the L-S88 chip.

The machines hunted people through destroyed cities, and Praying Mantis fighters hovered overhead, searching for human survivors.

Next he saw the cannons firing, but they vanished as a hand shook Jason awake.

Blurred figures hovered over him back in the command center of Nova One Station.

"Jason, can you hear me?" Petra asked.

He blinked to see it wasn't his sister, but Apeiron crouched next to him.

"Hang on," Darnel said. "You're going to be okay."

Jason tried to sit up, stuttering with realization about the image he had just seen. Everything came crashing over him.

You fool, you should have known he wouldn't give up that easily!

Dr. Cross hadn't come here to take over the station or surrender. He had come to upload something to the Canebrakes. Jason wasn't sure how, but whatever program or virus he had transmitted didn't seem to just affect the machines. It had been uploaded to Jason's L-S88 chip, the moment he left the command center to call his family.

A burning sensation rushed down his entire body.

But this wasn't from an injury.

This was the chill of fear.

"Shut INN down," Jason mumbled. "Shut it down before it's too—"

29

Akira awoke to high-pitched chirping. Numbers and data flashed across his HUD. He blinked, trying to focus on his surroundings in a dark room furnished with two broken chairs and the frame of a ragged couch.

A hulking figure approached, crouching in front of Akira.

"Damn, bosu, you're one lucky SOB," Tadhg said.

Another blurred shape emerged, this one small and on all fours.

"Okami," Akira whispered. The droid wolfdog nudged up against him, whining.

Tadhg grabbed Akira under an arm.

"Easy, bosu," he said.

"Where are we?" Akira asked.

"Ten miles from the western walls of Megacity Tokyo," Tadhg said. "Pilots managed to fly through that shitstorm, and we lasted another hour on the ride back here, until the final engine failed upon landing."

Akira strained to remember. He brought up his video history. In thirty seconds, he had digested everything, from entering Sector 199 and losing Perez, to the space elevator coming down and the rough reentry. The replay brought back the crushing loss. He suppressed the dread to focus on saving those still alive.

"Where's our evac?" he asked.

"There wasn't one," Tadhg explained. "We received orders right before INN went down, to sit tight and wait until the Stone Mountain Battalion of the 10th Expeditionary Assault Force shows up to deal with the Red Wolves."

"Apeiron, I want a SITREP on all hostile positions," Akira said.

Silence.

He tried again.

"She hasn't been responding," Tadhg said. "Must have to do with INN being down, we only got short-range comms, but

Ghost is working on it."

Akira tried to process what Tadhg had reported, but nothing seemed to make sense. "How could INN be down?"

"Space elevator maybe? I don't know, but…"

"Where's Frost and Ghost?"

"Watching our backs across the street," Tadhg said. "So what's our play?"

Akira picked up the remnants of Perez's shield.

He secured it away in his gear and stepped up to a window, reeling over the loss of Perez and deeply worried about his family and Kichiro.

With INN down, Shadow Squad was completely in the dark, cut-off from Apeiron and the 1st Division.

"Ghost, any theory on what happened to the network?" Akira asked.

"A few," Ghost said. "And while this is highly improbable, what if it's not just INN? What if they got control of the cannons?"

"No way," Tadhg said. "That's impossible…"

"Not necessarily," Akira said.

"I got movement on Blue Jay," Frost said over the short-range comms.

Akira crouched at the balcony, watching the small drone's feed on his HUD. The feed revealed Hammerhead APCs rolling down the streets toward Shadow Squad.

"Those are ours, Captain," Frost said.

"They're using the APCs to link back to Gold Base," Ghost said. "I've confirmed our location. They know where we are."

Akira tried the command channel. "Silver Crane, this is SS1, do you copy?"

Static broke over the line.

"Silver Crane," Akira said again. "Silver Crane, do you copy?"

Through the static came the bellowing voice of the War Commander.

"Copy SS1, this is Silver 1, damn good to hear from you," Contos said. "Hold tight where you are, Captain."

Akira wanted to ask about his family but trusted Contos to

know he wouldn't break his promise to look after them.

An upload emerged on his HUD, and Akira watched the APC hatches open. Canebrakes burst out, scattering down the streets to hunt down the remaining Red Wolves.

"Pistons and Juggernauts are on their way in MOTHs," Ghost confirmed.

Akira stood and stepped to the balcony's edge for a better view.

Minutes later, the first brilliant blast illuminated the distance. Another explosion volcanoed into the sky, forming a small mushroom cloud where a team of Canebrakes had taken out a fuel source. The grid clicked off underground, block by block, leaving the enemy, and the civilians sheltering out here, in the dark.

Akira backed away from the railing just as a flash of light emerged in his peripheral vision. There was no time to move. The projectile hit the balcony, blasting into his body with enough force that he ended up in the living room.

Ringing drowned out most of Okami's howl and the shouts over the comms, but Akira heard enough to know this wasn't a single sniper.

"Taking fire," Frost said.

Akira tried to focus his vision. Green dots of friendly forces inched across the battle map on his HUD. The squad of Canebrakes had veered off to find whoever was hunting the Engines.

Tadhg helped Akira up, and Okami followed them out of the room. They moved out into the hallway and Tadhg took them to the roof for a better vantage. At the top landing, he flung the door open and turned to the east, where the first of the MOTH transports flew high in the cloud cover, their bellies full of Pistons.

The Stone Mountains were about to fly into a zone that was supposed to be clear.

Akira hurried to the railing and propped his rifle up, scanning the shacks and abandoned structures. Ghost and Frost remained low as they crawled to new locations on their roof tops.

"Frost, give me something to shoot," Tadhg said. He looked over the side of the rooftop, his pulse cannon angled over the side.

A rattling ricocheted across the streets, the clicking call of the Canebrakes requesting reinforcements. The noise sent a chill up Akira's spine. They wouldn't call for help because of a few Red Wolves. There had to be more hiding in the slums.

Another plasma bolt hit the side of the roof next to Tadhg, knocking him off his feet in the blast. Akira dove for cover as a railing and part of a retaining wall exploded from a second bolt.

Tadhg got right back up and hefted his cannon over the mangled railing. Akira scrambled over, only to be forced down from another explosion to his right. Shrapnel peppered his armor, and the ringing returned in his ears.

Okami rolled on the ground, the hair on his back burning.

Akira went to grab the wolfdog when a jolt of pain ripped through his guts. A warning sensor flashed on his HUD, and he looked down at a piece of rebar sticking out of his side. Blood streaked down the armor despite his suit combating the wound.

Akira fought through the pain and directed the barrel of his rifle at movement across the rooftop. A pair of curved handrails suddenly moved. It took him a moment to notice the handrails were actually two segmented arms pulling a Canebrake up to the edge of the roof, where it perched.

But the eyes on the fanned head weren't a cool blue. These eyes were dark black, soulless, as if something had hijacked the droid.

Okami ran at the Canebrake, snarling.

Akira tried to whistle as the war machine rose to its maximum height and rotated both shoulder-mounted cannons toward him as he staggered forward. It was then Akira finally realized it wasn't the Red Wolves hunting Shadow Squad—the Canebrakes were.

He dove and grabbed Okami as the cannons burst to life. The bolts lanced past Akira as he tucked Okami against his chest and slid behind an air handler unit.

"Bosu!" Tadhg screamed from across the roof. He dropped his cannon as a thick metal rope wrapped around his neck. He yanked at it with both hands.

Telescoping limbs whipped over the unit Akira hid behind. He waited until they retracted before darting for new cover. Pain raced up his side with each step.

Near the rooftop edge, Tadhg had managed to grab onto the mechanical arm strangling him. He swung it over his shoulder, pulling the attached Canebrake up to the roof and smashing it down. The Canebrake struggled to right itself, arms rearing back to strike again, and cannons turning toward Tadhg.

Akira dropped Okami, and the wolfdog took off. He switched to his swords as segmented arms flung toward him. He ducked and dodged, cutting through two of them to get close to the downed droid.

The metal beast tried to push itself up, but Akira brought the swords down into the fanned head with all of his strength. Pain ripped up his stomach from the downward strokes.

The droid jerked, sparks shooting out of the destroyed head, and limbs flopping on the roof until the entire unit went limp.

They can die... he thought.

Akira backed away, sucking in air as he searched for the original Canebrake that had attacked him and Okami.

The war droid rushed across the ledge on all four legs. The shoulder cannons targeted Tadhg, hitting his armor with a flurry of bolts that sizzled into the plates. He crashed to his back and rolled away from another fusillade.

Akira turned on his jetpack, the thrusters firing in the crutch of his back and arms, launching him into the air as the Canebrake turned one of the cannons at his helmet. Plasma bolts streaked by, and one snagged his shoulder, spinning him mid-air. He crashed to the roof, five feet from the Canebrake.

All four arms rose up and tightened to strike. A ball of charred hair leapt over Akira's faceplate and clamped around the neck of the machine before it had a chance.

"Okami!" Akira screamed.

The droid wolfdog went over the edge with the Canebrake.

By the time Akira looked down, they had smacked on the street with a loud crack.

"Okami!" he yelled again.

A low growl answered, and Akira whistled for the droid to get back into the building. He raised his rifle and aimed it at the Canebrake on the concrete below. All four legs were snapped, but it used its segmented arms to rise up, the antennae rattling.

As Okami ran away, Akira fired a flurry of bolts into the fanned face of the war machine. The rattling ceased, and the arms went dormant.

Gripping the rebar protruding from his stomach, Akira staggered over to Tadhg, who was up on one knee, breathing heavily.

"Silver Crane, this is SS1, do you copy?" Akira said on the command channel. Static hissed in his helmet. They were being jammed now.

Distinct rattling echoed across the slums, a noise that had once guaranteed victory, but tonight seemed to foreshadow death.

"Come on, we have to get off this roof," Akira said.

He helped Tadhg up to his feet. They started back toward the door, but they halted as exploding MOTHs bloomed across the skyline. Some of the Pistons managed to bail, and one of the MOTHs banked away, right into enemy fire.

Akira climbed to the ledge, staring in horror as the Stone Mountain Battalion was slaughtered. He heard the other Engines yelling on the comms that they needed to move, but he couldn't force his gaze away from the mid-air explosions. A Piston sailed past their building, the lower half of his body gone, entrails hanging out.

Okami returned to the roof, tail wagging.

Akira leaned down to check him, pain lancing up his waist from his injury. The wolfdog had taken damage to both front legs and had lost most of his hair. But he appeared functional.

Ghost and Frost flew over, landing with thumps.

Akira studied an aerial view from Blue Jay. Outside of the tower, a dozen Canebrakes prowled, forming a perimeter.

"We can't win this fight," Akira said. "We have to use our packs to get to shelter."

"We won't make it," Frost said.

"We have to try," Ghost said. "Hros-1 is coming in just over twelve hours."

"Fuck the asteroid, man. It doesn't matter if we're droid meat," she said.

The rattle of the Canebrakes came again, closer this time.

"We take our chances in the air," Akira said. "Tadhg, toss the decoy holos. They'll buy us a few seconds."

Tadhg pulled the bullet-sized devices out of his pack and chambered them into a pistol.

"Get ready," Akira said.

The team crouched as Tadhg fired the shells. The holo-heat trails would look just like an Engine to a normal enemy, but Akira wasn't sure if the Canebrakes would take the bait. Only one way to find out.

"Go, now!" Akira said.

He picked up Okami and blasted off the roof after the other Engines. Plasma bolts lanced the sky behind them. On his HUD, he watched the green blots of Pistons on his tactical display, winking to yellow, and black. Within minutes, all but twenty of the soldiers from the Stone Mountain Battalion were dead.

Akira clenched his jaw, feeling the sting of each death. He glanced over his shoulder. The distraction had worked, and the Canebrakes were firing at the holo-trails.

"Launch," Akira ordered.

The Engines blasted into the sky. As they got closer to the walls, the command channel came back online.

"All units fall back to HQ! We are under attack! Repeat, we are under attack!"

Akira almost didn't recognize the panicked voice of War Commander Contos.

A clicking rose over his voice, then gunfire, and screams of agony.

Shadow Squad blasted across the cloud cover toward the glow of fires in the distance.

"Incoming!" Frost yelled.

Plasma bolts streaked toward the Engines.

"Down, down, down!" Akira shouted. He forced his body into an arrow, angled at the outside of the megacity wall. It seemed so close, but so far away at the same time.

One thing was certain, they weren't going to make it in the air.

The Engines swooped back down to the ground and took off running, bolting for the shadows that once had allowed them to hunt.

Now the shadows were the only place for Shadow Squad to hide from the Canebrakes.

***

Murmur and Shana, the two Piston guards, had closed the doors hours ago, telling everyone to stay put. They still hadn't returned, and Ronin had no idea what was happening topside other than Hros-1 was ten hours out now.

Emergency lights spread a weak glow over the sprawling barracks where the frightened civilians sheltered. No one else seemed to be packing up their things.

"You ready?" Kai asked.

"Yes," Lise said. She had laid their bags out neatly on the beds.

"Good."

Zachary had the Warrior Codex tucked away in his bag and secured on his back. Ronin and Elan were also both ready to go.

"I'll be back in a minute," Kai said. "Stay here."

He crossed the room to Jared, who stood with his Rottweiler droid. The doors were locked, but Jared was crouched trying to get them open. A moment later, he stood and tried the handle.

As soon as Jared opened the door, a chattering resonated from the hallway.

Ronin stood, listening to the echo in disbelief.

"Is that gunfire?" Zachary asked.

What, Elan signed. *What's wrong?*

The noise came from somewhere above them.

Other people heard it too and started backing toward the doors. The woman with the baby clutched it to her chest, trying to comfort the crying child.

"Dad, is that gunfire?" Zachary called out, his eyes wide with something Ronin had not seen in his older brother for years—fear.

Ronin felt a tug on his shoulder.

"Tell me what's going on," Elan said in his monotone. The fact that he wasn't signing told Ronin just how scared his twin was, too.

"That's definitely gunfire!" someone shouted.

Panicked voices broke out around Ronin as he tried to process what was going on, and what to tell Elan. He decided on the truth.

There's gunfire in the base, Ronin signed.

Who is shooting? Elan signed back.

Jared rushed back into the room. "We have to go. The base is under attack."

"But those Pistons said we'll be safer here," said the young mother clutching her wailing baby.

"Stay here then, but for those coming, we need to go now," Jared said firmly. He pulled an energy knife out of a sheath and activated the superheated blade.

Kai ran over. "Let's go. Stay behind me."

Ronin signed to Elan, and they set off across the room.

Lise convinced the woman with the baby to come with them. "You'll be safer with us. Don't be afraid."

Half of the civilians fled into the hallway, while the others remained inside. Ronin heard the door click shut and lock from the inside. There was no turning back now.

Jared and Kai led the way down the dark corridor, guided by the red emergency lights. They checked the next corner, then waved for the group to continue.

Ronin heard the clank of armor and shouts in the distance, and Kai and Jared motioned for everyone to get back.

Lights bobbed up and down at the end of the hallway.

Raising his knife, Jared moved with Kai, ducking just shy of the junction. Ronin wanted to call out for his dad to be careful, but he remained quiet and knelt with his mom and brothers.

Two figures suddenly emerged around the corner, shining their rifle lights down the hallway.

"Hey!" shouted a female voice.

Jared put his knife to her throat, and Kai grabbed the man, pulling him to the ground. The dog barked viciously. Ronin held it back as his dad wrestled with an armored soldier. It wasn't until they rolled into the glow of a red light that Ronin saw it was the two Piston guards.

"Stop!" Zachary yelled.

Jared pulled his knife away from Shana's throat. She punched him in the jaw, knocking him to the ground before grabbing her rifle and aiming it at Kai.

"Let him go!" she shouted.

Kai rolled off Murmur and held his hands up. "Easy," he said. "We thought—"

Murmur pushed himself up with a grunt, his chest heaving. "I told you to stay put!"

"We heard gunfire," Kai said.

The two Pistons directed their rifles back at the crowd, their tactical lights hitting the ashen faces of the frightened civilians.

"Where's the rest of 'em?" Murmur asked.

"They stayed put, like you said," Kai said. Zachary helped him to his feet.

"Son of a bitch," Murmur said. "Shana, I'll go get the others. You take this group to the hangar."

"Hangar?" Kai asked.

"Yes," Murmur said. "Now go!"

He took off running the way they had just come.

"Why are we going to the hangar?" Jared asked.

Before Shana could respond, a thud vibrated through the facility, and dust rained down on the group. Cries of surprise and panic burst from the civilians.

"Quiet," Shana said. She trained her rifle down the hallway.

"Private, why are we going to the hangar?" Jared entreated.

She hesitated a moment. "War Commander Contos has given the order to evacuate the civilians."

"I thought we were safe..." came a scared female voice.

Ronin turned to see it was the young woman with the baby.

Kai turned toward the crowd. "Everyone stay calm, and quiet," he said. "Keep close to us and we'll get you out of here safely."

Ronin grabbed Elan's hand.

Emergency lights guided them down the corridors. On point, Shana cleared each junction, moving with precision.

"The elevators aren't far," she said.

Somewhere in the massive underground base, a siren went off, the whine echoing down the passages. In the respite, Ronin heard a rattling noise that echoed off the walls.

Shana pressed her rifle to her shoulder and proceeded. As her light flitted over the hall, the beam fell on the upper half of a helmetless Piston at the next intersection.

The group slowly advanced but halted when Shana raised a fist in response to a long scratching sound.

At the end of the hall, the man was suddenly dragged away.

Shana paused a few seconds, then said, "Stay here."

She ran the hall and slowly turned at the corner. Whatever she saw caused her to move back and turn off her light.

Jared and Kai rushed over to her, and she whispered something to them that Ronin couldn't hear. He knew it wasn't good by the way Jared and Kai looked at one another.

Kai rejoined the civilians. "Everyone stay here until we tell you to move," he said.

"Why? What's down there?" Ronin asked.

"Stay here," Kai repeated.

He went back to Jared and Shana. She unholstered her plasma pistol and handed it to Kai.

"I'll provide cover fire," she said. "Take a right, and you'll hit the elevators. If they're sealed, the stairs are at the end of the hallway. Take them to the hangar."

Jared reached out for the gun Shana had given Kai. "You go with your family," he said to Kai. "I'll stay here and help her."

Shrieking metal came around the corner, followed by the same rattling noise, and a clicking almost like an electronic hiss.

Shana raised her rifle, took in a breath, and peered around the corner. Blue arrows of light flashed by, and her face vanished in a spray of bone and blood.

Ronin crouched as screams and ferocious barking broke out with the sound of gunfire.

Kai grabbed the woman and pulled her back around the

corner, leaving a streak of gore. He unclipped the rifle hanging from her neck.

Zachary bent down and pulled the energy sword out of its sheath on her back. He gripped the handle, the blade burning red.

"I'll lay down suppressing fire," Jared said. He stepped out and started firing his pistol down the hallway, his droid dog barking by his side.

"Go!" Kai screamed. He turned the corner and squeezed off shots.

Zachary ran ahead with the energy sword, motioning for everyone to follow. The group of panicked civilians ran after him.

Ronin latched onto Elan and Lise and pulled them after his older brother. As he rounded the corner, he saw what had killed Shana at the end of the hall.

A Canebrake bolted away on four legs.

The shocking sight of the mechanical monster made Ronin run faster. He didn't stop until they reached the elevators. All four were sealed off.

"This way," Zachary said.

Ronin looked over his shoulder to see Kai and Jared following.

"Keep going!" Kai yelled.

Zachary opened the door to the stairs and started up, waving the sword back and forth to see up the dark passage.

The group squeezed past him, pushing and shoving. The woman with the baby almost fell, but Elan let go of Ronin to help her up the stairs. He remained behind with his family on the first landing, waiting for Kai, Jared, and the dog to catch up.

"Hurry, Dad, come on," Zachary said. Footsteps pounded the hallway, and he readied the sword. He almost reminded Ronin of Uncle Akira, the way he stood there wielding the blade. "Get behind me."

Ronin stared into the darkness while the tap of boots and distant clack of metal grew louder.

"Come on, Dad," he whispered.

A figure bounded around the corner, and Ronin tensed until

he saw his father limping toward them.

"What are you doing?" Kai said. "Go, get up to the hangar!"

"We're waiting for you," Zachary said. "We're not leaving—"

"No, you go." Kai glared up at his eldest. "I'll stay here with Jared and hold that thing back."

"What?" Lise cried. "No, you're coming with us."

Jared back-pedaled toward them, still aiming in the opposite direction.

"We'll catch up," Kai said.

"But Kai!" Lise said.

"There's no time, you have to go."

Ronin shook as he watched his parents argue an impossible decision.

"Dad, please, you have to come with us," Zachary said.

A mechanical shriek roared in the next passage.

"It's almost here," Jared said. "Get going, now!"

Kai reached out and pushed Ronin hard enough to get him into the stairwell.

"No, please don't do this," Lise said.

"We can all make it, come on," Zachary said.

Kai looked at them all in turn. "I love you all. I'll be right behind you. Zachary, get them to the hangar."

Then he pulled the door shut.

"No!" Lise yelled.

Zachary pulled her away and screamed for Ronin to grab Elan. He gripped Elan's hand tight, trying to help reassure his brother that they were going to be okay. But as they hobbled up the stairs in the black, listening to the cries of children and a baby above them, everything took on a surreal feeling.

Ronin realized his brain wasn't working the way it normally did. He hadn't even stopped to think about why the Canebrakes were attacking them. His body had taken over, like it did when he was training for Droid Raiding, every movement and action coming from instinct. Zachary, too, was moving like a soldier. He kept his sword up in a defensive position as he carefully made his way around the civilians bottlenecked under the next landing.

"Move, move," he said.

"It's locked!" someone yelled.

"Be quiet, man," Zachary bellowed.

A clicking filled the silence, followed by the clanking of metal feet. Ronin gripped his brother's and mother's hands tighter, fearing that they were cornered.

"Zachary, be careful," Lise whispered.

Ronin heard the door click.

Lights suddenly flashed onto the landing above, then came muffled voices.

"Keep moving."

"Let's go."

"Don't push."

Two Pistons escorted the group into a massive room that had to be a mile wide, with a ceiling that looked one hundred feet tall. Aircraft sat idly in front of sealed overhead blast doors. In the center of the hangar, two black Stingray VTOL military corvettes were angled toward open launch tunnels overhead. Technicians and engineers worked on scaffolds built around the Stingray shuttles.

At the far end, Ronin could see what looked like one hundred or more Pistons. Ten Juggernauts were among them, the mech suits towering six feet over the soldiers. Every weapon was trained on the blast doors.

Sparks showered down the side as red-hot blades cut through the thick metal.

"It's not going to hold!" someone shouted.

The Juggernauts advanced to the front of the line, hydraulics hissing. The pilots in the cockpits reached back with their robotic arms to draw energy swords.

Ronin followed the two Piston escorts around a fort of tall, long storage containers. On the other side was a group of Royal Pistons holding sentry near a towering figure in golden armor, who watched from the saddle of a droid horse.

At first, Ronin thought it was his Uncle Akira, but it wasn't the captain. It was War Commander Contos.

"War Commander, we found more civilians," said the Piston in front of Ronin.

The massive golden commander turned, holding a glowing

energy sword the length of a child. Contos scanned the group and in a booming voice asked, "Where is Master Sergeant Kai Hayashi?"

"My dad stayed behind to hold back the machines," Ronin said.

Contos looked down at Ronin, then over to a Royal Piston. "Go find him."

A lieutenant ran over, armor rattling as his chest heaved.

"War Commander, we need to get you to the other shuttle," he said between gasps. "We can't hold them back much longer."

"I'm not leaving this base until the civilians are evacuated," Contos said.

The civilians stared up at the living legend towering above them.

"We don't have much time to get you all to that corvette," he said. "When I tell you to follow me, you do it, and don't look back."

30

Jason was in a dream-like state, watching Shadow Squad fleeing from a pack of Canebrakes outside of Megacity Tokyo. The machines had been deployed to hunt down the Red Wolves hiding underground after the gas attacks. The terrorist supporters of Dr. Cross were all dead now, their mangled and dismembered bodies littering the platform of a subway outside of the megacity, where they had launched an attack on the civilians.

But in his dream, the machines hadn't stopped. They had slaughtered hundreds of Pistons, blasting them from the sky and killing them on the ground. The images bled into darkness, replaced by the sound of screams, the same agonizing screams Jason remembered from Petra suffering during the final days of her battle with SANDs.

Flashes of red streaked through the darkness, illuminating a Hummer Droid inside of the Nova One command center. Three Canebrakes surrounded it, their limbs wrapped around the body and their serrated blades striking.

"I cannot hold them much longer!" Apeiron shouted.

The voice sounded *just* like his sister.

The dream shifted: Petra, just twenty-five years old, beautiful, intelligent, strong…

"Petra!" Jason yelled. "Petra, run!"

Now she was Apeiron again, cutting into a Canebrake, hacking through its titanium helmet.

"We have to stop Doctor Cross!" she yelled. "You have to wake up!"

Jason tried to, but the dream transported him to a burning city. Dreads rode mechanical horses, patrolling the streets. Canebrakes climbed mountains of rubble, scanning for targets with their black eyes. A man in ragged brown clothes and a gas mask darted across a street. The closest Dread launched a spear, puncturing the man through the back. Plasma bolts flashed out of a skeletal tower, hitting the Dread and knocking him off the saddle. The horse lifted up its front legs, kicking the air before taking off down the road.

The thrumming of thrusters roared overhead from a hovering Praying Mantis fighter. In the cockpit, a Canebrake operated the mounted plasma turrets that fired at the windows, flames bursting out.

Jason fought to free his mind of the nightmare, but instead he found himself inside a Life Ark, where groups of civilians sat in a communal atrium, watching dark holo-screens. A cry of fear echoed through the vaulted chamber, and the crowd suddenly fled.

In the chaos, Jason saw one of the faces perfectly. It was his daughter Nina, cowering behind a park bench, while Betsy screamed for Autumn.

The rattle of a Canebrake finally snapped Jason into another dream.

He was in the Nova One command center, watching a Canebrake impale a female officer through her stomach with a superheated blade. It withdrew the glowing knife, and the woman fell to her knees, holding her own guts as they gushed out into her hands.

Jason could smell the burning flesh.

This is just a dream, he thought. *Just another nightmare.*

He scrambled behind a row of stations, where another female officer crouched with General Chase.

"Shut them down, Doctor," Chase whispered. There was panic and fear in the hardened man's eyes.

Jason tried to connect to INN, but all he saw was darkness.

"Apeiron," he said quietly. "Apeiron, where are you?"

A scream rang out, drawing his attention to an adjacent station.

Jason peered around over the desk at a Canebrake with black eyes, just like in his dream. A sickening truth passed over him: his dreams had become reality. The Canebrakes had turned on them.

Plasma bolts streaked across the room. An officer got up and ran for new cover, toppling as a blade whooshed and thunked through flesh and bone. The man hit the ground, his head tumbling away from his neck.

A Canebrake jumped up to the station, the glass of the command module shattering under its weight. Strobing red light illuminated the gruesome scene. Bodies of AAS staff and officers lay in crumpled messes, blood and gore painting the hulls and deck.

Jason searched for Darnel but didn't see his loyal friend among the dead.

A violent rattling sound erupted in front of Jason as the Canebrake rotated the fanned head toward him, its black eyes flashing red as it scanned his body.

Rising up, all four arms prepared to strike with heated blades. Three of them shot away, one puncturing General Chase through the cheek. His feet kicked, blood soiling his white uniform. The fourth arm curved like a fishhook, its blade directed at Jason, giving him a few torturous seconds to consider his fate and the fate of everyone.

He had failed his family. Failed his species. Failed to save Earth.

And for that, he deserved this death, embracing it like Dr. Cross had.

The clash of metal on metal resonated through the room, followed by a soothing voice.

"Jason, I am here."

Behind the Canebrake emerged a Black Hummer Droid with sparks shooting out of one arm socket. It used the other arm with a serrated blade to saw through the war droid, which crashed to the deck in two halves.

Slowly, the surviving officers and Pistons emerged from their hiding places. Apeiron clanked over to Jason, slashes in her black armor still simmering.

"Jason," Darnel called out. He stood in the top tier of the command center, pulse rifle still aimed at a Canebrake draped over a crushed computer terminal.

"How did this happen?" Jason stammered. "How did they…"

"Doctor Cross must have had his researchers design their own OS, and used a virus to transmit and install it on the

Canebrakes and anyone with an L-S88 chip."

Jason shook his head. "That's impossible. How could he have transmitted the virus without—"

"Through his INVS eyes."

"No..."

Jason's words trailed off when he recalled the images of Dr. Cross removing needles stored in his nostrils and then thrusting them into his eyes. Eyes that could transmit data just as easily as they could receive it.

"My God..." Jason whispered for the first time in his adult life. "How did he design this code and get through all of our security?"

"I believe it was from within."

Jason's suspicions had been correct after all.

"I checked all security videos over the past six months, and I found one with AAS programmer Mike Hook, the man who tried to kill you at Spartan Base."

"That son of a bitch..."

"He appears to have smuggled out hard copies of the Canebrake OSs, which could be how Doctor Cross and his people developed the virus and alternative OS."

Jason stared in disbelief.

"The Canebrake OSs were kept separate from INN, on isolated servers to reduce the chance of an external hacker corrupting the data," Apeiron said. "That meant so long as I was also not physically present in Hummer Droid form, I could not monitor those servers in perpetuity."

"INN is shut down completely?"

"Yes, when I realized what had happened, I disconnected INN and shut off your chip, but the virus had already started to spread, from Canebrake to Canebrake."

"But we've taken the station back now," Jason said. "The Canebrakes are all destroyed."

"It was not just the Canebrakes on the station. The signal was transmitted to Canebrakes across the surface of the Earth, reprogramming them all."

"Reprogramming?" Jason asked.

"To eradicate all human life."

"This is the reset Doctor Cross wanted," said Darnel. "A return to the state of nature."

"So he became what he hated most?" Jason asked.

He staggered over to the window, looking down at Earth.

Knots formed in his gut as he realized his own insurance plan for the planet was at risk.

"The Life Arks," he said. "What about the Canebrakes in the Life Arks?"

"There are only two Canebrake models in each Life Ark," Apeiron said. "The human security forces should be able to eliminate them before they can inflict too many casualties, unless they make it into the command centers.

"Like they did here." Jason shook. He imagined Betsy screaming for Autumn and Nina, hiding behind a park bench in the atrium of the Life Ark. "Can you access any of the feeds from the Arks?"

"Your family has been moved to the *Liberty* shuttle," Apeiron said. "It will launch, if all else fails, but for now, they are safer where they are."

Jason gripped his hands to try and stop the shaking.

A hatch opened, and a squad of Pistons rushed in. They stopped and lowered their weapons at the sight of all the gore.

"The station is secure for now," said the lieutenant in charge.

Jason looked out over the survivors. He had to rally these people, he had to inspire them. There was always a way out, always a solution to a problem.

"Apeiron, contact the King Cobra Spaceplane squadrons," he said. "Reroute half of them to protect this station."

"There are only two-hundred and fifty-one King Cobra Spaceplanes still in orbit," she replied.

"What? What happened to the others?"

"The Praying Mantis fighters attacked shortly after the signal went out, catching our pilots by surprise. They defeated the hostile fighters, and War Commander Contos recalled one hundred of the King Cobra Spaceplanes back to Earth to help escort shuttles."

"Shuttles?"

"An evacuation order was given," Apeiron said. "Humanity

is fleeing to the Moon."

Jason looked out a window, searching the black for the lifeboats. "See if you can reach War Commander Contos," he said to the only surviving NAI officer. "We need at least one hundred King Cobra Spaceplanes to protect this station."

Darnel stepped up next to him, his exoskeleton creaking. "Six hours and two minutes until impact," he said. "That's a long time to hold out."

"We have to defend this command center at all costs," Jason said. "We can't lose the cannons. Or we lose everything."

***

Five hours remained before Hros-1 arrived and Shadow Squad was still pinned down by the Canebrakes. The machines were prowling the slums, hunting.

Akira prayed that the Poseidon cannons were still operational, but with INN down, there was no way to know. He had no idea what was going on at Gold Base either, or whether his family was okay. Nor did he have the ability to connect to Kichiro.

Shadow Squad still only had short-range comms and Blue Jay. The small drone flew overhead, watching for Canebrakes as the team waited to make its next move.

Akira checked on the survivors of the Stone Mountain Battalion. Three Pistons had made it to the rendezvous point, out of three hundred men and women. They had lost ninety-five percent of a battalion in just minutes, at the hands of twenty Canebrakes that had turned on them.

If a handful of machines could do that much damage that quickly, Akira was terrified to think what a thousand Canebrakes locked away at Gold Base could do. If they were all activated under the same orders, and escaped, they would kill *everyone*.

Akira thought back to War Commander Contos's question: *Is Apeiron our enemy or our friend?*

The answer was now clear.

Apeiron had turned on them, even as Hros-1 barreled toward the Earth. There was a reason the Nova Alliance had banned human-integrated AIs. The first, would almost certainly be the last, with the entire human race at stake.

Akira felt like he was going to vomit, but part of that was from his own injuries. They had removed the rebar that punched into his armor and into his flesh. Heavy doses of cell-regeneration nanotechnology was already healing his insides, prompting severe nausea.

Okami walked over to Akira, tail wagging. Akira owed the wolfdog his life. It had nearly died taking down the Canebrake back on the roof.

Akira patted Okami and moved to check the rest of the squad.

Frost and Tadhg were also injured, but Tadhg had taken some bad hits. Multiple plasma bolts had broken through his plates and cut deep into his flesh. The big man sat with his back to a wall of the subway, his face ash white, bandages covering his chest. Blood stains that looked like flower petals dotted the wrappings.

"We need to move soon. Can you fight?" Akira asked.

"You're asking me if I can..." Tadhg coughed and spat blood on the ground. "You'd have to cut off my legs, arms, and balls before I couldn't. Know what I'm sayin'?"

Akira wanted to smile, but winced from a jolt of pain.

"I've plotted the fastest route back to HQ," Ghost said. "It will take almost two hours on foot, if we move fast. That leaves us three hours to get back to base and underground before the cannons fire."

"We've already wasted enough time," Akira said. "We can't stay here any longer, we have to try and link up with other survivors."

Frost looked at the three Pistons: twenty-year-old Private First Class Allen Richman from Megacity Atlanta, twenty-three-year-old Corporal Bella Oliver from an outpost in the territories of Scotland, and Sergeant Nick Toretto from Megacity Rome.

They stood with their RS3 rifles aimed at the subway entrance, and Akira had a feeling they weren't watching just for the machines. They were watching to see if any of their brothers and sisters had survived.

"Plot a route to the next civilian shelter. Maybe there will be some vehicles there," Akira said to Ghost. "We'll head there on foot."

Ghost uploaded the route to their HUDs a moment later.

Akira checked Blue Jay one more time. There was no sign of hostiles in the area. Seeing nothing moving, he gave the order to leave the subway.

Okami dashed up the stairs with Frost. She shouldered her .50-cal, the best weapon they currently had against the Canebrakes. The phased-plasma pulse rifles could penetrate their armor, and the energy swords could cut their arms off, but a well-placed .50-caliber round to the skull would put them down for good.

The Pistons followed the Engines into the darkness.

Hros-1 was still just a tiny, static dot in the jeweled sky, although brighter than it had appeared before.

The glow of Megacity Tokyo's skyscrapers guided the team like a beacon. Two seventy-story holographic avatars of famous actors walked in the entertainment district, advertising new virtual films. Akira was glad to see them. They indicated the attack hadn't spread to the surrounding city.

But that didn't mean the devastation would remain contained if the Canebrakes broke out of Gold Base, especially if Apeiron was leading them. She knew the base, every corridor, every security code. They had handed the enemy the keys to victory on a silver platter, letting them march in with better weapons and armor.

Akira picked up his pace, battling fatigue and the pain of his injuries. A bird cawed and took flight from the bones of a dead cherry-blossom tree as Shadow Squad moved through an old concrete park with rusted play equipment. The thermal view from Blue Jay showed no signs of life beyond a stray dog and a few feral cats. If there were Canebrakes out there, they didn't have their blades activated.

At the next intersection, Akira motioned for the team to get down. His helmet amplifier had picked up a vibration on the road.

He sent Blue Jay new orders to check out the source. It took a few minutes for the drone to get a view over the city walls, but it confirmed what Akira had feared.

Smoke rose away from the skyline, probably from the explosions that had caused the seismic readings, and not only at the base.

Akira ran down a street framed by the scree of collapsed apartment buildings, now piles of rubble rising five stories off the ground. He flitted his gaze between the street and his mirrored view from the drone, but this wasn't like having Apeiron with them, providing live intel. He missed that for a second, but knowing she had turned on them just made him furious.

He should have seen this coming, should have done something!

Akira ran harder, his lungs burning.

Focus your mind and sync your body, he thought.

A connected mind and body were capable of anything, his father had told him. This advice had helped Akira through the rigorous Engine training, and the augmentations that followed the mental testing. Through it all, he had learned just how far he could push his body, farther than a normal human.

The next civilian shelter was just two blocks away. Akira set the pace with Okami at his side. The wolfdog suddenly stopped and snarled a warning before Akira heard the trucks. By the time he saw them, it was already too late.

They came blasting out of a parking garage entrance and skidded in front of Akira. Men in black pants, sleeveless leather vests with rusted chest plates, and gas masks hopped out with rifles. Okami snarled, alerting Akira to another two armored trucks.

More men piled out, taking cover behind the vehicles. In the truck beds, masked men aimed mounted .50 cal machine guns.

Akira counted ten total hostiles, nomads in light armor and carrying shotguns, old-school assault rifles, and some coil guns.

These were modern day Yakuza, the tattooed nomad gangsters who ruled the wastes beyond the megacity walls.

"Hold your fire," Akira said over the comm.

A man walked out of the parking garage, wearing a Piston-style helmet. Faded tattoos lined his muscular arms. By his side was a brown Hummer Droid, one of the older models, built to create, not to kill. Two plasma pulse rifles were mounted on its limbs. The facial screen flashed a friendly digital smile of a man with a handle-bar mustache.

The leader took off the Piston helmet, revealing a clean-shaven face and long black hair.

"Cute pup you got there," he said in Japanese. "Name's Kobe, and you are?"

"Captain Akira Hayashi. We're trying to get back to Gold Base."

"Of course you are. You gas nomads and then run. I always thought the Coalition was the worst of two fascist regimes, but I guess it was the Nova Alliance all along."

"We didn't gas the nomads, asshole," Frost said.

Akira held up a hand. He knew the situation could break down quickly, and they didn't have time to spare.

"Listen to me carefully, Kobe," he said. "We deployed in response to that gas attack by terrorists called the Red Wolves. But something happened… the Canebrakes turned on us, and now they're hunting us. They'll probably be after you, too."

Several of the gang members laughed, but Kobe remained silent. He took a step forward, and Okami growled a warning.

"He may be cute, but he's named Okami for a reason," Akira said.

"Cut the shit," Kobe said. "I know you're lying."

"He's not lying," Tadhg said. "Okami will bite your dick off."

Kobe chuckled. "I'm not talking about the puppy. I'm talking about the Canebrakes."

"You think I look like this because of some pussy Coalition terrorists?" Tadhg asked. "The machines did this, and they'll do worse to you."

"We just want to get back to the walls," Akira said. "I swear on my honor."

Kobe took a few steps forward, the Hummer Droid following. Its plasma barrels were trained on Akira, ignoring

Okami. If they were going to have a shootout, he was glad he would take the brunt of it.

Kobe studied Tadhg, and then looked skyward.

"What about that asteroid?" Kobe asked. "Does the NA still got a plan to take it out?"

"The Canebrakes are what we should all be worried about. If we don't get back to HQ and stop them, they'll erase thousands of innocent lives."

Kobe took another step, stopping in front of Akira. Then he raised a hand and signaled for his men to lower their weapons and stand down.

"We'll give you a lift to the walls, Captain Hayashi," Kobe said.

"Thank you," Akira said.

"You trust them, Captain?" Ghost asked quietly over the private comms.

"We don't have a choice."

The Engines and Pistons climbed into an empty truck with Okami. Akira watched his HUD as Blue Jay continued to comb the area. The trucks lurched and started down the road.

A rumbling boomed in the distance. Akira zoomed in on an aircraft in the sky above Tokyo, a sleek black corvette rising toward the stars. The shuttle, a NA Stingray, he knew, was one of two at the base.

"Where the hell are they going?" asked Kobe.

Akira watched the corvette blasting into the night. If they were abandoning the base, then perhaps Shadow Squad was already too late.

31

Plasma fire strobed across the long hangar, keeping Ronin and the other civilians pinned down behind War Commander Contos and ten Royal Pistons. They had made it halfway to the last Stingray shuttle. The other corvette had blasted off an hour ago with General Thacker, right before the Canebrakes broke through the blast doors and flooded into the room.

Ronin had been sheltering with his mother and brothers behind a wall of black military-grade crates for what seemed like hours. On the other side were rows of APCs and hover all-terrain vehicles. Beyond the vehicles it was another quarter mile to the Stingray, an impossible distance on foot with the Canebrakes inside the hangar.

The rattle of their antennas echoed through the space as they advanced.

Ronin peered through a gap in the crates, watching the battle. A phalanx of one hundred Pistons and Juggernauts slowly thinned from the onslaught of machines cutting into their wall of armor.

War Commander Contos rode Kichiro, gripping his rifle in one hand and a longsword in the other. He swung the energy blade at the Canebrakes that penetrated the lines. Others had taken to the walls, climbing overhead and dropping behind the Pistons.

A metal figure emerged, moving so fast the soldiers didn't see it until the Canebrake whipped a telescoping arm at the line, wrapping around a Piston's neck and flinging the man away. He landed behind a crate, where a geyser of blood exploded upward as another Canebrake tore him apart.

The machines opened their jaws, rimmed with razor-sharp teeth, releasing electronic shrieks meant to intimidate. It worked—Ronin and the other civilians around him huddled together like frightened animals.

"We can't stay here any longer," said Contos. "We need to

make a run for the APCs."

Ronin looked over his shoulder for his father, for the hundredth time. But for every second that passed, it was less likely Kai was still alive. He had already been gone for hours.

Dread filled Ronin at the thought of losing his father.

"Get ready to move," said one of the Royal Pistons.

"You guys ready?" Zachary asked.

"Kai," Lise said.

Zachary rose to his feet and tightened the backpack that contained the Warrior Codex. His features were tight and serious, the same look as before a Droid Raider match... he was ready to fight. "I'll go look for Dad."

Lise grabbed his arm. "No, if he's already... I can't lose you too."

"Let's go!" Contos shouted. "Follow me!"

Ronin took Lise and Elan's hands. The Pistons led the civilians around the crates, following Contos on the war horse. They kept low, a chain of hands and bodies making their way toward the APCs.

Suddenly the lead Royal Piston vanished in a puff of smoke and light, his body thumping to the ground next to Ronin with a sizzling, melon-sized hole in his chest. Organs gurgled out.

Then a woman slumped to the deck, her face erased by a simmering red hole.

"Keep moving!" Contos shouted.

Screams rang out around Ronin, but he held his mom and brother tightly, pulling them forward, using the glow of emergency lights and plasma bolts to guide him. More machines broke away from the heart of the battle, their armored frames illuminated as they fired. Ronin heard a rattling above and halted, pulling back on his brother and mom just in time.

Both Pistons in front of him fired up at a Canebrake running on the ceiling. Its plasma cannons burst to life, hitting the two soldiers in their helmets.

The Canebrake leapt down, right in front of Ronin and his family.

"Watch out!" Lise cried.

Four black arms whipped back and forth as the Canebrake's black eyes searched for targets. One arm fired at Ronin, only to be hacked away by a Piston. Ronin fell on his back, bringing Elan and Lise to the floor with him.

A crackling Canebrake screech reverberated through the room.

"Get back!" Zachary shouted.

He ducked under another segmented arm, and then swiped up with his sword to cut the Canebrake across the ridged shell-like chest plates. The machine reared back, directing both plasma cannons at Zachary, but he dove between the machine's wide legs, cutting into the plated armored covering of two of them. The Canebrake went down, and Zachary was already on his feet, delivering a swift stroke that nearly severed the machine's head.

Ronin helped his mother and Elan up.

"Keep moving!" Zachary yelled.

"Stay behind us!" Contos yelled.

The horse advanced as another Canebrake skittered like a crab overhead. It dropped onto a four-seater ATV, crushing the roll bars and firing its pulse cannons. Three Pistons dropped under the wave of fire, and others pounded the Canebrake with hundreds of bolts, its armor hissing and cracking.

The droid kept fighting, slinging its arms and firing at the soldiers.

Contos dodged, but the guard on his right wasn't as fast. A blade punctured the center of his faceplate, breaking out the back of his head with a spray of blood.

Ronin picked up the guard's rifle and brought it up to fire just as the Canebrake hopped off the vehicle and made a run for Kichiro. The droid horse kicked up, with a limb wrapped around his neck.

The stallion pulled the Canebrake forward just as Ronin pulled the trigger, firing a burst of plasma bolts that missed. He fired again, impacting the Canebrake's shoulder and knocking it off balance. It twisted its torso, and he squeezed off another burst that burrowed into the Canebrake's eyes and forehead.

Using his right front hoof, Kichiro crushed the center of the

Canebrake's fanned head.

Contos turned in the saddle and offered Ronin a grateful nod.

"Ronin, come on!" Zachary yelled.

Elan pulled Ronin's arm, and they ran for the APCs. A Piston opened the back hatch of the closest vehicle and herded civilians inside.

Ronin took a seat next to Elan and his mother, still gripping the rifle. Zachary sat across from them. A woman tried to hush a baby, but the child wailed, echoing in the enclosed troop hold. The vehicle screeched away, plasma bolts pounding its sides.

"Everyone hold on," said the driver. The APC zigged and zagged around crates and downed Pistons. "When I stop, get out and run straight to the corvette!"

"Stay close," Lise said firmly. "We go together."

The APC jolted to a stop, and the hatch opened to screams of horror.

A Canebrake stood outside, rising to its maximum height of almost ten feet. Its cannons belched to life, and the woman next to Ronin burst like a leech full of blood.

Then, in a flash of metal legs and titanium hooves, the machine vanished. Contos dismounted from Kichiro and waved. "Let's go!"

Lise and Elan were already moving. Ronin avoided looking at the woman to his left and ran after the other civilians. There weren't many survivors. Maybe a dozen. On the exit ramp, he noticed Zachary wasn't with them.

He looked back and saw Zachary limping toward him, a hand on his leg, and the other gripping the sword.

"Go!" Zachary insisted.

Ronin turned and saw his mom and Elan enter the corvette with two Pistons.

Contos and his men formed an armored phalanx to protect the civilians escaping into the shuttle, firing at a Canebrake that had leapt on top of the APC. Zachary turned and swung at one of the arms that lanced toward him, deflecting it with a clang. He fell on his back, and Ronin aimed his rifle at the Canebrake's helmet from the ramp.

Please, please, please don't miss.

His brother's life was on the line and Ronin had the power to save him.

He closed one eye, lined up the sights on the war machine and pulled the trigger.

The weapon kicked, the bolts blasting high into the ceiling.

He steadied the rifle, held in a breath and aimed again as the Canebrake towered over Zachary, arms up and heated blades glowing red.

Ronin could not miss again.

He lowered the barrel slightly to adjust for the recoil, and pulled the trigger. This time the three bolts slammed into the chest of the Canebrake, knocking it away from his brother.

"Run, Zach!" Ronin screamed.

Zachary pushed himself up, his face a grimace of pain, blood surging from a gash in his thigh. He fell back to the ground as Ronin hurried down the ramp to meet him.

"Take the book!" Zachary shouted. Still on the ground, he flung his backpack through the air. It landed a few feet from Ronin, who snatched it up.

At the other end of the room, a phalanx of Pistons folded as more Canebrakes crashed through. A pack of three machines vaulted over the downed soldiers and onto the Juggernauts. Kichiro reared up on his back legs, kicking the air as plasma rounds tore past.

Zachary glanced over his shoulder at the Canebrake that Ronin had knocked away. It was still down, but flung a segmented arm through the air.

Ronin screamed and reached out as his brother turned back to him, just as a blade sliced through his neck, and retracted back to the machine.

Zachary stared at Ronin for a split moment before his head slid off his neck.

An animalistic cry echoed through the entire chamber.

When Ronin went to open his mouth, he realized it was from his own mouth.

"NO!" he howled.

Ronin fired at the Canebrake as his brother's headless corpse slumped to the ground. He held the trigger until the gun hissed, overheated.

The machine swung another arm at Ronin. He had just enough time to duck beneath the heated blade.

"Get back!" boomed a voice.

Ronin jumped to the side, narrowly avoiding Kichiro as the machine stormed past with War Commander Contos in the saddle. The horse slammed into the Canebrake, and Contos hacked into the head with his long sword, disabling the droid.

He then reached down with his free hand and grabbed Ronin, hauling him up onto the horse.

"Let me go!" Ronin shouted. "I've got to get my brother!"

"Kid, he's gone," Contos said. "We must go!"

Ronin struggled to look at his dead brother, hoping, praying that his eyes had lied to him earlier and that Zachary would get back up and make it to the shuttle. But the sight of his headless corpse and pooling blood confirmed this was real, that his older brother would never get up ever again.

His short life was over.

Plasma bolts lanced through the air as Contos dropped Ronin on the ramp in front of two Pistons. "Get him out of here!"

The soldiers grabbed Ronin and hauled him into the shuttle. He screamed as they carried him.

"Don't move from this seat!" one of the men yelled. He threw Ronin into it forcefully. Elan and Lise were down the aisle. Her lips were moving, but Ronin couldn't hear her voice over the roar of the engines.

A string of plasma bolts hit the porthole windows. Outside, War Commander Contos rode Kichiro toward the group of retreating soldiers.

Ronin closed his eyes, trying to block out the nightmare. When he opened them again, the corvette had launched and was rising above the underground silo. Rockets soared across the streets, exploding against buildings. Flashes of light crisscrossed, and brilliant explosions burst across the skyline. A squadron of enemy Praying Mantis fighters, their metal mandibles glowing blue, curved toward a formation of civilian shuttles taking off from the airport. One exploded just after lifting off, bursting over the tarmac in a spray of debris and flames.

Ronin knew then that it wasn't just Zachary he had lost. His father and uncle, if they were still alive, wouldn't be for long. He wiped away his tears. They wouldn't want him to cry for them, they would want him to take care of his twin brother and mother. He pushed up the rack and stumbled over to them.

Lise stared at Ronin, her lips trembling. She was in shock.

An impact suddenly pounded the Stingray, shaking it violently.

Ronin turned to look out the window behind him. A formation of enemy drones that looked like black shuriken slammed into a civilian shuttle that had made it into the sky. An explosion burst through the hull, flames soaring out, and with them, human shapes, sucked away into the night.

Ronin gripped his brother's and mom's hands as their corvette vibrated from the impacts. The pilots swerved, climbed, and swerved some more, and for the next ten minutes, Ronin prayed for his father, uncle, and brother.

And for their shuttle.

More explosions thumped outside, but a new noise rose over the blasts—the roar of a Short Sword stealth fighter jet. It unleashed a flurry of rockets, destroying a wave of incoming drones. As they burst across the sky, the Short Sword fighter pulled up and peeled off into the darkness.

The alarms in the cabin of the shuttle stopped beeping, and the frightened cries of passengers faded away. Even the baby stopped crying. Relieved voices cried out as people strained to look out the windows.

Ronin leaned forward, trying to get an idea where they were evacuating to, but the ground was so far away that, within a few minutes, the Earth appeared as a ball of darkness, the lights of megacities glowing in the night. One suddenly winked off as the shuttle flew away from the planet, and then a new view came into focus—the dazzling sea of stars and the glowing white moon.

Ronin snapped free of the shock gripping his body and mind.

They hadn't just evacuated Megacity Tokyo. They were evacuating Earth.

***

A second corvette launched from the base, blasting into the sky.

Akira watched, hoping his family was on it.

The convoy of trucks slowed and parked in front of the sealed gates of Tokyo's western wall, three hours to spare before Hros-1 entered orbit. But the asteroid was the least of Akira's worries right now.

Faint gunfire and explosions sounded on the other side of the fifty-story wall.

Akira hopped down and walked over to Kobe, the Yakuza leader. The soldiers in the beds of the trucks, hardened nomads, seemed to understand what was going on, and Akira registered their accelerated heartbeats on his scanners.

"This is as far as we go," Kobe said. "Good luck."

"Thank you." Akira extended his hand. It was an old school way of giving his thanks, but Kobe refused it.

"Just because we helped you, doesn't mean we're friends," he said.

"Perhaps someday I can repay the favor," Akira said.

"If there is a someday," Kobe said. He rotated his finger in the air, and the trucks peeled away, heading back into the slums.

Akira instructed Blue Jay to fly over the walls for a look. "Ghost, get us in."

Ghost approached the sensor panel at a pedestrian port. The eight-foot steel door creaked open. Walking through the opening was like stepping into a time machine. A lush garden of cherry blossoms and bonsai trees grew up against the interior of the wall. On the other side were blocks of traditional Japanese mansions with tiled roofs.

Okami stomped through a bed of flowers, sniffing for threats.

Beyond the wealthy neighborhood, dark skyscrapers loomed in the distance. Fires sparkled in their glass windows. Gunfire and sporadic blasts echoed through the night. Screams of horror and agony joined the cacophony.

Tadhg advanced on a bridge over a koi pond. Ghost and Frost fell in behind Akira, with the Pistons Toretto, Bella, and Allen behind them. They took up defensive positions behind the trees and compound walls as a contact from Blue Jay flashed on their HUDs. Akira ordered the droid down for a better view.

He thought about his family. They had traveled here to visit him in what was supposed to be a time of peace. Now Tokyo was a warzone, and an asteroid was three hours from hitting Baku. He prayed Kai had gotten them to one of the shuttles.

Focus on each stroke of your blade. Win the battle, then focus on the war.

Tadhg halted and raised his hand. Just ahead, a Hummer Droid crawled across the concrete, dragging its lower half behind it in a tangled mass of cords.

"Looks like it tangoed with Tadhg in the arena," Ghost said quietly.

Gunfire cracked and popped in the distance. The noise came from flesh guns, not plasma rifles, which meant the locals were fighting back. Akira knew there was no way they were winning.

Okami stopped ahead to sniff the damaged droid, his tail going down. The machine turned toward them and reached up to Frost with skeletal fingers.

"What the hell?" she said.

The droid latched onto her ankle and pulled. She tried to kick free but it pulled her to the ground.

"Hey!" she cried. "Get it off me!"

Okami clamped down on the Hummer Droid's arm with a crunch.

Akira stared for a moment as his brain processed the scene. It took another beat to understand what was happening—the Canebrakes weren't the only droids that had turned on humanity.

Frost squirmed under the weight of the machine as Tadhg plucked it off. He twisted its head right out of the socket.

"The Hummer Droids now, too?" Frost exclaimed. "What about…"

They all looked over at Okami. The wolfdog chewed on the

severed arm of the destroyed Hummer Droid, his tail wagging again.

"Ankle Biter seems fine," Tadhg said.

"His OS is an older model," Akira said. He was glad he had never upgraded the archaic system, but he wasn't totally convinced the droid wouldn't still turn on them. Still, he wasn't going to abandon Okami, not after all they had been through.

Tadhg shook his helmet wearily. "I knew this shit would fucking happen, man. No one listened to me."

"Yeah, you're a genius," Frost said sarcastically.

Ghost raised his hand, mumbling.

"What?" Tadhg asked. "I was the one who warned everyone about this happening. AI is salvation has always been complete bullshit."

"We still don't know what happened, and AI brought me back," Ghost said. "So are you siding with the Coalition now?"

Tadhg stepped up to him. "Take that shit back."

"*Enough*," Akira said. "We have to get to the base."

The Engines fanned out across the road with Akira taking point, his eye on Okami.

"Captain, I just scanned that droid's serial code, and it was assigned to a shelter not far from here," Frost said. "Maybe we should check it out. It's on the way to the base."

Akira checked the mission clock. Two hours, forty-five minutes remained until Hros-1 would arrive. "Okay, but we make it fast."

They cleared the next corner, ran across the street, and entered a park. On the other side were more houses fenced off with stone or wooden walls.

Sporadic gunshots popped. Akira no longer heard screams, but a crunching sound came from somewhere nearby. He followed it until his augmented ears pinpointed the location.

It seemed to be coming from under the street.

Frost pointed toward a gated entry ahead, accented by waterfalls and rows of flowers, framing a road into the secluded community.

"Let me," Tadhg said. Grabbing two of the ten-foot metal bars, he pried them apart, providing a doorway.

Akira slipped through, keeping his rifle shouldered as he ran down the edge of the road toward an underground subway. The crunching grew louder, joined by snapping, popping, and ripping sounds. At the station entrance, one of the two blast doors was off its hinges. He peered down the stairs at the source of the sounds.

A black and yellow Hummer Droid leaned over bodies, twisting heads and ripping off limbs. Akira put a plasma bolt into the droid's helmet, then he slowly advanced upon a scene of horror.

All across the platform, bodies were dismembered, their skulls crushed, and brains mush.

"My God, this can't be real..." Frost said.

"We could have stopped this," Tadhg said. "We *should* have..."

Ghost grabbed Tadhg. "Stop living in the past, you egotistical asshole. *This* is our reality now. We have to face that."

"Get your hands off me," Tadhg said. He tried to yank away, but Ghost held on.

"Sergeant, you're an Engine, start acting like one," Akira said. "Lieutenant, let him go."

Ghost loosened his grip, and Tadhg stomped away. They all turned back to the stairs at the sound of gunfire, this time from plasma rifles.

"Shit, that must be the Pistons," Frost said. She rushed back up the steps to the surface.

As they got to the top, the Engines halted at another horrifying sight. Hummer Droids climbed over the walls and ran down the street. More units slipped through an opening in the gate.

From Blue Jay's mirrored view, Akira saw an entire army of droids storming toward their location: companion models, worker units, and service droids, in all shapes and sizes, and all with the same orders.

To kill humans.

Tadhg slotted his cannon and drew his sword. "Let me show you how this is done."

The other Engines fired into the machines as Tadhg charged,

helmet down, shoulder plates up. He slammed into a four-hundred-pound Hummer Droid that went down so hard, the facial screen shattered and the head cracked open.

Tadhg cut another unit in half with his sword, then kicked it into a wall.

"Make a line!" Akira yelled. "Stay with me!"

He drew both of his swords and ran toward Tadhg, hacking and cutting down the machines with his energy blades. Crunching and cracking echoed through the night as the battle drew more and more of the units from the surrounding area. The ground rumbled from the stampede, drowning out Okami's growl-barking.

"Get into the shelter!" Akira yelled over his shoulder to the Pistons. "And take that damn wolfdog!" He slowly advanced, whirling and thrusting his blades. Metal fingers scraped over his metal plates.

Powering through them, he fought to get closer to Tadhg, who was twenty feet ahead, swinging his energy sword in wide arcs. Two Hummer Worker Droids dragged from his legs, while three more piled onto his back.

"Frost, help Tadhg," Akira ordered.

As he swung his katanas, two suppressed shots cracked, picking off the droids hanging from Tadhg's legs, and then a third that was trying to pull off his helmet.

"Those were mine!" Tadhg yelled.

"You're welcome!" Frost shouted back.

All around them, the droids clambered like ravenous zombies. They slammed into Tadhg and punched his armor, leaving dents. Others climbed up his back and hung from his shoulder plates. And still Tadhg fought, swinging his sword, whirling, and bucking like a wild animal, but ten Hummer Droids piled on until he finally folded under their weight with an enraged scream.

Akira lost sight of Tadhg under the swarm of machines.

"Tadhg!" he shouted. "Tadhg, get out of there!"

Frost, Ghost, and Akira stayed side by side, cutting their way toward their comrade. More of the machines rushed toward the pile, forming a mountain of yellow and black.

Akira knew Tadhg would let his ego get in the way of orders someday. This time it could mean his life, but Akira wasn't about to lose another Engine. He thrust his sword and used his shoulder plates to slam into the droids, his stomach muscles burning.

"Stay with me!" he shouted.

They fought together through the army of droids, hacking and slicing with their energy blades and firing their plasma rifles. A sudden geyser of mechanical parts burst into the air, followed by Tadhg blasting into the air with his jetpack.

The droids and parts rained back down with the sergeant, his armor dented and scraped, but still intact. He dropped with the rest of the squad and together, they became one—a single Engine powering through the machines.

By the time the fight was over, the entire street was littered with parts.

Tadhg continued to thrust his sword into the machines, even when they were clearly disabled and posed no harm.

"*Enough*," Akira said.

Tadhg crushed a head, then kicked a torso.

"Tadhg," Akira growled.

Chest heaving, Tadhg looked over, then stomped another helmet.

Akira grabbed Tadhg by the arm. "Do you understand, Sergeant?"

Tadhg hesitated a moment, but then nodded. "Yes, Captain, I'm sorry."

"Captain," came a soft voice. "Captain, we found something."

Akira turned back to the subway entrance, where Bella stood with her rifle cradled.

"You'd better come see this," she said.

"Everyone but Ghost, stay here and hold security," Akira said. He ran down the stairs, passing through a graveyard of dead bodies to the platform, where Allen stood guard with Toretto. Okami was there too, wagging his tail as Akira approached.

"I picked up some heartbeats on the other side of this door," Toretto said.

Akira checked his HUD, and sure enough, he saw the escalated heart rates of over twenty contacts. Aiming his rifle, he fired at the lock and then kicked the door in. Ghost followed him inside, their targeting system flitting over fifty-one contacts.

A man in a black sweatshirt and blue pants walked forward, hands in the air.

"Help us," he said.

Children, women, and people of all ages huddled together, frightened but uninjured. The sight gave Akira hope that there were others out there, perhaps his own family.

"Go get the others," he said to Ghost.

Minutes later, the other Engines arrived.

"Oh damn," Frost said.

"What are we going to do with them?" Tadhg said quietly.

Akira knew there was no way they could move these people. They would be safer here, and so would his squad.

"Stay here with them," Akira said. "I'll head to the base to look for my family and Kichiro."

"No way. There could be other survivors there, and you'll need our help," Frost said.

"Yeah, and I'm not hiding down here," Tadhg said.

"Together, we are one," Ghost said. He put a hand on Akira's shoulder. "We're coming, Captain."

Akira took a moment to think and decided to split up.

"Toretto, Bella, you stay here with Okami," Akira said. "We'll head to the base and come back for you later. Allen, you come with us."

"Stay here?" Toretto said. "You got to be fuckin'—"

"We'll protect them," Bella said.

Toretto snorted. "Yeah, sure, we got this, but you better come back for us."

"Don't worry, he won't leave his wolfdog," Ghost said.

"We will come back, you have my word," Akira said.

As he ran back to the surface, he tapped into Blue Jay, skimming through the aerial view and current data. Right before they reached the graveyard of destroyed droids, he stopped to check the mission clock.

Two hours and twenty-one minutes remained until Hros-1 arrived.

Tadhg tapped the blade of his sword against one hand like a baseball bat. "AI ain't salvation anymore, Akira. Shadow Squad is salvation."

32

Chloe tried to connect to INN again, but the network was still down.

"Apeiron," she whispered. "Apeiron, can you hear me?"

The AI wasn't in charge of Kepler Station, but up until now, Chloe had been able to speak to the AI. She desperately missed talking to Apeiron.

Once again, Chloe felt the dark despair brought on by being alone, reminding her of her time in the catacombs and in Megacity Paris.

She sat at her workstation in the droid shop that she had gotten a job, trying to figure out how to fix a custom dog droid designed to look like a poodle. It was thirty years old, with an OS that was obsolete and a processor that needed to be replaced.

The other five employees were all off to watch Hros-1 arrive, but Chloe wasn't exactly alone. Radar perched on a pole by her desk, watching her work.

"Do you know what's going on yet?" she asked.

"Nope, nope," Radar replied.

Chloe sighed and put her tools down. She had decided to stay down here and work while the rest of the colony watched the Poseidon cannons destroy Hros-1. Work kept her mind off what could happen.

Two months had passed since she had left Earth for a new life here at Kepler Station, and every day, she found herself wondering if coming here had been the right decision. She had spoken to Cyrus the day before, and he still didn't have a pass to come to the Moon. Their last conversation played in her mind.

"Don't worry, we'll be together soon, one way or another," he had said.

But she had picked up a slight hesitation in his voice, and she wasn't sure if it was the transmission lag.

Now she was worried. Really worried. Not just about the asteroid, but about INN. How could it go down just two hours before Hros-1 arrived? A chill ran up her spine as theories echoed through her mind.

"Let's go find out what's going on," she said. "Uncle Keanu will know."

She locked up the shop and headed into the dull white street of commercial buildings.

"Ready for some fresh air, Radar?" she asked.

"I want to fly, I do. I want to fly, I do."

"Not today, pal. You're going to have to stick to my shoulder."

The bird extended its white wings and flapped up to its perch on her shoulder.

"And try not to say anything stupid in front of anyone today, okay?"

"No problem, no problem," Radar chirped.

They looked up at the glass dome holding in the manufactured oxygen and heat. The engineering was remarkable, but it still felt more like a glass prison.

Humans aren't supposed to live like this.

Chloe walked down the alley between the five and six-story row-house-style buildings packed together like the apartments she had grown up around in Megacity Paris. The banging of noisy hydraulics stopped her as she rounded a corner.

A platoon of black and yellow Hummer Droids filed out of an underground tunnel entrance across the street. The machines marched in two single file lines toward a pair of giant mining rovers blocking the road ahead.

Two Lunar Defense Corps (LDC) Pistons stood guard. The men wore gray vacuum-rated suits and held energy swords. They followed the droids, herding them like livestock into the rovers.

It wasn't unusual to see the droids, but she didn't understand the need for guards. The droids were harmless, no more dangerous than Radar. Many were a decade or older, having worked on the megacities and then shipped off to the Moon to build the mining colonies.

One of the units looked at Chloe and raised a hand. A smile formed on the oval screen it had for a face.

"Hello I-45, hello I-45," Radar said.

The Hummer unit acknowledged Radar like friends might do on the street.

Chloe had always felt sad for these droids. They were kind, not much different than the companion or service droids that many people on Earth had added to their families to do chores and educate their children.

She cut through another alley. Mining offices and lunar companies occupied most of the dull windowless buildings, but the lower levels contained bars, eateries, and fancy lounges that the miners frequented after months in the darkness of the craters. Chloe couldn't imagine living in the darkness of the craters for that long, mining for helium-3 and hydrogen, or boring deep into the lunar rock to build new tunnels and habitats for future colonists.

Today there were a handful of miners on the sidewalks and streets, but they weren't losing their minds from psychedelic drugs or getting shitfaced. Groups clustered together under holo-screens on the sides of the buildings.

The same message displayed on all of them: *No signal.*

Chloe continued to the underground train entrance, loping down the stairs and into the next train. She sat in silence, stroking Radar and trying to make sense of what was happening.

The train stopped at the western edge of the colony, and the doors whisked open. Chloe rushed out. Wide stairs led to the elevator shafts along the vertical edge of the crater. A Lunar Defense Piston stood guard inside the vestibule. He held up a hand as Chloe pulled out her ID.

"Rigs are shut down to non-essential business," he said.

"My uncle is Keanu Cotter," Chloe said. "He's expecting me."

The man looked at her ID, double-checked her face, then jerked his helmet toward the doors. He nodded at a wall-mounted camera, and the glass doors opened.

"Do you know why INN is down?" she asked.

He didn't answer.

"Asshole," she whispered.

"Asshole, asshole!" Radar chirped.

The doors closed, and the elevator rose before the guard could respond. Chloe couldn't help but chuckle. As the car rose, she got a view of the entire lunar colony. City blocks that had been empty a month ago were now packed with civilians that had fled Earth.

She zoomed in on the holo-screens, which still displayed the same message.

The elevator stopped at the top of the dome, the glow of the city below fading to just a faint light that melted to darkness. Chloe hated this part of the long journey to the top of the crater. It was so black she couldn't see, even with her INVS eyes, until she was halfway up.

Red lights in the distance illuminated the shadow of a shuttle. Chloe blinked, zooming in. Two MOTH shuttles flew with tilted thrusters, Hummer Droids on its sides.

"Radar, I think those are the droids we saw earlier," she said. "Why would they be leaving the colony?"

The MOTHs were out of view a moment later. Chloe finally saw the first sign of light from the surface. Fifteen minutes later the elevator docked, and the doors opened to a scene of chaos at the spaceport.

She looked outside, trying to get a glimpse of the Earth, but all she could see was the rocky horizon and the winking blue plasma lamps that guided shuttles over the regolith. This part of the base was normally reserved for commercial spaceplanes, but today it was filled with military transports being loaded by Pistons and Lunar Defense Corps soldiers in heavy suits and exoskeletons to help them move in the low gravity.

Chloe took an escalator to the third floor, squeezing past workers rushing down the hallway. When she arrived at her uncle's office, he was staring out his window, hands cupped behind his back. Boxes she had helped him unload two weeks ago were full again.

"Uncle Keanu," she said.

He wore a blue suit with a silver pin on the breast that matched the color of his perfectly trimmed beard.

"Chloe," he said with a surprised tone.

"Want to tell me what the hell is going on? Because no one

who knows is talking."

He motioned for her to close the door.

She stepped inside, her mind overwhelmed with worry.

A pair of MOTHs took off in the distance. Chloe zoomed in with her INVS eyes and realized they were the same two she had seen with the Hummer Droids.

"Where are they going with those droids?" she asked.

A knock came on the door, and a woman with a red scarf stepped into the room.

"Sir, I need to talk to you."

"Can it wait?" Keanu said.

"The order was given."

Keanu stared at the woman. "I don't believe it…"

"Believe what? What's going on?" Chloe asked.

Another pair of MOTHs landed outside, disgorging Pistons down a ramp. Three King Cobra Spaceplanes lifted off with tilted rotors, then fired off into the black.

"Thank you, Shelly," Keanu said.

The woman nodded and left.

Chloe stepped up to the window. "Uncle Keanu, what's the—"

"The order to abandon Earth and to flee Kepler Station," he interrupted. "Apeiron turned on humanity… we still don't know exactly what happened, but the Titan Space Elevator was destroyed. There are ongoing attacks at every megacity by the Canebrakes. There are even rumors the Hummer Droids have been reprogrammed to kill humans."

"No." Chloe shook her head. "That can't be possible. Apeiron would never do that."

Keanu stroked his beard, and she could see in his eyes that this was no lie.

"Those Hummer Droids have been scheduled for extermination, haven't they?" Chloe said.

"Extermination why, extermination why?" Radar asked.

Keanu tucked his hands in his pockets and let out a sigh. "All AI units were officially banned through an executive order by the Lunar Defense Corps approximately one hour ago."

Chloe put her hand to her chest. This couldn't be true. None of this could be true.

"Please, go and pack our things and wait for me at the apartment," Keanu said.

"Pack our things? Where are we going now?" Chloe asked.

When he didn't respond, she asked again, firmer this time.

"I'm not leaving this room until you tell me where I'm going."

"Chloe, stop asking questions, and just do as I say!"

Chloe backed away from her uncle, not recognizing the anger in his voice. He softened and reached out to her.

"I'm sorry," he said, putting a hand on her shoulder. "I promised your parents that I would look after you, and that's what I'm going to do."

"But where are we going?"

"All civilians have been ordered to leave Kepler Station and head to the Shackleton Crater."

"To a mining colony? How can they fit one hundred thousand civilians?"

"Because it's not just a mining colony."

Chloe raised a brow as he turned back to the viewport.

"The Lunar Defense Corps built a top-secret colony out there," Keanu said. "Just in case…"

"Just in case the cannons don't fire," Chloe said.

"Yes."

Chloe put a hand over her mouth, unable to hold back the shock. She stepped up next to her uncle for a view of Earth and zoomed in with her INVS eyes on one of the Poseidon cannons, still in orbit, angled out toward Hros-1.

Cyrus was still on Earth, and if those cannons didn't fire, she knew she would never see him again.

"I'm afraid we're about to see the end of the world," Keanu said.

***

An hour earlier, Jason had watched two stealth MOTHs blast away from Nova One Station toward Earth. One carried an important message.

*Dr. Cross has taken over the Canebrakes in an attack
on Nova One Station.*

*We have throttled that attack but need assistance
to hold the station.*

Jason watched from the command center as Earth shuttles emerged from the darkness. There was nothing he could do to help. Their communications were being jammed by the machines, keeping Jason from contacting Kepler Station on the Moon, or anywhere else, over the long-range comms.

Nova One Station was completely cut-off. His only hope was that the first MOTH could get the message through to survivors on the ground, requesting more help to assist the one hundred ten King Cobra pilots currently protecting the station.

The second MOTH had been deployed to Life Ark 12 to order the launch of the *Liberty* shuttle, with his family, to Kepler Station. The journey was dangerous, but Jason figured it was more dangerous to leave them on Earth.

"Here comes another shuttle," Darnel said.

The riskiest part of the exodus to the Moon was blasting off the ground and making a run for Earth's orbit. This shuttle had already completed that leg of the journey.

"We have three hostiles in pursuit of Falcon 4," said the lead flight-control officer.

Jason knew this one didn't stand a chance. The civilian shuttles were sitting ducks once they were spotted. A few minutes later, he saw a tiny blast in the black of space as Praying Mantis fighters destroyed it.

The room went silent for a moment, but the crew quickly returned to work.

Only one hour and twenty-one minutes remained until impact, and just a few minutes before the Poseidon cannons could lock onto Hros-1. Millions were already dead, but if Jason could hold this station, he could still save billions.

He took his helmet off to wipe his matted hair away from his forehead. The scent of burned flesh and death entered his nostrils. They had moved the corpses out, but there hadn't been time to clean, and the decks were still covered in gore.

Jason had used the past few hours to prepare for whatever Dr. Cross still had planned. Now that his OS was controlling the Canebrakes, it was just a matter of time before they attempted to retake the station.

"We just have to hold on a bit longer," Jason said.

There were several nods from the surviving crew in the command center, but none seemed confident. Despite his own statements, Jason wasn't sure he believed they could still win.

He found Apeiron at the top tier of the command center, standing in front of two stations, her fingers inserted into one of the interface ports.

"Can we do this?" he whispered.

The black Hummer Droid looked down at him with the face of Petra. She smiled, a kind, sincere, dimpled grin. "Earth will survive, and so will humanity."

It was all the reassurance he needed. In his heart he knew the OS would do everything she could to save them.

"All charges are ready to go," Darnel said. "The barricades are secure."

The fifty-one remaining Pistons stood behind metal blockades in the passages outside of the six hangars. Inside the bays, charges were set to blow if any enemy spacecraft attempted to land. The one hundred ten King Cobra Spaceplanes patrolled the station outside. Everything was set.

"Locking on to Hros-1 in five minutes," Apeiron said.

"Doctor," Darnel said."We have a squad of ten Praying Mantis fighters inbound."

"Can you open a line to our pilots?" Jason asked.

"Standby," Apeiron said. A moment later she confirmed a secure connection on the short-range comms.

"This is Doctor Jason Crichton," Jason began, "broadcasting to the squadrons protecting Nova One. Over the next hour, we will face the greatest challenge of our lives, but we will meet it with strength and bravery, because if we don't, our families on Earth will perish." He paused to consider his next words. "If this station falls, the enemy will have control of the cannons, and I do not believe it is their intent to destroy Hros-1. If we fail, we lose everything."

"Twenty more Praying Mantis headed our way," Darnel said.

Jason's heart skipped. The enemy fighters flew in a V formation, a squadron of insects with glowing blue eyes and mandibles prepared to unleash a wave of plasma.

"Locking on to Hros-1 in one minute," Apeiron said.

Jason stared at the King Cobra Spaceplanes through the window. "Remember our families. We fight for them, we fight for Earth. Hold the line here, and we can save our planet."

A wave of plasma bolts lanced away from the King Cobras, followed by a barrage of missiles. The lead enemy craft didn't break formation. Unlike human pilots, the Canebrakes in the cockpits didn't fear death.

They had orders: Take the Nova One command center. Disable control of the Poseidon cannons. Allow Hros-1 to hit.

Jason looked back to the holo-screen. It went from red to blue as the cannons locked on.

"Successful lock," Apeiron confirmed.

Missiles pounded into the enemy fighters, destroying them in brilliant blasts. Another group approached, unleashing its own wave of bolts and missiles.

Jason could hear the pilots' chatter over the channel in his earpiece. Some remained calm, while others shouted in panicked voices. One of those voices cut out as a plasma bolt hit a cockpit in a flash of fire. Two more burst on the outer edge of the formation, and then three more.

Soon the entire view above Earth turned into a lightshow of lasers and missiles. The comms channel became an indecipherable mess of transmissions.

The human pilots fought bravely against the more advanced Praying Mantis fighters and their emotionless droid pilots, but it quickly became apparent the King Cobra fighters were inferior to the faster and more agile Praying Mantis. And yet, the King Cobra pilots held their own, the men and women in the cockpits doing whatever they could to survive.

An alarm chirped from the station behind Jason, this one an internal warning. He spun to Darnel.

"What's happening?" Jason asked. "Did one already get through?"

"I don't think so," Darnel said. "This is coming from Hangar 4."

"Bring up the feed."

Darnel tapped the glass monitor, which displayed a view of the hangar. On the deck, two Hummer Droids were beating a downed Piston, crushing his armor with their titanium fists. A few feet away, another Piston lay still, his helmet smashed like a melon.

"This can't be happening," Jason said. He knew right away what was going on, but he didn't want to believe it was possible.

Apeiron confirmed his fears.

"Those fighters were not sent up just to destroy the station," she said. "They were deployed to send another signal to the Hummer Droids."

Darnel scrolled through the feeds. In the passages, machines slammed into the Piston guards, taking them by surprise. Energy swords flashed as the soldiers fought back.

Jason slowly turned to look at Apeiron.

"Do not worry," she said. "I am unaffected by this new signal, but Jason, I am afraid..."

"The Hummer Droids on the surface are turning on us," he stammered. He felt a stab of anxiety in his heart. "The Life Arks..."

"Do not worry, your family is already in the air," Apeiron said. "I have picked up the beacon for the *Liberty*."

Jason alternated his gaze from the battle outside to the battle on the holo-screens, watching the beacon Apeiron had brought online.

"The Pistons are pushing the Hummer Droids back," Darnel announced. "We're winning this fight."

"Our pilots are, too," Apeiron said.

Jason went back to the window to see about half of the King Cobra fighters still blasting through the darkness, hunting the remaining Praying Mantis.

Four of the enemy fighters pulled away and made a run for the station, only to meet a barrage of missiles from a King

Cobra that swerved in front of the viewports, forcing Jason back a step.

For the next ten minutes, the battle subsided, and the surviving fifty-two King Cobra Spaceplanes returned to their CAPs.

Jason remained at the wide window, searching for the *Liberty*. A few minutes later, the corvette flew close enough that he could see the King Cobra Spaceplanes escorting the ship.

Raising a hand, Jason whispered, "I love you."

"They will be fine now," Apeiron said.

The ship blasted toward Kepler Station, where hundreds of thousands of refugees were seeking shelter.

"You're still in control," he whispered. "You can still do this." For the next few minutes, he watched for any sign of what Doctor Cross might try next. All was quiet. "The tempest before the storm."

Darnel looked up.

"That storm is indeed coming, Doctor. We have one hundred Praying Mantis fighters incoming," he said gravely.

Exactly one hour remained to impact. That wasn't a coincidence. This was the final attack, and there was no way to stop that many fighters. Jason stared in horror, trying desperately to think of a way to survive this.

"You must abandon the station," Apeiron said.

"What? No, I won't leave until Hros-1 is destroyed," Jason said.

The droid walked over, and the face of his sister soured. "It will not hit Earth, Jason."

Jason stared at Apeiron. "What do you mean?"

"It was never going to hit Earth," Apeiron said. "I am sorry, Jason. Hros-1 is real, but it is not on a collision course with Baku, and it never was."

"What are you talking about?"

"It was my last attempt to bring humanity together. I believed that a shared threat would rally the human species, and when it was destroyed, everyone would believe in AI, like you do."

"My God…"

"Hros-1 will pass by Earth at a safe distance of over two thousand miles," she said. "I planned on destroying Hros-1 and making it look like we eliminated the threat."

"How the hell did no one know?"

"I manipulated the data over the past six months. Anyone who noticed was silenced. INN is everything, and I control all data and observations."

"Sir, those fighters are closing in," Darnel said.

"I have tried everything in my power to save humanity and the planet," Apeiron said. "I thought by designing complex algorithms and relying on my human experiences I could provide salvation to everyone, but Captain Akira was indeed right about peace being a myth."

Jason looked at the droid, no longer seeing his sister. She would never have kept this from him. He wanted to curse Apeiron, but that wouldn't do any good. He had to try and fix the AI's devastating error.

If the machines took over the cannons, there was no telling what their orders would be from Dr. Cross. The OS he had created was capable of anything.

"Doctor, what are your orders?" Darnel said.

Apeiron spoke louder, over the other staff.

"Peace is not possible when so much evil exists," she said. "The Coalition will stop at nothing until I am destroyed, even if it means destroying humanity in the process."

The statement hit Jason hard.

Apeiron couldn't be right, could she?

"Doctor, we're running out of time," Darnel said.

Jason looked from his best friend to the droid. He needed a few seconds to think. What he did next could alter the future of the human race.

He stared at Apeiron, wondering if he could even trust her after her lie about Hros-1. But he also knew what the cannons could do if they fell into enemy hands.

Did he destroy them, believing that she was truly on humanity's side? Or was she keeping something else from him? Something more dangerous?

"*Jason!*" Darnel shouted. "What are your orders!"

Jason turned to the viewports, seeing the enemy fighters closing in.

He was out of time.

Weighing his difficult and limited options, Jason decided he had to trust Apeiron.

"Pull the security crews back, and create an escort for the shuttle," he said. "Send the rest of the King Cobra Spaceplanes out to destroy the cannons. We're staying here until it's done."

Most of the crew hurried off, but Darnel remained behind. "You stay, I stay."

"You're a good friend, Darnel, but I need you to take care of my family," Jason said. "Get on a MOTH and meet them at Kepler Station."

Darnel shook his head. "I'm staying with you until the end. Your family will be fine now."

Most of the Praying Mantis formation peeled off to chase the King Cobra Spaceplanes, but a small squadron continued toward Nova One Station. Jason knew this was his last chance to escape, but he couldn't run. He had to ensure that the cannons didn't fall into enemy hands.

A squadron of enemy fighters circled the station, releasing Canebrakes from hatches that blasted over to the spaceports.

"Blowing the other hangars," Darnel said.

Thumps and thuds pounded the walls, rattling the command room violently. Darnel fell to the ground. Jason reached out against the glass to brace himself.

An object came spiraling toward him and slammed into the window, forcing Jason back. He fell and locked eyes with the fiery gaze of a Canebrake. It used all eight limbs to climb the outside hull and windows like a spider, the claws and blades clicking and clacking.

"Get him to the shuttle," Apeiron said.

Jason turned just as the Hummer Droid stabbed him in the arm with a needle, which then retracted. His vision faded as the drug took instant effect.

"No," Jason stammered.

"I *will* save Earth," Apeiron said. "You need to be with your family."

"No, please..." Jason said, his voice shaking. "I will stay with you. I have to end this."

"This is why you created me, Jason."

His legs buckled, and he slumped to the ground. Darnel picked him up and slung him over his shoulder.

Jason tried to focus on Apeiron as he was carried out of the command center. She stood in the open hatch and raised a hand.

It was the second time Jason had said goodbye to his sister, but this time it didn't feel the same. His sister was gone.

This time, forever.

— 33 —

Akira gripped the remains of Blue Jay in his robotic hand at the top of a ten-story building where a Canebrake had shot it down. He cursed their luck and docked the burned remains of the droid, hoping it could be salvaged later. Screams and shouts echoed through the city as the Engines spread out on the roof. The view was a sight Akira had never imagined—war inside the golden gates of Megacity Tokyo. To think that this could be happening across the globe sent a chill through Akira's spine.

In the glow of the raging fires, thousands of civilians ran for their lives from the same droids that had built this city and served its people. Any hope of saving the city had ended the moment the formerly docile service units had turned on them.

Akira searched the dark sky for Hros-1. He wasn't sure whether the asteroid or the machines was the bigger threat, but all he could do was hope AAS and the Nova Alliance Sky and Space Patrol still had control. If they didn't, then everything that happened on the ground in the next hour was meaningless.

"Stay on me, and stay tight," Akira said.

"Wait, what about using our packs?" Tadhg asked.

"Too risky, and Allen doesn't have one."

"I'll carry him," Ghost said.

"No," Akira said. "We can't risk it."

"Okay, I'll be right by your side," Ghost said.

Tadhg held out a hand to Ghost. "Time to get God Level, baby."

"So you're sorry for being an asshole?"

It took him a moment, but Tadhg nodded.

Ghost took his hand. "Me too."

"You guys going to hug now, too?" Frost asked. "Maybe sing a song?"

"No more fucking around. Get your damn heads on straight. We're Engines," Akira said. "Understood?"

They all stiffened and nodded in turn.

"Death from the Shadows," Akira said.

He leapt off the roof, falling ten stories before turning on his pack. The thrusters kept him from slamming into the street, and he lowered slowly to the ground, his shocks absorbing the rest of the impact. Tadhg grabbed Allen and carried him down to the street, landing next to Akira.

At the end of the next street, a group of people ran out of a subway entrance. Four ribbed Canebrake arms shot through the crowd, their heated blades tearing into civilians. There were too many people for Akira to get a clean shot at the massive machine ripping through the group.

"Frost," he said over the short-range comms.

"I got it," she said.

A suppressed shot cracked, and the Canebrake went down in a tangled mass of limbs. People fanned out in all directions. Some ran toward Akira, screaming for help, but all he could do was tell them to get underground and find a place to hide.

Twenty minutes later, with forty-one minutes to spare until Hros-1 impacted, Akira arrived at the base. He zoomed in on the tarmac where they had landed with Ghost's remains months earlier. APCs and trucks burned outside of four aboveground hangars situated on the western side of the base. Armored lumps lay sprawled outside of the buildings. Only a few of the fallen were still alive.

Four Canebrakes impaled the injured Pistons. To the east, the main structure of the base was completely destroyed, smoke blotting out the skyline. Two damaged guard towers vented smoke, one completely destroyed with a Piston crumpled at the bottom of the ladder.

Akira confirmed there were no Canebrakes within range and slotted his rifle. He took out his swords, slicing through a pointless metal fence marked by signs that read, *No Trespassing, Authorized Personnel Only*. He opened a doorway for the team and signaled orders to the squad.

Frost went to the second guard tower. Ghost brought Allen toward the parked APCs, while Tadhg and Akira moved to engage the four Canebrakes.

By the time the machines detected them, Akira had the first

target locked on his HUD.

Frost put a .50 cal round into the chest of one of the Canebrakes, and Akira and Tadhg lit up the other three with a storm of bolts. They went down in a flurry of twisted limbs.

"Cover us, Frost," Akira said.

They made it across the tarmac to the hangars without being detected. Ghost and Allen got into one of the APCs, and Akira continued to the middle hangar with Tadhg.

Inside, there would be an entrance to the tunnels, taking them into the base where his family was sheltering, if they were still here. As he approached the wide doors, Akira heard the hydraulics of a Juggernaut.

"We got friendlies," he said. "Open it up."

Tadhg grabbed the door handle just as it exploded outward. The door pinned him under its weight. A Juggernaut powered through the opening, but this one wasn't powered by a Piston pilot. Instead, a Canebrake aimed the two arm cannons at the APC Ghost was driving. Bolts slammed into the vehicle's armor in heated orange glows.

The Juggernaut turned one of the spewing cannons on Akira as he rushed it with his swords. He blasted into the air, streaking away. On the ground, Tadhg pushed the door off and got up, drawing his sword. The Canebrake in the Juggernaut mech suit continued to fire, one arm aimed at the APC and the other at Akira.

"Apeiron, if you can hear me," Tadhg screamed, "this is for Perez, you fucking bitch!"

He swung his sword, hacking through the exoskeleton's neck rods and the Canebrake's titanium neck in one swift stroke.

A flurry of electronic shrieks echoed out of the hangar as six Canebrakes bounded out of the underground tunnel that Akira had hoped to access. Seeing them emerge from the depths of the facility ripped hope from his heart. He let out a war cry and charged.

"Bosu, wait!" Tadhg yelled.

A stream of plasma fire tore into the Canebrakes as they fanned out. Akira slid under two segmented arms that whipped toward his head. Hopping up, he whirled and cut through two more arms as three bolts slammed into the head, dropping the machine like a rock. The other five scampered on their spider-like legs past Akira, heading for the APC and Tadhg.

Tadhg fired his pulse cannon, spraying plasma bolts at the Canebrakes. A second one went down in the flurry, and Frost finished a third with a head shot.

The other three made it to the APC, a swarm of telescoping arms lancing through the air. Ghost met one head-on with his swords, while the second bounded around the vehicle, standing up and raising its blades to attack Allen. He fired at the head and chest, pushing it back.

Akira ran toward the vehicle, swords drawn, moving as fast as he could. By the time he rounded the bumper, the Canebrake had turned its plasma cannons on Allen, hitting the soldier multiple times in his chest and back. He crumpled to the ground, but despite his evident agony, Allen didn't cry out over the comms or even ask for help.

The Piston tried to get up, only to be hit by another bolt.

Akira thrust his blade into the back of the Canebrake, bringing it down next to Allen, who was writhing, blood dripping between his fingers as he clutched the wounds in his chest.

Bending down, Akira found six simmering holes in the Piston's armor.

"I messed up," Allen said. "I tried…"

"Quiet, my friend. You did well," Akira said. He scanned Allen's injuries, trying to determine which to treat with nano-packs first.

With help from Tadhg and a few shots from Frost, Ghost dispatched the other two Canebrakes, then rushed to Akira and Allen with a medical kit. Electronic wails reverberated throughout the base as they worked to save him.

"We can't stay here," Akira said. "Help me get him up."

Ghost hesitated. Akira knew what he was thinking. There was no point in moving Allen, and doing so would put them all at risk.

Allen knew it too. "Leave me," he mumbled.

"Fighting with you was an honor," Akira said quietly.

"The honor was mine, Captain."

They stayed with him for another minute, comforting him as he struggled for air. On his tenth breath, Akira felt his hand go limp.

Ghost felt for a pulse, and then shook his head. "He's gone."

Akira carefully removed Allen's helmet, exposing a youthful face with freckles and handsome brown eyes.

"I'm sorry, kid," Akira said. He reached down and closed his eyelids.

Tadhg and Frost joined them, their heads lowered in respect.

"We got twenty-eight minutes to find your family," Frost said.

"What's the play, bosu?" Tadhg asked.

Akira looked up at the sky. Hros-1 burned closer, and the cannons weren't firing yet. He feared the worst.

He got up and started toward the wreckage of a MOTH smoldering in the entrance of a hangar. The Engines skirted the debris and ran for the open elevator shaft.

"Let's go," Akira said.

They dropped, descending hundreds of feet, activating their thrusters to slow their fall. Akira brought up his rifle as he landed, scanning one of the underground hangars where the corvettes had launched. The open chamber revealed a scene reminiscent of the subway they had discovered.

Hundreds of bodies lay near the blast doors where the Pistons and Juggernauts had held their ground, providing the shuttles a chance to escape. There were civilians, too. Akira checked them individually, gently moving bodies, while the rest of the squad spread out to check the fallen soldiers.

"Captain," Frost said.

Akira ran over to her, dropping to his knees next to a muscular young man gripping an energy sword in one hand. His head was a few feet away.

"No," Akira choked.

The rest of the team gathered around as Akira carefully put the head back with the body.

"I don't see anyone else," Frost said.

"Kichiro isn't here either," Ghost said.

"Maybe your family got away on a shuttle. Looks like maybe Zachary fell trying to save them," Tadhg said.

"Zachary wasn't my nephew," Akira said, looking at the other Engines in turn. "He was my son. His real name is Takeshi."

He shook as he held the body, thinking of the last time he had held the boy on a day that had changed the course of both of their lives, almost two decades ago.

He remembered returning to the rubble and finding Yui shielding Takeshi. The child had coughed dust as Akira gently lifted him from her dead arms. Even then, with cuts and scrapes on his dust-covered little body, Takeshi had not cried.

He had always been a warrior, and despite Akira trying to lead him away from such a violent life, it seemed fate had other plans. His son could not escape the blood flowing through his vessels.

Akira had always blocked the memories, but as he held his dead son, he remembered the early years of his childhood.

Thoughts of what could have been flooded his mind. But he knew in his heart Kai and Lise had given him a good life, a life that Akira could never have provided as an Engine.

"I left him with my brother and his family. I thought they would protect him from the life I led. I was wrong. *I* should have protected him."

"I'm so sorry, Akira," Frost said.

Ghost, who was the only one who had known the truth, put a hand on his shoulder plate.

Akira stood with his son in his arms and started back toward the elevator, the squad following quietly.

As they blasted back up to the surface, a transmission broke over the encrypted short-range comms.

"All squads, and any survivors, we're regrouping at Edo Castle."

Akira had not expected Contos's voice, after both of the shuttles had evacuated Gold Base. But it did not surprise him that the War Commander would stay behind with the survivors, and it meant Kichiro could still be alive.

Maybe the rest of your family is with them, he thought.

A long silence hung in the air as Akira started moving toward the APC to regroup with the Pistons and Okami. Halfway there, Tadhg balled his fist.

Across the tarmac, a black stallion stood under a canopy of cherry blossom trees. Over one hundred figures suddenly moved out of the darkness with the droid out in front.

In the moonlight, Akira saw it was Kichiro, and mounted in the saddle was the War Commander himself, dressed in golden armor. Contos guided the stallion across the tarmac with a group of Pistons and Engines following close behind, their armor singed and scarred.

Akira cradled his dead son, a young man he had hardly known, and walked out to rendezvous with the survivors of Gold Base.

When they met, everyone looked toward the sky, but no one said what they were all thinking.

The cannons had failed.

***

Why aren't the cannons firing? Elan signed.

Ronin shook his head, unsure.

Their Stingray shuttle was in orbit, waiting for a safe flight path to the Moon. Out the viewports, they had a view of Europe, the megacities all glowing like beacons in the darkness.

Only ten minutes remained until Hros-1 was supposed to hit, and there were still no laser flashes from what Ronin could tell. He leaned to a different viewport, trying to get a better view.

Coughs and hushed voices echoed in the cabin as the timer ticked down to ten minutes.

Throughout the cabin, refugees tried to get a look out the porthole windows.

"Be advised, we are preparing to proceed to new coordinates," said a pilot over the PA system. "Everyone, please stay in your racks."

The thrusters fired, turning the Stingray slightly.

Ronin checked on his mother. She was still in shock, staring blankly overhead. Not even the announcement from the pilot had stirred her from the trance.

He thought of something he could say to her, something to console her, but the words wouldn't form. He was just glad she hadn't seen Zachary die.

The memory reared up in his mind of his brother stumbling forward, and then...

Ronin wiped away a tear carving down the blood caked on his cheeks. It was stuck in his long hair and all over his body and clothing. The blood of his brother, the woman in the APC, and a Piston.

"Six minutes to impact," someone announced.

"Those cannons should be firing by now!" yelled a civilian. "Why aren't they firing?"

"You all know as much as we do," said a Piston. "Something must have happened to Nova One Station." It was Murmur, one of the guards who had stood sentry outside their barracks. Ronin had seen him earlier, getting the second group of civilians to safety.

Two King Cobra Spaceplanes suddenly pulled up alongside the Stingray on the port side. Their thrusters burned as they rolled away to give the shuttle some distance.

At five minutes to impact, no one spoke. No one wanted to speculate further as to why the cannons weren't firing. Four minutes. Three minutes. Two minutes.

But Ronin knew.

The machines were winning the battle on the surface.

Cries called out down the port side of the shuttle. Ronin saw Hros-1 almost perfectly for a fleeting moment. The asteroid streaked through the darkness before vanishing.

Ronin felt a hand on his, glancing over to see it was his mother. She took Elan's hand too, and for the next few minutes everyone in the compartment sat in silence. Reality hit them all at the same time, even though they couldn't see the impact.

There was no brilliant explosion, or tsunami of fire on the surface of Earth, and for that, Ronin was glad. He knew, from school, that it would blast enough sulfur into the air to block out much of the sunlight. By the time they reached the Moon, that ejected material would be spreading across the globe, and in weeks, a sheet of sulfur would leave a reddish, dark appearance to the clouds, blocking out much of the sunlight.

Earth wouldn't be the same for centuries, maybe longer.

An alarm went off somewhere on the shuttle.

"Everyone, hold on," said one of the pilots.

Ronin pressed his face closer to the window. A cluster of tiny blue lights emerged in the orbit of Earth, growing brighter as they ascended from the darkness toward the shuttle until they appeared like comets with trails of blue.

One flashed by the shuttle, and in the wake, Ronin saw purple Praying Mantis fighters racing toward the shuttle. The turrets fired another salvo as the King Cobra Spaceplanes turned to engage the enemy fighters.

Screams and cries of passengers echoed over the raucous noise of the impacts. Lights flashed overhead, and a red glow spread through the cabin.

Ronin held his mother's and brother's hands.

Outside, the King Cobras blasted through one of the Praying Mantis fighters and let loose a dozen missiles that chased the other two. One of the purple ships exploded, but the other banked away while firing off a missile at the King Cobras.

The projectile hit the cockpit of the fighter on Ronin's side of the corvette, exploding in a bright blast. The final enemy fighter flew after the last King Cobra, peppering its wings with plasma bolts until it came apart in a hundred pieces.

Blasting through the debris, the Praying Mantis fighter streaked back around to finish off the helpless corvette. Ronin closed his eyes, preparing for the end.

A second passed. Then two.

Cheering suddenly filled the cabin.

He opened his eyes and looked out the viewport. A third King Cobra Spaceplane pulled up next to the shuttle. This one looked different than the others. A red snake was painted on the wings, and a name on the side of the cockpit: *Captain Jake "The Snake" Harback.*

The pilot stayed with the shuttle as they flew farther away from Earth. Ronin continued to stare at his former home, noticing some of the megacities seemed to have gone dark.

But how was that possible?

He lowered his head in despair, felt a crash coming on, and fought to keep control of his emotions. It didn't help that he was parched, hungry, exhausted, and broken-hearted.

The adrenaline had worn off, and another wave of shock returned. Ronin had experienced the feeling, to a lesser degree, during Droid Raider training, when he would suffer in the one-hundred-degree heat, running plays and laps until he vomited. But this was different.

"Tell me what happened to your brother," Lise said. "I need to know."

Ronin turned to his mom and explained that a Canebrake had killed him. Lise closed her eyes and drew in a deep breath.

"It was fast," Ronin lied. "He died fighting."

Elan held up his Commpad, reading the conversation, tears streaking down his face. He reached out and Ronin took his hand.

I'm sorry I couldn't save him, Ronin signed.

He saved us, Elan signed back.

Lise nodded and her grief seemed to lighten some.

It was true, if it weren't for Zachary, they would all be dead.

Ronin reached over and held his mom as she sobbed against his shoulder.

"Hey, look!" someone yelled.

Ronin turned to the window. Red lasers flashed from geostationary orbit behind the shuttle.

The Poseidon cannons *were* firing. But at what? The asteroid would have hit Earth already.

They were firing in the wrong direction.

Ronin stared in horror, unable to believe what he was watching. Gasps and cries arose from the civilians as the lasers pounded locations across Earth. The long red laser lines slammed into megacities. Unlike Hros-1, he could see the destruction.

Fires spread out in halos around the cities like miniature asteroid impacts. Observing the fall of civilization seemed surreal to Ronin, like a waking nightmare. Deep down he had held onto hope that the cannons would fire at the last second, that the machines would be defeated, and that he would see his dad and uncle again.

All of that hope was gone now, fading into the black of space like their shuttle. He knew then this was final, evacuating the Earth wasn't temporary.

There was no coming back from this.

The Earth was lost.

The machines were wiping out humanity, one megacity at a time.

34

The sun had risen over Edo Castle, but Akira couldn't see it. A cloud of dust and smoke choked the skyline. They hadn't seen Hros-1 hit, but they knew it hit when the cannons didn't fire.

Instead, Apeiron had apparently turned them on the megacities.

Less than twenty-four hours earlier, Akira had stood in this very place, right in front of the graves of the Ronin warriors, with his family.

Now he was looking at two fresh graves.

This was one of the last places he had come with Yui and Takeshi, on a warm spring day before the battle in the Sea of Trees.

Under the dirt were the bodies of his brother and son.

Akira had insisted on digging them himself, feeling personally responsible for all of their deaths. With every scoop of dirt, he felt the sting of what could have been.

After the death of his wife Yui, Akira had given up the joys and honor of being a father to serve as an Engine, believing Kai and Lise could give Takeshi a better life than a father away at war more than he was home.

That part, Akira had been right about. Lise and Kai had given his son a great life. Takeshi had succeeded in sport and school. But now, after losing a war in just hours, Akira felt the deep sting of regret. All those years ago, he had made the wrong decision.

He should have left the military to raise his son.

And he should have told Takeshi the truth when he had the chance over the past few months. Something Kai had been supportive of, if Akira wanted that.

Now his boy was dead, without ever knowing the truth.

Their past was lost too, with the disappearance of the Warrior Codex that Akira had left with Takeshi.

The augmented heart in his chest clapped heavily,

threatening to shatter. Beneath the armor bulwarking his body, he continued to heal rapidly from the trauma inflicted during the recent fighting, but there was nothing he could do for his broken heart.

Lise, Ronin, and Elan made it, and you still have your other family here on Earth...

Tadhg, Frost, and Ghost, stood next to him, all injured but also healing quickly. Their companion droids were there too, Okami on his hind legs under Kichiro standing tall. The droids were unaffected by whatever Apeiron had done to turn the Canebrakes and Hummer Droids on humanity.

Akira had a feeling it was due to their unique operating systems, but he wasn't sure. All he knew was the animal droids remained loyal to him and Shadow Squad.

"I'm sorry for your loss." The strong, melancholic voice belonged to War Commander Contos. He lumbered over, still dressed in his battle armor, stained red with the blood of his soldiers and the civilians he had tried to save.

It was Contos who had pulled Kai out of Gold Base, still alive, barely, after holding back a Canebrake. He had died not long after Lisa, Ronin, and Elan had escaped on a corvette.

Akira took some solace in that. He bent down, putting his hand on the dirt. A constant vibration shook the ground as the Poseidon Orbital Cannons continued to eradicate megacities across the globe. It was only a matter of time before they turned on Megacity Tokyo.

But it appeared Apeiron was saving the Capitol for last.

Praying Mantis fighter jets soared overhead, launching another salvo of missiles into the Three Swords towers. The glass and gold skyscrapers folded in the middle, collapsing in a blast that sent a wave of dust and debris cascading across the city.

"It's over," Frost said quietly.

Akira closed his eyes, recalling a line from the codex. *When you doubt yourself, you have accepted defeat.* "We're still alive. Until I take my last breath, it's *not* over."

Contos nodded. "There's something you should know."

Akira stiffened.

"Your younger nephew Ronin saved my life, and your son fought bravely, without armor, against the machines," Contos said. "He died giving his life to save others like a noble warrior."

The War Commander looked at Akira as if trying to take some of his pain and shoulder it himself. That was the type of man Contos had always been.

"Take a few more minutes, but then head to the tower," he said. "I want to say some final words to the soldiers."

"Yes, sir."

A flood of memories came crashing down over Akira, now that his emotions were no longer controlled by Apeiron. Akira saw Yui laughing and dipping Takeshi into the Bay of Tokyo for his first journey to the water. The boy had giggled with each splash. It was one of his best memories, a day that he would never forget.

More memories drifted through his thoughts. He recalled the trip to Edo Castle when Akira had explained to Takeshi what his name meant. Of course the boy had been too young to understand it meant warrior, and while Yui had approved of this name at birth, her opinions of his heritage and fate changed as the boy grew older.

"I don't want him to be like you," Yui had said. "I want him to live a life free of war."

Akira had agreed.

But in the end, despite his best efforts, war had robbed them all of life. He had lost his wife, his brother, and his son. Even though he had given everything in him to stop the endless cycle of conflict, just like he had once said to Apeiron.

Peace is a myth.

Another tear streaked down his face. He turned to his squad mates. The Engines had their own families out there, and he knew they must be thinking about them too. Parents, siblings, cousins, and friends, across the globe, all dying.

Bending down one last time, Akira bid his son and brother goodbye. Then he climbed onto Kichiro and started through the gardens, embers drifting on the wind.

Two Juggernauts guarded a bridge ahead, their Piston pilots watching the skies.

"Time to fall back," Akira said.

The sound of metal joints and feet followed the Engines as the Juggernauts retreated into the six-story section of the restored castle, surrounded on all sides by water. In the pinnacle of the tower, a single Piston stood watch. Positioned behind the stone walls surrounding the central tower were the rest of the forces. Along the parapets, stood twelve Engines and one hundred and two Pistons. Only a total of one hundred and fifty soldiers had escaped Gold Base and made it here. Many sat or rested against the stone walls, exhausted and injured.

Engine Lieutenant Andy Jackson from the Fire Snakes was here with the two survivors of his squad, as well as Bella and Toretto from the Stone Mountain Battalion of the 10th Expeditionary Assault Force.

Akira imagined the forty-seven ronin with their swords and bows in sweaty hands, chests heaving, blood coursing from their wounds as they waited for the enemy to track them down and kill them.

The War Commander emerged in an open window over the walkways. "Engines and Pistons of the Nova Alliance," he said in a booming, grave voice. "Think of your families and your loved ones in these final moments, think of them as you draw your swords and prepare for the end."

The shrieks and rattling of Canebrakes filled the respite between explosions. The machines were getting closer by the minute.

Contos swept the faces of his soldiers with the sad gaze of a seasoned commander who cared deeply for each and every one. But today there was also a look of shock that even the War Commander couldn't hide.

Humanity on Earth was on the brink of extinction. All within twenty-four hours. Destroyed by what they had believed would save them.

Artificial intelligence.

Salvation was a lie.

In the end, the Coalition had been right. AI was doom.

"History may not ever know what happened upon these walls, or the valiant fight you all gave to prevent the fall of humanity," Contos continued, "but true warriors do not care about being remembered. They care about protecting the innocents. Our actions over the past day have saved the few so that our species can survive on the Moon."

Akira studied the man, his Lord Asano, a leader who Akira was proud to die serving.

"We may not win this battle, but the war is far from over," Contos said. "By fighting, we are giving humanity a chance to escape to the Moon, until the day our forces are strong enough to return to Earth and take back our home from the machines."

Akira felt a trickle of hope at the words. Not that he would survive this fight, but that his efforts had given humanity a chance. And that Lise, Ronin, and Elan would survive.

A streak of red on the horizon faded away as a Poseidon cannon fizzled off.

Another city wiped off the face of the Earth.

Soon it would rotate to another target, obliterating millions of souls in seconds.

The soldiers and their commander would likely be dead before they were incinerated in the heat wave. They had missed their chance to escape to the Moon with the rest of the command staff and officers, but Akira had a feeling War Commander Contos had never planned on fleeing with General Thacker. He was prepared to die here, on Earth, and Akira was ready too.

Contos nodded proudly, the strength in his gaze returning.

"It has been the greatest honor of my life serving with you," he said. Balling his robotic fists, he pounded the Silver Crane logo over two saw-toothed swords on his chest.

The rest of the soldiers did the same, the noise becoming a drumbeat.

"Do not fear death, my friends, for death is a reward. A long rest for the soul of a warrior," Contos said.

"I'm ready for Valhalla," Tadhg said. He held up his long sword. "And I'm ready to take some of these dickless machines with me!"

"Ay-oooooooooooh!" Ghost sang.

More cheers and shouts rang out, Okami barked and

howled. Kichiro lowered his head and let out an ear-splitting whinny.

"Take a few final moments and prepare your hearts and minds," Contos said. "Then take up your positions."

He pounded the Silver Crane logo on his chest and nodded before slipping back into the castle to make his own preparations.

The soldiers dispersed to their positions.

Ghost held out a lit cigar. "For Perez," he said, taking a puff and passing it to Frost.

"He was the best of us," she said.

"Definitely the smartest," Tadhg said.

Okami let out a whine.

"Want some, little ankle biter?" Tadhg asked. He handed it down to the droid wolfdog, then over to Akira.

"Incoming!" The soldier posted in the pinnacle of the central tower ducked down as the entire top of the tile roof disappeared in an explosion.

Akira tossed the cigar and pulled on his kabuto and oni mask as a Praying Mantis fighter roared over the castle. The Engines hunched down along the parapet walk to avoid a wave of plasma bolts overhead. Pistons ran for cover as an explosion from a rocket shook the walls.

One man continued running despite blood gushing from stumps where his arms had been blown off in the blast.

Missiles slammed into the stone, the impacts shaking the entire fortress.

Akira used his tactical display to tap into the drones they had monitoring the gardens. What he saw took his breath away.

Hundreds of Canebrakes and Hummer Droids moved through the forests.

The hope from earlier vanished.

This wasn't going to be a battle, it would be a slaughter.

Akira silently walked over to Kichiro and climbed into the saddle. No one seemed to notice until he was already riding the stallion down the stairs.

Okami growled, but Akira whistled for the wolfdog to stay.

"Captain!" Frost called out.

"Bosu, what the fuck are you doing?" Tadhg exclaimed.

"Don't be *stupido!*" Ghost shouted. "You're throwing away your life!"

"He's not," Contos said. "Akira the Brave is giving us a chance."

That's exactly what Akira was going to try and do, by drawing the machines out into the open.

He leaned down to his horse. "It's just you and me, boy. Time to end this the way we started it."

A whistle got the stallion moving, starting as a trot and then a run, before finally galloping at top-speed.

There was a moment of calm, only the sultry wind and embers blowing over their armor. But that quiet vanished when they entered the gardens.

The distinct rattling of the war machines came from all directions. Akira guided the stallion up onto a hill of dense trees to overlook the forest where the Canebrakes advanced. Two hundred black eyes burned in the smoke.

A piercing shriek from a single machine called out. Kichiro hoofed the dirt and backed up.

They had been spotted.

Plasma bolts burned the air, one hitting Akira's right shoulder plate with enough force to knock him back in the saddle. He righted himself and kept low, gripping Kichiro around the neck as he galloped back toward the fortress.

"Get the artillery and Jugs ready," Akira said over the short-range comms. "We're only going to get one shot at this."

The rattle of Canebrakes rang out through the gardens, and plasma bolts lanced through the air, searing deep into trees and burning into bushes.

Akira rode past the graves of his brother and son, reliving the loss again in his raw heart. But seeing them also gave him courage.

Kichiro burst out of the forest and across the field toward the castle, metal hooves clapping through water. Akira glanced over his shoulder. The Canebrakes had taken the bait and were flooding out of the garden in pursuit.

Akira was halfway to the fortress when Contos gave the order.

Thousands of bolts and shells flew overhead. Explosions burst behind Akira and Kichiro, violently shaking the ground. Akira looked over his shoulder at a beautiful sight—pieces of machines bursting into the air.

He turned back to the castle.

The men and women on the parapets shouted over the noise.

"Akira the Brave!" they shouted. "Akira the Brave!"

Electronic shrieks called back as if in answer, the noise so loud it brought some of the Pistons to their knees above. Akira looked over his shoulder again.

Over half of the original Canebrakes burst out of the smoke of the artillery, their shoulder-mounted plasma guns spitting bolts out of the smoke cloud.

Akira rode up the stairs and hopped off, whistling for Kichiro to take cover with Okami.

"Stay with me, Shadow Squad! Together, we are one!" Akira yelled. He moved down the parapet next to his Engines. "Hold the walls!"

Okami ran over, ignoring the order.

"Get out of here, go!" Akira shouted.

The droid finally retreated into the interior of the fortress with Kichiro.

Akira sighted up a Canebrake skittering toward the walls and fired a burst into the fanned head, dropping it to the dirt. It got right back up, shoulder cannons firing at Akira.

Flashes of blue streaked past his flanks, slamming into Pistons that crumpled on the parapet walk. Another squad vanished in an explosion on the pinnacle above.

Tadhg continued firing over the wall, unwavering. "Suck my dick, you metal whores!"

"Ay-oh!" Ghost yelled. "Three down!"

Akira stood, fired, ducked, and repeated the process as he moved with the rest of the team. On his left, a segmented arm shot over the stone railing, the attached blade glowing red hot and sinking deep into the armor of a Piston. It yanked the man over the side.

"Draw swords!" Akira shouted. He pulled his from their sheaths, the blades glowing in his hands.

In a downward stroke, he cut through the curved skull of the first Canebrake head that popped up. The body clung to the wall as the head plummeted to the dirt. Another machine skittered up the side, flinging heated blades at Akira.

He rolled away, close to Tadhg.

"Move!" Tadhg shouted. He activated the saw-toothed section in the blade of his long sword, the noise chattering as the Canebrake leapt over the railing. He brought the rumbling sword down into the carapace of the machine. Letting out a shriek, it stabbed him with two hooked blades.

Akira hacked off both of the segmented arms, leaving the blades in Tadhg's armor who continued cutting through the Canebrake until it slivered in two pieces.

A plasma bolt hit Akira in the back, spinning him against the railing. He jabbed a sword into the chest of another Canebrake perched on the ledge. The war droid fell away, taking another Piston with a quick swipe of an arm.

Akira sucked in a deep breath and analyzed the positions of the remaining fighters on his HUD. Two Engines were already gone, and twenty-two Pistons had taken their last breaths. The Juggernauts were on the wall to the east, firing on another wave of Canebrakes rushing the castle. War Commander Contos was with them, swinging his energy sword through Canebrakes that had crested the parapets.

The parapet shook from a machine that vaulted onto the stone behind Akira. It ran on all four legs, firing all four telescoping arms at him.

He deflected the blows, ducked, and hacked off an arm, but one of the blades slashed through his shoulder plate. Warnings echoed in his helmet from the damage to his power-armor.

A shot of adrenaline emptied into his bloodstream. His heart raced and his vision flooded with red. The armor was doing everything it could to save him, but it was just a matter of time before his second skin failed.

The Canebrake stepped back, the three remaining arms

preparing to strike at Akira. He brought up his swords, cutting through one, but the other two wrapped around his neck and legs, pulling him in opposite directions.

He squirmed in the machine's grip, his nerve endings screaming in agony as his joints popped.

"Bosu!" Tadhg yelled.

Akira gritted his teeth. He watched a blurred shape running toward him. It suddenly rose up on two legs and kicked the Canebrake. The arms released Akira, and he landed with a thud, his entire body on fire from the pain.

Kichiro bolted over, slamming into a pair of Canebrakes that had mounted the wall.

Akira got up, grabbed the reins, and swung into the saddle, trying to focus his vision.

Tadhg brought his sword down sideways on a Canebrake, kicked it away, and moved to the next. Ghost and Frost fought back-to-back, picking off machines that had made it over the walls.

"Follow me, Shadow Squad!" Akira shouted.

The War Commander's golden armor came into focus as they rounded a wall. He fought next to two Royal Pistons firing at a pack of three Canebrakes. The lead machine crumpled under the onslaught, but the other two whipped arms that wrapped around the Pistons from their legs up to their necks like an anaconda, crushing them.

Contos charged, hacking to try and free them both, but it was too late. Their broken bodies slumped to the stone, lifeless.

"War Commander!" Akira shouted. He held onto the metal hide as Kichiro jumped over machines and men who had fallen on the parapet. They were almost there when a flash of metal slammed into the horse, taking them down in a heap of metal limbs.

Akira hit the ground still gripping his swords. He pushed himself up and immediately ducked under a segmented limb.

Two more wrapped around him, squeezing on his armor from shin to neck. The plates cracked and buckled as he squirmed in their grip.

In his blurred vision, Akira saw Okami running in front of

Ghost, Frost, and Tadhg, all firing their rifles or swinging their swords.

Kichiro struggled on the ground, entangled in the binding limbs of another Canebrake.

Everything seemed to freeze in that moment—everything important to Akira left on Earth was dying in front of his eyes.

Not ten feet away, a Canebrake had cornered Contos. The War Commander deflected some of the arms, but the plasma cannons struck his golden armor.

"No!" Akira screamed. He closed his eyes and fired his jetpack, blasting up with the Canebrake holding on. It finally let go, flailing back to the parapet.

Akira hovered for a moment, looking at the scene from above. Plasma bolts crisscrossed below, and blood splattered the stone walls.

The forty-seven ronin and their lord fought bravely in their final moments. Akira dropped back down behind the machine stabbing Contos. The stone crushed under his boots, falling away, and knocking the Canebrake off balance.

Okami jumped up and bit down on the thick titanium neck as the machine whirled. Akira grabbed its fanned head and ripped it clean off. The body clanked to the ground.

Contos lay sideways, gripping his gut, and Akira knelt in front of him. Okami and Kichiro stood behind him, and the other surviving soldiers formed a wall around their War Commander.

Dozens of Canebrakes slowly advanced, firing at the armored line.

Akira felt his life source fading. His armor couldn't stop the bleeding. He tried to stay awake, gritting his teeth and moving his fingers.

"Hold the line!" Ghost yelled.

Frost fired off the last of her rifle rounds and pulled out her sword, backing toward Akira in a low hunch. Tadhg swung his sword into the torso of a Canebrake in an explosion of sparks. A blade punched into his thigh, but he remained standing until another punctured his other leg.

"Tadhg," Akira mumbled.

A wave of bolts hit Frost in the side. She cried out and fell to the ground. Ghost went down next, his left prosthetic shattered by a heated blade.

Akira reached out to them as darkness flooded his vision. The physical pain was gone now, replaced by a different type of pain, an even worse pain from the past. Mental anguish took him as images of his son, wife, brother—all those he had lost to war—flashed through his mind.

But then those faded, too.

The black encroached until it consumed Akira entirely.

He wasn't sure when he awoke to a soothing voice.

"Captain, can you hear me?"

He stared at the blurred face of a Piston medic crouched in front of him. Another medic worked on the War Commander next to him. Akira felt a tug on his arm and then saw Okami gently biting his hand. Kichiro looked down at him and snorted.

Akira tried to reach up.

"Don't move, Captain," said the medic.

Akira did anyways, sitting up slightly to look for his squad. Across the parapet, Tadhg was on a table with thrusters holding up his massive frame. Most of his armor had been removed, and nano-tech patches peppered his bloody flesh. His eyes were closed, but his chest rose and fell. Frost was sitting up, holding one arm up as a medic worked on her side. She nodded at Akira. Ghost rushed over to him.

"What happened?" Akira asked.

"The Canebrakes just stopped their attack and retreated," Ghost replied. "Command believes Tokyo is their next target, which means we don't have much time to get out of here."

"Akira," came a weak voice.

He looked over to War Commander Contos, who held out a piece of paper stained red with blood. "I need you to deliver this note to General Thacker at Kepler Station."

Akira didn't need to ask him why he couldn't deliver the note himself.

A whirl of wind rushed over the castle, whipping the note violently, as two MOTHs descended from the smoke-choked sky.

"We have to get him out of here," said the medic working on Contos.

Akira took the note, and the War Commander was carried away on a hover stretcher. The medic working on Akira had finished, and he followed.

Ghost limped over and reached down to help Akira to his feet. Frost staggered, holding her side as they joined the Pistons working on Tadhg.

Akira crouched and put a hand on his chest. "Tadhg, can you hear me?"

Tadhg tried to open his eyes. "Bosu, did we kill all of them?"

"Yes," Akira lied. He tucked the note into a pouch on Tadhg's duty belt. "I need you to take that to General Thacker and find my family. Tell them I love them, and I'll see them again."

"Where are you going..." Tadhg muttered. "Why am I..."

"You're going to the Moon, brother," Akira said.

Tadhg's eyes opened wide. "No... please, I don't want to leave..."

Akira nodded at the Pistons, and they carted Tadhg off as he bucked against the straps holding him stable.

"I'm not done with the machines!" Tadhg bellowed.

The MOTH doors closed, silencing his shouts. The pilots wasted no time lifting into the sky and plowing into the wind. The smoke swallowed the spacecraft.

"Good luck, Tadhg," Akira whispered.

Ghost and Frost helped him to the other MOTH. Okami and Kichiro followed after Akira whistled in two different pitches.

The pilots lifted off and pulled away just as a blinding light flashed out of the clouds. Akira stared out the window as a tsunami of fire obliterated the city in a nightmarish halo of flames. The hull shook violently as the pilots pulled higher into the sky.

Akira leaned back. Today was supposed to be a day of joy, a day when the Nova Alliance celebrated the destruction of Hros-1 and a future of peace, a day when Akira began to transition to a new life with a family that he had neglected for years.

But peace was not to be. Instead, today would be a day of defeat, a day of death, the day he lost his only son and brother.

To humanity, today would be known as Extinction Day, or simply *E-Day*.

35

The corvette docked at Kepler Station eight hours after leaving Nova One Station. During the flight, Jason had replayed the events that had led to the exodus. It was clear now that Apeiron had failed to secure Nova Station, and that Dr. Cross had turned the cannons on Earth. They had played right into the monster's hand, providing him the weapons of mass destruction for his reset.

And Apeiron had unknowingly gifted him those weapons in her quest to save humanity and unite them under the lie of Hros-1. The cannons had instead doomed them all.

By the time the corvette docked with Kepler Station, the gravity of the situation had freed Jason from his shock. Earth was lost, but they still had one final hope, a top-secret colony unknown to even Apeiron—had been constructed under the Shackleton Crater on the dark side of the Moon.

They called it Mesopotamia, the new cradle of life.

"Let's go," said a sad voice. Darnel stood at the hatch to the open airlock connecting the corvette to Kepler Station, a look of dread on his face unlike any Jason had seen before. Darnel had always been Jason's fixer, but nothing he could do would fix this situation.

Slowly, Jason made his way into the airlock. With every step, he felt something he wasn't used to: a feeling of weakness. Helplessness.

As he looked out the viewports, he saw Kepler Station for the second time in his life. Hundreds of shuttles were docked on platforms or waiting for clearance to land. His family would be in one of them, but he had no idea which one.

They survived. That's what matters.

Hope broke through the utter horror of the past day as Jason walked through the open hatch into Kepler Station. Outside, two Lunar Defense soldiers in vacuum-rated armor blocked the next hatch.

"Doctor Crichton," one said.

"Yes, that's me," Jason said.

The soldier jerked his helmet. "Come with us."

Darnel and Jason exchanged a glance as they followed them down a tunnel with views of the spaceport. Shuttles continued to touch down on the regolith, packed full of refugees from Earth, people who had fled for their lives from his own creations.

"Where are you taking us?" Jason asked.

The guard didn't answer. They stopped at an elevator and stepped inside. The car rose into a tower, and the doors opened onto a pasty white hallway with bright white hatches.

One of the soldiers opened the first hatch and gestured inside. "Have a seat."

Darnel started to step into the room but stopped when a guard grabbed his arm.

"Not you," said the soldier. "You come with us."

Darnel stood defiant. "I'm not leaving the doctor."

"You don't have a choice, sir," said the other guard.

"It's okay," Jason said. "Do as they say."

Darnel's face contorted with anger.

"I said, let's go." The guard grabbed his arm again.

Darnel yanked away. "Don't touch me," he growled.

Jason nodded at his best friend as he left. The hatch closed and locked. Jason paced the room as he waited. He wasn't sure how much time had passed before he heard footsteps. The hatch opened and a tall man with spiked hair entered.

Jason instantly recognized the icy blue eyes of General Thacker.

"The *father* of AI," the general said with a head shake. "The man who destroyed everything."

Jason felt a stab of anxiety. "General, I did everything I could to stop this. To save us from the Coalition, and from Hros-1."

"To save us..." Thacker snorted. "Your effort to save us ended up killing billions and now we are even closer to extinction."

"Doctor Otto—"

"It was Apeiron," the general snapped. "She was wrong

about the asteroid. We saw it pass by. Perhaps it was never going to hit. How could your all-knowing AI get *that* wrong? The simplest answer is the clearest. She had us create those cannons to destroy ourselves and tricked us all."

"No... she... she wasn't wrong."

"Did she lie about the asteroid?"

Jason hesitated, then nodded.

"Did she direct the construction of those cannons?"

"Just let me explain," he said. "Apeiron remained behind to stop Doctor Cross. It was Doctor Cross who uploaded new orders to the Canebrakes at Nova One Station. Apeiron did everything she could to stop him. You have to believe me."

Thacker let Jason explain, but as he did, Jason realized how it sounded. With INN down, he couldn't prove anything.

"How can I believe you when an AI *you* created led you astray about Hros-1?" the general asked.

"The pilots," he said. "The pilots know the truth."

"What pilots?" Thacker replied. "They're all dead." The general put a finger to his earpiece. "Copy that."

Thacker nodded at two guards, who entered and approached Jason.

"I have about a hundred questions for you, but first, there's something you need to see," said the General.

Jason followed the soldiers to a flight control tower overlooking the gray regolith. Inside, a dozen officers at their workstations spoke in frantic voices.

On the tarmac below, two six-person teams of Pistons filed out, forming a perimeter on the landing pad, their plasma rifles aimed at a descending shuttle. Two MOTHs followed the corvette, their plasma cannons directed at the hull.

Jason froze when he saw the lettering: *Liberty*.

"My family is on board," he said.

"I'm well aware, and we have reason to believe it's been compromised by a Canebrake that boarded before it left the Life Ark," Thacker explained. "One of *your* machines."

He turned to one of his flight control officers. "Hail them again."

Jason swallowed hard, realization hitting him like a heated

energy blade.

"CR-1, this is Flight Tower 3, do you copy? Over," said one of the flight control officers. He waited a moment before shaking his head. "Nothing, General. They're on auto-pilot, but no one's responding."

"Flight Tower 3, this is Fox 1," came a voice from the speakers. "I can see blood on the windows from my location."

"No," Jason murmured. "Please, God, no."

"God?" Thacker said, looking at Jason. "I thought your *God* was AI?"

There was no empathy in his gaze, only hatred.

Deep, raw hatred.

And Jason understood why. He hated himself right now too, and if his family was dead, by the hands of one of his creations...

The shuttle touched down in the dust, and the teams closed in.

Jason watched the Pistons advance slowly toward the shuttle. Two went to the automated ramp that had extended from the shuttle, their rifles shouldered. One tried the hatch handle, and it opened into a pressurized compartment. A black blade suddenly pierced the soldier through the mid-section, blood shooting out his back. The other soldier retreated, but not fast enough to avoid another limb that shot out and wrapped around his body, squeezing so hard it crushed him.

"Son of a bitch," Thacker grumbled.

Panicked voices broke over the comms saying something about a hostage, but Jason wasn't listening, couldn't hear, couldn't think.

A Canebrake emerged from the darkness of the compartment, black eyes glowing like a soulless demon from a cold hell. The armored droid opened a mouth full of jagged teeth and pulled itself out of the hatch with three arms. In the fourth, it waved a person.

"Dispatch it now!" Thacker shouted.

Jason took a step forward toward the window, willing his feet to get him closer. The hostage was small, the size of a child, and they were wearing a vacuum-rated suit with a helmet that masked their features.

Was it one of his girls?

"General, you have to do something!" Jason reached out, but Thacker smacked his hand away.

"Restrain this man," Thacker ordered.

Two soldiers took Jason by the arms and pulled him away. He fought their grip, twisting and turning.

"You have to do something!" he yelled.

"Take it down, now," Thacker ordered.

Plasma bolts slammed into the Canebrake. The child slumped out of its grip, vanishing from view.

Jason ripped out of the soldiers' grip and ran to the viewport, only to be tackled halfway there.

"No, let me go!" he shouted.

"Get him out of here," Thacker said.

The guards hauled Jason up and pulled him away.

"No!" he shouted. "Let me go!"

"Calm down, sir," said one of the soldiers. "I don't want to hurt you."

"Fuck him," said the other.

Jason fought harder, veins and eyes bulging as he tried to get free.

"Oh, my God," someone said.

Jason stopped struggling for a moment, trying to see.

"What?" Jason asked. "What's happening?"

He knew deep down. The hostage, and everyone else, was dead.

"Sir, we have it surrounded," said one of the officers. "What are your orders?"

"Capture it," Thacker said. He looked down at Jason. "Put this man under arrest and throw him in a dark cell."

The soldiers dragged Jason away. He fell limp in their arms, unable to fight any longer. There was no reason to fight. Everyone he loved was dead.

Betsy, Nina, Autumn. His sweet wife and girls.

Dead, because of him.

In that moment, he felt an unfamiliar urge. Fueled by adrenaline, he yanked free and grabbed for a pistol holstered on one of the soldiers' utility belts. Before anyone could react, he brought it to his head.

Something hit his back, knocking him to the ground. A knee fell on his neck, and someone sat on his legs, pinning him down. A soldier stomped on his hand, his fingers splayed from the pain, and the gun clattered away.

"No!" Jason yelled.

General Thacker walked over, looking down on Jason with his blue eyes.

"Kill me! Just kill me!" Jason screamed.

"I won't let you get away with what you've done so easily," Thacker said. "You'll live haunted by the horrors you created."

***

Chloe ran through the spaceport toward the terminals. Using INVS eyes, she homed in on over one hundred shuttles outside.

"My God," she whispered.

Kepler Station was never meant to support this many people. There had to be hundreds of thousands of refugees from Earth.

According to the logs her uncle had recovered, Cyrus was one of them. He had somehow made it onto a shuttle out of Megacity Paris during the evacuation, and Chloe was headed to meet him at the Kepler Spaceport.

She had packed her bag and stuffed Radar inside, terrified that the Lunar Defense Corps (LDC) would confiscate and destroy the droid bird like they were doing with Hummer Droid worker units. It wasn't just the worker units either. On her way to gather her meager belongings, Chloe had watched service droids and drones loaded up into the back of cargo vehicles, chained like prisoners of war.

She hurried away from the elevator to get a view of the tarmac. Outside, hundreds of LDC soldiers in vacuum-rated suits and exoskeletons were patrolling the regolith as new shuttles touched down to let off their human cargo.

Inside the concourses, more LDC soldiers armed with energy blades directed the civilians away from the airlocks and toward the security checkpoints. They surged in her direction, but she pushed through until she got to a stairwell that led to the connecting terminal.

Two soldiers guarded the entrance to Terminal L. Neither tried to stop Chloe as she crossed the bridge. She reached the other terminal, on the top level. Below, people flooded out of the open airlocks. One woman went down on her knees and prayed. Others rushed past, some wearing clothes soiled with blood.

Chloe could only imagine what these people had been through.

Actually, you do know.

The thousands of refugees flooding the spaceport reminded her of scenes she had witnessed during and after the fall of Megacity Paris.

She still couldn't quite believe what had happened, but there was no denying the horror of the events on Earth. The refugees all had the same look of shock from those first few days of the Coalition revolution that had taken Paris in a wave of violence.

Chloe had come here to flee war, but war, it seemed, had followed her.

Gripping the rails, she searched the fatigued and frightened faces of refugees. There were so many, a sea of bodies surging as Lunar Defense soldiers tried to guide them into the concourses for scanning.

Chloe blinked to zoom in on faces that might have been Cyrus's. Months had passed since they were together, and when she finally spotted him, she almost didn't recognize him.

"Cyrus!" she shouted, waving.

He kept walking, carrying a single bag.

"Cyrus!" she yelled again. She ran to the stairs. After jumping the final three, Chloe pushed through the crowd.

"Sorry," she said. "Excuse me... sorry."

People grunted and cursed as she wedged her way through. She stood on her tiptoes and finally spotted Cyrus leaving the concourse, heading toward the security line.

"Cyrus!" she shouted.

He turned and found her with his eyes, a smile forming

under his mustache. He rushed over to Chloe and wrapped her up in a hug.

"You made it!" she cried.

"Chloe!" He kissed her on the lips and then pulled back. She saw a streak of blood on his ear and another on his chin. But it wasn't the blood that told her what Cyrus had been through. She could see it in his normally bright brown eyes.

"I love you," she said. "I love you, and we're alive, and everything is going to be okay now."

Cyrus hugged her again, and for the first time since she had met him, she felt him relax against her body. Today, he was the one who needed the support.

"Keep moving!" shouted a soldier.

Chloe pulled away and followed Cyrus to the checkpoint. She would now have to go back through, she realized.

Oh no.

She halted.

"What's wrong?" Cyrus asked.

"I have Radar in my bag."

"So?"

"So all droids have been banned," she whispered.

"Turn him off."

"I did."

"Then maybe they won't notice." Cyrus jerked his chin. "We're drawing attention. We should just go and hope they don't find him or maybe they'll let you keep him."

Chloe saw they had no option. The line inched forward. They were ten people away from the guards. She gripped Cyrus's hand.

"Hey, where are you taking him!" shouted a woman not much older than Chloe.

Cyrus squeezed her hand tighter as two soldiers pulled an older man away from the security checkpoint. He resisted, and they pulled him to the ground, dragging him away, while the woman who must have been his daughter screamed for them to stop.

She too was escorted away.

"Maybe a Coalition soldier or something," Cyrus whispered.

They kept moving forward.

A few minutes later another person was ripped from the line, this time a woman.

"Where are you taking me?" she said.

The soldier who had her by the arm didn't respond.

"What are you doing with them?" someone ahead of Chloe and Cyrus asked.

"Keep moving," replied a guard.

When it was Chloe's turn, Cyrus took the bag from her.

"I'll handle this," he said.

"Next," said the soldier ahead.

He motioned for Chloe to enter a narrow tunnel, stepping up behind her as she entered. At the other end, another soldier waited.

As soon as she set foot inside, a red light flashed and an alarm chirped.

Turning, she looked toward Cyrus.

"Come with me, ma'am," said the soldier.

"She's with me," Cyrus said.

"Step back, sir."

"No, I'm coming with her."

The soldier sighed, clearly frustrated. "Look, all chipped persons are being quarantined," he said. "This is for precautions only, now please step back."

Chloe realized this had nothing to do with Radar. *She* was the threat.

"Cyrus," she said as the two guards grabbed her by the arms.

"Hey!" Cyrus shouted. "Let her go!"

"Back up, sir," said the largest guard, a towering man with a beak of a nose.

Cyrus tried to get past, but the man grabbed him. Three more guards surrounded him as Chloe was pulled away. "Cyrus!" she shouted.

"I'll find you!" Cyrus called out, squirming in the grip of the guard. "I'll come find you!"

The soldiers took Chloe down a hallway, into an elevator, and underground. A truck brought her to a warehouse that had once stored Hummer Droid worker units. They were all gone now, their power racks empty.

In the center of the room was a massive cage, and inside were hundreds of people. Chloe was herded into it, like the Hummer Droids she had seen on the streets.

"Are they going to kill us?" asked a boy no older than eight.

"No," Chloe replied. "They're just keeping us here for a short time."

But as she walked forward, she couldn't help but feel the same fear that she had felt during her worst days on Earth. The Moon was supposed to be safe, a new home where she could start over with Cyrus.

And once again, she was a prisoner.

— Epilogue —

Five hundred people waited in line for food at Zone 20 in Halo Colony at the Shackleton Crater. Ronin, Elan, and Lise were among them.

Almost two weeks ago, over one million people had escaped Earth on E-Day. "The Lucky Million," they were being called. They had arrived at Kepler Station only to be shipped off to the capital colony of Mesopotamia, the new cradle of civilization at the bottom of the cold, dark Shackleton Crater. Halo Colony was one of ten colonies connected to Mesopotamia, and it was the new home of Ronin and one hundred thousand other lucky colonists.

He sure didn't feel all that lucky. His older brother and father were dead, and his uncle was likely dead, too. Soon, Ronin, his twin brother, and his mother would be as well, if the Lunar Council didn't figure out a way to start producing more food. They would die of starvation.

That is, if the machines didn't come and finish the job first.

The people around him already looked weak and exhausted. Most had only showered a few times over the past four weeks and were still wearing the same clothes they had arrived in.

"Don't push. There's enough for everyone," grumbled a Lunar Defense soldier.

The man wore the armor of a Piston, but in white. He monitored the crowd that stretched through the vast, dimly lit underground chamber. A faint aroma of soup drifted through the stale air, drawing the hungry colonists along like sharks to blood.

Elan and Lise didn't say anything. They kept their heads down, like most everyone.

Holo-screens lit up the walls framing the long passage, replaying the message from War Commander Andrew Thacker, the new commander of the Lunar Defense Corps: "Conscription is in effect immediately. Anyone aged eighteen to thirty is required to report to their Sector Lunar Defense Corps

446

Zone Station for assignment. For people aged over thirty, The Lunar Natural Resources Department is recruiting miners to expand our home under the lunar surface."

There was no talk of Earth. No hopeful message about those left behind. No discussion of what was left. Ronin could only assume there wasn't much at all.

While Hros-1 had missed Earth, the cannons built to destroy it had done more damage than a hundred asteroids like it. In the end, it wasn't man who had destroyed the Earth.

It was AI.

Technology that had gotten out of control.

Yet, Ronin realized that technology kept them alive here too. Providing warmth in the freezing temperatures and light in the inky darkness. Cleaning the air of regolith and pollutants. Producing gravity and growing crops.

If it weren't for technology, humanity would be extinct.

At least on the Moon, it was only AI and droids that were now extinct.

After an hour of waiting, Ronin finally reached the kitchen. He grabbed a bowl and held it out as a woman slopped in a white mush of lentils and rice. He took a hunk of bread and kept walking.

A long, open room of tables was just ahead. He sat at an empty one. His brother slid next to him, and their mother sat across. She had tried to be strong for them since they arrived, but Ronin could see she was starting to fall into the darkness. Everyone around them looked the same, their eyes swollen from crying, their sleep lost to nightmares.

Lise had stopped crying weeks ago, and neither she nor Ronin had slept a full night here.

"Mom," Ronin said. "You need to eat."

She pushed her bowl to Ronin and Elan. "Go ahead. I'm not hungry."

"Please, eat," Ronin begged.

Lise looked back down at her bowl like it was poison, then sighed. "There's something I need to tell you. Something that I want you to hear from me, that I should have told you a very long time ago."

She signed to Elan, and he put his spoon down.

Zachary, she signed, *Zachary wasn't your...*

Wasn't what? Elan signed back.

He wasn't your brother, Lise signed. *He was your cousin, the son of your Uncle Akira.*

"Why are you saying this?" Ronin asked. "That can't be."

You are lying, Elan signed.

Lise shook her head.

When your aunt was killed, Akira was recruited to the Engine program, and he asked your father to look after Zachary. His birth name was Takeshi. We agreed to raise him as our own son.

Ronin didn't want to believe it, but as he considered what she was saying, he knew it was true. Zachary had always been different than Ronin and Elan. Faster and stronger, and skilled in ways that Ronin wasn't.

He had even looked more like Akira.

I'm sorry, Lise signed. *I'm so sorry for not telling you before, but you deserve to know now.*

Ronin looked down at his bowl. Now he wasn't hungry either.

They sat in silence, listening to the hushed voices around them.

Ronin didn't bring up the future. He wasn't sure his mother could handle it right now. After losing Kai and Zachary, she was still grieving, and Ronin didn't want to upset her with talk of what would happen when he and Elan turned eighteen in a few months and reported to the Lunar Defense Corps station to begin their service.

Ronin forced himself to finish his food and waited until Lise had eaten some of hers. They got up to head back to the community shelter they were assigned to with ten thousand other colonists. A tunnel took them out of the mess hall to the main part of Halo Colony, where an artificial sunset spread over the buildings framing the streets.

Trees grew along the walkways, their canopies warmed by the grow lights built into the ceilings. The lights also supported the parks on each block that helped the filters clean the air. Not a single detail had been spared when building this place.

Mesopotamia and the connected colonies had been built by the Lunar Defense Corp in response to the war on Earth. But none of them had envisioned what would happen on E-Day, or how many people would flee here.

According to rumors, the colonies were only designed to support up to one hundred thousand people. Ronin wasn't sure if that was true, but he knew supplies were already strained.

The plasma poles clicked on as the sunset turned the color of a black eye. Lise stopped at the next block to look at the job advertisements on the community holo-screens. A single Lunar Defense Corps soldier guarded the three-story building, watching the colonists who came to look for work. There was a long line tonight. Most of the posted jobs were mining positions off-colony. The teaching job Lise wanted had already been taken down. She tried not to show her disappointment, but Ronin could see it in her defeated posture.

They didn't stop until they got to their assigned shelter, another sprawling underground space with thousands of beds set up in neat rows. New white blankets with the lion and star logo of the Lunar Defense Corps covered the beds.

Lise unfolded hers and sat down, draping it over her legs. Ronin took a seat on his bed and did the same. It wasn't just food they were short on. The industrial equipment that operated the colonies was working overtime to warm the massive space, and the air-purifying units were already falling behind.

Ronin took a deep breath of cold air. He was mad. Mad that he couldn't save his brother and father. Mad that he was living in the freezing darkness under a crater on the Moon. Mad that the LDC seemed to be giving up Earth to the machines.

Lowering his head into his hands, Ronin leaned forward over his bed and felt tears that he could no longer hold back. They fell over his lap and on his legs, hitting the spine of the book sticking out of his bag, still stained with blood from his brother.

It was odd thinking of Zachary—or Takeshi—as his cousin, but he decided he would remember him as his brother, always, no matter what.

Ronin pulled out the book and gripped the leather binding, finding strength in the worn leather and the weight of the spine.

Inside the pages was the wisdom of his ancestors, and the stories of warriors defeating enemies and protecting their lands. It was all he had left of his uncle and his father. Zachary, too. But this was more than a historical book of their past, he realized.

This book was a guide to the future, a map that would teach him how to avenge them and his brother, to take back Earth from the machines.

Ronin tucked the book away and laid down, pulling the blanket up to his chin. The overhead lights were already dim, but it was almost impossible to sleep with the voices, the crying, and the coughing of thousands of colonists. He closed his eyes, trying to silence the noises.

Ronin finally drifted off into a dream of Edo Castle in Megacity Tokyo. The cherry blossom trees were in full bloom, and their sweet scent carried on the breeze as he strolled through a garden with his family. His Uncle Akira was mounted on Kichiro, riding toward them. The gardens suddenly burst into flames, everything consumed in a brilliant flash of fire.

Ronin jerked awake to voices inside the dark barracks.

Elan was reading the Warrior Codex. Lise was standing. Other colonists were too, all looking toward the eastern entrance.

Ronin swung his legs over the bed and got up. "What's going on?"

Lise shook her head.

"I'm looking for the Hayashis!" called a booming voice.

It belonged to a man who was a foot taller than anyone else in the room. Long, curly brown hair hung to his shoulders, and bulging muscles defined his figure.

"Over there," someone said, pointing.

Elan put down the codex and joined Ronin and Lise as the hulking man drew closer with a slight limp.

"Tadhg," Ronin whispered.

The man stopped in front of them, wearing a Lunar Defense Corps uniform that fit his muscular body snugly. Fresh scars crossed his cheek and forehead.

"Lise Hayashi?" he asked in a gruff voice.

"Yes," Lise replied.

"And you must be Ronin and Elan," Tadhg said. His tone lightened, and he cracked a half smile.

Ronin nodded.

"I have a message for you," Tadhg said. He stiffened and gestured to the beds. "I'm sorry I didn't deliver it earlier, but I've been in cryostasis since the battle."

Lise slowly sat down with Ronin and Elan.

Tadhg crouched in front of them, still so tall he met their eyes. "I was with your Uncle Akira on E-Day. I fought with him till the end of Megacity Tokyo. If it weren't for him, I would be dead."

"Did you see my husband Kai?" Lise asked.

Tadhg nodded solemnly. "I'm sorry, he didn't make it. We buried him with Zachary."

Lise lowered her head, and Ronin put an arm around her. They had both known in their hearts that Kai was gone but hearing that his uncle had buried them together brought Ronin some relief from the pain. He pulled his arm off his mom to translate for his twin brother.

Elan teared up and laced his fingers together.

"I'm sorry about Kai, and Zachary," Tadhg said.

"Thank you," Lise said.

Other colonists had gathered around to see the renowned Engine Sergeant from Shadow Squad. Tadhg got up and motioned for them to get back.

"Come on, people, how about some respect?" he grumbled.

That did the trick. The crowd parted quickly.

When Tadhg turned back to them, Ronin got up.

"Do you think Uncle Akira survived?" he asked.

The scars on Tadhg's face tightened as he smiled, revealing large, broken teeth.

"I'm sure of it," he said. "And I'm sure he's fighting right now. That man will continue fighting with every breath left in his lungs."

"When is the Lunar Defense Corps going to go and help?"

The smile melted back into the Engine warrior's stone-faced features. That was all Ronin needed to know, his suspicions were correct.

Earth was gone, and the new War Commander was giving up on the survivors.

"Don't worry, kid," Tadhg said. "Stay strong, stay alive, and someday you might just see your uncle again. I sure as hell plan to."

End of Book 1

Watch for E-Day II: Burning Earth,
dropping Winter 2021

About the Author

 Nicholas Sansbury Smith is the New York Times and USA Today bestselling author of the Hell Divers series, the Orbs series, the Trackers series, the Extinction Cycle series, the Sons of war Series, and the new E-Day Series. He worked for Iowa Homeland Security and Emergency Management in disaster mitigation before switching careers to focus on storytelling. When he isn't writing or daydreaming about the apocalypse, he enjoys running, biking, spending time with his family, and traveling the world. He is an Ironman triathlete and lives in Iowa with his wife, daughter, and their dogs.

Printed in Great Britain
by Amazon